THE ABOLITIONISTS

The Abolitionists:
A Star in The Void Book I
by Christian Lemar







First paperback edition 2022

Cover and Interior design by CoverKitchen

ISBN 979-8-9866119-1-4

Published by JCLW Publishing, LLC in the United States of America

# ACKNOWLEDGEMENTS


Very special thank you to my biggest fans, Samuel and Mary Ann Wilson. Thank you, Deuce, Marlon and Samaya Naomi and the Simmons and Wilson families.

Special thanks to my editor, Kevin Miller.

Thank you, Anjlee Khurana, Madia Willis, Kate Hallinan, Alan Calder and Ilan Ben-Zvi.

# PROLOGUE

*On SiqT' Qkar. Dark God. The Container. Lord of the Void.*

In the beginning there were two, and God created light to see, to spite his second face in an effort to prove which was older. God saw his marvelous reflection and abandoned duality to create a universe in his image. The God without image remained in the dark, watching what the God of Light would do with his reflections. He called himself SiqT' Qkar, and he created the black void in between the God of Light and his reflections. SiqT' Qkar holds the black container that supports the fragile, violent expansion of God's reflections. SiqT' Qkar facilitates darkness in all its manifestations in God's universe to create balance and to remind the God of Light that the darkness enables his reflection.

# PART 1 – IGNITION

# GRANNY SELENE TELLS A STORY

## AKRON, OH – 1993

"Granny?" Hermod said. "They can't both have been the same person? That's crazy, right?" He was lying on the floor of his bedroom, his forearms perpendicular, his chin cupped in the palms of his hands. Granny was sitting in a chair some seven feet away. He stared up into Granny's eyes, kicking his feet back and forth.

"That would be tight though! If you could change and be anyone, girl or boy." His gaze wandered around the room with his thoughts.

"We are all one, chile," Granny Selene said.

"What?" Hermod hopped up onto his hands and knees. "That's crazy, Granny." His jaw dropped as he shook his saucer-eyed head at her.

"In God we are," Granny Selene said matter-of-factly. She pursed her lips in an attempt to hide a smile, the wrinkles crawling through her skin around her mouth and chin. Her amber eyes met Hermod's, which were slightly browner.

"So, I'm God then?" he asked. He smirked at her as if daring her to agree.

"Yes, boy," Granny Selene told him, straight faced. She nodded. "You'll see."

"That's crazy, Granny," Hermod said. His head was awkwardly large for his thin neck. Like an apple on a shoestring, he whipped it up and around and stared at the ceiling. "But maybe not." He stopped and whipped the apple back around at Granny. "So, something happened to me the other day in school. If I tell you, you have to promise not to laugh or tell Auntie."

"I promise, chile," Selene said, drawing an X over her heart with her right index finger. Hermod drew a similar mark on his own breast.

"I could hear what these two girls were saying," Hermod said, "but I was down the hall like maybe . . ." He paused and shook his head. "I don't know . . . thirty feet away. I thought I was imagining it, but one of them, Kala, is in my class, and she has this low voice like a boy, and it was her! She was saying, 'Get Hermod to ask him for me! Get Hermod to ask him for me!'"

Granny nodded as she continued to listen in silence.

"So, that's when I knew it was, like, actually happening. I went and asked Kala what she wanted me to ask, and she punched me—not Kala, the other girl, Monique. She's kinda ugly, and I don't like her anyway."

"Oh, you boy," Selene replied before nearly doubling over in laughter. "That's how your uncle started, hearing voices."

"Uncle Cissy?" he asked, smiling while knowing and not knowing what he had just done. He sank to his knees.

Selene silently admired Hermod's round eyes and the small dimple in his right cheek when he smiled. "You are a Vincent through and through. Burning in you like fire. What about your friend? Isaiah, the redbone?"

Hermod's brow crunched down into two folds, and his lips twisted. "I don't know," he said, confused and embarrassed. "We just like hanging out." He shrugged.

"OK." Selene tightened her lips and smiled, wide and mischievous.

"What?" Hermod asked, chagrined.

"Don't be afraid to be a Vincent, chile," Selene said.

Hermod crawled around and then sat with his legs folded over each other. He threw his hands into the pit between them and frowned.

"I like him," Hermod said into his lap. "We like the same video games, and we read the same comics. And he eats the marshmallows in the cereal last too! It's nice to be around him."

"And that's alright, chile," Granny replied, still smiling. "Don't ever be afraid of how you feel."

"But that's not what Auntie says," Hermod replied. "She says boys like me, and Isaiah need to go to the altar every Sunday. I hear her too when she isn't talking, just like I heard Kala. She thinks I'm gonna die of AIDS when I grow up."

Selene's lips coiled, and she squeezed her eyes shut. "That ol'—" She paused and censored herself. "She wouldn't know joy if it kissed her on the mouth."

Hermod looked up from his lap, wide eyed. "I think she needs to get some."

Hermod's eyes and mouth sprang open, and Selene leaned her smiling face in toward him. They both erupted in laughter.

"She's jealous. Don't pay her any mind," Granny said.

"Am I going to hell, Granny?"

"Never!" Granny exclaimed. "Why would you? Who told you that, chile?"

"They say that all the time in church. About homosexuals." Hermod leaned his head back down to stare into his lap. "I knew they were talking about Brother TD and Brother Keith, but," Hermod shook his head, "I felt like they were talking about me too. So, I looked it up in the dictionary. I'm pretty sure that's me."

Granny Selene's smile disappeared, and wrinkles webbed away from her pursed lips and furrowing brow.

"Sometimes I dream I'm on fire," Hermod said. "It doesn't hurt. Maybe hell feels good." He shrugged, his eyes still fixed on the space between his crossed legs.

"Look here!" Granny Selene snapped her fingers at him, and his head shot up at the sound. Her eyes bored into his. "You are Hermod Patrice Augustin Vincent, and you are beyond all of this." Granny spread her arms out wide as she scooted forward on her chair. "You hear me? Don't you mind nobody. Ever. Understand me?"

"Hermod!" A stern woman's voice rang through the hall. "Who are you talking to?"

Startled, Hermod got onto his knees and "ran" on them to the door, his fists balled at his sides.

"Never be afraid," Granny said. "Not even of her. Heffa!" Hermod turned around, and Granny smiled her patchwork-toothed smile at him and then disappeared.

"I told you . . . Granny!" Hermod yelled. He was smiling from ear to ear at Granny's final insult. He began breathing heavier and faster as footsteps thundered closer. His smile melted, and his lips and eyes squeezed shut.

"And I keep telling you . . ." the woman said, her voice louder, closer than before. Hermod hopped up to his feet and stepped back a few paces from the door. It swung open and slammed against the wall. "You ain't got no damn Granny!" she screamed.

Her open palm smashed into Hermod's face. He had no time to see it, but he had braced for it. He was still thrust to the floor. The apple led the shoestring along with the rest of him, hurtling into the wall. Hot pain spread in waves from where she had slapped him. His elbow was also spreading pain through his right arm.

His aunt stood over him. A tall, beautiful woman who would have never sacrificed her body, career, and social life to bear such a burden as this, Hermod Vincent. He had been thrust on her when her sister died a year ago. She hated him for ruining her sister, and now he was here to ruin her. They were both silent for a few seconds. Then she turned and started back down the hallway.

"'You *don't have a* damn Granny," he said into the wall, correcting her. She stopped and rolled her eyes as far to the right as they would go. Her cheeks and palms were getting warmer.

"Excuse me?" Auntie Beatrice said. He was forbidden to call her anything else, though even the IRS referred to her as Bea. She whipped her body around, and her sheeny mane followed. Curls rolled through the air and bounced around her shoulders and neck. She stood in the doorway, her hands on her hips.

He uncurled himself from a ball and rubbed the place where she had slapped him, glaring at her. "You said it wrong."

She marched at him and raised her right hand.

He brought his own in front of him instinctively and closed the fist. Auntie Beatrice fell to the floor. She slept there for nineteen hours.

## SOLON, OH – 1999

"Sis, you heard about that there demi they locked up?" Deacon Edmund said, excited. He turned to his right and smiled at Auntie Beatrice and then turned back to the road.

"Yes!" Beatrice said. "The man who could walk through things. They caught him!"

"Yeah! I was watching a special on it last night. They said they have to keep him in an induced coma or something like that. But yeah, they got him."

"The world is going to hell! Demons popping up everywhere," Beatrice said. <And I'm living with one of 'em,> she continued in her head.[1]

"They sure are!" Deacon Edmund replied.

"Listen here!" Auntie Beatrice said, "He's got four months and then he can do what he wants! I won't be around to pray for him anymore." <Ungrateful evil faggot!> her mind hissed.

Hermod sat directly behind her in the sedan, his arms folded tight around each other.

"You hear me?" Beatrice yelled and then began coughing uncontrollably. Her bony body hunched over in the front seat, and she tried to muster the strength to control the heaving.

"Yes, ma'am," Hermod mumbled in response. He felt bad for feeling good about her suffering. Just four more months.

<Homosexual devil! Why can't it be him instead?>

"Your mama—" Beatrice was interrupted by a wheezing gasp. "Your mama, what would she say?"

They were silent for several seconds.

---

1 Thoughts and telepathic conversations will appear in between brackets: <Thought>

"Ya auntie's talkin' to you, boy!" Deacon Edmund said. <Crazy lil' homo.> He'd driven them to church once Beatrice had become too frail to drive them. He had learned not to look Hermod in the eye. Beatrice had warned him.

"I don't know," Hermod said. "Bet she wouldn't call me a faggot though."

Beatrice had refused to stop going to services even after her doctor had advised her to remain home. "I'm not the one who needs prayer," she would say to everyone as Hermod wagged along behind her with his head down.

"God will free you," Beatrice said, then lowered her head to her handkerchief and coughed, "from that awfulness."

*Would he? Could it come soon?* Hermod wondered. He stared into his lap, the infinitely low rise of his wide-leg pants spread out between his legs. He was beginning to think that only he could free himself from it.

"You mind ya auntie boy," Deacon Edmund said. "She takes good care of you! You get right with God, and you'll see she loves you."

*You go and die!* Hermod thought.

The car jerked to a halt and then continued on the road. Edmund turned around and looked at him. Hermod lifted his eyes to Edmund's. The man whipped his head back to the road before their eyes could meet. They drove the rest of the way to the Second Pentecostal Church of God in Christ in silence. Hermod was already scheming his escape from the processional to run to the dollar store at the corner to buy that week's sermon distraction, *Masters of the World*, issue twenty-four.

Deacon Edmund steered the car toward the front of the church.

"Help me, boy," Beatrice said.

Hermod could feel her disgust at the thought of Deacon Edmund or anyone else handling her. He wanted to feel empathy for her, but there was a lot more disgust for him inside of her. He loathed needing to assist her more than she did.

He opened the door and stepped out of the car. Beatrice pushed her door open wide with the end of her cane. She twisted her body and lifted one leg out of the car, placing it gently on the ground. She paused and then lifted her other leg. Hermod stared down at her, his shadow spreading over her. She braced her left arm on the cane and peeked her head up and out.

Their eyes met briefly.

<Handsome devil.>

She pulled her eyes away from his. Hermod held his right arm out, bent at the elbow. Beatrice grabbed it and pulled herself up. The warmth of her body was a shock to him, her sentiments were always so cold and negative. They turned and faced the stairs of the church.

"Hey, Sister!" Sister Elaine, a cheerful-looking wide-hipped woman called out to them. "Hey, Hermod, such a handsome, honorable young man of God. You look sharp this Sunday."

"Thank you, Sister Elaine," Hermod replied.

The two shiny young boys trailing Sister Elaine smiled and waved at them. "Hi, Sister Bea. Hi, Hermod." They said in unison. Then they followed Elaine quickly up the stairs.

"I'll have the nurses put some tea on for you, Bea!" Sister Elaine called out as she reached the top stair. She held the door open and waved her boys inside. A breeze threatened the strength of the hairpin that held her lace chapel cap on her head. She reached up to secure it and then looked down at Hermod and smiled.

He smiled back at her. It was the first time he'd smiled that morning.

"Go on," Beatrice grunted, pinching her fingers around his bicep.

As he stepped forward, a sharp pain stabbed through his right eye and drove in deep behind it. His vision flashed white, and the stabbing pain receded. He could not see with his eyes, but the image in his mind was as clear as the waking moment. He was in a hospital room, seated near the window, softly kicking his backpack and staring out the window at the Case Western Reserve campus beyond. He was angry. The hospital door opened. He turned his head and closed his eyes as they passed over the bed.

A man with no features entered the room.

"Hermod!"

<I'm sorry, Hermod,> the man said. No one had ever called out to his mind intentionally before.

"Boy!"

Hermod shook his head. The pain was gone, and he could see again. He felt Beatrice gripping his arm. She was trying to shake him but could not.

<Dammit, boy!>

"What's your problem this morning, Hermod?" Deacon Edmund yelled from inside the car.

Hermod turned himself and Beatrice back toward the car and then kicked the door shut.

<You go do what I said,> Hermod told him. Deacon Edmund glared at him for a moment before he drove away to park the car.

Hermod ascended the stairs and found a place in the front of the church. Someone brought Beatrice her tea. They experienced the service. Hermod zoned out of everything that didn't involve the choir. No one mentioned homosexuals, perhaps due to Elder Turner and Minister Paul's absence. They were at the state clergy meeting in Columbus. Perhaps this was why Beatrice was mostly unmoved, even during the collective healing prayer dedicated to her, until the altar call. She never missed an opportunity during altar call; the pastor's coup-de-grace for the hellbound, where the weakest of them would submit to public shaming and would be forced to speak in miraculous tongues.

She elbowed Hermod once the organ got going.

"Get saved, boy," Beatrice whispered angrily. "Get saved!"

He sat still and ignored her.

<Well, burn in hell then,> her mind growled in response to his refusal.

Beatrice Vincent-Maxwell, MD, died three weeks later.

That day, Hermod sat beside her near the window in the hospital room and watched the man open the door and stand in the threshold, just as he had in Hermod's vision weeks ago at church.

<I'm sorry, Hermod,> the man said. He was tall and had two colors. He was harder to feel than anyone else Hermod had met before.

<Who are you?> Hermod asked, standing up.

<Don't be alarmed. I know what you are.>

"Who are you?" Hermod demanded.

<I will show you that you are not alone.>

<Who are you?> Hermod screamed at him in his mind. His backpack caught fire.

"Calm, now," the man said and then exited the room.

Hermod looked down at his feet and then jumped up and down on his backpack. Seconds later the man reentered the room with a fire extinguisher.

As Hermod stepped away from the blaze, the man aimed the canister at the backpack and extinguished the flames. He set the extinguisher on the floor and looked into Hermod's eyes. They were Juno's: curved like almonds with pupils glistening brown. Staring into them, he heard her voice in his head.

*"The blood will flow again."*

His twin minds warred with each other. The darker one wanted to destroy Hermod right then and there. The fair one understood that they might die in the attempt. Together they agreed there was much to gain from harvesting from this young, fresh fount of power.

"I'm Dr. Scott Gaskill," the man said, extending his right hand. "I'm here to help you thrive."

# UNCLE CISSY

## GRANITE FOREST AT THE FOOT OF ARABIA MOUNTAIN – FLAT ROCK, GEORGIA – 1822

A low barley moon shone gold as far as it could against the sun. Peach cloud haze bled out into plum. They stood above the treetops on the edge of a towering rock. Night shadow spread over Arabia Mountain, behind them in the east.

They had tarried in transition for several hours now, contemplating their fortune and those of their allies. Their eyes were fixed on the pearly big house, twinkling on an island in between the black-green expanse and the white cotton ocean.

"We need to end them all now and be done," she said.

"It is not time for the culling," he replied from the same mouth.

"Will it ever be?" she rasped.

"I will decide when to cast the blood spell."

"The rot won't hide, brother. It will grow and choke us."

They were silent. Their skin, muscles, and organs melded and settled totally into her for several seconds.

"Father would be proud."

"Enough!" he shouted.

Her soft, round breasts slowly deflated and spread into his broad chest as his design assumed their flesh. Sickened by her insistence, he remained silent for a moment.

"I allowed you," he said finally.

"Always hubris," she replied, offended. "I saved us. This is what matters."

He did not respond.

"Crown Moon hides their thoughts from us," she said.

Crown Moon, Sister, Uriah, and the dozens of warriors in their host would normally rouse themselves with food and drink and orgy in anticipation of a breaking. The sensation was impossible to ignore. This evening their thoughts were scattered and indiscernible.

"I am also weary of their double mind," he replied, understanding that her malice had fully drawn the ire of their company. "We will allow them to air their grievances after the breaking."

"Curse them," she hissed. "I'll find a stronger, braver league once the spell is cast!"

He ignored her. His jaw clenched and then softened.

She moaned as Siq'T Qkar's sacred words echoed in her mind. They could end the traitors and the crackers tonight with blood and a whisper.

"Maybe Mo' Jo will ride with us," she said, excited. She sighed and then continued, relenting to his command. "When we set everything right."

"What a league we would be," he replied.

Lighting splayed through the cloud ceiling in the distance. Thunder sounded moments later.

"We should go," she said. "Paul is waiting."

"Many are waiting."

Their belly throbbed and loosened. It was a pleasant anticipatory feeling. They yearned to reunite with the void before the sun returned and took it back.

Vincent assumed them. Juno diminished. He broke their fixation on the glistening big house and flew down from their perch to find Paul in Crown Moon's encampment.

Paul's blood raced through him the moment he saw Vincent part the tent curtain. Their penises hardened. Paul leapt up from the cot and enveloped him. He haphazardly unfastened his pants and dropped them just enough to allow Vincent to fill him. Pulling and pushing deep in his groin made him come fast and hard. They sang their breathy lover's song as Vincent spread and pulsed in him. Their lips folded around each other as Vincent withdrew, and Paul collected himself back into his pants. They disconnected, and Paul gathered his weapons before Vincent led them out of the encampment to show Paul where he had hidden the rock.

Vincent held his hand out ahead of him. A bright beam shone from it and cut through the darkness of the forest, revealing the fallen trees and winding brush obstructing the path ahead.

"There are foxes in here," Paul said. "I know they're your buddies." He held his rifle upright near the butt in his left hand while he hacked a path through the thick brush in front of them using a machete. He could still feel Vincent inside him, and the pleasure wafting deep in his belly contrasted with the uncertainty that had gripped his mind and heart since the last breaking three weeks ago. Crown Moon and Sister had shunned him ever since. Fucking had settled his nerves a little, but he still felt like something was chasing him.

"Shine it over there a bit," he demanded, nodding his chin to the left ahead of him.

Vincent redirected his hand slightly and illuminated a boulder almost the size of a shack standing in their way. Beyond it, the faint beaten path meandered through the thick vines on the forest floor.

Vincent held his left hand out. Shadow shrouded the boulder, and it disappeared. He turned to Paul and beckoned with his other hand for him to proceed.

He leaned in and kissed Paul's lips. Paul pecked his mouth at Vincent's and then walked across the shadow where the boulder had been. Vincent followed, and they continued down the path. Shadow released the boulder as Vincent moved farther away. They walked in silence for several yards.

"Would you still want me if I was like y'all?" Paul asked finally. The anxiety of the evening forced the years of bottled inquiry from him. He had to know. He stopped for a second and looked straight ahead, then continued walking.

"Dark?" Vincent asked, squinting as his lips curled in confusion.

"Well, maybe," Paul said, glad that Vincent had brought it up. "I meant, like, magical. Like gods, like you and your posse. But, yeah, maybe if I wasn't passing."

"You aren't passing," Vincent said, annoyed. "You're black."

"What if I was more familiar to you in any way?" Paul asked, shaking his head. "Would we still have all this?"

"I found me in you," Vincent said. "So, no. I would only want you if you were this Paul."

"What's wrong? You're afraid."

"I am not!" Paul snapped. He turned away from Vincent to wipe his eyes in secret.

"Show me."

"No, you go on!"

"Show me." Vincent knelt beside Paul and grabbed his hand.

"Dammit, Vincent." Paul jerked his hand from Vincent's grasp and stepped away from him. "I can't," he said, his back turned. "All this killing. I'm just human. I just—I can't do it anymore." He kicked the dirt, rubbed his hands along his arms, and shrugged.

"Lover, don't you see?" Vincent asked, still kneeling. "Once we have finished, you won't ever have to think about passing for any white man, ever again." He stared at the center of Paul's back. "The nation will be right for the work we do now."

Paul jerked his spine straight up and was silent for several seconds. Vincent's words stung him, and he had chills all over his creamy skin. Indeed, he was afraid and unsure where he would fit into Vincent's new world, should he survive to see it. Would he be too white? Did he deserve to enjoy Vincent's America too? Passing had allowed him to thrive. Smart and doe eyed, he had smooth brown curls that were just loose enough to keep the whites from guessing about his parentage. He'd gone to school and played in the church yard with his all-white half brothers and sisters. These siblings, whom he had loved, deserved only death, according to Vincent and Juno.

Paul had another sister, Miriam, with whom he shared a mother. Miriam was too dark for a life beyond the chains and fields and kitchens. She was sold on New Year's Day when Paul was nine. Anger replaced the nostalgia for his white family as he thought about her. What atrocious life had been thrust upon her because she was darker than he was?

"What about Ursula, huh?" Paul asked Vincent and himself. "What if I die tonight?" Vincent, who had let his gaze wander into the shadows, quickly turned his head to look at Paul. "Quadroon babies give you a good surprise when they start growin' up," Paul said, kicking the dirt again. Vincent stood and approached Paul. "Which daddy is she gonna look like? Is she going to school, the kitchen, or the field?"

"You doubt me," Vincent said. "You doubt us." He pointed his finger between the two of them.

"I'm human. And I'm losing my ability to know when I should run or kill or fuck." Paul shook his head and drew his pistol. "I've got so much blood on my hands." He looked down at them, one palm up, the other holding a gun.

"See?" Vincent began. "You are a god."

"Fuck you!" Paul said. "Everybody lookin' at me like I'm some cracker. They might not be able to hurt you—"

"Calm down Pa—"

"No, Vincent!" Paul yelled. "You calm down. Have you even noticed what's been happening since your last show?" Paul approached him with wide red eyes, spittle flying from his mouth as he talked. "My platoon won't listen to me. Sister stalks my tent at night. While you're out here having fun with Remus and them under that rock, I'm running out of chapters." Vincent approached him with open arms, but Paul shook his head and scowled, backing away from him.

"Don't speak such things upon yourself." Vincent said. He let his arms fall to his side. Paul had been so self-sufficient and loyal he'd never felt like Paul needed his protection. Until now. He had indeed noticed the dust unsettling between him and Crown Moon and Sister. What really troubled him was that he could not see where and how it resettled. They locked eyes and neither looked away for several seconds before Vincent closed his.

"Alright. I take it back, then." Paul took a deep breath and unsheathed his machete. He wanted to be fucking again. That way he wouldn't have to think so much about dying. He pointed to the ground and turned forty degrees to find the path. He pushed the brush aside without the assistance of his blade. Then he turned around and saw Vincent smiling at him. Vincent raised his arm and laid his hand on Paul's shoulder. Paul looked ahead, and they both stood still for a moment. Vincent's warmth radiated through him.

"We will part ways with Crown Moon, after the breaking," Vincent said. Paul whipped his head around and stared into Vincent's brown eyes.

"We'll see," Paul said. He faced forward, and they both continued walking.

Wind whipped up a frenzy in the tree limbs. "Shouldn't be much farther," Vincent said against the thrashing branches and crunching of leaves and sticks underfoot. He could see the clearing up ahead, and the towering rock in the middle of it. Moonlight reflecting on its zenith, contrasting with the black night beyond it.

"Do you remember the way?" Vincent asked.

"Yes," Paul replied. "We will meet you around here at midnight."

Vincent left him at the edge of the clearing and floated toward the deep black shadows underneath the rock. He would ask the void to show him how to settle the dust.

Paul turned and retraced their steps back to the encampment.

## CROWN MOON'S ENCAMPMENT – THE GRANITE FOREST (SOUTH OF ARABIA MOUNTAIN)

"Juno must die," Crown Moon's twin voices spoke in unison. "Vincent must die."

Sister stood silent and did not reply. Rubies in her staff glowed with the fire.

"They scourge themselves even," the Crown Moon twins continued. "They are too strong."

"Would you kill me if I was too strong?" Sister asked.

"You are formidable as you are," Crown Moon said. "But you are not our enemy."

"And Vincent is ours?" Sister asked them.

Crown Moon remained silent.

"It is a last resort," Sister said finally, "but I don't think we have reached that end."

Three men and two women in the host agreed verbally. Crown Moon was not assured.

"She would cast the blood spell to end them and us!" Crown Moon shouted, "We cannot abide with such wanton destruction of life, not even the transgressor's."

Crown Moon spoke to no one in particular. Uriah, the tree-talker, and the host of warriors inside the camp looked at Sister in silence, waiting for her to respond. Sister turned to them. Even their warrior's eyes were wide with fear and hope.

He's right, Sister thought. Earth herself would rise up in fury against them for the bloodshed. But would she rather have Juno and brother Vincent or Earth's wrath? It had not risen up against the white masters for all the blood they had spilled. She tried to ignore this counterargument, but it returned louder and louder. No one ever kills them. Well, not until she and Juno and Vincent and Crown Moon and Uriah and the dozens of others they had amassed started their crusade. Maybe, Juno was right. Maybe it was time to stop fighting these costly battles and end the war once and for all.

"Juno is our sister," Sister replied. "We will stand by them."

"Juno says we have not yet burned enough to build a new world," Uriah replied, finally speaking up. "Trees don't like to burn."

"Yes, tree-talker," Sister said. "Burning won't get us what we want."

"Neither will their madness and blood spells," Crown Moon responded. "Nyemhaa's Star is here. He will make the task easier for us."

They all fell silent. Wood crackled and popped in the firepit.

"And the creature?" Sister asked. She had no doubt that Nyemhaa's miracle star would aid them, but the void and its spawn held secrets untold.

"SiqT' Qkar's Web will hold Remus," they replied.

"SiqT' Qkar won't allow it!" Sister said, incredulous. Gasps and whispers sounded around the tent.

Crown Moon waved both right hands at Sister.

"Dark God serves us all," Crown Moon replied. "I still have favor with the void."

"It will hunt you forever after this betrayal," Sister warned.

"So be it," Crown Moon replied. They would seek forgiveness from Siq'T Qkar, if necessary, once they had removed the threat to their ascension. They clapped their hands together, and two of their attendants parted the tall dark curtains of the tent. Moonlight poured in and mixed with the firelight.

The twins circled the tent and met behind the group of warriors filing out of the entryway. Sister sat and sipped from her cup, watching Crown Moon. One of them laid a hand on Uriah's back.

"Our mission is blessed, friend. Be courageous as always," Crown Moon assured him. Horses neighed and huffed outside of the tent.

"The shadow is neither Vincent nor Juno," Sister said, she and Crown Moon remaining. "Might we try the chant again, to spare casualties?"

Crown Moon stood near the entrance holding the curtain open, ignoring her last question. Sister placed her cup on the bench that surrounded the firepit and then stood and approached the door. Horse hooves clapped the dirt, and the host chattered just outside the tent.

She exited and saw warriors in the host mounting their horses. Some of the unpowerful had their rifles drawn. Crown Moon let the curtains go and followed Sister to her horse. Uriah rode past them, and they watched him continue to the head of the line that was forming.

"Sister!" Crown Moon called. They cut their four eyes at her and she shuddered, fixed in between them. "Do what needs to be done," they said through tightened jaws and then walked to their horses and mounted them.

One of the twins grabbed the reins of his horse and moved on. The other remained with Sister, who sat still. They both watched as the other twin met Uriah at the head of the line and led the host out of the encampment.

Crown Moon, who had stayed behind, saw the worry in Sister's eyes. She would comply. To hell with her guides and stones and blood magic. Their double vision had shown them the futures, and those that they preferred would never be realized so long as Juno and Vincent lived.

Paul met Crown Moon and Sister on the eastern slope of Arabia Mountain, and they followed him into the forest. Two miles away, Uriah and the host hid near the forest path that would take them all, once reunited, to their ultimate destination: Forest Edge Plantation.

Dry leaves swirled and hissed at them. Buffeted by the wind, tree limbs beat against each other throughout the thick forest. Paul stepped onto a large tree root and slipped. His hand whipped out and nimbly maneuvered his arms and hips to steady himself before he stepped down on the other side of the root. He brought his other leg over it and then glanced back. "Careful, y'all."

Crown Moon helped Sister over the root and then the three of them continued behind Paul. The hissing crescendoed, and trees groaned at the wind's prodding. Paul scanned the forest. The full moon, his only source of light, dimmed and brightened as the wind dragged clouds across it. He heard a sharp pop in the distance ahead to his left, followed by several more. A large swatch of the darkness shifted, and several birds lifted into the air, the dark flock flapping away from the commotion. Several loud snaps echoed in the forest. The trees' squealing persisted, and the leaves hissed even louder. Paul drew his pistol and crept toward the disturbance. Crown Moon closed their eyes and started whispering.

"There," Paul said, looking back at Crown Moon as a moonbeam slipped through the forest ceiling onto the twins. Their hands were clasped in front of their sternums.

"Ninixetlau SiqT' Qkar. Hraqk Sisvumm Qkorthqk. Ninixetlau SiqT' Qkar. Hraqk Sisvumm Qkorthqk," Crown Moon whispered.

A wall of tree leaves waved at Paul in the distance. Moonlight shone down to the forest floor in the clearing. They were near the rock. Though dozens of yards worth of trees still obscured it, he could discern its shadow. It was darker than the trees' shadows. He'd resolved some time ago that even under a new moon, that thing would still cast the darkest shadow.

The rock. It was as tall as a big house turned onto its side, long and almost perfectly rectangular. Its two wider sides were flat with small grooves here and there. The shorter sides were textured with flowing grooves. The rock's crown was jagged in the moonlight, as craggy, sharp, and fissured as its underside. Perhaps it was a broken piece of some longer rock.

The rock rotated slowly in place some twenty feet off the ground. A figure moved in the deep shadow beneath it. Paul was dozens of yards away from this deepest blackness, but he still felt uneasy looking into it.

As Paul stood and stared through the trees at the rock face, Sister stepped beside him. Paul felt her arm brush his. She smelled like roses, hot hair, lavender, and smoke.

Sister watched the shadows darting between the faint moon glow that cut through the trees and the void beneath the rock. Paul felt the air move in the tiny space between them; she was shivering. Crown Moon was apprehensive as well. Paul had nothing to fear from them, the beings in the void. Some of them were like what an angry child might dream up with time and pen and paper. Paul had seen monstrosities with tentacles, webbed and feathered wings, paws and hooves and human hands, arms, and even faces. Creatures made of just as much shadow as flesh. Hulking beings who displayed an intellect and an understanding far beyond what God had given to Paul. All of them were in his lover's charge and, as such, were his friends and protectors. The stuff of derelict nightmares. The allegiance thrilled him. He felt safer around them than his current company.

"Their dance is beautiful, no?" Sister asked as she stared into the shadow. "They are free. Free!" Her eyebrows jumped, and Paul heard her excitement in the words. He struggled to keep his eyes fixed straight ahead.

"That's up to you, really," Paul said as he continued to watch the creatures move around them.

"Ninixetlau SiqT' Qkar," Crown Moon whispered, their pace increasing with each repetition of the chant. "Hraqk Sisvumm Qkorthqk. Ninixetlau SiqT' Qkar. Hraqk Sisvumm Qkorthqk. Ninixetlau SiqT' Qkar. Hraqk Sisvumm Qkorthqk."

Shadows spread out from the forest beyond them and obscured the moonlit trees just behind Paul's left shoulder. Something darker than the shadows emerged from them and crawled into the small space between Paul, Crown Moon, and Sister. Paul jumped back, brandishing his pistol and unsheathing his machete before his feet landed. A moment later he relaxed, and Crown Moon stopped chanting.

"You!" Paul said, shaking his head as he holstered his pistol.

Remus stood up straight and looked down at Paul. The creature was one and half the size of a man. Born from the void, moonlight struggled to shine through the shadow that it wore over its thick coat of fur. Paul could see a few of its stripes every so often, through the shadow. Remus nodded at him, and Paul replied in kind, wondering whether the thing was ever really there or just constantly reaching out of the void.

<She is waiting,> Remus said. It had no voice and communicated instead through the chorus of its victims and thoughts and fears and other feelings. It stared at Sister. She kept her head down, reluctant to make eye contact. When she finally did, their eyes locked for a moment before Remus turned to face Crown Moon. They stood with their eyes closed and clapped their hands three times.

"Sisvumm Siqtr'qk!" Crown Moon yelled, pressing each right palm into Remus's abdomen. Remus clawed at them, and his shadow passed through them, but they did not move. Remus was preparing to pounce at them when the ground beneath it crumbled and fell away into a deep sinkhole. Paul and Sister scrambled away from the chasm, and Remus grabbed at nothing as it fell into the abyss. Its silent roaring seared Paul's mind, and he gripped his head and fell to one knee. Crown Moon clapped their hands thrice, and the forest floor was whole again.

His mind quieted, Paul gasped and sighed in relief. Then he stood and faced Crown Moon, drawing his machete. Sister slipped behind him and grabbed his other hand as it moved toward the pistol at his hip. She twisted his wrist and brought the blade of her staff to his throat. Her breasts and the gold bands she wore around them pressed into his back.

"You will be silent now and comply," she said. Gold claws dug into his wrist and penetrated his skin just enough to draw blood. She released him and then stepped around to face him. Paul grabbed his wrist and pressed the butt of his palm into the wound. It burned, and the pain dug deep into his bones.

"You will be silent now and comply," Sister repeated.

"Traitors!" Paul sheathed his machete despite his desire to cut her deeply. His entire body shook as he turned to face Sister and then Crown Moon. They stood bone still, their hands at their sides.

“You will be silent now and comply,” Sister said for a third time. She held up her hand, the tips of her gold claws glistening in the moonlight. She brought them closer to her face and licked the red liquid from them. Paul’s wrist burned where she had scratched him.

She waved her claws in a circle in front of her, and a flat, reflective surface appeared. Paul could see a woman in it. She was holding a baby in one arm, and together they strolled in between lines of bed linens strung up to dry, billowing in the wind. A younger woman with a basket of freshly folded sheets approached her. Then the disk vanished.

“Ursula,” Paul gasped. "You touch her and—"

“And you would never even know,” Sister said. She pointed the pronged blade of her staff at his throat. “Continue as you were, usher. Remus never arrived.”

Paul clasped his wrist, smearing the droplets of blood. The tremors in his body had lessened, though his heart was racing and felt heavy in his chest. Silent and forcibly complicit, Paul led them closer to the rock. Summer night changed to winter as they moved closer. Darkness became blackness. and shadows became indistinguishable from the rock’s base. Something beneath it howled. Paul found some comfort in the sound.

Paul’s mind wanted to make his hand reach for his machete and hack Sister’s throat, but it could not. What had they done with Remus? What else had they planned?

<Is that you, Paul?> Vincent asked.

The thought struck Paul, startling him. Sister looked at him and flexed her clawed fingers. Paul’s back briefly contorted, and he gasped and looked at her. He would have cut her down if not for her blood spell.

“As you were,” she whispered.

Crown Moon meddled with the thoughts Paul broadcast to Vincent. The twin sentinels appeared large and menacing in his mind’s eye.

Paul drew in a deep breath and looked at the forest floor. He raised his eyes and saw them in the flesh now. Crown Moon. Ninexetlau, he’d heard Vincent call them that name. The Double. The Twin Temples. One was fair with ruby eyes, and the other had skin like red chocolate and eyes like gold. Their other features were identical. They wore a crown of long hair cut to the middle of their lips. The tops of their heads were shaved bald and shone like water. Their lips were dark, round, and long. Dark sparkling scales made a parabola from the corners of their mouths to the tips of their ears. Small lines coiled in a meandering tattoo all over their bodies. Several mystic glyphs were also tattooed discretely between them. The lines converged into a large crescent moon on the left breast of one twin and the right breast of the other. Dense leather covered their loins, and aprons of large black buzzard feathers and bear claws hung from their gilded belts. Dark jewels sparkled in them. They wore hand-sewn ox-hide boots covered in downy eagle feathers.

"As we were," Crown Moon insisted.

They all advanced in silence until they were at the clearing the rock had made. Moonlight shone starkly onto the rent earth, upturned roots, and broken trees scattered around the rock. Its glow pressed into their eyes as they stood. Paul could feel Sister staring angrily into his back. She dug her gold claw tips into the air in front of her, and they pricked sharply into Paul's back despite the distance between them.

"Go on, boy," she rasped.

Paul broadcast his thoughts. <I am here. We are here.>

He advanced alone into the clearing. Crown Moon and Sister watched him surmount the debris of the torn forest and then disappear into the shadow beneath the rock.

Unseen things were moving around him. Large beings darted out of his way, the wind of their passage ruffling his clothing and hair. He heard them breathing and croaking, growling, and even calling his name. He continued forward into the blackness, a darkness to which his eyes would never adjust.

Straight ahead something was shining. He stopped and smiled, then took a deep breath. Vincent approached, a nude brown man glistening in the void. Paul stood there, frozen. Vincent opened his arms as he came closer and placed his hands on Paul's shoulders. Paul knelt and wept, and Vincent held Paul's face in his hands. Creatures bayed in the shadows around them.

Vincent looked beyond the shadow to the edge of the clearing. Sister and the twins were standing there in the moonlight. Often, the void would speak with him and show him outcomes, to guide him. This evening it had shown him the rock aflame and its smoke smoldering the dawn.

"Shall we go to them?" Paul asked, standing up. Their eyes met and then they wrapped their arms around each other, holding tightly for several seconds.

Finally, Vincent unclasped himself from Paul, grabbed his face, and pulled him in for a long kiss. Paul's wrist was wet on his back.

"You're hurt," Vincent said, pulling away.

Paul smiled and started walking back to the edge of the forest. Vincent followed. "It's nothing," Paul replied. He had wanted to say something else entirely, but he was rendered all but a flesh marionette strung and maneuvered by Crown Moon and Sister. He stopped walking and turned to face Vincent. "Got caught on a tree is all."

Beings snarled and growled louder than when Paul had approached earlier. Maybe they had seen and heard. Maybe they were warning Vincent.

"I see." Vincent's eyes met Sister's from within the darkness, where she could not see him. Where Juno had none left, he had some faith in Sister. She would not betray them completely. He and Paul walked in silence for several dozen feet. Sister greeted them the moment they cleared the void.

"Welcome, brother," Sister said, kneeling as Vincent approached. She grabbed his hand, and he held it near to him as he floated past her to Crown Moon. Vincent could feel Juno threatening to usurp his resolve and war with the mages right there at the rock. He smiled at the twins, and they bowed their heads and knelt.

"Brothers," Vincent said.

<Break them now,> Juno whispered inside him.

"We laud your return, friend," Crown Moon said in unison, "blessed by the void and ready to do the work."

Paul stood near Sister, who was still kneeling. Vincent looked around the forest as he filled his lungs with the night air. His eyes fluttered, and his head swam around his shoulders for a moment. When he opened his eyes, he nodded at Sister, and she stood up.

"Where is Remus?" Vincent asked

"Oh, Vincent, you've grown too used to it," Sister replied. She approached Vincent holding a beautiful white court dress adorned with a variety of sparkling sequin flowers. She held the shoulder caps and furled the dress into a hoop, then lowered it to the ground before him. Vincent's stern face broke, and his worry for Remus dissolved as he set one foot into the dress and then the other. Sister watched his eyes soften and his shoulders settle as she pulled the dress up over him and helped him slide the shoulder straps over each arm.

"Be with your family for the moment," Sister said, as she zipped up the bodice of Vincent's garment. "Remus will return. Has it ever missed a breaking?"

They all began walking.

"Yes," Vincent said, looking down into his dress. He remembered a time before the rock, before Remus. Before Paul even. He and Juno and Sister and Crown Moon were united in their bloody and furious campaigns. What great work they had accomplished with their will and gifts combined. And tonight he prayed to SiqT' Qkar to help him destroy them. How had they come there? What had Juno's malice wrought? He turned to Crown Moon and grasped Sister's hand. "Yes, Remus has missed quite a few fine breakings. Nothing is set in stone, I suppose. Not even the nooks in this one." He turned to the rock. It loomed over them. Surely, they had done something to Paul and Remus. Sister, the Impervious Witch and Crown Moon, the Double. Even as he felt like it was crawling around him, Vincent's skin shone radiant where the moon's rays touched him. "There was commotion here before?"

Paul started, and Sister could barely prevent herself from doing the same. Crown Moon tightened their fists behind Vincent. One of them watched him, and the other watched Sister as they marched.

"It was nothing, Vincent." Paul replied, walking a few feet ahead of him. He had his machete drawn, rending any overhanging branches and vines that were in their way as they approached. The smell of his exertion was a perfume for the four others behind him. "Just a beast in our way," Paul said as wood cracked and splintered beneath the machete's blade.

"Yes," Sister said. "Boars get mighty bold in the nighttime. I loathe slaying the innocent creatures."

"It would have made a nice butt roast," Paul remarked. His mind drifted away from the immediate peril to the first time he'd met Vincent in the shadow of the rock. He'd had no idea how to proceed in the extreme darkness. He'd widened and focused his eyes as far as they could go, but still he could not see. So, he used the tightening of his scrotum and the jitters in his pistol hand as a guide and stopped when he nearly shot a hole in his own foot. He'd never seen such darkness before, not in caves and not even in dreams. And then Vincent had appeared, glistening stark chocolate brown against the blackness. Paul's scrotum had relaxed instantly, and then his entire body followed in a wave of peace and joy, the likes of which only Vincent would be able to show him. That first time they had embraced, he had led Vincent away from the shadow, from the rock, through the forest, and back to the plantation to break it.

Everything changed the night Juno came back instead. Paul, in his bewilderment, had tried to kill her at first. But Juno was able to calm him and show him that she and Vincent were one and the same. Paul had been frightened and disappointed. He wondered why she had not come sooner. But he hid his frustrations well and even grew fond of her. Sometimes Vincent wouldn't return for weeks or months. Eventually, Paul grew to love her in a way that he could not love Vincent. After she bore them a child, their souls were locked in agreement forever, and Paul had decided to trust them and love Juno and Vincent for his daughter's sake. He used to wonder what went on in that rock whenever they would abscond until after the time Juno came back with Remus. One of the riders, a weather mage, dropped dead when Remus entered the camp. Juno had explained that the creature's presence could inspire that reaction in lower beings. She had been surprised no others had fallen. Five other riders ran away into the night. Paul had decided then that he would never inquire about the rock other than where it would be upon his lover's return.

"I hope Remus arrives in time," Vincent said. He turned and stared up at the rock, gleaming in the moonlight. His lips slowly widened as his head was filled with vivid imaginings of what might become of Master Clarence Thomlinson in the morning.

# TYPICAL TUESDAY

## SPACE, 40000 MILES FROM THE EARTH'S SURFACE 11:21 AM EST – 2022

"Hermod, you've got about ten seconds till disconnect."

"I'm on it," Hermod said, shaking his head. He was speaking with Gloria from the Deep Space Climate Observatory. Though he still wasn't quite able to explain it, he could communicate directly through radio waves, even at tremendous distances from Earth. He'd lost count of how many people were on the comm line for this "Sun Run," the moniker they'd termed for Hermod's geomagnetic storm deflection assignments. This was his fifteenth. He was told this was the most dangerous solar radiation event in five years. Two days ago, an X Class solar flare had launched nearly five billion tons of solar material directly at earth. While that might yield an opportunity for the layman in Miami to view some spectacular night auroras, said layman would probably be without power and other resources for weeks as a result of cataclysmic electromagnetic disruption. More importantly, a crew of astronauts was delivering supplies to one of the far-side lunar stations in a hauler shuttle with degraded particle shields. They and their haul would be shredded by trillions of energized protons, electrons, and the other subatomic goodies spewing out of the sun at them. It was cheaper for the US and Chinese governments, the sovereignties who ran the lunar station, to send Hermod and his magnetic field than to get the stricken astronauts back to Earth and fail at trying to heal solar radiation poisoning over god knows how many agonizing years that would take. Hermod was going to keep them alive while making sure that Florida could keep the A/C running.

"And then another ten seconds until direct impact, OK?" Gloria asked.

"Got it," Hermod replied.

"Five, four . . ."

"You really don't have to do that," Hermod said. He had no idea what to expect the first time this happened. They told him to watch for what would look like a halo around the sun rushing at him. Minat, at NASA's Solar and Heliospheric Observatory, had warned him that given the gravitational and magnetic fields that he maintained in his combustive state, he might get a little "antsy" when the magnetic cloud and radiating force wave hit him. "Antsy" was an inadequate description. He'd been so tickled that he couldn't stop laughing and barely was able to absorb the radiation wave.

Forty thousand miles from Earth, he faced the sun and watched the haloing radiation approach. Blazing just about as hot, he smiled in anticipation of the wave of . . . orgasm? The storm of radiation surged into him like a hard erection. He was instantly aroused and moaned and breathed in and out audibly. Even in his nuclear ignition he could feel his erection pumping hard. He was panting.

"Oh my god," Hermod said. "Aaahhh." He moaned loudly and then started panting.

He heard laughter in his ear. Someone whistled.

"Did you get his number?" he heard faintly. It sounded like Minat.

"We . . . we must have our comm back," Hermod said, chagrined.

"We've got everything back," Gloria said, chuckling.

"And the radiation cloud?"

"Completely dissipated. You've saved everyone from Idaho to St. Lucia a lot of candles."

"It was a pl—" Hermod stopped himself.

Gloria burst out laughing. Minat joined her. Two other callers joined them.

"Guys, I will find you," Hermod said, embarrassed while trying to recall how many people were on the line. He laughed and looked back at the sun and then down at his great world, swirling blue, brown, white, and green.

He laughed to himself, wondering how much the homos would pay for a "Classified: Demi No-Hands Solar Storm Cum" vid.

## ELEANOR ROOSEVELT PROJECTS, BROOKLYN, NEW YORK – 2:47 PM EST

"They sent this faggot," the shirtless young auburn brown man in sagging jeans said. He was covered in black tattoos.

It's always the hard "F" that drives it home, Hermod thought. "Faggot." There was something about when straight people said it with that hard "F." It was always shocking.

The shirtless man was holding a young chocolate-skinned girl by her neck. The man aimed his pistol at Hermod as he descended into the housing complex courtyard. The crowd that had gathered made room for him as he approached the young man. He couldn't see the girl's face due to the way her captor was holding her, but Hermod couldn't help but admire her hair.

"Please don't call me that," Hermod said. "Just let her go, and I'll be on my way."

<Hm. Why he talk like that?>

"Wow, it's Hermod!"

<Of course this damn app won't load!>

<Damn, ain't no service?>

<He's beautiful.>

<This faggot-ass nigga is the most powerful nigga on Earth?>

"Help her Hermod!"

"Save my baby!" a middle-aged woman whose face was wet with tears screamed. He turned and locked eyes with her.

<Hermod! Don't forget dinner at 8:30, and bring me some Haribo bears on your way home,> Lee called to him.

<Kinda busy, babe,> Hermod replied. The rationale behind his husband's sweet tooth had escaped him until Lee had pointed out the similarity between it and Hermod's weed cravings.

"This punk-ass nigga ain't gone do nothing to me." The shirtless man yanked his captive's hair and spat at Hermod.

"Help!"

Six police officers were rounding the building, and two of them were holding their pistols in their holsters. A third was reaching for his.

<Oh great, fucking mega nigger is here.>

"Fuck that faggot! I'll kill him too!"

Hermod took a deep breath and waved his hand at the young man.

"Fagg—" The young man dropped his gun and fell to the ground. The captive girl wriggled free and ran to her mother. Policemen converged on the young man with their guns drawn.

"Officers, he is no longer a threat," Hermod said, standing between the downed young man and the drawn weapons. He nodded at the ring of officers, who slowly holstered their pistols. One of them reached for her handcuffs.

<This self-righteous fuckin' demi faggot,> Officer Nalbeck thought. He reluctantly holstered his gun last.

Hermod sighed. One day he wouldn't pick up on every single "faggot" thrown his way.

He ascended and looked down on the crowd.

"Thank you, Hermod!"

"Thank you!" the people yelled up at him in unison. Even two of the cops waved goodbye. He smiled.

<Why he gotta talk like he white?> the sudden thought crept into Hermod's mind.

He sped away.

## CLINTON HILL, BROOKLYN, NEW YORK – 3:16 PM EST

Hermod squinted and stared at the curtained window just inches in front of him. He was floating one hundred feet in the air adjacent to the Ashland Place Tower. Harold and Marguerite Dinnow had started fighting about an hour ago. One minute ago, a single thought pulled Hermod from his patrol over Bed Stuy toward the Dinnows' fourteenth-floor apartment.

<Harold, you wouldn't!>

He'd read enough minds and been on enough of his voluntary patrols to know when a person truly thought they were going to die.

Hermod could barely see enough of the living room through the blinds concealing the tempered-glass curtain wall. He was focusing on a plate of food on the dining room table.

<Don't forget about the reservation and my gummy bears! And get some letters too!>

"Lee, baby," Hermod said. "I'm busy."

<Well, just don't forget.>

Hermod heard Marguerite's muffled scream. He squinted at the plate, and the food on it began to burn. A small flame spread across the table. Smoke spread around the table and wafted through the dining room. Seconds later he heard the muffled squeal of the smoke detector. Harold burst into the dining room.

"Gotcha!"

<Put out the fire, Harold,> Hermod told him.

Harold shook his head and stumbled around the table and then darted out of the room. He returned with a bag of flour and poured a mound of it over the small fire. He dropped the bag and stared at the window.

<Open the blinds, Harold.>

Harold walked toward Hermod and obeyed. Now Hermod could see clearly into the apartment. There was blood on the couch to his left, and two beer cans were tipped over, spilling their contents onto the carpet.

<Go get your wife and bring her to me.>

Harold disappeared into the hallway and reappeared, dragging his wife into the dining room. She was bleeding from her nose and a small cut on her forehead. Harold pointed at the window, at Hermod, and his wife looked up and then backed away from Harold, shuddering.

Hermod smiled and winked at her as she fell to her knees, crying.

<Go to sleep, Harold.>

Harold folded to the floor.

<And not the ones from the bodega!> Lee demanded. <You know the ones I like.>

<Babe!>

## DOWNTOWN BROOKLYN, NEW YORK – 3:58 PM

"Code eighty-eight at the corner of Jay and Tillary. Need DOD response. Code eighty-eight."

Hermod frowned. He would tap into the police radio frequency right when they needed demi backup. "Code 88" was police code for a violent crime involving two or more demis. He was tempted to ignore it and switch back to his podcasts. The Pentagon was pretty pissed at him after the last time he intervened in a code 88. Three cops and a demi had died in the battle. But since they really couldn't do anything about it except hand out cash, they tasked Dr. Gaskill and his demi-policing operation, SPASE[(1)], to "handle" it. Or rather, make the world feel less afraid of demis, of Hermod.

Intervening might also conflict with his Haribo run. He'd need to leave in the next hour or so if he was to get Lee's gummy bears and be back in time for dinner. There were surely SPASE-appointed DODs (Demis on Duty), who'd heard this call. He ascended several hundred feet until he cleared the glistening high-rise towers to get a better view of the corner of Tillary and Jay Streets.

---

1 SPASE = Special Protections Armory & Supernatural Enforcement

Police cruisers formed a semicircle around three people who were too small to see clearly, though he did recognize the bright orange prison onesie on one of them. He hadn't the patience to dive into their minds. Criminals' psyches were so dirty. Commandeering them was like diving into a mound of shit. The stink remained long afterwards.

The street opened up beneath two of the cruisers. Hermod could feel the officers' fright as they tried to flee their vehicles.

"Code 88. Need a DOD now! Hostile Demi situation at Tillary and Jay."

Hermod watched as one of the cruisers lifted into the air and twirled toward the apartment building on the northwest corner of the intersection. He descended five hundred feet and caught the cruiser in his hands, then placed it on the ground. The wide-eyed officer inside leaped out of the vehicle. Hermod smiled at him.

<Jesus! This guy.> One of the assailants was starstruck and frightened simultaneously.

<God! You are fine,> Hermod told him.

They locked eyes: Hermod's were admiring while the young man's were wide with dread. He knew instantly that the young Latino man was a sister. He had a tattoo of a dagger on his neck with the word "Espada" in beautiful script beneath it. The young man threw his hands toward the asphalt, and the street began to ripple and crack. Gawkers nearby were shaken to the ground, and trees adjacent to the road fell. People climbed out of their cars and fell to the road, disoriented by the violent tremor.

"Yo, Juicy! Help!" the handsome young man yelled as he ran away. He clapped his hands twice and began whispering something.

Hermod held out his hand, and a dome of fire rose up around the young man who clapped twice again. He was still whispering.

"Not so fast, gorgeous," Hermod said. He imagined himself lying with the boy, fucking orgasms out of him.

<Enjoy that for a while,> Hermod planted the scene in the young man's head. He crumpled to the ground and rolled out flat, unconscious, an erection growing in his pants. The fire dome extinguished. Seconds later, shadows pooled black around the young man, and he sank down and disappeared into them.

"Shit!" Hermod exclaimed, annoyed.

A fist as big as a cinder block smashed into his shoulder, a second drove an uppercut into his abdomen, and a third smashed into the right corner of his jaw, sending him flying. Officers scattered as he collided with an empty police cruiser. He shook his head as he peeled the wrecked cruiser from around him, just in time to see another vehicle flying at him. He caught it in his powerful gravitational field and raised it into the air. A beautiful dark-brown woman as large as a bear was charging at him. She had three massive arms. "KIL" was painted in white on her black leather T-shirt. Hermod smashed the police cruiser onto the brute woman.

"I'm not going back!"

Hermod turned around to see who had spoken. Then he noticed the hole high up in the façade of the Supreme Court Building two blocks away on Jay Street. He'd stumbled on a prison break in broad daylight. The man in the bright orange prison uniform was standing in front of him. Students from the tech universities nearby, office workers, and other gawkers had gathered behind the man. He raised his hands, and the crowd rushed Hermod and pummeled and thrashed at him. They couldn't hurt him, and he had an obligation not to hurt them. Swarmed, he watched the three-armed woman tear through the police cruiser that had crushed her. She punched all three of her fists together.

"Juicy!" the man in orange screamed. "Get Espada. Let's dip!" He traded garments with the man of similar stature standing next to him and then ran up Tillary St.

"Fuck this," Hermod said. "Down!"

The throng collapsed to the ground. Hermod charged Juicy and quickly caught her third arm and broke it. He punched the side of her skull, knocking her unconscious before she could scream. He turned and looked up Tillary Street. The escaped puppet master was about 500 feet away. Hermod took aim and set himself to charge.

Green lightning flashed, and thunder shook the air. Hermod stood still and ascended. In his mind he felt the escaped man succumb. Mingo had arrived, which meant that he needed to leave.

## LEE AND HERMOD'S APARTMENT – DUMBO, BROOKLYN – 11:35 PM

"It's going to take another three months to get a table, there now," Lee said, disappointed.

"I couldn't help it, Lee," Hermod replied. "There were hostages!"

"I had to pay them seventy-five dollars! And you forgot the letters."

"They were out of letters, babe. He said they would have some in two days."

Lee frowned at him, then slid a green gummy bear into his mouth and began mashing it up with the others. His frown faded as the sweetness spread his lips into a childlike smile.

"At least they aren't melted this time," Lee said. He leaned across the bed and pecked Hermod on the lips. "Thanks, baby."

Hermod smiled at him and ran his fingers through Lee's thick black hair. Then he stood and removed his T-shirt and then pulled his pants off and exited the bedroom in his boxer briefs.

"Dinner's in the oven, babe," Lee said. "Knock yourself out. I'm going to bed."

"Not before you brush your teeth!" Hermod yelled from the kitchen. "All that candy."

"Hush." Lee countered. He licked his teeth and folded the half-eaten bag of Haribo bears. He stared at the Turkish copy on the packaging and smiled, then he opened the nightstand drawer and placed the bag back into his stash. Lee swore that Haribo treats from Istanbul were like crack, and he refused to eat any others. He maintained a stash that needed to be replenished regularly.

"You know," Lee said, yawning, "you can just tell me you were fucking some Turkish boy." He laid his head on the pillow and looked at the bedroom door. Right on cue, Hermod poked his head in.

"Babe," Hermod said through his chewing, "it's all over the news!" He retreated back to the kitchen.

Lee smiled deviously. He had seen the news notification about the foiled terror attack at Ataturk Airport. He patted the empty space in the bed beside him. "Come here. I need cuddles."

"Brush your teeth."

Lee complied. Hermod finished his sauteed spinach with orzo and branzino filet, then brushed his own teeth before climbing into bed. He and Lee traded spoons for several minutes. Lee got hard first. Hermod took his lover into his mouth and made love to him. The taste of Lee's semen was sweet and exhilarating. He wanted more of it in the way that Lee wanted more Haribo bears.

Hermod gently pushed his erection against Lee's hole, still moist with spit. Lee moaned and arched his back in offering. He gasped as Hermod entered him deep and then coaxed and welcomed his cumload. They fell asleep still connected.

## 3:12 AM

Lee faced his own reflection in the window before stepping out onto the apartment terrace. He'd woken up a half hour earlier, alone.

He looked out at Manhattan, sleeping in shadow. White moonlight spread up and down the East River. He shook his head.

<Hermod! Where are you?>

Beyond the city, across the river in New Jersey, a bright flash punched out the black night. Downtown briefly had a small sun of its own. A half a second later, the night silence exploded. Lee clapped his ears and shuddered.

## SPASE HOLE – MAXIMUM-SECURITY SUBAQUATIC DETENTION CENTER – 280 MILES OFF THE COAST OF DELAWARE

"I was bound to end up back in here sooner or later," Hermod said. He looked at the floor and smiled and then looked back at Tig Forster's bearded, inquisitive face.

Hermod's confinement space was lofty enough for him to take flight in. Large windows lined the walls, which was nice. Over the last couple of days, Hermod found himself wondering whether glass was more cost efficient for building a pressurized enclosure. There was no sunlight that far below the sea, but he did get some visitors from time to time. Ugly, fascinating things from the deep, they were probably as mystified by his body as he was by theirs. The ceilings had eyes, and when they opened, they had a nasty sting like those sabers the human guards held. Large squares in the slick-looking walls shone like sunbeams on wet stone and illuminated the lofty prison.

His living quarters were some twenty feet behind him. He had been given a bed, a small library, a refrigerator, a sink, and an HD flatscreen for monitored entertainment and telecommunication with SPASE and approved outsiders. Another sink, a toilet, and a shower were separated from the living space by an opaque Plexiglas perimeter. It was raised one foot off the floor to allow his guards and handlers to watch his foot traffic behind the partition.

"I suppose it's a good thing I can't kill myself." He laughed. Though he kind of enjoyed the time with Tig, being put on suicide watch was a little bit much.

Tig shrugged. "And how do you know that?" He stared at Hermod, who looked down at the floor and then back at Tig several times.

"Wha—"

"I mean, have you ever tried to kill yourself," Tig asked, "since the Rain?"

"It was a nightmare. I wasn't trying to die or kill anyone else," Hermod admitted, shaking his head. He considered how much damage he'd caused and the people he'd accidentally killed on the job and asked himself why everyone was in tizzy about one accidental explosion that didn't hurt anyone. "I really don't know what happened, but I wasn't trying to kill myself or anyone else."

Tig was reluctant to pursue the documented attempt about thirteen years earlier. "And what made you say that?" he asked. "Have you been thinking of ways that you might try and fail maybe?"

Hermod huffed and smiled. "I've definitely asked myself how high the cliff would have to be. Just thinking about my powers and their limits but nothing serious."

"What cliff?"

"You know, if I jumped. Would probably have to be from Mars, right?"

Tig looked at him and then they both laughed.

"From Mars," Tig said, chuckling. "Right? I wish we could smoke in here; I really do. You heard about the cops in Newark?" He was suddenly animated, startling Hermod. Tig twisted around in his seat, digging his hands into his pockets. He paused and grinned, and his hands reappeared, one of then clutching a pack of chewing gum. He plucked a stick from the packet, his eyes fixed on it as he unwrapped it. Thumb and index finger pitched the stick onto this tongue, and it curled perfectly in the humidity of his eager mouth.

"No," Hermod replied.

"Bronders and Volkoski? The ones who killed Marshawn Butler?" Tig asked.

"No, I haven't heard. Are they dead yet?"

"Well, Bronders is."

"No shit?"

"Yeah, and Volkoski has been missing for days now."

"Do we care?"

"Well, sorta," Tig said. "Gaskill thinks it's a demi. Feds want him to look at it. Two unexplained suicides, three strokes, and now these two within six months. All killer cops."

"Any suspects?"

"Me? You? Everyone we know. I mean . . ." Tig began to chuckle.

"You got that right," Hermod said. The news was a strange relief. Justice for Marshawn. It was calming. He'd been searching all over for calm since they brought him into holding. This grim news was how he found it. He reflected on his "Cavanaugh" meditation earlier in the afternoon. He chuckled as he wondered whether or not meditating was even working for him. Tig, still chewing, withdrew the pack of gum from his pocket again.

"Man, you really need to quit smoking," Hermod said. He chuckled and shook his head in admonishment. "You can't heal your own cancer. Or did you forget?"

"Yes," Tig replied between his chewing.

"Don't smack," Hermod said, his lip curling briefly.

"As you wish." Tig nodded and chewed. "So, you failed. Tell me about the first try."

"Why?" Hermod's lip curled a bit tighter this time. "I mean no. I haven't tried to kill myself. Why?"

"Because . . . that's why I'm here, Hermod."

Hermod looked at Tig and then took a deep breath and sat up in his seat. "I understand," he said

Tig nodded in response, acknowledging the unspoken permission to unload.

"You say shit like, 'Man, without Lee I don't think I could even be here anymore.'" Tig added a tenor to his voice and hunched his shoulders a bit to imitate Hermod's delivery. "Or 'I really wouldn't know how to live' etcetera." Tig stopped for a moment, and they both tried not to smile or look into each other's eyes.

"So, when shit hits the fan and we have Pentagon mandates to bring you back in here and provide them a thorough report on your stability, hindsight matters when you say stuff like that in here." Tig pointed to the floor. "We clear?"

"I got it, T," Hermod said. He held his hands up, palms out, and shook his head.

Tig rolled his eyes. "Now we gotta write a report to try and calculate how many people you might kill in an attempt to kill yourself. You shoulda been a comedian if you didn't want to deal with shit like this." He opened his mouth as he chewed, and the sucking sound popped against the walls of the room.

Hermod shrugged. "Demi comedian's still gotta register with SPASE though."

"Look, the Demi Protection Act has all demis by the balls, even me. So, if you're not gonna stop being sad and exploding everywhere," Tig paused and held out both of his hands as if he were dropping something, "then at least give us a heads-up or something."

Hermod's lips were drawn apart, and his jaw clenched for a moment. Then it softened.

“I still get a little depressed, but it’s never anything that extreme,” Hermod replied with a straight face. He drew in a deep breath and shook his head, his hands clasped between his knees. “You guys think that little of me, huh?”

“I mean, you just had a minor nuclear meltdown in your sleep two nights ago,” Tig said. “which could be written off a little easier as an ‘accident’ or a ‘field exercise’ if you didn’t have a history. No casualties or private property damage even. Healthy and stable Hermod is a lot less of a liability than sad Hermod.”

“Ha!” Hermod laughed. “Sad Hermod. I’m not sad!”

Tig smiled and chewed. He was smiling too wide to talk, and he struggled to bring his lips back together. He was grateful for the moment of laughter. It helped hide his anxiety. He felt weird about lying to his friend. There would be no suicide report. Hermod was not on suicide watch. His accidental explosion was an alarming anomaly considering Hermod’s cognitive abilities, field expertise, and weeks of psychic training. The day prior, Dr. Gaskill had ordered this lengthy, fabricated examination and would not disclose its purpose to Tig. Disturbed, Tig was compelled to contact Gaskill’s right hand, Alexander Cyral, for clarity. He’d had trouble believing the thoughts Cyral had exchanged with him. Supposedly, they were Gaskill’s centuries-old memories. Tig was certain the violence and malice he’d seen were beyond Cyral’s imagination. The visions were almost too disturbing to believe at all. He was afraid that something awful was going to happen, though he would remain as optimistic as he could in the meantime.

“OK, being serious now. We also want you to get outta here and back to your normal life. But you’re the most dangerous man alive and still the least deadly. You’re kind of a demi poster boy.” Tig’s eyes widened, and he rolled them around the room, then nodded at Hermod. “Lot less roadkill than a lot of demis with a fraction of your power.”

“Ouch,” Hermod said. “Roadkill?” He eyed the four men standing around the room’s invisible exit behind Tig. Two of them were armored SPASE detention wardens. One was his SPASE-appointed power dampener or “Demi Diaper,” Davi. The other was his SPASE appointed handler,

Ian Domingo Montes, the Dominican superman affectionately referred to by many as "Super Mingo" or just "Mingo" for short.

Davi was staring into his phone, periodically looking up from it to ensure that things were still alright. He was the strongest demi dampener that Gaskill could recruit. Hermod required two or more junior dampeners when his Demi Diaper wasn't available. Hermod thought he was a pretty nice guy, but the very nature of his power made him a real pain. Almost as much of a pain as Mingo.

Hermod didn't even need to use his powers to discern Mingo's bias. Just the dictionary. He and Mingo had gotten into a small scuffle during their first SPASE briefing together after Mingo addressed him as Super Mono. Super Mingo vs. Super Mono. Super Monkey. Thankfully, the Diaper was there. Hermod had fantasies about pummeling him, and he was assured Mingo had similar urges toward him. Hermod imagined it would be a pretty good fight. Mingo was an impressively powerful piece of shit.

"I mean," Hermod began, "I say all that about being depressed, but I don't . . ." he shook his head and pursed his lips. "I don't mean it. I just still have some work to do, you know." He looked at Tig and then out the large window to his right and then down at his shoes. "It's something that happened to me in high school after my first breakup. My first boyfriend broke up with me *and* outed me to the whole school."

"That sounds rough."

Hermod shrugged. "Being queer was lethal in the nineties. Had to be tough, and a good liar." He paused and smiled from ear to ear.

"What?"

"I did try to hang myself with my belt. It was about three days after the breakup. My aunt had just died. So dumb."

Hermod shook his head again and then looked out the window. "I started hooking up with Igor, my geometry teacher, about two weeks later and completely forgot the whole thing."

Hermod looked at the corner and then back at Tig. Tig stared at Hermod with a straight face.

"No!" Hermod exclaimed. "I have not tried to kill myself since then." He laughed. "Since I started getting dick for real."

Tig's lips parted slowly at first and then burst open as waves of laughter spilled out of him. "Hermod," he said, shaking his head.

"Apologies," Hermod replied. "I have been meditating a lot though. It helps."

"That's great! Is that what you were doing when I walked in?"

"Yes."

"What do you find has changed since you've started meditating?"

"Anger." Hermod pointed at Tig and then retracted his finger and held it in front of his face, blowing on the tip of it.

"What type of anger?"

"The angry kind."

"Would you care to explain?" Tig grimaced in confusion for a second. Hermod's cryptic sarcasm was a little dense for him sometimes.

"No," Hermod replied, and his expression flattened.

"Alright then," Tig replied. <Asshole.>

<I heard that.>

They were both silent for a few seconds. Tig started laughing first and then Hermod. They kept it going, even doubling over for a moment. They calmed down several seconds later, taking a few deep breaths. Tig wiped his eyes.

"Can you ever turn that off?" he asked, then raised his hand and tapped his head. "The antennae?"

"No. But PT has helped tremendously. I can choose what stations I want to hear now. Understanding how radio receivers work has helped a lot. Apparently, the antennae aren't all psychic."

"That's amazing."

"Yeah. I've been diving into quantum mechanics and stellar mechanics. It's like I'm learning about what my dick does!"

They both laughed.

"I feel it though," Tig said. "After I came out of that coma, psychic therapy was the only thing that saved me. Got me talking to the machines again."

"They thought you were brain dead, right?"

Tig shook his head. "Enough about me. I'm glad you're meditating."

"Thanks."

"Ready for your big interview next week?" Tig asked.

"You watch RSVP?" Hermod replied. He didn't take Tig as the underground news type. Though he was tremendously excited for his streaming primetime debut, he was not ready at all.

"Sometimes," Tig said. "I like Yusef Droitkin. He actually talks to demis, you know, like we're citizens too. It feels good to feel welcome in the conversation and not always the topic."

"I was kind of floored when he texted me," Hermod said. "I'm surprised Gaskill is letting me go."

"We can't stop you," Tig said, shrugging.

Hermod shrugged in response. SPASE couldn't stop him, but the United States federal government had given Dr. Gaskill and his army of demis permission to do anything necessary to try to do so as long as it added up to making regular Americans feel less afraid and more powerful than demis. Anything except go back to the moon. That's how this business all started, the day Dr. Gaskill returned from the moon and brought the Rain down on them all. To date there were 100,000 documented demis and an estimated 500,000 in total.

"Anything else you want to share?" Tig asked.

"I mean, I—" Hermod hesitated.

"Spit it out," Tig said.

"I've been having weird dreams lately. I rarely remember my dreams." Hermod raised his head but stopped before his eyes met Tig's.

"Why are you remembering these?"

"I don't know. I guess . . . well, they're happening at home." Hermod looked at Tig then and widened his eyes slightly. "They're kind of creepy, to be honest."

Hermod sat up straight in his chair and looked around the room, squinting his right eye and then closing them both, shaking his head. "So, I wake up in the middle of the night and get out of bed. I walk out of the bedroom, and I notice it's really chilly, as if we left the patio door open."

"Mm-hmm."

"And it's really dark." Hermod paused and looked down at his shoes. "Pitch black. But I know my way around my own apartment, you know? Even in the dark, right?"

"Yes," Tig replied, nodding. "I suppose so, depending."

"So, yeah, it's a lot darker than usual, and it's cold. I walk on into the living room, and I see the curtains blowing in the wind. I see the patio door and I, like, you know, I'm not thinking, I keep walking toward the door to close it, and then I notice this sort of black . . . thing . . . taking up half the living room to the right side of the patio. So, you know I'm panicked and immediately jump into the air, you know, like, what the fuck?"

Tig nodded as Hermod pantomimed the scenario. Hermod pulled his shoulders up as high as he could beside his head.

"It was this massive thing, crouching in the corner near the patio door."

"What did it look like?"

"I never really saw it." Hermod looked into Tig's eyes, and his own eyes and lips lost their animus for a few seconds. Hermod shook his head slowly. "It was like a shadow that I could feel, like out there." He pointed to the windows along the far wall that looked out at the deep ocean. "I couldn't see it at all . . . just its eyes." Hermod put his hands up to his face and drew circles in the air in front of him with his index fingers. "Big shiny eyes. But the whole room was *dark*, darker than anything. And it was just, like, there. I felt it . . . looking at me."

"What color were they?" Tig asked. "The eyes?"

"It . . . they were shining like white lights."

"Were you having one of these dreams when you exited your apartment last Thursday evening?"

Hermod nodded. "Yes."

"So, what happened next?" Tig tried to keep from being visibly disturbed. Cyral had shown him a similar vision, a black shadow stalking with white piercing eyes. It had crept into Tig's dreams last night. He saw it in his mind's eye as Hermod described it. Was it true? Was Hermod being possessed?

"Well . . ." Hermod hesitated as he remembered. Bits and pieces of the night came back to him. For a moment he felt like changing the subject, lest he commit some sort of betrayal. "I don't know, really. I . . . I want to say that it walked over to me and then we went out onto the terrace, but . . ." Hermod squinted and shook his head. "I don't know."

"Did the creature say anything to you?"

"No." Hermod hung his head. "I . . . I don't know. It's all a blur after I saw it. I remember jumping into the air and vaguely being on the terrace." He frowned. "Something happened on the terrace . . . and that's it. I woke up in that pit and was surrounded by SPASE agents, and they escorted me here."

"What do you think might have happened on the terrace?"

Hermod shook his head. "I don't know. I mean, maybe a fight, but I doubt it. There was something very familiar, almost friendly, about this sort of—" Hermod stopped talking and looked at Tig. "Like we knew each other and were about to go kick it. Me and this monster." Hermod laughed and shook his head, then looked away. "How crazy is that?"

Tig smiled. "I mean, it's a dream. And I can talk to machines and heal people and you . . . you do everything that you do. It's not crazy at all." Tig shrugged. "Have you had that dream since you've been here?"

"No. I don't really sleep here."

"How's that working out?"

"Fine, I guess. I'll get out soon. I just watch the shadows in the deep while I wait." Hermod's focus drifted back to the windows and the ocean ripples reflected in a small rectangular patch that ran along the floor and up the wall behind him.

# THE CRATER

## SECAUCUS, NEW JERSEY

Sean Mathers missed wearing pants sometimes. In his flight suit, his penis was rigged, so he could let his urine flow anytime he wanted. Somewhere situated in this hunk of sentient metal enveloping him was a waste-management system. The armor that he wore, MASS,[1] literally had bowels of its own. Sean's piss would flow through the system of pipes and eventually deposit itself somewhere near the thing's left "hip." Any salvageable nutrients would be filtered out and stored for emergency life support. Any waste would burn up eventually in the jet engines.

Inside the machine, Sean could move freely in an oxygen-sealed pressurized bubble. Inside the massive bubble, Sean held his hands out in front of him like Superman would. The billions of circuits that coursed through the body armor fed into nano chip bundles conveniently located throughout. By way of their unique symbiotic relationship and some of his and

---

[1] MASS = Mathers Anomaly SymbioSis. MASS is a symbiotic humanoid giant made from Sean Mathers' proprietary composite of the Ojun fungus, titanium, gold, and iron. Sean is its chief designer engineer and operator. It is outfitted with anti-nuclear, anti-aircraft, and anti-demi weaponry. It is powered by a mini fusion engine system and the energy permeating from the proprietary compound itself. Its communications systems manipulate a network of satellites along with a hacked and encrypted feed of every communications channel on the planet. Even when he is not physically piloting the device, it can do his bidding.

Tig's brilliant engineering, the messages transmitted by Sean's muscle movement and neural activity activated the many functions that MASS could perform.

This morning the pair sped through the air at 2,000 miles per hour at Sean's request. He was headed north just ten minutes outside of Jersey City. He was coming up on a bulbous white wall of cloud, the southern edge of a massive system headed up to Maine. He had been advised by the Coast Guard to beware of a lightning storm along the Delaware coast.

"Cyral? What are you getting?" Sean asked.

"Nothing," Cyral replied. He was always curt with Sean, and the word spat out of him like old chewing gum. "You tell me."

"What about the anomaly?" Sean asked. "Any blips last night?"

"Hermod is his name. Hermod Vincent."

"I thought he was already taken," Sean said. "You OK?"

"Sorry. I mean I know the guy."

"You mean you fucked him?"

<Excuse me?> Cyral roared in Sean's head.

<Gotcha! You're fucking the inmates!> Sean's brow crunched over his green eyes, his smile set squarely in between his fine-lined jaws. Cyral could see it clearly.

"Can't shit where you eat, huh?" Sean said.

"Would Ade agree?"

Sean laughed.

"We used to date, yes," Cyral said.

"Oh." Sean was caught off guard by his own sense of empathy for Cyral. Cyral did not share too much about himself and his queer life. Sean had seen him hungover more than a few times, but he had never gotten a glimpse into his personal life until now.

"Tell me about that."

Cyral snickered. "Not today."

"I'm picking up all kinds of residual energy signatures already and I'm ten miles from the aqueduct," Sean said.

"It feels strange, Cyral said. "Even from here."

"Approaching. I can see it now."

The world projected onto the surface of Sean's control sphere. The whole front side opened up to him as if he were standing outside, and not encased in a massive machine. It connected a series of thin gold and Ojun fibers via a two-inch-square port behind Sean's right ear. MASS transmitted visual cues directly into his optic nerves. The same was the case for all of his senses. He heard what the machine heard, smelled what it smelled, and felt what it felt. They continued to soar through the air until the hundred-foot crater opened up before him. It was still smoldering.

At SPASE headquarters, Cyral sat with his legs straight out in front of him, his feet resting on a conference table. A four-foot projection of MASS's video feed was broadcast on the wall in front of him. In it, the crater grew closer and closer. Cyral's stomach twisted, and he felt pressure in his eyes and in his jaw as the crater opening swallowed his view.

"I was watching this as it happened," Cyral said. "It woke me up.

"How?" Sean asked. "You're not fried? You see this?"

"Lots of questions. I was almost fried. It hurt. A lot." Cyral squinted for a second. He couldn't recall many images from that evening, but he certainly remembered the experience. There was a figure in a beautiful white gown. He wanted to call it a woman, but he couldn't tell for sure. It was much like his first meeting with Ade. The figure was beautiful and desirable, but he couldn't see its face. There was a skeleton, burnt black beyond black. It was angry. More anger than he'd ever sensed. Several people's anger. He'd had trouble distinguishing whose fire it actually was, but it raged like he'd never seen Hermod rage before. After the episode, he understood why the doctor had taken so many precautions with Hermod after his first ignition. Hermod had brought out a new face in Dr. Gaskill, one that Cyral had not seen on him in the fifteen years they had worked together. Cyral understood the face a bit more after that night with Hermod in the crater. He'd confronted the doctor about what he felt in the crater with Hermod.

On the screen the MASS arm reached out to the crater's wall. Even before it could make contact, a great portion of the wall dissipated into a cloud of ashy debris. The screen went gray, and flecks of black and carbonated dirt flew every which way. Cyral swallowed hard and brushed his tongue against the back of his teeth. He shut his eyes for a second. The on-screen cloud rushed at him with such a suddenness that he backed away from it.

"Damn thing!" Sean cursed.

"I didn't copy," Cyral responded, peering at the screen.

"Never mind."

"This guy is absolutely intriguing. He can increase his personal gravitational and magnetic fields to sustain this fusion process as easily as he can blink his eyes. He was unconscious during all of this, right?"

"Yes," Cyral said. "So, something internal or reflexive must have controlled this reaction, fusion or fission. Or something else."

"Exactly. Gravity, magnetism, magic, mind, maybe all four? But all of it coming from him." Sean's voice brightened. "Maybe this is what we need to get approval for renewed Ojun extraction."

"He'll never comply," Cyral replied.

"Scott?"

"Oh," Cyral said, sounding surprised, "of course Scott can't go back up there! They might allow you and me. I was talking about Hermod. He's obviously far too powerful for us to contain against his will. And I doubt he's interested in voluntarily allowing us to systematically dismantle his powers."

A hole opened in one of the tips of the MASS armor, and a sample of the cloud was suctioned into a depository within. "I'm taking a sample so we can do some more testing on this environment," Sean said. "There was a gas line in that mass of dirt that Hermod just disintegrated in a dream."

The machine moved to the opposite corner of the chasm and consumed another set of samples from that side. "I believe the Coast Guard and Con Ed took preventative measures on their end, but why wasn't there a massive gas explosion during the event? They surely couldn't have anticipated Hermod's arrival. Why isn't this area a lake of fire right now?"

"Because it was a controlled burn," Cyral replied, volleying Sean's cynicism.

"I don't even know if we would call it burning," Sean said. "I mean, the gas never ignited and sustained its own explosive fire. It's like he was—" Sean couldn't finish the sentence. There was a lump in his throat, and he was unsure of what he was saying. It made no sense. "It's him. If he were setting things on fire, like a flamethrower, they would still be on fire, or they would have burned up all their fuel and would have been incinerated. That gas line would surely have exploded and burned for a long while. For that matter, if he decided to just set things on fire, he might have exploded and destroyed an area roughly the size of Houston, given what we're seeing here. This fire was self-sustained. It was kind of alive and growing and retracting, choosing what to burn and what not to. Feeding."

"But we already knew that his pyrokinetic abilities were attached to the manipulation of his gravitational and magnetic fields," Cyral replied.

"You thought you knew, but you never proved what that apparatus is."

"No. Because the last time he burned like that, unconsciously, we controlled it. It hurt a lot, but Scott and I, we . . ." Cyral paused as he recalled the experiment, how Scott had not wanted to be the point of entry in Hermod's psyche, how he was almost overwhelmed and nearly caused a nuclear explosion at the base. He remembered thinking he might faint, and then he had felt someone behind him. Two people, actually. They helped him back to his feet. One was darker than the other. They whispered something in another language and then vanished. Then the experiment was over.

"You alright?"

His voice startled Cyral out of his memory. "Yes. Just remembering that experiment. It almost failed but then . . . something happened."

"Exactly, and it wasn't really science, was it?"

"No."

"How hot did he get in that experiment?" Sean asked. "I bet you it wasn't nearly as hot as he was when he did this. I watched that tape after that incident. Gaskill was remote even? Why? He never told me."

"You know he's always skittish about Hermod," Cyral began, "They can't ever be too close or something like that. It's like his phobia."

"Mmmm," Sean groaned. Cyral was right. The rain happened and then this kid, Hermod Vincent, became a dark cloud that wouldn't go away. He and the machine looked from side to side, surveying the chasm. "He must be massive and getting even hotter! And he knows it now."

"Not yet."

"He will soon."

The view on Cyral's screen scrolled up. From a worm's-eye view, the crater opened up some forty feet above MASS. A helicopter flew over the opening.

"Shit," Sean said. "MASS, hide." This machine obliged and set itself to absorb its heat and light to make it nearly undetectable to any physical or electronic eyes.

The view changed as Sean and MASS soared out of the crater. More carbon dust dislodged and shot up in MASS's wake, like an eruption. Workers ducking their heads into the hole to get a better look shielded themselves from the up rushing dust cloud. Sean flew directly out of the center and noticed them looking up, their eyes wide as they scanned the sky for the source of the jet engines that had just passed over them.

"I'm headed back," Sean said.

"Davi and Mingo were on their way to HQ to escort Hermod back to the city. Should they connect with you beforehand?"

"No need. Just fill them in. I'll upload a field report on the way back."

## LEE AND HERMOD'S APARTMENT – DUMBO

"I blacked out at some point," Hermod said, "but it wasn't like fainting; it was like 'car over the bridge' panic. Like I'd never wake up again." There was so much fire, he remembered, but it wasn't out of control, burning everything. It's just that he wasn't sure who was controlling it. He'd never raged intentionally like that outside of a SPASE lab. It had scared him in a way that he couldn't describe to Lee.

"And then you woke up in a crater in Jersey," Lee said, "and they took you to the SPASE jail?"

Hermod nodded. "Pretty much. I woke up near the aqueduct and then yeah, SPASE jail."

"And those three hours, you don't remember anything?"

"A little." Hermod shook his head. "Well, I remember this name, Nyemhaa. Weird. I don't know anyone by that name." He shrugged. "I remember waking up, and I remember feeling angry and jumping out the window there." He pointed to the patio. He had decided to omit the details about the shadow that had stalked him in the living room and escorted him away from the terrace. "I remember some of the flight there. I was talking to someone, yelling at them. And then I remember feeling like I was dying, for real."

"But you can't die," Lee said. Hermod had told him that several times, and Lee had seen it with his own two eyes. Still, the uncertainty in his husband's voice threatened to plant the doubt in his mind. "Why would you be feeling that?" His biceps squeezed tighter against Hermod's ribs, and Hermod's brown fingers sank farther into the spaces between Lee's hairy sandy-white skin. Their pelvises slowly pushed in opposite directions, and Lee's erection pressed flat between his hips and Hermod's fuzzy behind.

"I think I've died several times in this bed," Hermod replied. He twisted his head and his lips grazed Lee's. The hair on their faces mingled for a moment. Lee licked Hermod's lips.

"I want to be serious for a second, baby. Who is Vincent?"

Hermod closed his eyes and tucked his head beneath Lee's chin. He didn't want to discuss this with him now, but he knew that doing so would help him retain the bits of memories that he did have.

"I mean, you told this old family story to me, but you said his name several times the other night."

"I'm black, right? Of course, I can die!" Hermod exclaimed and then laughed to himself, ignoring Lee's inquiry. He rested his face on Lee's pillow and stared out beyond the bed, into the Lower Manhattan skyline. Sunlight reflected off the One World Trade Center in the distance, the facade glistening like a diamond. He smiled and moved his gaze to a cluster of courthouses around Foley Square. Voices whispered in his ear from the grave nestled nearby on Duane Street. He shivered and grimaced, trying to drown them out. Rage filled him, and he wanted to flatten the building in that instant.

"Puta!" Lee shouted.

The sound of Lee's voice was like cool water on a fresh burn. Rage quelled, and Hermod opened his eyes and smiled at his love. The anger was so sudden and foreign.

"I don't know. I just, that night . . . you scare me a little," Lee said, deciding to drop the discussion of Vincent for now.

"That's a first," Hermod whispered. He wondered if he might benefit from being a little more anxious about the episode himself.

"Yes, it actually is." Lee sat upright, jolting the bed, and their fingers released.

"I don't like hearing you talk like that." Lee inched closer and cupped Hermod's sleepy head in his hands, then rested it on his lap. "I'm serious, H. You really scared me, and all this Vincent business and such—" Lee ended the sentence abruptly. He'd anticipated some unforeseen territory in their relationship, especially given how quizzical Hermod could be sometimes. He thought about the limitations of his own thresholds: patience, willful ignorance, and pain.

"I'm sorry." Hermod's lips curled into a smile as he anticipated Lee's frustration about the words he was about to speak. "I spoke with Tig about everything during the lockdown. I mean, Cyral's gonna give me a scan later this afternoon. I don't want to worry too much about it, baby."

Lee's face held for a moment before he clenched his teeth, his lips quivering. He huffed and thrust his body weight down hard on the bed. Hermod's body hopped up and twisted ever so slightly in the air. Lee was on him when he landed, straddling his abdomen, pushing all of his weight down onto him. Hermod coughed due to the sudden loss of air. Lee held either side of Hermod's face with his hands and forced him to look into his eyes.

"You can't scare me like that and then tell me to wait for your ex to fix things."

The air sizzled. and Hermod held his finger up to Lee's lips.

"He's not my ex, babe." He reached up and pulled Lee closer to him. "You were there too. All this gloom and doom." Their lips locked, and he thrust his pelvis up beneath his lover, shifting ever so slightly so that his penis fell forward, the tip reaching to his navel. Lee positioned his abdomen exactly over Hermod's, and their hard penises lay side by side as his body came to rest. Lee's lips touched the tip of Hermod's ear. "You know I would never hurt you."

"This is less about me than you, Hermod. Are you OK?"

Hermod let the rhythm of Lee's heartbeat echo in his own body, closing his eyes.

Lee felt his own body warm up. His skin tingled, and he felt the hair on his arms and legs rising. He moaned. They levitated off the bed. Lee wrapped his arms tighter around Hermod, and their hips squirmed together.

"No," Lee whispered defiantly. Hermod opened his eyes. Lee held his chest and head up, cobra style. "No," he said, louder.

They fell back to the bed, Lee still on top of him. He pressed down as hard as he could. "No, we're talking about this, Hermod." Lee pushed his lower body down firmly against Hermod's while he held his wrists down on the bed.

"You're serious?"

"Yes."

"Lee, I, you—"

"¡No me digas eso! 'No me entiendes.'" Lee flexed his fingers in air quotes. "¡Te entiendo! ¡Tengo un corazon! Te siento ahí dentro, Putamadre."[(1)]

Lee paused for a moment. "Yo tengo una alma también," he whispered and then turned away.[(2)] He grabbed a fistful of his own thick dark brown hair and held it above his head. Then he released it, the strands landing in a haphazard clump. He turned back to Hermod. "I may not be able to jump over buildings and, like, fly to Jupiter," he slapped him gently on his leg but couldn't yet form the smile to accompany it, "but I know a trick or two. About people . . . about you. You leave breadcrumbs, you know."

Hermod was silent for several seconds. "I know," he finally replied. He smiled and closed his eyes.

"I can lift you; I swear." Lee bent forward and kissed Hermod on his lips. "Eres el superhombre más hermoso que," Lee paused and kissed him quickly again, "jamas haya vivido. Mi Superhombre."[(3)] Lee kissed Hermod again, harder. He tasted the tip of his tongue, and warmth spread out from his sternum and deep into his armpits and scrotum.

---

1 "Don't tell me that· 'You don't understand me·' I understand you! I have a heart! I feel you inside it· motherfucker·"

2 "I have a soul also·"

3 "You are the most handsome Superman that has ever lived· My Superman·"

"You can be modest about it if you want to, but I'm the luckiest man alive. The only thing that can destroy you . . . is you. You hold on to these archaic notions and let them weaken you. '¡Que lastima! ¡Llorra, Llorra! ¡Soy maricón!'"(1) Lee pretended to rub his eyes fiercely and stretched his face down into a frown. "Yes, you're a fag. Yes, you're an American nigger man, since you like calling yourself that for some damn reason." Lee twirled his eyes in his head. "But I can't see why you don't see how you transcend that. Every second you exist."

"This . . ." Hermod stopped as Lee floated into the air and moved away from the bed, the sheets unraveling from around him and falling to the floor. Hermod remained still, his arms still above his head where Lee held them. "This is all new," Hermod said as he rose from the bed and levitated about four feet away from Lee.

"That faggot is thirty-eight years old. That nigger is hundreds of years old. Your super boyfriend, he's just a teenager, sorta. All this new power doesn't mean I'm OK all of a sudden. Shit, it means the opposite. Everything means everything in America. You can't just chill no matter how powerful you are. Being rich used to work, but now that's fucked too. There is no chill in the USA, baby."

"Well, first off, that's why I'm begging you to go in with me on that place in Málaga. Second, I didn't fall for your power." Lee was still floating, his erection subsided. "You wrapped your head around being the most unique and dangerous being in the world. Don't get in your own way over bullshit. Throw those thoughts away and let me help you."

"You are. You do."

"I mean with this." Lee closed his eyes and felt himself tumbling into an inversion. "Who is Vincent?" Lee opened his eyes and met Hermod's.

"Not now."

Lee's face dissolved into frustration. He felt a series of small pecks on his neck as Hermod's soft, invisible hands caressed his shoulders.

"Later, I swear," Hermod vowed. "Vincent was my great-great-great-something-uncle. Somewhere around there. He was also a demi, or the

---

1 "Oh shame· cry· cry· I'm a faggot·"

equivalent, it seems." He had vaguely mentioned Granny Selene's stories about Vincent a few times to Lee. He thought about her from time to time. Granny Selene had stopped visiting after Aunt Beatrice died. He had not mentioned to Lee or anyone that Granny Selene was not even his mother's mother. In college he began to dig into his lineage and found the Mueller Farm tax and plantation fiscal records. Selene Vincent was listed in slave property audits. There were several other Vincents on the plantation between 1778 and 1816: Jaqueline, Juno, Clyde, Mariah, and Aristotle. Mueller Farm records end in 1816, despite what appeared to be a lucrative operation. He had been able to track Selene beyond the plantation through the birth records of her first two children, one of whom was his Great-great-great-grandfather Leonard. Selene died in South Carolina in 1870. Hermod did not want to dive into that right now though. It wouldn't help. "I'll tell you a sad story another day, babe."

Lee frowned. "You're a bitch sometimes, you know?" Hermod set him upright in the air, and his hair fell over his face. "If we're not having a heart to heart then come and fuck me."

"I just want to watch right now." Hermod took a deep breath and waved his hand. Lee shut his eyes, and his shoulders and hips snaked in opposite directions. His left knee bent slowly and wrapped around the other. He threw his head back and gripped his pecs, his erection stiffening.

"You had enough last night, I guess?"

"Last night?"

"You don't . . . Ahhh," Lee moaned. His neck relaxed, and his head hung backwards

Hermod started stroking himself, floating up from the bed as he watched his lover's skin blush. His erection was as stiff as it could get, veins of varying widths webbed all over the shaft. The head was fully exposed, dark, and wet, from the foreskin. His nipples were hard pegs. He tossed his head around his shoulders, his hips thrust out, and his back straightened.

Lee's body stiffened, and every muscle in his core tightened. Veins began to rise across the area around his navel and down his legs. His scrotum drew up and nearly disappeared behind his penis. His shaft flexed hard once, and then it flopped around violently, tossing thick ropes of semen in every direction. Lee wailed as his body convulsed and spewed his cum around the room. Hermod collected it all and held it in the air. Lee's body relaxed, and some veins sank back beneath his skin. The small pool of semen flowed across the room, and Hermod drank it down. Lee's erection subsided as he floated back to the bed. Hermod looked down at him as the sheets rose from the floor and blanketed him.

"Lover," Lee moaned. He was tempted to press further. Did Hermod really not remember anything from last night? The things they'd said and done to each other?

"Yes."

"Don't hide from me," Lee said, deciding to drop it.

Hermod floated back down to the bed and tucked into Lee's big spoon. Lee wrapped his arms around him and rested his chin on Hermod's shoulder. For an instant Lee's touch was cool, the sweat soaking in the hair on his chest. Hermod felt the matted hair wipe back and forth against his shoulder blades as Lee pressed his body close. A burst of hot breath warmed the back of Hermod's neck as he felt his outer buttocks being squeezed by Lee's quivering thighs.

"I can't hide from you." Hermod scanned his lover's memories of the last several hours and started to piece together the events of the previous night. He was chilly with guilt. Lee was the only one he couldn't hide from.

<You're trying hard AF,> Lee thought.

# BIG HOUSE

## FOREST EDGE PLANTATION – FLAT ROCK, GEORGIA - 1822

Lois stood on the wide porch staring into the pitch-black beyond where her light could reach. Deep-rooted trees grew close together in the forest hiding in the dark. Roots, fallen branches, and low swooping branches and vines all made exploration difficult—running too. The fool slaves were always caught snared in some ungodly vine or speared by some broken tree, bleeding so badly that whipping wouldn't have been physically possible. Lois had seen a few. And then there were some she had not seen again. Hiding was easy in the Granite Forest, just as easy as dying.

Lois recalled the evening Martha Ruth came back to their sewing room in the big house attic with ashen skin. Martha fell to her knees and huddled over a napkin she had been clutching beneath her bib. She had looked around the room like there were hoods waiting to burn them both and then quickly unfurled the napkin, which was lined with a handwritten letter. She discarded the napkin and flailed the crumpled letter in Lois's face.

"Dey's killed—" Martha could say no more, tears rattling in her eyelids, her entire body trembling.

Mr. Seymour Scott had sent a letter to Senator Clarence Erick Thomlinson's plantation home addressed to Martha Ruth Scott. She remembered how Martha trembled as they held each other that night and read it. Martha's tears soaked deep into the shoulder of Lois's blouse. What had they done to Jacob to make him spill her name? How offended had Master Seymour been to spend paper and ink and postage to tell a nigger that he'd made her a widow? What had they done to Jacob? What had Master Seymour collected? Lois didn't think of Jacob often; such thoughts led down a craven trail filled with spite and violence.

Lois closed her eyes and let the wind wipe her cheeks. Her blouse's shoulder caps and skirt hem flitted in the warm evening breeze, the hem tickling the skin above her socks. She set the lamp on the porch ledge and decided not to risk her skirt on the stairs. Henry didn't sweep them on Tuesdays.

She took a deep breath and wrapped her uniform cardigan tighter around her as she saw a bluish green streak of light dart through the forest. She was startled by the flash and alarmed at her level of fright. It was a stark contrast to the anecdotal vision of torchlight hopping and flickering between the trees as people guessed their way through the knotted root quagmire of the Granite Forest. Several powerful snaps sounded in unison, followed by a squeaking noise like the trees would make during tempests and twisters. But it was much louder, like all the trees were bending over.

*Pop! Pop! Pop! Pop! Pop!*

The treetops in the canopy flailed and bounced, some falling down. Birds scattered in the night air and cut a black flurry across the night sky. Cocks and chickens and sows in the barn screeched and thrashed in a frenzy. Springs squealed on the door hinges forty feet down the porch to her left. Ned, Jessica, and Leah darted down the porch toward her.

"Is it her?" Ned asked, excited.

"I heard the rumors that she might come," Jessica said, as she whipped her head toward them. "Talk of sick overgrowing trees and a living shadow as big as two men in the forest." She moved closer to Lois and bumped her soft, curvy hip into her, then grabbed her and hugged her from behind. "Cheer up, girl," she whispered. "We might be free in a minute!"

Jessica released her and then lifted her skirt slightly and descended the stairs. Once at the bottom, she smoothed her head and removed the bandana covering it, shook her head twice. Hair hung around her head three times as big, a mass of black shiny curls and kinks.

"If it's that rock then it's her," Leah said. "Minister Jacob seen it while he was escortin' the master's guests to the main road. He says him and Master Greenley and Gerdie saw it as plain as a cloud."

"If it ain't we's all got lashes comin'," Lois said. "Standing around like it's a Sunday evening." She thought it best to quell her anticipation. If it wasn't indeed the rock, she would surely face more cold meals, crowded wet cots, unwanted advances and fingerings, and Miss Sara Eugenia's rages. At least he never hurt her, Master Clarence. Not yet at least. Not like the others. He'd probably sell her in a rage, but she would have to do something far worse than lazing outside the house. Lois wondered what a new master would do to her; whether or not she would enjoy the train ride if she was sold to a master far away.

"Maybe she'll break him!" Jessica said.

"That's just talk," Ned said. "To scare young uns."

"You wait and see," Jessica said. "Miss Pertonia told me she overheard Massa Clarence reading a letter from his Aunt in Atlanta, and she was goin' on about Massa Illiam at the Olympia Plantation out toward Columbus." Jessica stuck her chest out. "Miss Pertonia don't tell lies."

"Look!" Ned pointed south of the house at a group of people leaving a long, dilapidated hut and hurrying toward the church about fifty meters farther south.

"Come now, Clara!" Miss Sara Eugenia called from inside the house. Lois started. A shadow moved over the moon, and several deer, coons, dogs, and fowl fled the forest and raced out into the fields away from the house.

*POP! POP! POP! POP! POP!*

An explosion rocked the four of them to their knees, back, butt, and stomach respectively. The rock burst through the face of the forest, launching whole and broken trees into the air. Chunks of tree trunks and gnarled root clusters as big as horses tumbled and tore through the field. Lois heard glassware and windows breaking and shattering throughout the house. She stood tall and watched the animals, trees, and dirt fly through the air.

Jessica, Ned, and Leah cowered and covered their ears. Towering and glistening, the rock glided to a halt in the middle of the field about 250 yards from the east end of the house. Shadows of a dozen people on horseback flew out of the hole in the forest behind it. One of the riders fell back and rode a little slower than the others. A figure exited the forest and followed the lone rider. It did not walk or ride. It wore a white dress with some decoration that Lois could not discern.

"It's him!" Jessica said. Several slaves emerged from the quarters and gathered on the lawn. Others came running from the fields on the south side of the plantation. The rock was here. They would be free today.

"It's them," Lois whispered. Jessica turned to face her. Her mouth was slack, her eyes were as wide as Lois's.

"I told you!" Jessica shook her thicket of hair and moved toward the porch stairs.

"What do you mean?" Ned asked even as he walked down the porch closer to the rock, not minding any of them.

"Come now!" Miss Sara Eugenia squealed behind Lois. The girl turned to see the door burst open and Clara's frail pale body stumbled out, nearly falling over her dress. Ned slowly stepped aside from the stairway not minding the commotion. Clara gathered herself from the porch floor and then stood up and looked behind her.

"Go!" Miss Sara Eugenia squealed as she pulled her rotund self across the door, quickly surpassing her daughter. Miss Sara Eugenia yanked Clara by the arm and forced her ahead. "Move, you sow! To the church!" Clara was shaking and nearly hyperventilating, but she found the strength to hobble along behind her mother.

Masters Clarence and George Thomlinson approached Sara Eugenia on the finest two stallions. Their white servants, Reese, Michael, and Daniel, followed.

"We have to get to the church!" Sara Eugenia cried, pointing to the rock. George's horse bucked under him, and he fought to regain control. Clara backed away and fell to her knees, pulling herself into a tight ball. One of the men on horseback spun around and rode toward the church. He would not stop for another twenty-five miles.

Master Clarence let his hat fly into the wind. He pulled out his pistol and tossed it to his son, George. George caught it and loaded it. Master Clarence looked back at the house and saw Lois and the other slave children standing there. He saw dozens more slaves advancing toward the rock. Some of them broke away from the herd to flee into the forest. There was a crash in the house, and a brown body flew out the door holding a large bulging bundle of things wrapped in one of Miss Sara Eugenia's linen tablecloths. He was wearing a pair of Master Clarence's shoes and his coat as well.

"Get here!" Master Clarence shouted. He fired his pistol at the man several times but missed. The man disappeared over the banister and rounded the house.

"Get to the church!" George screamed at Clara. Shadows covered them as thick clouds moved in, obscuring the moon. The air was still, the silence broken only by a child's piercing cry.

Lightning struck the Thomlinsons' man, Reese. Another bolt struck the field. All them, except for Clarence, were smitten to the ground. Reese laid on top of his horse, both of them broken and charred. Thick smoke rose from their bodies. Their third servant, Michael, and his horse lay dead as well, their bodies a bit less burnt.

George Thomlinson wriggled his body slowly beneath his dead horse. Miss Sara Eugenia Thomlinson rolled onto her belly and crawled toward her husband, Master Clarence. He and his horse were unscathed, though he was having trouble hearing over the ringing in his ears. Clara lay on her side, groaning and struggling to bring herself upright.

Clarence turned his horse around and helped his wife to her feet. He held her hand as she steadied herself against the horse. Clarence looked up at the house and caught Lois staring down at him. From where she stood, the shadows on her face created an expression that he had only usually seen on hardened men in fits of bloody rage.

The sound of galloping grew louder in Clarence's ears. He turned his horse to face the noise. The rock towered above the riders and the crowd of slaves gathering around them, its shadow crawling over them all, closer to Master Clarence and his family. A man yelled, and the horses neighed. The throng of slaves parted, and several men rode through the break.

The slaves cheered and hollered, and some danced, tears streaking several faces. A man with a child on his back hurried away from the crowd and into the woods, holding hands with a woman who was cradling an infant.

Clarence gasped. Down the field, through the crowd of slaves, he glimpsed a figure in a white dress that shone against the shadow void cast by the towering rock.

Ten men on horseback approached. Uriah, the tree-talker, large, hairy, and dark brown, hulked over the strongest horse. He held a coiled whip. His torso was wrapped all over in thick twisting roots. He reared up suddenly on the horse and lashed the whip out ahead of him, then swirled it around above his head a few times, brought the whip down around him, and wrapped it several times around his torso, where it blended in with the other roots there. Clarence watched with dread. He was familiar with handling a whip, though he could never have wrapped the whip around his own waist in such a fashion.

Miss Sara Eugenia held Clara in her arms, and both of them stopped behind George. He held a pistol in one hand, a rifle resting in his other arm, and his fingers crept near the trigger. Master Clarence rode his horse beside George and nodded at Sara Eugenia and Clara. Sara Eugenia's mouth and body quivered as she held Clara's head down, absorbing her tears and cries in her bosom.

As Lois stood on the porch watching Reese's horse burn, she felt sorry for it. She descended the stairs as the riders passed. The rock's black shadow cast directly onto them. Dust kicked up into her eyes, and she closed them briefly. She was within twenty yards of the horsemen and just then noticed that a handful of them were white men.

The large man wreathed in knotted roots cracked his whip again, and the horsemen slowed. Lois noticed the rock catching up with them, floating over the end of the warriors' line. She sneezed, and the nearest horsemen looked at her and moved his hand to his waist, holding the position for several seconds. Feeling his eyes crawling over her, she backed away several feet. He nodded at her, and her knees shook. She almost fell down, but she steadied herself, blinked her eyes hard, and took a deep breath. The large brown man turned forward and let his horse lead him with the rest toward the Thomlinsons several yards ahead.

As the rock approached, Lois tried to recall whether she'd ever seen such grim shadows in the night. She closed her eyes for a moment. Even that was no match. She hadn't believed that anything could be darker than the back of her eyelids.

The shadow moved over the crowd of the enslaved. A woman yelped, and two more ran from under it back into the moonlight. Lois was just tall enough to see the people vanish beneath the shadow as it crept over them.

Forty yards down the field away from the Thomlinsons, the army and the rock stopped their advance. The enslaved started to file behind the army. Clarence held his pistol high in his right hand. He held his left hand out to his side and slightly behind him, waving at Sara Eugenia and Clara to stay behind him. The two of them continued cowering, not really needing his permission.

Lois rubbed dirt from her eyes with the knobs of her twisted wrists. A small arm reached around her waist and then a head pressed into her side just beneath her arm. Lois stopped rubbing her eyes and lowered her hand, rubbing her palm in circles on Jessica's back. Jessica hugged her a bit tighter for a moment and then let one arm go and waved to Ned, who was standing on the porch. He clung to the post, one foot half off the step, the other behind the post. He was transfixed by the brown men on horseback lined up just a few yards away. He didn't know brown people could ride horses. Jessica waved her arm again and again until Ned took a deep breath and then finally stepped down onto the stair. He walked slowly toward Jessica and Lois and stood between them, staring at the horses and the glowing brown men on top of them. They were bigger and healthier than he'd ever seen brown men get. Moonlight reflected on their skin, which was slick and dark like wet stone. The small army of men was ten lines deep, at least as far as he could count. Ned was short, and there might have been more men that he couldn't see.

Hearing growling, Lois looked up—and shuddered. The rock was just thirty feet away above the center of the warrior pack directly ahead of her. Moonlight glowed on its back, and the void hid its front and everything its shadow cast over. She heard the growl again followed by something like a bird shriek. She was suddenly shivering and covered in gooseflesh. She realized then that Jessica, Leah and Ned had run back up the porch stairs. She took careful steps back toward the stairs, only glancing away from the rock twice to get her bearings. She continued to stare up at it as she mounted the stairs, one foot behind the other. She stopped at the top just on the edge of the first step. Being that much farther away from the rock gave her comfort, though the chill remained.

She noticed movement in the group where the moonlight shone. Something moved from the rock, and the crowd parted around it. Lois saw Sara Eugenia shuffling on her knees around Clara and swatting at something that was hidden by the throng of warriors. Lois stepped a bit to her right to see that it was indeed Clarence, as she had imagined. She could hear Sara Eugenia swearing and Clarence screaming something. They got louder and then they were silent. Lois turned around briefly and saw Jessica hugging her knees on the porch and Ned and Leah kneeling beside her, whispering in her ear.

"They're gonna save us, Jessie!" he said. "Save us."

Jessica shook her head once and then hid it in between her knees.

Lois turned back to the Thomlinsons. Sara Eugenia was on her knees holding up Clara, who was half conscious. Clara's head rested on her mother's shoulder. Sara Eugenia was staring at someone, shaking, her eyes were wide, and her right hand clutched the fabric near her sternum. Lois couldn't tell if she was shaking her head on purpose or not.

"I'm the master here!" Clarence yelled.

Lois turned to Leah, Ned and Jessica. She heard something tear apart, loud and deep. Screams jolted her into the air. Blood pounded in her head for several seconds and then also in her chest. Two people continued to wail. Lois covered her ears and dropped to her knees. Ned clutched his head and crouched close to Jessica. Lois unclasped her ears and pulled them into a huddle, her back to the Thomlinsons. Her hands were busy; there was no way to silence the screaming.

Crown Moon looked at each other and then ahead at the family of four some twenty feet away. Uriah and Sister sat atop their horses on either side of the twins. The four of them traded glances and then turned their attention to the commotion behind them. The men there were guiding their horses to step aside. Crown Moon watched Vincent glide through the partition that had been made, Paul galloping beside him. They both came to a stop in front of Crown Moon. The host reformed their line.

"Welcome to Forest Edge, home of the honorable Clarence Thomlinson, Senator of the State of Georgia," Paul said, then paused and looked at Vincent. "Residing White Wizard of the Georgia Kuklos.[1]" He waved his hand in front of him and pointed it at the Thomlinsons.

"Yes!" Vincent hissed. "He is a succulent, evil pig, isn't he? His Cyclops?"

"There were two," Paul said.

"Were?"

Paul nodded.

"Excellent."

"They're usually falling apart at this point," Paul remarked without smiling.

"The Honorable Clarence obviously wants a show," Vincent said as he moved forward. Paul drew his pistol and followed on horseback. Sister and Uriah were behind Paul, and Crown Moon held guard at the front of the line. Vincent approached within spitting distance of the cowering family and looked down at them.

"Don't move!" George shouted. He was shaking violently but able to muster enough focus to keep his rifle aloft.

Clarence stood directly beside him, his pistol drawn and his rifle at his side. Sara Eugenia was bone straight but on her knees. Clara was unconscious now, drooling heavily onto Sara Eugenia's shoulder.

"Jesus, Jesus, Jesus, Jesus . . ." Sara Eugenia whispered over and over.

Vincent looked into her eyes and smiled. He held out his right hand and lowered himself to the ground.

"I said don't move!" George said and then he fired and missed. Paul aimed his pistol and responded in kind. A clump of dirt and grass flew

---

1 Kuklos: Ancient Greek translation of "Circle·" Believed by historians to have been an inspiration for the naming of the Ku Klux Klan·

from the ground two inches shy of Clarence's foot. George glared at Paul's stoic face.

Vincent looked at Clarence.

"Who is master here?" Vincent asked.

Master Clarence looked Vincent in the eye, and anxiety straightened his back. George took a deep breath and hoisted himself. Grass fell from him, and his hair was standing up on end in some places. He had not stood up since falling from his horse. He stumbled for a moment, but Clarence grabbed him and held him steady.

"Up, boy!" Clarence whispered into George's ear. He dug his fingers deep into the bones in George's forearm and yanked him up to his feet. "No time to be a woman!" The words echoed in George's head, and he felt himself jerking upright. Clarence's vision was blurry, but Vincent's eyes were bright and clear.

"Who is master here?" Vincent asked again.

"I'm the master here!" Clarence yelled.

"We'll see," Vincent said, then rose into the air, turned around, and nodded at Uriah. Uriah prodded the horse and then galloped to the Thomlinsons and whipped a long root out in front of him. Its tip cracked the air as dozens of thick roots wriggled out of the ground in between and around the four Thomlinsons. Some of the roots were thin and long and others were as thick as the warrior's limbs. They writhed around like weeds in a lake, floating nimbly and whipping and wriggling at Uriah's whim. The three conscious Thomlinsons wailed from fright and pain. Clara, still inert, moaned softly as she was tossed about by the roots, which groaned as they snaked around the Thomlinsons' wrists, ankles, and necks.

Vincent crossed his arms as he watched the roots snare and knot in front of him. When they were finished with their writhing formation, the Thomlinsons were strung up in a line, the root snare dangled them a few inches from the ground tilting toward it, their backs exposed to the moonlight. The nooses at their necks were just tight enough to help stabilize their weight without suffocating them. Smaller manacles held each wrist and ankle.

Sara Eugenia continued to scream.

Vincent floated toward Clarence, grabbed his cheeks, and pulled his head up to look into his eyes.

Clarence curled his lips so tight that all his teeth showed. He huffed and spat at Vincent. The glob of phlegm sizzled and evaporated as it neared Vincent's chest.

Vincent's eyes flared, and his gaze bore into Clarence's. He held him by the flesh in between his upper and lower jaw and pinched it with more and more force.

Clarence wiggled his body. "Aaarrrllggh!"

"What was that?" Vincent asked.

Clarence groaned again, and Vincent released him.

"We will have the trial at dawn," Vincent said. He looked down the line. Sara Eugenia had stopped her screaming and was whimpering again.

"Jesus, Jesus, Jesus, Jesus, Jesus . . ."

"Stop saying that!" Vincent yelled, yanking her hair as he passed, causing her noose to tighten around her neck. She gagged and was silent for several seconds.

"I'll take a small penance now," Vincent said. "We don't want to make the property too anxious. It's bad for the harvest, right?" He looked at Clarence, who was now arching his body and neck to see Vincent at the other end of the vine that held them.

"No!" Clarence said. He wriggled vigorously in his snare, his belly flopping around his body and his wrists chafing and bleeding where his bones met the edge of the noose.

"We need calm minds and strong backs to get the most out of this here land, right, Master?" Vincent asked.

"God is our strength!" Sara Eugenia called out. "Clarence! George! Clara! My babies! God's love is our strength!"

Vincent neared Clara, at the end of the line.

"No!" Sara screamed. "Take me, please!" She tried to hoist her body to turn her head as much as possible to look at him. She shook her head in every direction and then craned her neck up to catch his eyes.

"No, please. Me! I'm sorry. Please! Take me instead!" The last syllable curdled into a sad cry in her throat. Tears lined the edges of her eyes.

She bared her teeth in a wincing frown, and her jaw shivered as it tried to remain closed. Vincent looked at her as he ran his hand through Clara's long hair. He dragged his fingers down a lock of it, and the instant their tips cleared the last strands, Clara's body was consumed by roiling blue fire.

"Nooo!" Clarence screamed. "Damn you! Damn you!" He jostled his body as hard as he could to break the snares. The vines swayed with his movements but remained strongly rooted in the ground. George fainted. His body jostled left and right with Clarence's movements. Sara Eugenia shook violently, looking straight down and ahead of her. She was quickly coated in ash, and her hair and dress were singed from the embers that rained on her. Some of the newly freed onlookers cheered. Others danced and sang. Their exuberance was the opposite of the host's reverence. The soldiers remained inert and stood bone straight.

Clara's left wrist disintegrated in the flames, and that same side of her swung down to the ground. Her right arm burned up seconds later, and what was left fell from the snare. Flames and embers sprayed out into the night when the charred remains hit the ground.

Vincent waved his hand to quell the flames around Clara lest they judge the rest of the Thomlinsons before the breaking at dawn. He looked up and down the line and then made his way back to the shadow beneath the rock. His host continued to look on in silence, as ordered. When he was no longer visible, secure in the void, the host broke their line and started to usher the freed men and women to their quarters.

Crown Moon, Paul, and Sister found food and space to regroup in the big house. Uriah saw to the camp setup, managing the guard and enlisting some of the newly freed men and women and children. In an hour or so, Uriah would lead a company, and they would ride out into the night in a vast sweep of the Thomlinsons' acres in search of the sixty-eight white staff members who had escaped, slaying any white men whom they came across.

## FOREST EDGE SLAVE QUARTERS

Three cocks crowed just shy of unison.

Lois stirred on the small sheet that she slept on. Hay crunched under her body and pricked at her through the thin fabric. She propped herself up on her right elbow and rubbed her eyes with her left wrist. She sat all the way up and stretched her long thin arms to the sky and yawned. Eyes barely open, she reached to the line above her sleeping pallet to retrieve her day dress. She stood, took off her nightie, and then put on the dress. She was careful not to stress the left armhole too much. It had been recently repaired. The dress was covered in patches from repairs over the last year and a half. She had hoped she would start shooting up a bit, so that she could grow into a new day dress.

Two shadows darted past the holes in the two adjacent wall boards nearest her. These and three others, strategically placed around the shack, served as windows. Lois heard laughter and tree branches rustling and cracking. She turned and noticed everyone else was still asleep, including Leah, who was sleeping in the cot next to her.

Lois knelt and looked at the girl for several seconds, wondering if she should wake her. She heard more laughter but from farther away this time. Only then did she recall the night before, deciding against waking Leah.

She remembered the way the Thomlinsons had been strung up in the vine and wondered what she should feel for them. Lois, Augustine's last daughter, had been purchased by Clarence Thomlinson almost six years earlier. Lois and Clarence had often thought of Augustine and the noises she had made when the merchandiser pulled Lois down from the block by the chains and handed her and her brother, Michael, over to him. Neither of them had heard such a sound of grief. Michael ran away from Forest Edge immediately. He never healed from the lashings and mauling he got after he was retrieved. Septic infection claimed him just two weeks after they arrived. Thomlinson had forbidden Lois to see him before he died and then had his body burned and scattered behind the church. "That's how the Thomlinsons treat runaways," Sara Eugenia had scolded Lois during a particularly loud mourning spell. "It's a waste of our money!" Lois wondered what price Juno would make them pay.

She stood and walked closer to where Ned and Jessica were sleeping. Ned was curled into a ball, completely concealed by his second sheet. It had been his granny's sheet, which he inherited when she passed. Few children had two sheets. Several of the pallets near them were empty, as were many of the small cubbies along the outer wall where her neighbors kept what few belongings they were allowed to own.

The cocks crowed again, this time out of sync but closer to harmony.

Lois shook her head, yawned, and headed toward the entrance. She scanned the floor for the tired limbs that usually spilled off their cots in the wee hours. Daylight had not yet mounted the hill. It was still dark, though the shadows were bluer at that time of morning when the orange horizon was still no match for the glaring white moon.

She opened the door and stood in the entrance for a moment. She could barely make out the left façade of the big house up the hill. Creatures made all manner of noises in the dark woods to her right. She looked at the sprawling field to her left where white cotton blossoms glowed in the moonlight. Hovering above the gloom of the dark field, she thought they looked like an army's worth of white heads watching the sunrise off to the east. Lois smiled to herself and wondered if Juno and her liberators could beat an army of white people.

She turned and faced the field, rounding the left side of the hut where the water buckets were hung. She retrieved one from a hook hammered into the hut board and continued past the hut to the well and the wash house.

A clump of shadows jostled in the field just to her right, closer to the border of the cotton field. Part of it was shimmering in the bright moonlight. Lois stopped and focused, and the clump revealed its features. It was a person kneeling in the grass—no, above the grass, rocking back and forth. Then she noticed the glistening prongs above the figure's shoulders. A golden arm held a long spear in its hand. The figure stopped moving and grew legs beneath it. The calves dazzled in the same manner as the arm and the spear.

Lois gasped and dropped the bucket into the grass as the figure turned and approached her. It was a beautiful woman. She held a swirling ivory staff with sharp gold prongs at the tip. Diamonds sparkled along its twirling, snaking length. Bright rubies decorated the handle's pronged swirling tips. The arm that held it lacked any other clothing or decoration. The woman's other arm was ringed from thumb to shoulder with fine gold bangles. Solid gold claws tipped her fingers. She was wearing boots with hide soles constructed in a similar fashion as her gold sleeve. A sliver of ivory cloth hid most of her vagina. The moist tip of her mound showed just enough for Lois to discern its curve. Her bare breasts were pierced at the nipples by thin cords of gold that draped down in looping semicircles along her sternum. Her round face shone dark chocolatey red. Braids of varying widths snaked every which way from her scalp and down her shoulders and back. They might have been alive. Lois was ashamed to look but could not tear her eyes away, her head craning up as the tall woman approached.

The woman's bulbous lips parted into a warm, toothy smile. Lois's fear subsided as she looked up into the woman's eyes. They were just a foot apart now. Lois had never seen a black woman who was so beautiful. The thought raced through her head even as the scent rushed into her nose. Roses and oranges, lavender, rain, and something mineral-like that Lois could only discern as dirt.

"Good morning, child," Sister said to her. She picked up the bucket and handed it to Lois. "You dropped something."

Lois accepted the bucket without taking her eyes from the woman.

"Are you—" Lois stopped, her mouth agape.

"No." Sister smiled. "I know what you would ask. I am not her. I am called Sister."

"I . . . I am Lois, ma'am."

Sister shook her head. Lois was briefly dismayed.

"I am your Sister, child. Do you understand?"

"Yes," Lois said, then cut herself off as her lips formed the "M." She smiled up at Sister. Orange light kissed the blue night higher in the sky now. The sun would be up soon.

"Were you praying?" Lois asked.

Sister nodded. "Yes. Not to your god though."

"Oh," Lois replied, confused. "What for?"

"Conviction." Sister looked up to the faint stars and then back at Lois. "Come, girl." She stepped past Lois, then turned and offered her hand. Lois turned to Sister and then looked back down the hill.

"That well was for the slaves, Lois," Sister said. "We wash in the tub. Come now."

Sister started walking, holding her hand behind her. Lois took a deep breath, smiled, then skipped to catch up with the woman. She grabbed Sister's strong hand and held it tight. It was cold, but she was comforted by it.

As they neared the crest of the hill, Lois looked up at the rock, which was still cast in darkness. Lois's pulse quickened slightly as she watched it loom. Then she noticed the woman in the white dress floating near its precipice. She slowed her pace, as did Sister. Just ahead of them at the top of the hill were several of the strong men from Crown Moon's host. They were standing in a circle around the Thomlinsons. Through the line, Lois could see the rack and Clarence dangling from it.

"Will you make him pay?" Lois asked.

Crown Moon appeared at the opposite edge of the circle of men.

"Yes," Sister replied. "Him and her. They will both pay."

Sister placed her hand on Lois's shoulder while her eyes watched Crown Moon. Lois stopped staring at Juno and turned around to face Sister.

"You've drawn a bath in the house before, yes?" Sister asked.

"Several!" Lois said, then shrugged. "But not for me."

"Well, go now and draw your own!" Sister said, smiling. She stepped behind Lois and gently prodded her bottom with the tail of her spear.

Lois held her breath, and her eyes grew wide as she looked up at the house. The white exterior was starting to glow in the first beams of morning light. She looked back at Sister.

"Go on," Sister said. Lois finally started toward the house. "And find some breakfast and a new dress."

Lois's mouth fell open at the last word, and she turned and looked back at Sister once again. Sister nodded, and the girl sprinted around the house to draw from the master's well.

Sister joined Crown Moon and watched Juno near the rock precipice. "Were any others taken in the night?"

"Uriah and the host found several," Crown Moon replied. "They will be cleansed."

"Have we any hands for ourselves?"

"Yes," one of the twins replied as he looked up at Juno and the rock.

"Two strong backs," the other said, turning to face Sister.

"And one girl," they said in unison.

Sister smiled.

"She is not of age to be used in your experiments and trade," the twin facing her said.

"They all are of age for something," Sister replied, then fell silent for several seconds. "She will join us soon."

In the distance behind the Thomlinsons' snare, smoke rose from the plantation church. Thick and black, it billowed into the sky, and fire licked higher and higher from behind the façade. Two riders appeared from behind the church and galloped to the big house. Fire roared around and above the white church façade, and it remained intact for several minutes as more flames whipped and danced around the steeple base. Sister could hear the blood boiling inside. The front door of the church burst open, and people wrapped in flames spewed out of it, along with the very inferno. Flames rippled up the façade and clung to the steeple. Racing up its height, they clawed it down into the heart of the blaze. Seconds later, the black skeleton of the Forest Edge plantation church collapsed. Orange flames whipped up and lashed the blue night sky where sunlight crept in. Black smoke billowed through the air above, indistinguishable from the night sky in some places.

"Dawn is here," Crown Moon said.

# BAD FAGS

## LANGSTON'S – BED-STUY, BROOKLYN 2022

Hermod stood in front of a wall of broad backs, most of them bare, all lined up against the bar jostling against each other in the struggle to get a drink. He dug his fists into his hips and huffed. In one of them he held several twenty-dollar bills. He closed his eyes briefly due to the lasers about to shine into them. Pink pressure grazed his eyelids for a moment and then he opened them. The wall of backs had not diminished. Several people were gathering around him now, forcing him to join the phalanx of thirsty clubbers.

A large, round, chocolate-skinned shoulder grazed him on the right, and he stepped forward a bit to retain his footing against the man trying to cut in front of him. He glanced to his right and smiled politely at the handsome man standing beside him. The man's two friends were standing directly behind him. One of them, still wearing his shirt, winked at Hermod and smiled. Blushing, Hermod returned the smile and then looked back at the bar and stood on his tiptoes to try to assess the bartender's productivity.

"That little nigga right there?" he heard over his shoulder. Then someone giggled.

<He looks white.>

Hermod turned to face the skinniest of the trio standing beside him. They made eye contact.

"He looks white," the man said. His brown skin shone and sparkled due to a coating of sweat. His head rattled slightly on his neck, and his mouth turned down on both sides. His shirted friend tapped him on the shoulder.

"Bitch, stop," the overdressed friend said before bursting into laughter. "You say that about me!"

The taller, darker man standing shoulder to shoulder with Hermod looked straight ahead. Hermod could feel the man's body jerking as he laughed silently. The man settled his laughter and peeked at the "white" guy next to him. He gasped, instantly transfixed.

"You're—" The man's mouth fell agape as he turned and glared at his two friends.

"Y'all, that's Hermod!" he whispered and then turned back to Hermod. "She's ugly. Don't mind her."

"I won't," Hermod said, smiling at the young man who quickly turned back to his friends. They were frozen, their eyes wide in their bewilderment.

Hermod felt warmth in his head and chest, and his arms tensed. Nothing supernatural. His hands were sweating, and the wad of bills was nearly soaked in his grip. He turned and smiled politely at the three young men. He focused on the mean skinny one who was, in fact, not very handsome, and nodded. The young man immediately doubled over and grabbed his crotch due to the uncontrollable flow of urine in his pants.

"You all have a good night," Hermod said. He wriggled himself around amongst the sweaty, musky bodies flanking him, took a deep breath, and then snaked his shoulders in between the throng. Hands gripped his abs and legs as he walked through, though his left hand shielded his bulge from gropers.

On the other side of the bar crowd, Hermod closed his eyes. Almost immediately, he smelled a body approaching him. He opened his eyes and then closed them again before they met the pair in front of him. Hermod swiveled his hips and pivoted away from the stranger. He opened his eyes again. *There he is,* Hermod thought. The bruise from the incident earlier lifted completely from his ego, and he smiled at Lee and danced closer. Lee clasped Hermod's waist and then leaned in close. Their cheeks brushed together for a moment. Lee smelled him and then danced away. Hermod clapped twice and twisted his hips, continuing to dance in place.

A stranger approached Lee and danced near him. They made eye contact, but Lee did not smile. The lights dimmed, and they were in darkness for several seconds. Bass throbbed beneath them, tingling their skin. Two hands grabbed Lee's butt. The stranger pulled their waists together, and he slid his dick against Lee's.

"That your man?" he asked in Lee's ear. Lee pulled his head away as the stranger attempted to bite it.

"Yes," Lee replied. In the swirling lasers, he watched Hermod dance from behind. He smiled as Hermod twirled around. Their eyes met briefly, and Hermod nodded and smiled wider, then continued twirling.

"Wanna be the third tonight?" Lee asked. He had one hand firmly on the man's backside. The man forced his hips to move along with Lee's to the beat. Lee twisted the man's thick, hard left nipple with his other hand. The stranger's erection was hot beneath his pants, pressing against Lee's flaccid bulge.

"I don't do darkies," the man said. "But I'll do you."

Lee stopped smiling and patted the man on the butt. "Nunca, imbécil,"[(1)] Lee replied. He twisted the stranger's nipple hard. The stranger winced and backed away. Lee pulled his shirt hem over his head and balled it up in his fist. Sweaty glistening olive skin rippled over Lee's muscular body. All of the men within five feet of him were looking now. Two of them whistled. Lee looked at the stranger and then turned around, bobbing his head and hopping around while tucking his shirt into his belt.

Hermod approached him from behind and grabbed him by the waist. He pulled him close and rubbed his dick against Lee's butt. Lee turned around and kissed him, pulling their hips closer.

"What was that about?" Hermod asked, nodding at Lee's bare chest.

Lee cut his eyes and huffed. "Cracker," he replied.

Hermod's jaw dropped, and he let out a laugh. "You can't be saying that, Lee." He continued laughing. "You got the brightest eyes in here!"

---

1 "Never, asshole."

"Pero no soy ellos, querido."(1) Lee made eyes with the smiling young man dancing in place behind them and then returned the smile. "Who's your friend?"

Hermod turned around to the young man and nodded. The man danced forward with his hand outstretched. Lee grabbed it and pulled him in for a hug.

"Hi, I'm Lee," he said into the boy's ear. Lee's hug was tight, and their sweat mingled where their skin touched on chests, abs, and backs.

"Omri," the young man replied. A jet-black helmet of buzzed hair contrasted with his golden desert-sand skin and silver-gray eyes. "It's a pleasure."

Omri smiled and continued to grind his hips against Lee's. Hermod approached Lee from behind, grabbed him by the belt loops, and joined in.

"He's beautiful, no?" Hermod asked.

"He sure is," Lee replied. Then he leaned over and bit Omri's nipple.

Hermod locked eyes with the stranger, now standing about fifteen feet behind Omri.

"Your friend wants in," Hermod said into Lee's ear.

"Fuck him!" Lee looked at him and snarled again.

Hermod released Lee's belt loops.

"¿Otro trago?"(2) Hermod asked.

"Sí, cerveza. IPA."(3) Lee let go of Omri's butt, and the two moved apart just a few inches. Hermod approached and grabbed both erections bulging through their pants. He winked at Omri.

"You want a drink, babe?" Hermod asked.

Omri looked at Lee and then back at Hermod. "Sure, an IPA as well."

"Three shots of Centenario then." Hermod smiled devilishly at the two of them and then looked beyond them at the stranger, who was still staring. The stranger raised his cup to take a sip, and Hermod nudged it so that drink flowed down the stranger's chin and onto his brown-haired pecs.

---

1 "But I am not them· dear·"

2 "Another drink?"

3 "Yeah· a beer· IPA·"

"I'll be back," Hermod said to the others. Lee smacked his ass as he walked away.

<Fucking lucky nigger!>

Alcohol and juice splashed up from the man's cup into his face and onto his hirsute body.

Hermod grinned as he pushed his way through the throng of writhing dancers and approached the empty bar opposite the DJ booth. Then he turned around and leaned against it, scanning the crowd. As expected, the stranger approached the bar some ten feet away near the opposite end. He grabbed a handful of napkins and patted down his hairy chest, neck, and chin. He threw the clump to the floor and fished in his back pocket with his right hand. Hermod leaned against the bar and watched the man. The stranger looked up, and their eyes met from across the bar.

Hermod stared into the stranger's, Louis's, face. They were approximately ten inches from each other now.

"You lovin' those protein bars, aren't you? You know they make you gassy, right?"

Hermod could have assumed any form he wished from the myriad images that comprised his and Louis's visual memories, but he appeared to Louis as his regular old milk chocolate self, only he wore a stocking over his face. It flattened his nose and pillowy lips. His eyes shone like light on the open night ocean. Both of the men were naked, and Louis had an erection.

"You excited to see me?" Hermod nodded to Louis's genitals.

"I . . ." Louis stood breathing silently, his body trembling and the movement making him sway to and fro.

"Let's talk." Hermod furrowed his brow and cut his right eye almost to a wink, just enough where he could clearly see out of it. It was the kind of facial movement that required absolute control and fluidity like Samantha's nose twitch hex on *Bewitched*.

"Why did you call me that? Lou, is it? Why do you hate me?"

Hermod hadn't been called a nigger in a year—at least not to his face. This was probably a record considering his standing with law enforcement, SPASE, and the Pentagon. Staring at Lou, he realized he hadn't really been called a nigger today in the club either, but there was something about this time.

In the blackness of his own mind, Louis stood glowing white, staring into the dark, cloudy vastness. Lightning and other things flashed in the distance, and clouds whipped around in the winds above them. They stood naked in the obscure terrain, face to face.

"You . . . We were just at the bar. How did we get in here? You were—"

"Just a lucky nigger."

"You're not! I was just—I'm—"

"No, you're not," Hermod said, interrupting Louis's false apology. "You should stand behind what you say. It doesn't really matter where we are or how we got here, Lou." Hermod leaned to his right, and out of the shadows a velvety ledge appeared for him to rest on. He glanced down at Louis's swollen penis.

"You like me, do you?"

"No!"

"You're a nigger lover!" Hermod pointed at Louis and perked up his ears. "I knew it." He stamped on the dark floor beneath him, and thunder clapped above. Louis saw lighting flashing far in the distance behind Hermod. He fell to his knees and covered his ears. His eyes were wide, and he curled his arms up into his chest.

"It doesn't feel too good though does it, Lou? Calling people hurtful names?"

"But I didn't call you a nigger. I just thought it."

"Why did you think me that? I want to know, Louis." A tear welled up in the bottom of the white man's brown eye, and the floor beneath Hermod turned to brick. Shackles descended from the black sky behind him. Hermod heard their jingling and turned his head just in time to see the black chains turn to mammoth ropes of gold, big enough for a grown man to climb on. Something glowed in the vast, deep, shadowy terrain around them, and the blackness warmed to deep blood red as massive clouds formed above them, and the ground flowed with blood-red water.

Objects from Lou's memory flew out of the tempest but then slowed down and flew around in no particular rhythm. A football. A half-eaten carrot and a jar of peanut butter with a cigarette hole burned into the cap. A tattered, soaking boy's Bengal's T-shirt. A typewriter. A broken baseball bat and a pair of skis that had been wrapped up nicely with green-and-red plaid bows. A door was attached to a hinge and threshold. It kept slamming, the number on it reading, "39B." A razor. A large clump of long, wavy brown hair. An Audi steering wheel.

"You know, Lou, you remind me of this guy I went to school with," Hermod began. "He liked me but couldn't deal with it, so he used to call me 'faggot' and 'nigger' all the time, so we would have to fight each other. I have to admit it kinda made me hard knowing I made him hard, and he had no way to deal with it besides try to hate me. It fucked me up though. We could have just gotten along and given each other hand jobs. Why are white boys so fucked up?"

A chair rose from the running water, and Louis stepped back and sat in it. He hopped up from the cold wooden surface and then sat back down, easing his flesh onto it. The chair was just like the chairs that Louis sat in at his country day school. A gold star was painted on the back, and in it an eagle spread its wings, its talons held in front, clutching a stone and a torch. The symbol was wreathed in olive branches.

"No way! You went to Stank Rock?" Hermod shouted.

Louis smiled without parting his lips. It was a warm, endearing, familiar smile. "Yeah, How'd you—"

"The flaming eagle. Well, that's what we used to call it."

"Friar's School?"

Hermod held his head up and at an angle, and his hands flew to his waist. "Yep."

"Yeah, you guys . . ." Louis's voice trailed off into laughter.

"This isn't funny, Louis," Hermod replied. "You know my husband was half-white. Well, not evil white. He wouldn't have liked you."

"What do you mean 'was'?" Louis asked.

Hermod blinked rapidly and looked away for a moment before turning back to Louis.

"I . . . Yes, my husband *is* white. Well, not American white. Still, he doesn't like you."

Louis looked at him, expressionless. "I want to go now."

From the inky blackness off to Louis's left, a double line of miniature men emerged. They marched in file, holding bayonets. Every fourth pair carried large drums around their necks. They wore gray military outfits, and all of their hats were a bit too large. The buttons and fasteners on the jackets glinted gold. Each boy was no bigger than a child's action figure. They moved just as the band itself had when Louis was a member.

"Hail to alma mater, we soar to glory's peaks," Louis whispered. Transfixed, and his head followed the miniatures as they marched farther and farther away from him.

"Why are you wearing a mask? Is this some sorta—"

"Nigger magic?" Hermod looked around, "Yes, of course I'm here to rob you." Hermod took off the mask.

"I was gonna say, 'demi trick,'" Louis replied. "I remember you now. You're that activist demi dude. Where are we?"

"Why do you hate me, Louis? Why do you hate us?" Hermod thought he might have been feigning earnestness, but he really did want to know.

<I pity you all, to be honest.>

Their eyes met.

"Why is that?" Hermod's voice reverberated. The clouds spread out, and the marquee burst into a cloud puff and dispersed into vapor, disappearing. Beneath him the clouds swirled and rose up. They solidified into a large wooden chair with a tall back. The cushion was covered with jet-black quilted leather. The back of the chair rose up into the red clouds and spread darkness there. Louis looked at it and then sneezed. "You people have it rough," he said. "Everyone knows it. And you'll always have it that way. It sucks, but it's never going to get better. Not in our lifetimes at least. But I mean, whose fault is it? Not ours!"

"Go on," Hermod replied, the black leather making an awkward sound under his bare bottom.

Louis looked up into the air and moved his hands in front of him like a professor. "I mean, this is how people feel nowadays. Get with it. We're over that Black Lives Matter shit. There're other dark people in this country who aren't fucked up. Shape up or ship out. And stop taking our fucking boys."

Hermod stood and looked at Louis. "So that's why you called me a nigger? How the hell do you get out of here?" Hermod turned and walked away from Louis. "Tell me, Louis, should I kill you now or when I get back?"

"What do you mean?" Louis said, running to catch up with Hermod. "Wait!"

A beautiful woman turned around and faced him. She was wearing a gorgeous white dress with sequined flowers all over it. She had the same chocolate complexion as Hermod and was just as tall. Her shoulders were soft and feminine, more delicate, but her arms and back were strong, the muscles moved under the skin like stones beneath a silken river of chocolate. Her breasts caught the dress magnificently. They hung firm and not too low. The dress moved about her well-rounded waist and he watched her legs glide against each other whenever the dress folded around them in the wind.

"You can't kill me!" Louis cried, stamping his foot. He saw fire in the distance, coming closer. He was in awe of her beauty, which made him that much more afraid.

"I can't?" she asked.

"Who are you? Where did the man—his name was Hermod, right? Where is he? Let me out of here. Who are you?"

"I am . . ."

"Who?" Louis demanded. He knelt and clasped his hands. "Please don't kill me."

"I am . . ." She—or rather, he—faltered again and looked down at his hands, now softer and slighter. He cupped them around his breasts and threw his head back, feeling the hair weighing it down and twisting in the wind. His dress flew up farther into his undercurve, deeper than it should have. It felt pleasant there, in a different way.

"I . . ." Of course she knew how to pronounce "Hermod," but she could not.

Blackness had surrounded her, and lightning flared high in the sky. Fire continued to close in on them, and the last red cloud rested above Louis's head. The ground beneath him crumbled, and Hermod, wearing Juno's body, raced to him as he fell.

The rubble of the foundation on which Louis stood fell into the fire that burned deep below them. The flames and smoke spread all around.

Louis landed on top of a boulder the size of a small house. Juno landed on her feet about ten feet away from Louis. Hand-stitched sequin flowers were luminous in the fire. She twisted her head in a coy, inviting way and smiled at Louis. A figure stepped out of the shadow behind Juno, and Louis screamed. It stood straight up behind Juno but much taller. Then it hunched down and wriggled its fingers, the claw tips dancing in the light.

Lightning flashed, and thunder echoed throughout Louis's mindscape. Fire grew in height and intensity as it approached them from the distance.

"You were just a man before. How is this happening?" Louis asked, looking around at the mayhem. Fire licked at him, and he ran toward her.

"I'm being rude. Louis, I'd like you to meet Remus," Juno said, motioning to the crouched beast made of shadow. Its glowing eyes stared at Louis. Remus crouched lower to the boulder's surface, one hand extended beyond it. The shadow dissipated briefly, and Louis saw a neat ridge of striped, blue-and-black fur snaking down Remus's back along its spine, disappearing in a small tail just where the creature's buttocks began to part. The creature's poise, stripes, and deathly essence were hypnotic. Louis could not look away.

"We've known each other for centuries." She looked down at Remus, and Remus looked back up at her. In a flash she was changed again. Her flesh disappeared, the dress clinging to a black skeleton which was nearly invisible in the dark. Louis could only see it for the dress flapping around it in the wind. Some of the bones were silhouetted in the firelight far off on the horizon.

The mandibles opened and closed.

"And that look usually means Remus is famished."

Remus opened his jaws wide and moved closer to Louis's face.

"Who are you?" Louis screamed. He was shaking and sweat and spittle and tears flew from his head as it shook.

"I am—"

"Hermod!"

A punch knocked the air out of him. Lee grabbed Hermod's shoulders and shook him.

"Baby, you alright?" Lee asked, he stooped and looked into Hermod's face. "Where's our drinks?" He nodded behind him to Omri. The young man was dancing nearby, his shirt dangling behind from his back pocket and bouncing off of his ass.

Hermod looked around, bewildered. Louis was on the floor now, being attended to by one of the security guards and a few concerned homos.

"What'd you do to your friend?" Lee asked, nodding at all the commotion around Louis.

"Nothing. I . . ." Hermod shrugged and looked again at Omri's ass and then at the strangers and then at Lee's back as he flagged down the bartender. A short young woman with well-kept curls came and spoke to Lee for a few seconds, then turned back to the bar.

Lee turned around. "You sure you're alright?" He jabbed his finger into Hermod's hip bone near his pelvis.

"Damn!" Hermod said. He jabbed Lee's pecs, and Lee stepped in and hugged him.

"You can hang?" Lee asked. "For some Israeli boy hole?" Lee nodded at Omri.

"I'm good," Hermod said. "I'm good. We'll have some fun." He looked behind Lee and made eye contact with the bartender. Lee turned around.

"Fifty-seven," she said.

# THE LOOK

## LEE'S AND HERMOD'S APARTMENT – DUMBO, BROOKLYN

"Baby, it came!" Hermod exclaimed. He rushed into the bedroom, a priority mailbox floating into the room behind him. Hermod looked at Lee with wide eyes and then at the white box with blue lines and then back to Lee. His smile slowly widened across his face.

"Just open it!" Lee said.

Hermod extended his hand, and the box disintegrated. Its contents, a gray suit cover, floated in front of him. Its zipper handle moved across the perimeter, and the suit cover fell to the bed while the hanger and garment inside remained afloat. Hermod grabbed the hanger and removed a sparkling white dress from it. He stepped back from the bed and let the garment unfurl to the floor. He held it up in front of him and looked it up and down. His jaw was slack as he handled the garment with a gentle touch.

"It's gorgeous," Hermod said.

Lee crawled across the bed toward Hermod and marveled at the back side of the dress. It was a beautiful hand-sewn A-line eighteenth-century court gown, nearly floor length. Its previous owner must have been tall, Lee thought. He leaned forward on the bed and extended his hand to feel the downy linen, cotton, and silk-blend textile. Dazzling sequin flowers of all kinds covered the entire garment.

Lee stood up and went to Hermod, kissing him gently on the cheek.

"Here," Hermod said, passing the garment to Lee.

Lee took the bodice and held it up in front of him. He shook his head. "I mean . . ." He paused for a moment and admired the sequin orchid, hand stitched on the left side of the bodice. He turned it around to see red roses, bright pink rhododendron blossoms, and lotuses with orange- and blue-tipped leaves all rendered in sparkling sequins along the backside. He turned it back around and noticed a fifth orchid on the bottom-right corner of the dress. "I haven't seen you in a dress this pretty before." They both chuckled. "You'll have to try it on, I'm afraid." Lee shrugged and continued to examine the dress. "It is beautiful though. Hopefully it fits better than that shift your friend made."

"It better," Hermod said. "Especially for four hundred and fifty coins." Hermod laid the dress down on the bed and looked at it as he disrobed. Once naked he picked up the dress and carefully took it off of its hanger.

"That vintage slavery sure looks good on you," Lee said, laughing.

"Don't call it that. I checked them out; they're nice people just making a buck. I was thinking maybe for special occasions like on the beach or camp," Hermod replied, trying to change the subject. He grabbed the suit cover from the bed and fumbled with the label, hoping to find the address:

American Epoch
501 King Street
Charleston, SC 29401

"Meanwhile, bitch, you bought that wedding dress, didn't you?"

"I didn't know its provenance," Lee said in his own defense.

"Pues, devuelvelo. ¡Puta!"[(1)] Hermod said and then turned from admiring the red, black, and green sequins in the rose that he was examining. He tried not to smile as he watched Lee, who was about to reply.

---

1 "Then return it· Bitch!"

"No," Lee turned his straight face to Hermod, and they both laughed. Lee stepped behind Hermod. "I only needed the bodice anyway."

"No te pondrás ese por nuestro aniversario, ¿cierto?"(1) Hermod said, laughing.

"Te pondras esa?"(2) Lee glared at Hermod's garment. "You have too much body for that. It looks small." He approached Hermod. "Those shoulders won't fit." Lee squeezed and massaged Hermod's shoulders as he watched Hermod handle the garment. He held it above his head and put it on headfirst, wriggling his body to help it slide down. His arms snaked through the arm holes, and his rippling chocolate-skinned back writhed and flexed as his shoulders and arms worked. He had trouble pulling the small, hidden zipper between his shoulder blades.

"You should wear it to your interview with Yusef," Lee said. "The kids will love it."

Hermod paused and sneered, imagining the thought of his streaming debut in this beautiful dress. He could use the good press, and, to Lee's point, the queer kids could also use a boost. Though he marveled at the prospect of the mentions and social media frenzy, it still didn't feel like a special enough occasion.

"Can I help?" Lee started to approach and then stopped when he realized the dress was rippling in a wind that he could not feel.

Hermod grunted and stepped away from Lee, waving his hand behind him. A gust of hot wind swept over Lee, so hot he began to perspire beneath his clothing.

"Vale," Lee whispered, backing away.

Hermod turned around and saw that Lee was fanning himself with a T-shirt.

"Sorry," he said while unzipping the dress. "I guess I'm just a little excited." He kneeled and stepped into it, pulling the straps up over his shoulders. The dress zipped up without the aid of hands.

"Clearly," Lee said, tossing the shirt away. As he watched Hermod fit the dress on himself, he gently squeezed his dick and balls three times.

---

1 "You're not wearing that at our anniversary are you?"

2 "Are you wearing that?"

"It has such an interesting silhouette on me," Hermod said. He stepped closer to the tall mirror near the closet and rotated. White silken linen and bright blossoms flew all around him for a moment. Hermod sighed deeply.

Lee's crotch felt fuller at the sound. He was suddenly not bothered by Hermod's mood swing. The sequin flowers were vibrant in the sunlight, pouring in through the bedroom windows. Hermod's neck was softer, less tense, as were his shoulders. His chocolate-brown skin shone, and his head fell to the right, the movement and the angle inviting Lee's kisses. Lee stepped closer and grabbed Hermod from behind. His crotch led, and then his kiss and then his chest.

Hermod turned around in Lee's embrace and pulled him in, Lee's arms wrapping tighter around him. Hermod gripped Lee's head and pulled him in closer, and they kissed deeply. Their erections crisscrossed, Hermod's beneath his dress and Lee's bulging through his underwear. Hermod kissed Lee's neck twice and then his lips climbed up to Lee's mouth. They held each other's lips and then Lee rested his head on Hermod's shoulder.

Hermod turned his body a little to relieve the pressure against his throbbing penis. It poked a tent out of the dress with a wet spot at the tip. Several smaller spots were sprinkled between the orchids and roses there. Their hard muscles intertwined. Lee kicked his shoes off, and Hermod held him aloft, gently removing his clothing. Lee hiked up Hermod's dress, and their erections fought beneath it. Lee's long fingers reached down and spread Hermod's ass. One of them slowly poked in. He licked another finger on the opposite hand and then switched them, the wet one dug slowly in, and Hermod straightened and moaned as it entered. Another finger slipped in. Hermod moaned and gripped Lee's sides. He reached beneath him and fondled Lee's balls. He moaned at the gentle rhythmic pressure of Lee's fingers against his prostate.

Something was different. Lee's grip was stronger, and his lips felt softer than usual against Hermod's neck. He moved his hips a bit easier. He smelled like a pleasant mixture of grass, stone, and wood. This lover was hungry but passionate.

Lee moved with an unusually aggressive rhythm. This type of sex usually required Hermod's coaxing. At that moment, Lee's erection was as hard as a bone.

His fingertips dug into Hermod's waist and tossed him around onto his belly. Lee pressed up hard below Hermod's navel, and Hermod arched his back. Lee spat into his other hand and stroked his hard veiny dick, then slapped it against Hermod's butt, making the flesh ripple and reform into a chocolate-skinned bubble. Hermod pressed his hands into the bed, keeping his lower back arched as Lee had set it. Lee pressed against Hermod's hole. Hermod closed his eyes and took a deep breath. The penetration was slow, and he invited more as he arched his back. A strong, wet hand grasped his mouth, and teeth nipped almost painfully at the tip of his ear. He exhaled as Lee filled him deeply and slowly. Hermod threw his head back and yelped. Lee swallowed it with a kiss and pushed himself deeper, mashing Hermod's butt into his hips. They continued their marathon until they finally expired six hours later.

"It's so pretty, chile."

Hermod opened his eyes and blinked rapidly. He could not feel anyone else in the apartment. His human vision was still clearing, but there were no strange shadows in the dark, in the bedroom. Not yet. Lee was still asleep in his arms. Hermod gently freed himself and sat upright. Lee turned around and moaned, then rested his head and arms on Hermod's thigh.

"Put it on for me, chile. Show me."

Hermod could see the room now, the bits that shade allowed. Lee was the only other person in the bedroom. He grunted and drooled on Hermod's thigh. Hermod gently replaced his leg with a pillow and then got up and stood beside the bed. Everything was still in the dark. Lights from South Brooklyn peeked around the edges of the closed curtains.

"Yes, show me," the voice requested.

In the dark corner to his left, the closet door opened slowly. Hermod looked back down at Lee for a moment and then lifted himself a few inches into the air and floated toward the closet. A patch of plastic reflected briefly, and he noticed the label on the gray suit cover. He smiled while recalling the white dress that it protected.

"Go on now!" the stranger urged.

Hermod turned around and scanned the room with his mind. Lee was still sleeping. Hermod's presence swept the entire apartment. He could feel no one else. He had wanted to call out to inquire about the identity of this enabler, but then his belly churned with excitement, and he was suddenly eager to put the dress on, as eager as he had been when it arrived. He reached for it and quickly unzipped the gray suit cover around it, removing the hanger and placing it back onto the clothes rack. He clutched the dress to his chest and turned around, pressing it tighter to his chest as he scanned the room again. Lee was still motionless.

Hermod's arms relaxed, and he held the dress out in front of him. He smiled at it and then reached it down to his foot and stepped into it.

"No, no. Over ya head. It should fit right now!"

Hermod paused and then pulled his right foot out of the dress. He held it up to his eyes and looked it up and down. It had not fit over his head so easily when he first tried it on. He turned the dress around to see the back of it and then lifted it above his head and raised his hands in the air. To his surprise the dress fell down smoothly over his body. The linen blend felt cool against his chest, pleasantly grazing his nipples and his bare penis. He adjusted the shoulders so that they fell parallel over his collar. Then he smiled, grabbed a handful of the garment at his right and left, and whirled around in the dark. He released the dress and it blossomed down and out from his waist, fluttering as he twirled twice more.

"Marvelous, chile! Come now, show ya granny."

Hermod floated toward the bedroom door, and it opened for him. The apartment was darker than usual. The city glow usually cast its night light through the dining room windows and even into their bedroom when they left the door open at night. He did not sense anyone else besides Lee, though he was instinctively driven toward the living room. *She must be there,* he thought. His cheeks stretched end to end on his wide smile. At the bedroom threshold, he saw her shadow in the living room far off to his left.

Something was standing just outside the door to his right, in the dining room. Hermod gasped and held his breath. Frozen in the air, he could feel it beside him. He rolled his eyes as far to the right as he could, and they met another pair shining down at him through impossibly obscure shadows near the ceiling. He tore his eyes away and focused them on the kitchen, directly in front of him. He wanted to continue examining the shadow, but he could not bring himself to look again.

He inched back inside the threshold, looking straight ahead. His focus drifted down to the hem of his dress between his feet. He exhaled, unable to bring himself to face whatever was in the dining room to his right, though he could feel it examining every inch of him. He could feel its presence in his mind, pervasive and electrifying, like grief. He was shivering. Even out of sight he felt the heaviness of the creature pressing on him like sauna heat.

"Quit it now," the woman said in a lower disapproving register. "Ain't nothing even there."

*Bullshit!* Hermod thought. He was too frightened to face the thing directly. Still staring at the hem of his dress, he turned his head to the right and then stopped. He looked at the floor where it met the cloud of shadow. Slowly, he rolled his eyes up the length of his body and focused on his right shoulder, hoping he might be able to see the being in his periphery. He saw only shadow, blacker than any he'd encountered. He found himself growing anxious about falling into it. He steadied himself and refocused on his own right shoulder.

Shining eyes crawled down the black form into Hermod's view and stopped at his eye level, about three feet in front of him. Hermod held his breath and rolled his focus slowly from his shoulder to the pair of eyes. They were set wide apart in a large head that did not reveal a single feature from within the gloom. The thing moved its shadow across Hermod's line of sight toward the living room, all the while maintaining eye contact with Hermod. The heavy darkness exposed the night glow in the dining room as it shifted its gloom to the living room. There, it eclipsed the light that poured in from the terrace. Hermod watched the thing move without form. Weight lifted from him, and he found himself thinking that he had been enjoying the thing's pressure. He sighed out the trapped breath. Though he still couldn't see through the creature's shadow, his fear subsided, and he felt a familiarity with it. He used to have a friend who made him feel this way. Isaiah. Isaiah had stopped talking to him after they finally made out.

"Come now, child," the woman said from the couch. "Actin' like y'all are strangers."

Hermod stood in the bedroom threshold. Granny was sitting with her back to him on the couch. She stood up and adjusted her blouse. He could see her left shoulder jostling, and she shuddered under her own weight as her body rose from the couch. She was obscured in the shadow that the creature had brought into the living room, though Hermod could make out some of her gray hair and the pale-yellow cuff on her blouse. He closed the bedroom door behind him and moved away from it, taking a deep breath. She waved her hand at him and then braced it against the armrest to assist her. Then she turned around and sank back into her seat.

"Granny Selene?" Hermod approached her and the creature. He would need to cross in front of it in order to get to Granny. He was about three feet away when the shadow sprawled slightly and sank down to the floor and settled. Its eyes looked at Hermod and then slid shut. It reminded Hermod of how a cat might dramatically yawn and then sink into its namesake nap. He crossed the mound of shadow and then stopped in front of the couch.

Granny's round face was Illuminated a bit more now that the creature was resting.

"If you don't look like the queen of Earth," Granny said, shaking her head. She stamped her feet a few times. Her eyes fluttered, and she raised her arms and waved them out and then in.

"Come on, sweetie!" Granny said. "I need a hug."

Hermod struggled with processing the impossibility of all that was occurring. Then he moved toward her, struggling to hold back his tears.

"Boy, if you don't . . ." Granny began. Her brow cut down between her eyes as it always did when she was frustrated. And, as always, Hermod struggled to keep a straight face.

Tears fell over his lips and into his smiling mouth as he fell into Granny Selene's open arms. They embraced for a long moment. Granny smelled like cinnamon and butterscotch. *She still likes butterscotch,* Hermod thought. He hugged her as tight as he could without squeezing her old frail body too hard. Her embrace was light but warm, and he wanted to evaporate in it.

"Still callin' me 'Granny,'" she said as she jostled him and laughed, nestling her head beside his.

"Tell me a story, Granny," Hermod begged. "Please?"

# GRANNY SELENE TELLS A STORY

## LEE'S AND HERMOD'S APARTMENT – DUMBO, BROOKLYN

"He sho' did!" Selene paused and giggled, her shoulders heaving up a bit as she wiggled in her chair. Her lips curled and smoothed the fine wrinkles around her mouth and chin.

"He stood up," Granny Selene continued, "and threw his robe to the ground. Massa Mueller stopped in his tracks and looked up!" She stopped talking and shook her head. Hermod looked into her eyes, rapt in her words. "Massa Mueller wasn't no small man. He didn't look up to *no*body." Her "no" was practically a shout. Hermod jumped and grinned simultaneously as he imagined this fabled man.

"But he looked up that day. Jesus, we all did." More raspy laughter erupted from her. "I remember," she said through her chuckles. "I heard a sorta scream like and thought it was yo uncle—Cissy, as they called him around the house." She shook her head, and her amber eyes met Hermod's own, which had a similar, more saturated luminance. He was lying on the floor, his forearms perpendicular, his chin resting in the palms of his hands. He stared up into Granny's eyes, kicking his feet back and forth in the air as she continued. "They told me later when I was old enough to get it, why it was ya Auntie Juno jus' disappeared. That dark business. Ya auntie an' uncle could kind of um, transfer, or no . . . immiti . . ."

Hermod's mouth tightened as he sensed Granny struggling to pronounce the word. She stopped talking and in the instant Hermod knew. Granny's face cleared for a moment and then she smiled knowingly as her eyes narrowed, zooming in on Hermod's.

"Cissy could change." Granny smiled even wider then. "I was so young. I didn't know anything about what all that meant—girls, boys, and what the difference was. They was always in some sort of dress anyway. All I knew was Cissy was the best cook that house had ever seen." Granny nodded at Hermod and danced her shoulders.

"Them plates saved many of 'em from that post, let me tell you. I was young, but I knew good eatin'. She spat in all of the Muellers' food that she made, and they would chomp on down and exclaim about it too. 'Ooooohhh, Cissy you did it again. Oooh, Cissy you'd give God a stroke with this here ambrosia!' You know them white folks' tongues, on and on." Granny Selene closed her eyes and shook her head. "Cut 'em on out!" She spat out the words in a whisper and brushed something invisible from her lap before opening her eyes again. "That was Cissy. Gave us all a fright sometimes, but she sure did put some backbone in the older ones. The ones who had been broken, torn from they husbands and wives, beaten, eaten by dem dogs, raped on enough. That was a good summer, when Cissy came. Was right after Mama died."

"I'm confused, Granny. I thought Cissy was a boy, Uncle Vincent." Hermod smiled and looked into her eyes, awaiting an answer.

"You rememberin' now?" Granny smiled her dentured grin. "I'm sorry, baby. Yes. When did I see you last?"

"Oh, God, Granny it's been twenty years at least!" Hermod smiled as wide as he could without separating his lips. His head sunk into his shoulders and then he spun himself around on his butt and brought himself upright. He sat with his legs folded, his back resting against the edge of the coffee table. Selene smiled down on him from the couch.

"Yes," she replied. "I shouldn't a been gone so long. Passing these here stories is important work!" Granny paused and frowned, then wrung her hands in her lap.

"Granny?" Hermod asked.

"I done forgot where I was," Selene said. "You so full of questions." She released her hands and then began again in her normal register. "So, the night it happened was one of the hottest nights in September. I'll never forget it 'cause Miss Nicolette had heatstroke and almost died out in that field. Massa Mueller came home in a fury 'cause she wasn't the only one passing out that day. He was cussin', saying all the niggas was lazy, that he wouldn't even match half the other farmers crops this harvest season. On and on you know, them tongues." Granny paused and wriggled her pinkie, laughing at her own insult. "That ol' cruel worm of a man. He was so mad that night, and he had a few choice names he was screamin' too. Everybody in the house was chilled to the bone 'cause Massa Mueller, he was a hot firecracker!" Granny snapped her fingers. "He was quick to give out lashes, hot brandings, scaldings. Long as you could get back to work within a day. That was Massa Mueller. But not that night. For some reason, that night he needed more than any of that. Massa was a wizard too. We thought he mighta brought out Higgins that night!"

"Higgins?" Hermod asked.

"You don't remember this part?"

He shook his head.

"Well," Granny continued, "Cissy had been cheating on him with one of the free niggas who had come to stay at the plantation on some gov'ment business that summer. Everybody knew—well, everybody who kept in the house knew—that that pretty nigga didn't like what us ladies was given. We also knew that Cissy could give both!"

"What do you mean, Granny?"

"Remember just now I said that Cissy could change?"

Hermod nodded.

"Well, Cissy and Juno, they were one and the same, remember?"

Granny stopped talking and looked at Hermod. "What about that song? You remember my song? I bet you don't."

"What song," Hermod asked, squinting. "I—"

Granny sang it:

*Go to sleepy little baby!*
*Before the bogeyman catch you.*
*Mama went away, and she told me to stay . . .*
*and take good care of this baby.*

"Cissy used to sing that song to me," Granny said. "I done sung that a million times, boy. You don't remember? After Aunt Isis died, they put me in the nursery with the toddlers. Juno helped tend to the nursery and used to sing me to sleep. Before Massa brought her into the house. When she left, Cissy would find me and sing it to me instead. That's how I knew they was the same."

Her voice echoed inside him, whispering the song over and over: 'Before the bogeyman catch you.' He felt heaviness deep in his chest, and he gasped and hung his head. Overcome with melancholy, his lower lip loosened. Sadness shifted to anger, and he clenched his fists for several seconds. He looked up at Selene. Her soft, round, wrinkled face smiled down at him.

"Yes," Hermod said, unclenching his fists. He looked down at the dress covering his knees and then back up at Granny. The mood swing alarmed him. He'd already forgotten what had brought it on.

"Exquisite, baby!" Granny said, poking her neck out at Hermod. Then she burst into laughter. "You see? So, Massa Mueller came sailing into that house demandin' attention, screamin', makin' all kinds of noise. His chil'ren knew to lock their rooms when Massa was in a fury, and Miss May didn't ever pay him *no* mind. I think she might have been having a small party in her parlor that night. They sho didn't come out to see what was the matter. We was all upstairs trying to find something to be busy with—you know, trying not to get caught in Massa's sights lest we get lashed."

"So, what happened?" Hermod asked.

"Oh, don't you remember yet?" Granny asked. "So, Cissy came out of the kitchen with a hot plate of food and dragged Massa Mueller into the dining room. He got all pampered and fed and drunk and all that, you know. And at some point, Massa dismissed all the maids and the butlers, and that's when I left the house. But on my way out the do', I walked past the dining room, and Cissy asked me to slide the do' on shut. Mind you, Cissy asked, not Massa Mueller. He just nodded me on—you know, all drunk, pants open, Cissy on his lap.

"So, you know the big houses had them oak doors you could slide out and divide up the house with? Them white folks snuck around in there like coons in the trash! So, I walked to the door and grabbed the latch and started hefting that old thing across the floor. Just when it was about to shut, Cissy looked at me and winked, and I winked back and—"

"Yes!" Hermod yelled, sitting up straight. Behind him near the terrace, the sleeping shadow roused and stood, swallowing the light spilling in from the windows. Hermod rose and hovered several inches above the floor, clasping his hands under his chin. He rested his head there for several seconds and then shook it. He released his hands and approached Selene, kneeling in front of her and grabbing her frail hands. She smiled widely, and he felt her breath on his face.

"Oh, sister," Hermod moaned, hissing the s's. He squeezed Selene's hands. "I remember!"

He held onto her hands for several seconds. His jaw rattled, and he shook his head and brought their clasped hands to his forehead. He looked up at her, his lips shaking and tears floating along his eyelids.

"I never saw you again," he whispered, then hung his head. Tears streamed down from his eyes to his chin.

Selene released his hands, and they fell into his lap. She grabbed his head and lifted it, staring into his sunken eyes. "But now you do, don't you?" She smiled and rubbed his cheeks between her palms. "Now, c'mon."

"What about Oscar, Mariah, Nicole, and Clyde?" he asked "Did y'all stay freed?"

"Shoosh now," Selene whispered.

"Where's—" He stopped and looked to his right and then stood up as he looked to his left where the shadow stood. Hermod almost froze in a stooping position.

"Is it . . ." He stood tall and looked up and down at the pillar of darkness. He felt it. "Did they fix it?" he asked. His eyes grew as wide as cups, and he turned toward Selene, who smiled and wiggled her knees beneath her shawl. He looked down at his body and gasped, his jaw agape. He ran his hands up and down his body and grabbed a handful of the garment in each hand, then closed his eyes and smiled as he ascended a few inches above the floor and whirled around to face the shadow.

"It's my . . ." He paused and stared down in awe at the sparkling dress. "My gown." He smoothed his hands over it then clutched handfuls of it and rubbed the cloth on his face. "How can this be?"

Selene flashed her patch-toothed smile at him. Bright blue flames danced around his body, though the dress remained intact. The shadow disappeared, its dark residue dissipating as it wafted through the apartment. Night light filled the room again. Towers sparkled on the other side of the terrace windows.

"Where are we, girl?" He turned and faced Selene. Larger flames coated him now.

Selene laughed at him.

"It's the future, Cissy baby," she said. "It's the future."

He looked down at his hands, all aflame.

"What spell?" he whispered.

"It's your kin," Selene replied. "No spell."

He turned to face the terrace. His lips fell open as he moved closer to the window, marveling at the buildings beyond it. Clouds snagged on the glowing beacon at the tip of One World Trade Center, the Freedom Tower. He opened the door and advanced out onto the terrace. Wind pushed the blue flames around him in a spiral. He stopped burning and lowered his body to the terrace floor. Grainy concrete cooled his heels. He pressed his hands against the railing and looked down the twenty-five stories to the ground. His gaze drifted back up and south toward the two bridges.

He whirled his body around, and it rose into the air again.

"Did they fix it?" he asked.

He saw his reflection in the terrace window and stared at it. He only recognized the dress.

"Hermod!"

"Hermod," he whispered. He raised his right hand and grazed his cheek with the index and middle fingers. He was shorter and chocolate-red, like Selene. He was handsome and strong and had been branded several times with ink, or so it looked. The hand that touched his face was sleek and pretty, like their mother's hands had been. He had her cheeks too. He had almond-shaped eyes like Selene's, like Juno's. He wondered which parent had given this boy those beautiful Vincent eyes.

"Hermod!" Lee yelled out a bit louder this time.

He passed back through the open terrace door and into the living room. Gloom still lingered through the space, and he could barely see Selene on the couch. She smiled up at him and wriggled her knees.

"How did you find me?" he asked. "Did they fix it?"

"Baby, where are you?" Lee called out. The bedroom light turned on.

Vincent looked toward the bedroom door and saw Lee's shadow approaching.

"You found me," he said, turning to Selene. The couch was empty now. He took a deep breath. Thoughts raced in his head, and flames licked around his eyes. He glanced behind him at the towers, bridges, and river, all begging to be explored.

"Hermod, what the fuck?" Lee yelled.

He felt the man in the doorway growing angrier. It aroused him.

"I remember now!" Hermod shouted. "I remember now!" Still aflame, he approached the bedroom door.

# THE BREAKING

## FOREST EDGE, BIG HOUSE YARD – 1822

George Thomlinson opened his eyes and blinked several times. His hands and feet were numb. He looked at his hands and saw that they were blue. He tried to twist his right arm, but pain exploded in his wrist and shot down his arm and into his back. His legs jolted from the pain, which only caused it to intensify in each ankle. He screamed and squeezed his eyes shut. Tears built up in the corners. He coughed and tried to scream again but could not. He wanted to cough more, but he felt a hot, excruciating explosion in his chest from when he landed hard after falling from his horse. He had been nimble enough to roll across the horse in the opposite direction so that he hit the ground before the animal did, saving himself from being completely crushed.

He tensed his core and struggled not to cough anymore. Even the jolts of the suppressed coughs sent waves of pain through his body. With his left leg and arm, he tried to brace his body, so he could take some sort of breath and let the pain subside. But flashes of new hot pain continued all over his body.

The warrior men were surrounding them now. He tried to crane his neck high enough to see their faces but could not. He felt a hot splash followed by ebbing waves of pain, which dowsed his curiosity. He could see their lower bodies mostly and the spear shafts, sword blades, and rifle butts of their arsenal. Behind the men directly in front of him was a shadow, darker than any he'd seen. He knew the rock was there, but he could not move his head far enough to see it. He shivered, his mind rattled by macabre fantasies of how Vincent's wicked enchantment would end them all.

"George?" Sara Eugenia called, her voice strained.

"Ma'am," George replied, immediately recoiling and suppressing his coughs. *Nothing has ever been this excruciating*, he thought as he tried to turn toward his mother.

"Oh, but that's not true, is it, George?" a voice called out, contradicting his thought.

"Stay away!" Sara Eugenia cried.

The ground beneath George churned, and the pressure against his wrists and ankles softened. Groaning and squeaking filled his ears as their vine snare came alive. George watched the vines swirl and shift, and his back relaxed as he was brought upright. He winced as the vines twisted, drawing his arms out and down. He was standing now. His wrists were bound to vines that were anchored in the settling dirt.

Then he saw her. A woman, wearing the same white dress that the man had been wearing that night. Last night. Her hair was thick and did not move easily in the wind. The white garment wrapped around her round plump hips and supple breasts. She had a soft, inviting face, and her round, shining cheeks were set high on the bones. He thought she was beautiful, and he smiled at her as she descended to the ground in front of him.

He could see the faces of the men surrounding him now. Some were bearded, some were thinner than the others, and some were scarred. Some were red; some were even white. A few faces were covered with leather masks painted with meandering lines. The rock loomed beyond them all. George shuddered at the sight of it and lost the strength to continue surveying. He sank to his knees and started wheezing.

"You must have forgotten that time," Juno said.

"Stay away!" Sara Eugenia screamed.

As George wheezed into his thighs, his nostrils filled with the sweet smell of spring water, and he felt fingertips on his chin. They raised his head slightly and held it there. The sweet smell brought pleasant memories to him.

"Let him be!" Sara Eugenia squealed.

George held his eyes shut. Tears gathered around the edges of his eyelids. He heard muffled screams to his right. He opened his eyes and stared into the woman's round, creamy face. Her almond-shaped eyes and round, supple lips invited him to enjoy the moment of relief that she offered.

"It's alright if you have," Juno whispered to George. He was nearly weeping now. His lips curled around his teeth as he struggled against the sobs and the pain in his body. Juno released his head, and it fell back into his knees. He moaned as loudly as his body would allow. He did remember.

Juno walked behind George and, hiking up her dress, stepped over him. Then she grabbed the back of his shirt and ripped it open. As George moaned and heaved his silent cries, she ran her hand over the ridges covering his back.

"I came here to break this plantation as is our custom," Juno whispered. "But your suffering has touched my heart, young George."

Each breaking ceremony was bespoke to the countenance of the plantation master and his family. Juno and Vincent had discerned this family's secrets. This one was particularly inspiring. A few years ago, George and his father, Clarence, had gotten into an argument during which George had sworn he was going to become an abolitionist lawyer and would shut down Forest Edge plantation. Clarence punched a tooth out of his face and told him that he'd whip him if he ever mentioned it again. George had thought his father was joking until the night their boy, Ruben, was punished two months ago.

"Twenty-six lashes it was?" Juno asked. She approached Clarence. Vines were snaking and wriggling all over his body. He was completely sheathed in them, barely visible, his moans and screams muffled. He jostled violently inside, but the cocoon of vines held him upright.

Uriah was standing not too far away from Clarence. Juno nodded at him, and Uriah held out his hands. The dirt and grass beneath Clarence churned, and the vine cocoon loosened around him. His wrists were pulled above his head, and he was pulled up so that his toes just barely touched the dirt.

Uriah let one hand fall to his side as he approached Clarence. Clarence gasped as Uriah unfurled a massive vine from the many in his armor.

He whirled it above his head several times and cracked it in the air. Clarence closed his eyes.

"You were asked a question," Uriah said. He lashed out his arm and whipped it back. *Crack!*

Clarence gasped again from the sound as his world flashed white. Red mist exploded from his body and lingered around him, glittering in the sun's rays. The vine had torn a footlong gash on the right side of his back. Several people on the other side of the line of men cheered. Juno waved her hand, and they all fell silent.

"Twenty-six?" she asked, her hands behind her.

"Twenty-six." Clarence whispered.

"That is a typical punishment here at Forest Edge?"

"Yes!"

The lash came again. Sara Eugenia screamed. Wounds crisscrossed each other and Clarence wrenched his body in pain. Urine spread across the front of his pants, soaking into the ground beneath him.

"What happened to Ruben that night?" Juno asked. She held her hand up to halt Uriah. "Speak now, Clarence."

Clarence squeezed his eyes shut and braced for the lash. He was shaking, and the vines that held him aloft had cracked open the skin around his wrists. Tears flowed down his face.

"Let him be, you devil!" Sara Eugenia screamed.

Sister stood in the line with the host not far from where Sara Eugenia was ensnared. Juno nodded at Sister, and Sister stepped forward, her naked hand holding her spear. She approached Sara Eugenia.

"Devil!" Sara Eugenia screamed. "Devil!"

Sister's citrusy floral musk filled Sara Eugenia's nostrils, and she turned away from Juno and saw Sister's dazzling gold claw tips reaching out at her. Sister's fingers entered the woman's throat as easily as they had flown through the air toward it. Sara Eugenia's screaming ceased, replaced by a gurgle. Sister moved her hand deeper into Sara Eugenia, closed her fingers around her windpipe, and ripped it out.

Still holding the bleeding, dripping flesh, she returned to the line and closed her eyes. Her lips were moving, but she made no sound. Crown

Moon closed their eyes as well. Paul stood in the line not far from Crown Moon. He wanted to yell and warn his lover, but instead he watched silently, still unable to defy Sister and Crown Moon's powerful hold on his body.

"No!" Clarence screamed. Uriah cracked his whip, and Clarence quieted himself, the muscles in his arms tensing as he shuddered, but the lash didn't come.

Sara Eugenia flapped about in the snare. Blood showered out of her, and she stopped flailing as the flow reduced to a trickle.

"What happened to Ruben that night?" Juno asked again.

"I . . . I took his hand," Clarence began. He was sobbing and drooling, and his words came out slurred.

"And what else?" Juno nodded at Uriah. He cracked the whip in the air, and Clarence jerked upright.

"I gave him twenty-six lashes too!"

"All because your son loved him," Juno said. "A beautiful black man."

"Witch," Clarence hissed. The air above him sizzled in response as another lash rent his back open, and Uriah cracked the whip in the air. Several onlookers beyond the line of warriors hollered in praise.

"Again," Juno said.

The whip tore open even more of the man's flesh. More cheers erupted from around the circle.

"And what did you tell your son after you maimed his lover?" Juno asked.

"I . . ." Clarence couldn't hold his head upright, and it bobbled left and right. Tears filled his eyes, clouding his vision. Ringing filled his ears, and he felt numb. "I told him y'all are good for fucking."

Juno nodded, and the whip gouged out more of the man's flesh. She walked from Clarence to George and ran her fingers through his hair.

"'The ugliest girl in that house out there could polish me off in her sleep far better than your mama ever will. You go find one of them instead,'" Juno said slowly. "Is that right, George? That is what he said?"

George raised his head, the breeze cooling his wet face. He'd managed to sustain a heaving and breathing cadence that allowed him to mourn and ignore the pain.

"I know it already, honey," Juno said to George through a thin smile. She looked back at Clarence, her brow cut down in between her nose and her lips spread across her clenched teeth. "Don't keep your master waiting."

"Yes," he replied. "Yes, that's what he said." He turned to face his father. "I'm sorry, Pa."

"Don't be!" Juno shouted. She whirled around, her jaw dropping as she shook her head at George. She raised her hand, and the whip lashed Clarence again. "It isn't your fault."

Juno approached Clarence, grabbed him by the hair, and held his head up, forcing him to look into her eyes.

"I'm not ugly, Clarence," Juno said. She pushed her face closer and kissed his slobbering lips. "Can I finish you off?"

She pulled her dress over her head, then set it on the ground. Then she cupped Clarence's cheeks in her hands. He was shaking violently, and spittle splashed on her round breasts. She caressed his neck and rubbed her naked body against his. She rubbed her round buttocks against his crotch, twisting her head back so that she could look into his eyes as she did. She kissed him on the right cheek. He groaned and winced. She was careful not to touch the wounds on his back as she draped her arms across him, rubbed her fleshy breasts against him, and tossed her hair around in his face. She rubbed her head slowly against his and smelled him as she unbuttoned his shirt. It had been ripped from collar to hem on the backside. She pulled the bloody, tattered shirt from him, tossed it to the ground, and rubbed her hands against his hairy chest. As she kissed his neck over and over, it went limp, and his head fell onto her shoulder. Within seconds, snot and saliva was dripping down her back. She fondled his groin and squeezed his penis and testicles through his wet, soiled pants. She unfastened his belt and unbuttoned his pants, and they fell to the ground around his feet. She fondled his bare, flaccid penis and testicles. Jeers erupted from the host of warriors, though many of the onlookers beyond the line were silent, caught between awe and fear.

"No?" she whispered into his right ear, kissing the space right beneath it. She pulled his head into her breasts and smothered his face in between them. "No?" she whispered again. She wrapped her arms around his neck and danced around until she was standing behind him.

Clarence jolted and howled in pain. He stood up as straight as he could on his tiptoes and braced for more waves of pain as he felt her body heat getting closer to his wounded back. Her nipples pressed into one of the long, bleeding gashes and then the full weight of her body was on him. He howled in pain, a sustained, agonized cry. Soft, hot, mushy meat, like pounded chicken, smooshed against her breasts, and his blood smeared all over her body as she pulled him closer, kissing the back of his neck.

"No?" she whispered again. Still holding him close, she kicked her right foot against both of his legs to spread them. Then she let him go.

"Maybe something else then?" she asked.

"Something different."

Clarence's body went straight upright as he braced himself on his tiptoes and shivered. The voice. A man had spoken that time. The faces that he could see were smiling from ear to ear, the crowd roaring louder than before. He tried to turn around, but massive hands braced his waist, and he felt a round, hot, hard pressure against his buttocks. One of the hands released his waist, and he squirmed until the missing hand slammed down into the wounds on his back. Clarence screamed a shrill, extended song of pain, and the jeers and whistles from the host swelled. The hand swiped down Clarence's back, pushing into the broken flesh, as deep as the fissures allowed. Vincent swiped down to Clarence's buttocks and then wrapped around the veiny erection perched there, smearing blood up and down the shaft. The hand returned to Clarence's waist and held him fast as Vincent's penis head forced the man's tight sphincter open. He thrust the shaft deep and unforgiving into Clarence's body.

Clarence's screams harmonized with the host's rebellious chorus. The remaining slaves watched mostly in silence. George shook violently on the ground, his face in his knees. Uriah stood with his whip in his hand and his arms crossed over his chest as he watched and smiled. Crown Moon stood in the line facing Clarence and Vincent. Sister stood in the line, still clutching the woman's windpipe. The three of them all had their eyes closed and were whispering beneath the warriors' uproar.

Vincent pulled Clarence closer to him, pushing deeper without regard for any friction. Clarence whimpered and then howled as Vincent pushed farther and farther into him, feeling the man's insides parting around his erection.

"No?" Vincent whispered into Clarence's ear. One hand gripped Clarence's throat while the other held Clarence's waist, his fingers digging down to Clarence's hip bones. "Well, I hope you enjoyed this as much as I did."

Vincent released him and stood up straight, his erection still deep inside Clarence. Clarence shook violently, suspended between the vine snare and Vincent. In a bright flash, Vincent's body ignited into a whirling fire that enveloped Clarence. Flames licked as high as the treetops. Vincent stepped backwards, withdrawing his penis from Clarence. Though the fire quickly extinguished around Vincent, Clarence was still consumed by the flames. His cries were no match for the crowd's frenzied song. As Vincent watched the man burn, his penis turned flaccid and dripped on the ground between his legs.

"Men and women of Forest Edge!" Vincent yelled, rising into the air just high enough to see the newly freed slaves who had remained. Many, including those with children, had fled. Some were having their way with the Thomlinsons' belongings first. "I have broken your master, his evil, his family, and his claim on your lives. You are free!"

The frenzy erupted again. His body felt warm inside as he was filled with their collective joy. Their energy coursed through him and gave him a vigor that no meal could. He looked beneath the rock, and the impossible void shook. The beings there bayed and howled their vicarious elation.

Cheering and roaring issued from the crowd. The line of warriors had given slightly as they too were bucking their horses, and a few of them even fired their pistols into the air in celebration.

Vincent looked out at the people in their celebration. The flames from Clarence's pyre had shrunk slightly, but they were still tall enough to be seen from afar. Vincent's smile spread wide as he watched a young man and woman laughing on the big house porch. She was wearing a beautiful blue gown. It was a bit oversized, her hips and bust looking comically larger than normal. The young man was round, as Clarence had been. The brown seersucker suit fit him nicely, Vincent decided. The young man grabbed the young lady and twirled her around the porch. They embraced and then the young man grabbed her hand and pulled her down the stairs, and they ran around behind the house.

In the field two of the freed slaves were kneeling by the rock with their heads bowed. One of them was an older woman with her head tied in a rag. She was holding a book in both hands and waving it frantically at the rock. She shook her head and hopped up and down on her knees and then began tearing pages from the book and throwing them at the rock. Her companion, also a woman, stood up and approached her. It appeared as if she was singing, her mouth agape, and then she started clapping and dancing around, the older woman tore more pages out of her book while tossing her head around.

Vincent descended and held his head high staring at the rock.

Sister opened her eyes, stepped out of the line, and dropped the handful of Sara Eugenia's flesh. She approached Crown Moon and Paul.

Vincent stepped forward to retrieve his dress from the grass. He held it in his hand for a moment, admiring one of the hand-stitched sequin roses near the right breast. There were thorns on the small stem. He smiled and looked up at Paul, who was about a hundred feet away. They locked eyes. Paul's face was pale and flat.

Vincent watched Sister step up and face Paul. Then she thrust her gold claws deep into his chest. The claws drove into him like fingers in mud, down to the last knuckles. She pulled her hand away and turned to face Vincent. Vincent stood motionless. He felt like his insides were being hollowed out. He had willfully ignored Paul's humanity, and now that it was too late to protect him, Paul's frailty was clearer than ever. How selfish had he—they, he and Juno—become. Did they deserve to survive the war if Paul didn't?

"Curse you, traitors!" Vincent said.

Sister lifted the dripping, bloody claw and swirled it in the air, making a large circle in front of her. She held her hand out and closed it so that the gold claw tips, glistening red with blood, met at a single point.

"Nyemhaa shine on us," Sister said. "Nyhemaaaaaaaaaaa." She sang the name in a low alto.

Paul fumbled for his rifle with his right hand and clutched his wound with the left one. He fired a shot into Sister's abdomen and fell. His rifle pitched into the ground, and he hunched over it and dropped to one knee as he strained to unholster his pistol. Crown Moon clapped three times. Sister recoiled briefly from the shot and looked down at her abdomen. She was bleeding from a small scratch. Unbothered, she continued chanting the name and stabbed her scepter into Paul's side, then held the bloody tip to the sky.

From the clear blue sky, a great bolt of lightning shot down into the spear, and thunder roared and shook the ground beneath them. The host around Crown Moon scattered. The twins clapped thrice more and then turned around and pushed their palms out toward the rock. Vincent dropped the dress and rose into the air. Sister launched her spear at the towering rock and where it pierced the stone, lightning struck again, and the rock exploded. Vincent and the rock base fell to the ground, and large boulders flew out in every direction. Thick black smoke billowed through the field and into the air, spreading through the sky until a dark, rolling shadow covered the entire plantation. Day turned into night again, and thunder grumbled as the shelf cloud expanded out over the county.

Several of the shadow creatures that dwelled beneath the rock had leapt out before the cracked base fell to the ground. The dozen or so creatures lashed out at Crown Moon's host with talons, teeth, tails, and tentacles, all fashioned from the unfathomable darkness of the void.

A shack-sized boulder crashed into the big house attic and rolled through the master bedroom on the second floor, crushing Sara Eugenia's parlor on the ground floor. Ned, Leah, and Lois, who had remained in the house, were all rocked to their knees when the boulder bounced through the kitchen and out into the backyard. Their little hands clasped each other's shoulders as the ceiling warped and crumbled onto them. A tub smashed into the floor and teetered on its side just inches away from where they huddled near the burning stove. All three of them scuttled into it. Ned and Lois moved each end of the tub and propped the edge onto their tiny backs, allowing the tub to sink over them. Leah lay beneath Lois, and Ned crushed himself into a little ball beside her. They trembled as they listened to the muffled crashes. In the kitchen, the wood-burning stove was overturned, and a small fire began burning on the floor. It spread slowly, inching closer to the dry wood beams in the rubble nearby.

Outside, Vincent's arm shook beneath him as he lifted himself up and knelt on the ground. Several large rocks were hurtling toward him. He waved his hand, and they all stopped where they were and fell to the ground. He stared at Paul's body for several seconds. His rifle barrel had planted itself in the ground, as he fell from the fatal blow, and his sternum had landed on the butt. Blood dripped down the butt and around the curves of the trigger mechanism. A pool of it was spreading out beyond Paul and beneath Crown Moon.

Vincent stood up slowly and stepped toward his dress. Little Ursula's face flashed in his mind. He was briefly comforted, knowing that even if he failed that morning, the Vincent blood would flow on. He focused on the twins, flanking his dead lover. He knelt and picked up the dress and raised his arms, snaking them through the arm holes. He let it slide down his body as he adjusted it and approached Paul's corpse.

Fire exploded from the back of the big house and raced up to the roof and danced along its length. Several of the free men came pouring out of the main porch entrance and the southern side entrance, along with the children who had been trapped in the kitchen. Smoke rushed out of the windows and doors and up into the morning air, joining the dark gray-green cloud that was already accumulating. The few remaining free people ran out into the fields and the forest, fleeing the battle, fire, and lightning.

"Please!" George yelled. "Don't leave me here."

Vincent slowed his pace and looked back at the boy's vain struggle against Uriah's snare. A horse thundered toward them carrying one of Crown Moon's warriors. A winged beast pursued him. It did not fly as birds do; rather it twirled through the air on six wings, all of them flapping in a devilish yet graceful synchronicity. It had one great arm like a lion's but with an opposable feline thumb. Four tentacles trailed it. Vincent stepped aside and let the chase pass him by.

George took a deep, painful breath and cowered, ignoring the pain in his shoulders. The horseman charged toward the snare, and the horse launched them into the air, clearing the snare and landing flawlessly on the other side.

The shadow paused its pursuit and swirled a foot or so away from Sara Eugenia's body, its tentacles flailing in a serpentine dance. It reached out its great paw and jostled her body. Four of the six wings stopped flapping, and the creature ceased its swirling. Thrashing its claws and wings and tentacles, the creature extracted Sara Eugenia from the snare, breaking the manacles fastened to George's left arm and leg in the process. The tentacles pulled her in close until the thing's black countenance enveloped her. It resumed the graceful flapping of its wings, its tentacles worming around each other. There was no trace of Sara Eugenia. Ignoring the horseman, it snapped up George in its tentacles and then turned around and flew back toward the shattered rock with him.

Vincent stood just six feet shy of Paul's body. Crown Moon stood motionless on either side of it.

"There is no future in butchery," Crown Moon said. Beyond them in the field, gunfire and magic flared in the darkness, briefly illuminating the clashing beasts and men, shadow against flesh. "Two hundred and eighty-four lives you have claimed this month alone, and what has come of it? She gave us no choice."

"We will allow it," Vincent replied. Black smoke blotted out the noonday near and far, and the vision he'd seen in the void unfolded in front of him. He rose into the air and floated a few feet above the ground. He grimaced as loneliness and the threat of failure pricked him. He thought about everything that had been lost to him in the span of a day. His lover, his friend, his army, his promise. "Your betrayal. No matter the outcome of this day, SiqT' Qkar's blood will remedy everything. Even if not today."

Fire spread across the pool of Paul's blood and then enveloped him. Crown Moon stepped out of the viscous pool before the fire reached them. They stopped moving when they were side by side.

"What did you do to Remus, traitor?" Vincent asked, suddenly more animated. His neck flexed, and the corner of his mouth coiled.

"It is banished," Crown Moon said in unison. "The Void King will return, but you must die."

Vincent extended his right arm in front of him, clenched his fist, and pounded his chest. Crown Moon, the fair one, snapped his head and shoulders back. Lightning crawled across the cloud above, illuminating several dark boulders flying toward them. The largest rock smashed into the darker twin.

The fairer one steadied himself, one foot forward, one foot back. He caught the boulder in both hands, pivoted, whirled around on his right foot, and then launched the thing at Vincent. Black tentacles wrapped around the airborne boulder and dragged it off of its path. The six-winged creature whipped along with it as it regained control of its flight.

Crown Moon, the darker, stepped out from the massive rock that had crushed him. He raised his hand at Vincent, and the fairer twin did as well. The winged shadow creature steadied itself and then started its body whirling in a frenzy above Vincent. The creature launched the boulder at the twins and then flew after it toward them. Arms still outstretched, Crown Moon, both of them, clapped one hand on top of the other, and Vincent fell to the ground. A sinkhole opened beneath him. Crown Moon, still pressing their hands together, glided apart, and the oncoming boulder flew between them. The winged shadow swept down on the fair twin and dragged him away. Tentacles held his arms apart, and his hands were swallowed in the creature's dark form, lest they craft more harmful spells against the master. With its giant claw, the creature gripped the fair twin by the waist and struggled to draw him into its void.

Vincent sank deeper into the hole as Crown Moon the darker continued to press his palms into each other. Vincent struggled to unpin himself from the bottom of the growing chasm. Crown Moon the fairer and the shadow creature swept their struggle across the field and collided with the darker twin. His palms separated, and Vincent flew out of the pit. A pillar of lighting struck down several times from the bubbling cloud ceiling through the darker twin, tearing the ground beneath him. After several bolts, he collapsed onto the burnt ground.

The fair twin planted his struggle with the creature not far from where his darker brother lay. Something shiny rushed past his face and struck the creature, and he was thrown to the ground. Screeching, the creature was motionless in the air for a moment before it evaporated in a glow of golden light. It diminished and the winged beast was gone. Sister's scepter fell to the ground.

She knelt near Crown Moon the darker and helped him to his feet. Vincent, who was just yards away, suddenly appeared right next to her.

He pounded her skull with a closed fist. She crumpled to the ground next to the darker twin. Vincent kicked him away.

A large man on horseback charged from the smoke and shadow in the distance. Instantly recognizing the knotted armor, Vincent raised his hand and closed it into a tight fist. Uriah fell off the horse, which bucked and then retreated. The roots around Uriah's abdomen tightened and then squeezed. His neck burst open and soft tissue sprayed out of him. His smashed torso seeped out from between the vines and pooled on the ground beneath him.

Vincent pounded his fists into Sister's breast and yanked on the thin gold bands from their piercings in her nipples. The gold burned in his grip, and he released them and grabbed her by the neck.

"Were you jealous of her?" Vincent asked. "Why would you make me destroy you?"

"You—" Sister struggled to talk through the grip on her throat. He held his knee over her gold-decorated arm, the weight of his void pinning her to the ground. "Your hubris is legendary—"

"Nyemhaa Nyemhaa Nyemhaaaaaaaaa," Crown Moon the fairer chanted. He held the last syllable, singing it out.

Vincent bared his teeth at Sister and tightened his grip. "How could you?" He turned around, Crown Moon the fairer stood just behind him now. "We shed blood against Nyemhaa!"

Vincent's heft had lightened, and Sister was just barely able to push her weight up to send Vincent backwards into Crown Moon's grip. The instant the mage's hands touched Vincent's back, an explosion of light blinded them. Crown Moon held Vincent firm, overpowering Vincent's fierce resistance. Crown Moon's touch was excruciating, and it was becoming harder for Vincent to move. Sister wormed her way out from beneath him and coughed. She stood up slowly, Vincent's eyes following her every move. Immobilized by Crown Moon's touch, he could only watch. A pillar of lightning shot down from the storm, striking the ground just a few yards from her.

"Your fight is vain," Sister said. She knelt and retrieved her scepter with her gold claw, which was still slick with Sara Eugenia's and Paul's blood. Her naked hand caressed her neck. "Nyemhaa will bring order," she said as she walked around and stood in front of him. Crown Moon the fairer, still singing the final note of his chant, held his palms on either side of Vincent's neck.

"Nyemhaa Nyemhaa Nyemhaaaaaaaa," Sister chanted. She held the final note in harmony with Crown Moon as she lifted her scepter into the air. Vincent's eyes followed the tip until it plunged deep into his right collarbone and through his left side, piercing the ground. Sister raised her hands and stepped closer to him, continuing to sing her chant.

"Nyemhaaaaaaaaaaa."

Crown Moon the darker approached from the gloom of the torn field and stood beside Sister. Vincent looked at his reflection in his own blood spreading beneath him. He brought his head up and watched the twin approach him.

"Nyemhaa Nyemhaaaaaaaaa," Crown Moon the darker chanted. He clapped his hands three times and placed them on Vincent's head. A bright light flashed from the spot where he touched Vincent, and the three of them shone through the darkness of the battle and the storm. Vincent bowed his head, gathered the blood-soaked dress in his hands, and looked for the hand-stitched rose at the breast.

"It's all rose red now," he whispered.

A great wind rushed over the three as they chanted. The light extinguished, and Juno stood up even with the scepter lodged in her.

"With SiqT' Qkar's blood," Juno said.

Crown Moon struggled to hold their hands in place against Juno's resistance. She was getting hotter to the touch, almost unbearable despite Nyemhaa's protection. Wind whipped Juno's thick hair around her face. She pressed her palms into the blood-matted dress and looked at it. Crown Moon's four eyes widened in surprise.

"Juno SiqT' Qkar Ln'tibm Tr'qkar," Juno said. She lunged at Sister, freeing herself from Crown Moon's hold. Juno pressed her bloody thumb into a spot near Sister's navel. Sister was suddenly unable to move or speak.

"My impervious Sister," Juno said, "you should have bandaged that." She nodded to the place where she held her thumb. "Before you caught fever." Sister was unable to move her eyes to the spot. They were frozen on Juno's stare. She remembered that Paul had gotten off a shot after she stabbed him. Her legs trembled and buckled, and she fell to the ground. She started convulsing, drool and mucus and then blood flowing from her mouth. Her skin started cracking and peeling, and she became emaciated, her braids turning gray and strands flaking away at the roots.

Juno turned around. Crown Moon's four hands were quickly closing in on her. She hopped back a half step and grabbed the lighter twin's left hand and the darker twin's right hand and thrust them downwards, dragging Crown Moon to the ground. Paralyzed, the twins groaned and shivered.

Juno's blood smeared over the twin's. She was beginning to feel weak, and her grip on them loosened slightly.

"I never did get to show you the power of SiqT'—" She stopped talking as she coughed up a large knot of blood and mucus and then fell to her knees. Blood issued steadily from her mouth, and a black mist flowed from her throat and nose, dissipating into the air around her. She gripped the twins' hands with all her strength. "SiqT' Qkar's blood!" she screamed. "We never had the time." She coughed, and blood and shadow spurted from her mouth. "We are out of time, Ninexetlau. But SiqT' Qkar's blood will flow again."

She held their hands to the sky, and lightning struck the three of them. Thunder groaned in the air, and beneath them tremors rattled the ground.

"You will see," Juno whispered. "The blood will flow again." She dropped Crown Moon's hands, and they fell onto the single chest that they now shared as one man. Juno fell to the ground beside him and rolled her head to look at Sister, who had finished decaying. Her skull was nestled in the small mound of dead hair that remained. Her gold sleeve and claw rested in the space between her rib and hip bones. Her nipple dress had unraveled, and the long thin lines of gold fell in between her ribs.

Fire crept over Juno's body, and she closed her eyes and wondered where the void would take her next. She was consumed into vapor as the battle between man and shadow waged in the field beyond. Her beautiful white dress flattened to the ground. Its red, purple, pink, yellow, blue, black, orange and green sequins reflecting the battle fire. The storm clouds would dissipate within hours, and the sun would illuminate the rubble and carnage. Men and shadow would continue the endless battle across the earth. Centuries later, those who remained would never forget the day that Vincent and Juno fell at Forest Edge.

# DOCTOR'S VISIT

## LEE'S OFFICE – WATER STREET & BRIDGE STREET – DUMBO – 2022

Lee placed his hands on the table and stared at the mood board in front of him.

Stacey, Lee's Executive Producer, looked behind her for an instant as she finished typing out her thought. "You heard about that officer, right?" she asked, eager to dive into the topic.

Lee did not reply. His phone buzzed beside him with a new text message: "We are still on for 9:45." The number was an unlisted contact.

"What's wrong, Lee?" she asked.

He loosened his lips. He had pursed them so tightly they were throbbing. He shook his head. "Oh, nothing. Why do you ask?" He stood up from the table and stepped two feet to his right to face his laptop. He opened it.

"Well, you're just now checking your email for starters," she said. It was 9:37 a.m. On most mornings there were at least five new notifications on her phone by 7:00.

The elevator sounded. Both of them glanced toward it and watched as Marcus emerged.

"And we've been talking about this case all week," she said. "I figured you'd have something to say about it."

"Morning all," Marcus called out as he marched past them clutching two brown bags and an overstuffed translucent one with three purple-filled Danish pressing against the inside. "I got breakfast. Y'all heard about that cop, right?"

"Good morning, Marcus," Lee replied, smiling. "And thank you!"

"Morning!" Stacey said.

"Which one was it now?" Lee asked.

"Officer Cavanaugh. From that Leroyce Keals shooting last month. This whole business is some scary shit, but at least there's some justice come out of it." Stacey shot Lee a curious glance. He looked at her and could tell she wasn't finished. She looked at her screen and started typing feverishly: *"You don't have your croissant or espresso; my inbox is empty . . . You good?"*

Lee looked at the back of her head. She turned and half smiled at him.

*"Come into my office,"* he replied to her.

Stacey scanned the room for Marcus. He was in the back prepping his morning tea and toasting a bagel. She got up and followed Lee into the back. Her eyes lingered on the mood board on the table and the adjacent whiteboard.

"And that frame set that I posted last night hasn't been hacked to pieces." She jabbed her thumb at the whiteboard. Lee looked behind him, stopped at the door, and let her pass. Then he stepped in and closed it behind her. He sat on his desk, and she landed casually on the chaise near the window and looked out at the river. Lee rolled up his sleeve.

"This, Stace." He moved closer to her. She turned away from the window and gasped.

"Lee?" she moved toward him and hovered near his arm, wanting to touch it but knowing better. Bandages were wrapped tightly around most of his forearm. They were speckled with small bloodstains near his elbow. Lee winced as he tried to roll his sleeve back down.

"Can you help me a bit?" he asked, nodding to his arm.

"Of course." Stacey gently unfurled his sleeve back down over the bandages and fastened the button at the cuff. Lee walked back to the desk, then sat down and looked at the ceiling.

"Last night, it happened again."

"The nightmare?"

"Yeah." Lee's head fell forward, and he looked at the floor, rubbing his injured arm.

Hearing the tremor in his voice, Stacey stood to approach him. "What did he say?"

"He had no idea what was happening?"

"What? I mean, what happened?"

"We were asleep and then I heard something, and I shot up out of bed. The room was pitch black and, like, filled with smoke, but it wasn't just smoke; it was like a black fog." Lee paused for a moment. "I was sitting in the bed, and I could hear Hermod." Lee clapped his hands. "He's, like, yelling at someone out in the living room. It was like yelling and laughter."

Stacey propped herself up on her left hip and raised her right hip, arching her back. Then she plucked a slim cigarette case from her back pocket and held it up, pointing to it.

"Oh yeah, sure, just out the window," Lee said.

She opened the window behind her, and the sounds of the street rushed in.

"But yeah, so I found him in the living room screaming his head off at someone, and he was wearing that goddamn dress."

"A dress?"

"Yeah, this goddamn vintage thing. It's really very pretty, actually, but yeah, it was really strange."

"What was he saying?"

"It was all strange." Lee squinted and shook his head. "He would ask 'How did you find me?' but he wasn't asking me."

Lee snapped his fingers and sat bolt upright. "Yeah, 'I remember now. I remember now,' he kept saying. And laughing. 'You had to come lookin',' he said. But it wasn't him. And then it would be him, like he was talking for two different people, arguing with himself and another person. It's all a bit of a blur."

Lee looked at Stacey, and her eyes met his even as her head was turned to blow her smoke out the window.

"I mean," he continued, "it was him, you know, because no one else was there, but it wasn't him. It was like he was someone else. And it was so hot!"

His eyes widened at the last word. "Like too hot. I was sweating so much that I panicked, you know? He's never really burning in the apartment or near me really. It was . . . I've never felt it like that. Even during the other two nightmares, he didn't ignite. This was different."

Stacey placed her arm on Lee's thigh and inched closer to him. "How was it different?"

"It was weird, like I couldn't tell if there was, like, smoke or what it was. And he wasn't burning anything. Like, nothing at all. Everything was fine."

"Except you." Stacey nodded her chin at his arm.

"Seriously, there wasn't even a whiff of smoke this morning. Not even the dress was burned or charred or anything. Pure white. It was so weird that I'm wondering how I'm not dead." He laughed. "Or what even happened."

"And your arm?"

"I was yelling his name, over and over. It felt like an eternity, but really. I was yelling his name and trying to yell over his shouts, and finally, I did."

Lee closed his eyes tight. "There was banging on the floor, like an angry neighbor banging. And then he called my name. 'Lee,' he said in his voice, not that other voice. 'Baby, what's happening?' he said, and then I got really scared."

Lee stopped talking and looked at Stacey. She looked at her cigarette, which was still lit, about half an inch of ash held fast at the end. She moved her hand out the window and let the ash drift away.

"I remember thinking, 'What do you mean 'what's happening'? You're happening,' you know?"

He laughed. Stacey chuckled too.

"So, he ran to me out of the dark, and I was standing there looking around, you know, like, God, what is happening? Sweating my fucking balls off! And he just appeared in front of me, his eyes glowing and jet black, if that makes sense, and he wasn't sweating at all, and his face was perfectly calm, and I was terrified for a second, you know? Like . . ."

He paused and looked at the floor then back at her. He held his index and middle finger toward her, and she handed the cigarette to him. He took a drag.

"He was so calm," he said, exhaling smoke. "I didn't know what to do, so I screamed and sort of punched him. I missed, but he grabbed my arm, and for a moment I saw that other person he was yelling with or for, and God if that didn't burn. ¡Maldita perra!" He nodded at his arm. "I screamed so loud, but even before I could, he'd already changed back, and his grip didn't burn anymore, but it was too late." He waved his bandaged arms in front of his face.

Stacey nodded. He took another drag and then reached out to return the cigarette, but she shook her head, so he dunked it in a nearby can of San Pellegrino.

"So, yeah, I was screaming, he was crying, and there was smoke everywhere. He was trembling like crazy and clearly had no idea what was going on. I've never seen him so scared."

Lee stopped talking, and Stacey took the silence to mean it was OK for her to query now.

"Are you OK?"

"Yeah." He shrugged. "I've been burned worse. It's no big deal."

"By him?"

"Comes with the territory," Lee said nonchalantly. "I usually just go see Tig if it's really bad. Jesus, Stacey, your face!"

Stacey laughed. "I mean, you're telling me he gives you second-degree burns on a regular basis."

"Not second-degree." He smiled at her. "But yeah, I mean . . . Tantra. You channel your chi and bang."

"Lee." Stacey looked at him with worried eyes. "What are you gonna do?"

"I have no idea. But I just have to figure it out."

"And so, what happens when you don't wake up and you're nothing but vapors?"

"He wouldn't hurt me, not like that."

"He just did." She pointed to his arm. "And you're telling me it happens by 'accident'" she air quoted the last word "on a regular basis. Shit, the next time he cums too hard you could just melt away!"

Lee smiled.

"I'm dead serious, Lee." Her voice was louder now, her hands gripping the couch.

"I know you are. I take care of myself, Stacey, and so does he. I'm worried, yes, but not about dying. He's shown me. I mean, it's weird, but he feels my pain sometimes now. It's this extreme empathy we have. He's probably somewhere crying about all this right now. Hermod would destroy the world to save me."

"Exactly," Stacey said, crossing her arms and straining to keep her glare from smoothing out into her wide bright smile. "Do you hear yourself?"

Lee rubbed his injured arm gently.

"You two are made for each other."

"I know." Lee smiled for a moment and then his mouth went straight, pensive. His phone buzzed in his pocket, and his desktop dinged. The speakers in his office broadcast the phone ring.

"Oooh!" Lee looked at her. "I have to take this." He pulled his phone out of his pocket.

"H?" she asked.

"No. Give me ten minutes."

Stacey jumped up from the couch, and Lee quickly wrapped his intact arm around her, gripping her as tightly as he could. She almost wheezed from the force of his embrace.

She threw him an exaggerated frown, a final scolding, then her face lit up with her smile, and her chocolate eyes shone. "Y'all are something else," she said as she walked out of the office.

Lee stopped smiling and put his headphone into his ear. He listened. The phone hung past his waist in his hand. Someone flew by the window behind him. He felt it. He could feel them. Sometimes he thought he was a latent demi. He had a high tolerance for physical pain and a similar emotional resolve that bordered on apathy sometimes. And they loved him. Well, Hermod loved him. Long before they started dating, some months after the Rain, Lee always found himself casually, often intimately, connecting with demis.

Lee raised the headphone mic to his mouth.

"Good morning, Mr. Sánchez," a voice said. "Is now still a good time?"

Lee closed the door and sat on his desk, facing the window. Another great shadow flew by. Definitely a demi.

"Yes, I'm OK to speak now," Lee replied. "Will Cyral be joining us?"

"No, he won't." There was a distinct heaviness to the voice, causing Lee to question which pronouns he might use in their conversation. Hermod had referred to Ade as "she," so he figured it would be safe in this conversation. "I am Adeseku Efe. I work closely with Alex. You may call me Ade."

"It's a pleasure to meet you, Ade."

"May I call you Lee?"

"Yes, of course." *Such an odd question,* he thought. Everyone called him Lee. But the moment of comfort swiftly ended, and he grew anxious about what trusts he might betray by approaching SPASE without Hermod's permission. Why wasn't Cyral there? Or was he? Who else knew about this conversation? Lee feared SPASE more than he feared the CIA. Everyone did.

"Great. Lee, before we begin, I'm going to ask you to do something for me. We know you can mute yourself from your lover whenever you feel like it."

"What?" Lee sat up straight on his desk. He hadn't shared that with anyone. Ever. His hand shook with rage. "Who told you that? Where's Cyral?"

"Please relax, Mr. Sánchez." Ade's tone was not begging but demanding.

"I won't continue this conversation without Cyral. Where is the doctor he spoke of? The psychiatrist who helped Hermod. Doctor—"

"Lee!" The name shot out, straight through Lee's thoughts. "If you finish that sentence before muting yourself he *will* hear it, and he *will* kill us all tonight! Now, do you want that?"

Ade's voice was calm. Too calm. Though he would likely be spared, Lee knew Ade was serious and that he understood they were on the same page now.

"I'm muting." Lee closed his eyes. "But I won't continue talking without Cyral."

"Good," Ade said. Lee expected Cyral to unmute himself at that moment and chime in. "Just a moment."

Ade's line went blank as if she had left the call, but a moment later, she returned. "Just a moment, Lee," Ade said. He heard another phone ring.

"Alex Winston speaking," Cyral said. Lee thought he sounded pleasant and a bit warmer than usual.

"Alex, Ade here. I have Lee Sánchez."

"Hey, Cyral," Lee said, a bit exasperated. "Listen—"

"Just a moment." Cyral replied from SPASE Headquarters. He looked at his office door and it closed and locked.

"Not here," Cyral said before the line went dead. He closed his eyes and put his hands in front of his chest, palms facing outward. It was mostly out of instinct. He really didn't need to position his body at all, just his consciousness.

Ade was sitting in a darkened conference room thirty floors beneath Cyral. She smiled and reached for the green backlit speaker icon and pressed its soft plastic coat to disconnect the call. She felt Cyral dragging her mind into the psychic conference.

Lee stood up from his desk and glared at the phone screen. He felt a sharp tingling in his head and then sat down quickly on the couch.

<I've taken us offline,> Cyral said. Lee could see him in his mind, just glimpses of him, as if he were watching a hazy flipbook where Cyral was sitting at his desk at SPASE headquarters staring out a window into the deep sea. There was another flipbook too.

<You must be Ade.> He felt like he was reaching into Ade's flipbook to take her hand. Most assuredly, Ade was a woman, the alluring, beautiful kind. He was chagrined by his earlier confusion and imagined himself rubbing the back and legs that he saw in her flipbook like he would his own husband's. He wanted to penetrate her, not as he had other women but in a way that no other creature without a prostate could appreciate. <It's a pleasure.>

<Likewise.> Ade felt him as if he were in the room. Staring at her. Wanting and wondering. He was just cute enough to not loathe it. Cute enough even to seduce? Ade enjoyed not hunting every once in a while.

<Seriously?> Cyral said. There was no humor or flirtation in his thoughts. <This was not supposed to involve me. You were supposed to brief him on you and Doc's findings and be done. Every second we're here—>

<Is one where we're at least a bit more hidden than we would be on the phone,> Ade interrupted. Lee watched her flipbook self swivel her head and cross her arms. <I mean you are *the* Alex Winston Cyral, correct?>

<We'll be fine, but you realize the severity of this, right? The risks?> Cyral asked. <And you too, Lee?>

Lee locked eyes with Cyral's flipbook image. <Yes and no,> he replied. <I wager though that whatever you and this Dr. G—> Lee couldn't say the name; it disappeared into a fog. Though frustration and angst dug through his mind for it, it wouldn't come out.

<I'm sorry I can't let you say his name on this channel either,> Cyral said. Lee felt a hand grip his own. He shivered as he looked down at it. <Trust me.>

<What is going on?> Lee asked.

<Cyral,> Ade replied, <it's time.>

<Time for what?> Lee stood up from his couch, and both Ade and Cyral felt the heat of his anger in their own thoughts. His flipbook self was burning bright red.

<Lee, calm down,> Cyral said. <Sit.> He let out a huff of air. <You're probably aware of some of what Hermod had to go through for him to be cleared to reenter society. SPASE was not only commissioned to sort of triage Hermod as one of those affected by the Rain, we are federally obligated to monitor this particular victim.>

<Monitor?> Lee asked.

<Yes,> Ade said. <Hermod, as you know, exhibits extraordinary abilities that defy typical demi categorization, abilities that cross the boundaries of nuclear and astrophysics, biology, metaphysics, alchemy, and magic. We believe he can even manifest speculative energies that we may not even be aware of. Anti-matter and dark matter even. Spirit energy.>

Lee did not respond. They both saw him staring down at the tablet on his desk. His reflection stared back up at him in its dark glass surface. Living images, memories of the life he had lived with Hermod, swarmed around him, filling the air. Hermod kissed his hand and stood and grasped him in a bear hug the moment Lee proposed. Lee opened the door to their new apartment for the first time and gasped. Hermod grabbed Lee's waist from behind and kissed his neck. He released him for a second and slid his hand into Lee's left back pocket. He left a set of keys there and removed his hand and slid it back down the contour of Lee's butt, squeezing it firmly.

<I wouldn't worry too much about it. SPASE has a mandate to monitor all the best demis> Ade told him. <Even me.>

Lee felt his hand being clenched again.

<Your husband is the greatest liability in the world, which is why we kept monitoring him. Keep monitoring. Both of you.>

<I'm well aware of your presence on the periphery of our daily lives. It came with the ring.> Lee laughed briefly.

<The doctor believes that Hermod's body and soul may be a target for a malevolent reincarnation.>

<Cyral, please,> Lee replied.

<Hear him out,> Ade said.

<The doctor was once in league with a slave witch named Vincent,> Cyral continued.

Lee took a deep breath. The first name grabbed his attention. He would finally get his answers about Vincent. But how trustworthy was the source?

<Vincent led a clan of runaway abolitionist sorcerers and demis from the late seventeen hundreds to just around 1820 when he was slain by his coven members at a plantation outside of Atlanta. The coven had its roots in South Carolina but roamed for years throughout the South helping slaves free themselves and striking down plantation families. Vincent became an unstoppable force who united the rebellious slave demis of his time. But the doctor saw pure evil in him then and banded together with the other demis to destroy him.>

<OK, pause.> Lee paced the room wishing he had one of Stacey's cigarettes. <Guys, this is a bit much. How were there even demis back then?>

<It's all true,> Cyral said. <Vincent and Juno did, in fact, exist. Hermod's maternal heritage links them directly.>

<And how did you discover this?> Lee asked.

<The doctor showed us,> Ade said. <There are plantation records.>

<Lee,> Cyral continued, <I know this may seem overwhelming right now, but from what you described to me, everything fits—his nightmare episodes, the persistent anxiety—it all fits.>

<It gets weirder, Lee,> Ade told him. He watched her bow her head a bit in her flipbook. They were silent for a moment.

<Juno,> Cyral said.

<The moon?> Lee replied.

<No. Vincent shared his body with another person,> Cyral explained. <Juno, Vincent's sister.>

<¿Que?> Lee said, perplexed.

<They could become each other at will, especially during ceremony, extreme battle or sex.>

<You're kidding,> Lee said. <And let me guess, they wore a beautiful couture white dress with fucking sequin flowers all over it.>

<What?> Cyral asked.

<Nothing. It's just this dress he bought the other day. Its—> Lee stopped and paced around the office for several seconds. Cyral watched him hold his chin in thought and stare at the floor for a moment. Lee really wanted a cigarette.

<Lee,> Ade prodded.

<Juno and Vincent shared an identity in as much as they were locked in the same body,> Ade explained. <Though Vincent seemed to be the most dominant twin, Juno was more aggressive.>

<¡Ay, Claro! > Lee said, exasperated. <¿Asi que basicamente ellas son brujas trans y bipolares que quieren dominar a mi hombre?>[1]

<Yes and no,> Cyral said. <They are not trans. They are two identities.> He waited for a moment before continuing. <The doctor felt Hermod's birth. He has been watching him ever since, waiting for—>

<¿Para que?> Lee asked. He was struggling to figure out what he was getting so angry about. <¿Para matarle de nuevo, Vincent? Y a Hermod, tambien?>[2]

<We hope it won't come to that,> Ade said.

<Qué dicen?>[3] Lee asked. His flipbook self was turning red again, the memories swirling around him in a maelstrom.

<We believe that the possession is pretty much inevitable,> Cyral said. <And frankly, you don't want to be there when it happens, Lee. You're telling me that he's having blackouts, hurting you.>

---

1 <So basically they are bipolar trans witches who want to take over my husband?>

2 <For what?> <To kill him again, Vincent? Hermod too?>

3 <What are you saying?>

<¿Celoso?>[1] Lee replied. <We don't' need relationship advice, Cyral.> He stopped pacing and looked down at his arm. He felt Cyral psychically gripping his shoulder this time. He shrugged away from the phantom sensation. Despite his anger, part of him still wanted to connect with Cyral. He and Hermod had both missed him in their lives outside of SPASE.

<So, what do you want me to do?> Lee asked. <Just . . . I don't even know. You're telling me my husband is turning into a two-hundred-year-old slave witch?>

<Yes and no,> Ade said. <You have a profound pacifying effect on Vincent in particular. He loves you in much the same way that your husband does.>

<The doctor told you this, huh?> Lee asked.

<Yes, in fact, he did.> Ade smiled. <He's been snooping, I suppose.>

<How?> Lee asked.

<Me,> Cyral admitted.

<Go on,> Lee said, frowning. The other two saw his flipbook go dark. The colorful memory storm had ceased. He sat in shadows, though, in fact, the sun lit up the entire space around him.

<I have been acting as a conduit for the doctor,> Cyral explained.

<You used me,> Lee said in disgust.

<While you were sleeping, to minimally engage Hermod.>

<Puto maricón,> Lee said. <You used me, Cyral?>

<You have a right to feel violated,> Cyral said. <But you shouldn't think of it like that, Lee.>

<We had to know,> Ade interrupted, <and now we do. Vincent is alive in there, and we have to stop him from coming back, and we believe we can. You can.>

<I almost burned alive last night while you and doctor . . .> He had the strange sensation of fogginess at the desire to say the name. <Him!> Lee shouted. He saw Stacey waving at him through the glass door, her face puzzled, a pantomimed query. He must have shouted aloud. He waved her off and smiled, exaggerating his gestures.

1 <Jealous?>

<The doctor has been keeping you safe,> Ade said.

<Hermod has been keeping you safe, in fact,> Cyral countered. <He loves you, and that is the secret weapon that will keep Vincent and his sister at bay. Their love for you.>

<We believe you can convince Vincent and Juno to stay at rest, to let their vengeance go,> Ade said.

<Ha!> Lee replied. <And what are they coming back to do? Who are they looking for? What was so evil about freeing slaves?>

His questions were met with silence.

Lee clenched his jaw. <So, what's the next move?>

<We need to gradually increase Hermod's awareness of the doctor's presence,> Ade said. <They need to meet face to face. When Hermod is ready, the doctor can open the psychic rapport that will aid your husband's defenses against Vincent and Juno's rage.>

<And how am I involved in that? They already know each other!> Lee asked. <It sounds like they should just schedule an appointment, right? I can brief him if that's all it takes.>

<It will take more than that,> Cyral said. <The doctor needs to continue to use you as a conduit. It's hard to explain, but his power signature would be immediately recognizable to Juno and Vincent in a face-to-face meeting at this point.>

<Was this your idea, Alex?> Lee asked.

<No!> Cyral said. <I had no choice, Lee. Please understand that.>

<I get it,> Lee said. Hermod always talked about Gaskill. He sounded like an intense, nosey asshole, and now Lee had proof of it. He paused to let things sink in before responding. <Doesn't sound like we have much time.>

<No, we don't,> Ade admitted. <The doctor slayed Vincent approximately two hundred years ago under what they called Nyhemaa's Star.>

Lee was chilled by the name. Hermod had mentioned it after he returned from his lockdown.

<This ritualistic celestial event is set to occur on the tenth,> Ade said

<Guys, that's in a few days,> Lee said. <In fact, it's the day before we leave for Morocco.>

<Well, we certainly don't want to hold you up from pretending to be straight in Morocco,> Cyral said, smiling.

<So, I can't meet the doctor, but he wants to sort of be up inside me is what you're telling me,> Lee said. <How does that work?>

<I must say your sense of humor regarding this is refreshing,> Ade said.

<I mean, you can't stay a boner killer forever, right?> Lee replied.

<Even in the face of death,> Ade replied.

<Especially then, honey,> Lee said. <Laughter makes it go quicker, I suppose.>

<You have quite a candor regarding death,> Ade said. <I know soldiers who wouldn't take so kindly to this burden.> Ade had been growing anxious in the weeks preceding this conversation. August 31, 2022, had been circled on her calendar for nearly five years now, ever since Dr. Gaskill had his vision. <I'm excited to be working with you, Lee.>

<My pleasure. You should join us for dinner and a nightmare one night,> Lee said.

<It would be my pleasure, I assure you,> Ade said. <Maybe a fitting reward should we survive.>

Cyral sneered.

<So, you still haven't told me what I need to do,> Lee said, looking at his arm.

<Nothing,> Ade replied. <Just be you. The doctor will continue to inhabit you during the night, during your sleep. Through your connection with Hermod, he will subtly ingratiate himself with Hermod.>

<Our aim is to be able to have the doctor fully reveal himself in five days, at which point the psychic suppressants will be in place,> Cyral said. <You won't know he's around. He will just be.>

<Starting tonight?> Lee asked.

<Starting now, the moment we cease talking, the moment you unmute,> Ade said.

<And this is gonna work?> Lee asked. <How do I not give him away? I don't even know the doctor exists! I'm hiding something I don't even believe is real.>

"But I am," Dr. Gaskill said.

Lee jumped up from his desk and pulled his breath deep into his abdomen. He spun around to face his office door. He gasped at the man looking at him. He was two toned, the right half of his head a smooth red-chocolate color with a golden-yellow eye and the left a fairer brown, like oats with a ruby eye. His hands matched the respective sides of his face. His dual skin tones blended in a jagged line that ran from the top button of his shirt to the back of his collar and presumably all around his body. He was slightly taller than Lee, balding, and had a long, wide nose. Gray hairs filled out his eyebrows and neatly trimmed mustache and beard. His skin was tight and shiny. His suit was tailored perfectly, and he wore no tie. The top button of his shirt was open. He stood perfectly still. His presence made Lee's skin tingle. The man smelled like ashes and fresh water. His gaze pierced through Lee, and it seemed like time stopped for a moment. The air was heavier, and he felt like it was not proper that he should share a room with Dr. Gaskill, like he wasn't clean enough. He felt on the verge of ecstasy that he'd only ever shared with Hermod.

Lee fell to his knees, his head filling with foreign memories of ex-slave men and women burning the bodies of their captors, urging dumbfounded slaves to find shoes and dance. He saw a beast clawing, rending white men's flesh in the shadows of a great boulder in the woods. He saw Juno caught up in a swirling maelstrom with twin men, one the color of Gaskill's left side, the other the color of Gaskill's right side. He saw Hermod as a boy, laughing with his granny. Saw him in the epic battle with Chris Upton, the water wielder. Saw himself screaming in pain that morning when Hermod gripped him.

"You can do this, Lee," Dr. Gaskill said. "Hermod needs you to do this."

Lee was unable to speak, his head filled with the sights and sounds of the day he first saw his love. The smell of the backseat of the cab mixed in with his own lavender scent. He remembered asking the driver to turn the A/C off, so he could open the window, letting in the honking of stalled cars on the bridge. He remembered turning to look out the window and locking eyes with the man five feet away from him stalled on the bridge as well, in the train car. That bright, almost crooked smile. He'd crawled over to the driver's side of the car to be closer to him, to smile closer at him. He'd looked toward the emergency exit near the train and then got out of the cab. The driver yelled after him. Lee told him he'd be right back. He watched Hermod walk between the people in the train car. Lee kept tabs on the traffic on the bridge to make sure he didn't miss his cab. The train was still stalled. He wasn't surprised when Hermod floated briefly out of the emergency exit and reached out to shake and kiss Lee's hand. He took Hermod's number and watched him float up and away from the bridge. He lost him behind the apartments lining the river. Traffic was still stalled. The train crunched and lurched away. Lee texted Hermod immediately, and they found each other that night, never leaving each other's side after that.

Lee knelt on the floor, closed his eyes, and wept.

"What's wrong, baby?" Hermod asked.

Lee looked up, startled, his eyes wide. He leapt up from the floor and grabbed Hermod, drawing him into a hug. He winced at the pain in his arm but did not lessen his grip or his weeping. Hermod tightened his left arm around Lee but held his other arm away. He was holding a large bag with a firm, flat bottom. Its contents were hefty, and Hermod didn't want to drop it.

Lee pressed his face against Hermod's, and stubble pricked his cheeks. He couldn't feel Cyral or Ade any longer, couldn't see their flipbooks. He was filled with a worry that he hoped he could hide from Hermod, a worry that the doctor had already begun to mask.

"I'm sorry, baby," Hermod said. He brought the bag between them, and Lee took a better look.

"Marge's!" Lee said, his mouth wide. "They were open this early?"

Lee pulled the heavy cake box out of the bag and admired it, his smile comically wide.

"I talked to Tig," Hermod said as he caressed Lee's arm. "I'm going to figure this out. I'll never hurt you again. I swear."

Lee grabbed the box from him and stared at it.

"Marge's," Lee whispered, placing the box on his desk. He returned to Hermod and wiped the tear from near Hermod's nose before pulling him in and kissing him deeply. Lee couldn't help feeling like he'd made a grave mistake, but something about the arrangement made him feel safer now. He wanted to trust Dr. Gaskill, Ade, and Cyral. He wanted to believe that things would be OK with their help. But he loved his husband, and deep down he could not bring himself to trust anyone more than him. He was trying hard not to cry and trying even harder to hide his feelings from Hermod. Marge's carrot cake helped.

"I really didn't need to know that Marge's was open this early," Lee said.

"I pulled a favor," Hermod explained. He smiled, and they embraced for a moment longer.

Gaskill felt a flash of anxiety, but there was something extraordinarily human about Lee that kept Hermod human too. This made Gaskill optimistic about the plan. Of the many shared moments he had stolen his way into, this one was one of the most genuine, one of the very few that made him feel guilty.

# HE'S JUST A DOORMAN

## LEE'S OFFICE – WATER STREET & MAIN STREET – DUMBO

Lee stepped out of the elevator and looked out the front door of the building. It was cloudier than he would have liked. He needed more sunshine. He hadn't wanted to return to the office after meeting Tig in Clinton Hill earlier. In fact, he'd wanted to stay there with him, watching him tinker with his robot pals and engineers. He'd wanted tomorrow to just happen and blot out today. At least it was early enough to catch happy hour.

His footsteps echoed on the tiles, and Myron looked up from his podium.

"¡Conquistador!" Myron said. "¿Sales temprano hoy, cierto?"[(1)]

"Si," Lee said. He hated when Myron called him that. They had struck up a conversation in Spanish a week after Myron started, Myron in his Caribbean and Lee in his Castilian. He had called him things like "Salvador' y 'Conquistador" and referred to Spain as the "Motherland" several times. Though it irked him every time, Lee had decided that Myron was ultimately

---

1 "Conqueror' you are leaving early today' no?"

harmless and often funny, and his personal struggle with history was his own problem. Lee paused near the podium and hiked his duffle bag up onto his shoulder. "Estoy muy cansado hoy y he fumado tantos cigarillos."[(1)]

"No sabía que fumabas."[(2)]

"Yo tampoco."[(3)] Lee laughed and leaned on the podium.

Myron smiled. He had a handsome smile, which was hidden by his unattractively meek resting face. He seemed to be always frowning, and he had a severe stare, and he stared at everything. But his smile. Lee thought he might have been a handsome man if not for visible impressions of the troubles he'd seen. His face looked worn, like a soldier's. His brow drooped heavily over his eyes when he wasn't greeting tenants and guests. There were long, thin barbed scars under his chin and along his neck. He was missing his molars on the left side of his face, though that didn't impact his smile too much. Myron never quite stood up straight either.

Myron looked up at Lee and held out an open pack of Newport 100's, one butt pulled out above the rest.

"No, gracias. ¿Sales?"[(4)] Lee pointed to the door.

"Yeah."

The men walked to the door shoulder to shoulder.

"Allow me." Myron hopped to the door before Lee could reach it and stepped through it. He held it open for Lee and smiled at him from behind his cigarette. He lit it and took a pull.

They stood in silence for a moment.

"You're waiting for your man?"

Lee nodded. "Yeah. We're gonna grab dinner."

"He was here earlier too. Must be serious."

"What?" Lee turned his attention from the traffic to Myron.

"I mean, he's never here like that." Myron raised his eyebrows slightly as he exhaled smoke and tapped the ashes from his cigarette. "You only see him on the news these days. I was a little starstruck."

---

1 "I'm so tired today and I've smoked too many cigarettes."

2 "I didn't know that you smoked."

3 "Me neither."

4 "No, thanks. You going out?"

"Yes, I suppose." Lee took in a slow breath.

"I mean, and you've been looking a little beat these days," Myron added.

"Huh?" Surprised, Lee squinted at Myron. He exhaled and looked up at Lee. "You're observant," Lee said, his lips curling slightly.

"I mean, I Google too." Myron laughed.

Lee took another deep breath. "Yeah, it's been a tough week." He looked at his watch. "But thank you for your concern, Myron. How's life on your end?"

"You're a solid-looking dude, too. Nice strong legs." Myron patted Lee on the back of his arm and pulled on his cigarette. "Pretty eyes. You'll be fine, Conquistador."

"Excuse me." Lee let his gym bag fall from his shoulder, and he caught the handle in his palm. Lee had never spent much time interacting personally with Myron. Standing there with him now made him feel uncomfortable, and it wasn't just Myron's irksome references to Spanish monarchy. He'd known Myron longer than quite a few staff members, and they'd exchanged a few words now and then, tips at holidays, a few drunken pleasantries. Myron was privy to his comings and goings, shipments, guests, office layout, and staff roster, along with all of the other details that the public had access to given Hermod's popularity.

"Thank you, Myron." Lee let the duffle fall to the ground and then turned and faced Myron, his lips taut. "But I'd prefer to keep our communication professional."

"Aw, c'mon. Don't be like that." Myron smiled, and Lee could see the shadows where his molars used to be. Myron's brow lifted slightly, and his eyes went dark. Lee couldn't see anything in them. They barely shone in the dusky light. They were dark brown, matte rather than shiny, like none he'd ever seen. He felt a revulsion and suddenly wanted Myron to be anywhere but next to him. Even dead. Dead would be best, he thought before scolding himself for thinking it.

"Be like what?" Hermod asked. He landed beside Lee, bracing Lee's waist with one hand while he knelt and picked up the duffel bag in the other. He kept his eyes fixed on Myron's. Something compelled him to do so. Even without reading his mind.

"Nothing." Lee leaned back slightly into Hermod's embrace and enjoyed his warmth. The tough but soft muscles in his chest and arms felt good against his back. He turned quickly and pecked Hermod on the cheek. Their eyes met for a second.

<Let's go,> Lee thought.

"It's a real pleasure, H." Myron smiled, then flicked the cigarette butt to the curb. Hermod's unseen flame burned it to nothing as it arced through the air.

"Can't say the same. You are?" Hermod's reaction was instinctive, cold, and defensive, as if he was an untrained hound in sight of a mailman.

"Goodnight, Myron," Lee said. He grabbed Hermod's hand and turned and walked away, pulling Hermod with him.

"He's watching us walk away, isn't he?" Lee asked.

"I . . ." Hermod opened his mind and tried to feel for Myron. "I can't." He slowed down.

"No, keep walking," Lee said, pulling Hermod back into stride. He grabbed Hermod's waist and pulled him in tighter, then exhaled deeply. "That was weird."

"Yeah. I can't see him." Hermod shook his head. "Like see him, his psychic presence I guess. That's never happened before. Like he was just a picture of an asshole and not a real one." They walked a few more steps before Hermod halted and turned around. Lee turned to look too. Myron was gone. A moment later, they continued walking.

"That's never happened."

"Yeah, that was strange. Myron's usually cool, but he got really fresh and mentioned something about my legs and googling us."

Hermod turned and looked at him with his brow cut down in a V. "That guy's off. We're finding a new doorman tomorrow." They walked farther up Main Street. "I still can't believe that. I could reach out and turn off the president right here and now, but I can't see that motherfucker for shit."

## HERMOD AND LEE'S APARTMENT – DUMBO, BK

<When will you be home?>

<It's quiet tonight. Thank Go—> Hermod stopped the thought. He was trying to stop using the word. <Thank goodness.>

<OK. I wanted to wait for you to eat, but I must settle down. Seven o'clock conference with Laura tomorrow morning.>

Hermod looked down and watched cars and people flow up and down Flatbush Avenue. Moonbeams glimmered in the Prospect Park lake.

<OK, babe. Well, it's pretty fucking boring tonight. I was just going to meditate for a little longer and—>

<Boring?> Lee stopped sipping his gin and tonic and chuckled. He looked out the window onto Brooklyn's south side before returning to the food waiting to be prepared on the kitchen countertop.

<Well, you know, it's August, and no one's really around to be bad anyway.>

<Baby, you're not looking hard enough. There's always bad in this city. Have you been in the Atlantic Target yet?>

<I mean, I can't hear anything . . . >

"Then come home."

<I do need some cuddles.>

"You know where to find them."

<Dope. Well, I'm gonna meditate a bit and do a round, I guess. Then I'll be on a cuddle hunt.>

<Where are you rounding?>

Hermod stalled. He looked away from the city, toward the ocean. The moonlit projects in the north.

<I don't know. I may not.>

<You ready for your interview tomorrow?>

<¡Si!>

<You know Yusef is a bitch. Maybe you should wear the dress for good luck.>

Hermod laughed aloud. The sound tingled Lee's ears and warmed his cheeks.

<I'm ready. I went over the interview questions with him earlier today. Should be pretty exciting.>

<Any hashtags I can get the jump on?>

<Hashtag save yourselves.>

"Maricón. Is shrimp OK tonight, babe?"

<Mmmmmm . . . is there some more of that bisque you made?>

"Just a bowl. It will be waiting for you."

<Eres el puto amo. ¿No?>[1]

Lee smiled and looked out the window again. A shrimp tail pricked his left index fingertip. He placed it in his mouth.

"¡Coño! ¡Puto camarón!"

<Huh?>

"Permiso, 'Ay, Hermod, sálvame, de esas camarones monstruosas y horribles! ¡Por favor ! ¡No puedo sobrevivir!"[2]

<I'll show you impaled.>

<You learned from the best. Where are you?>

<Near the park, headed north.>

<Show me.>

<What do you mean?>

"Show me!"

<Where are you?> Hermod countered.

"In the kitchen."

Hermod didn't need to dive into his mind to see Lee staring out the window.

<¿La esquina?>

<Si, 'the cut.'> Lee giggled and looked for a moment at the bowl in the sink beside him where he had discarded the prickly shrimp shells. He looked back out the window as he turned on the faucet and let the warm water rinse away the shrimp slime.

Hermod ignited. Air rushed into his nostrils, and he felt a similar pressure, intake, across every inch of his skin. A tingling sensation spread around

---

1 <You are the fucking best· No?>

2 "Excuse me· 'Hermod· please save me from these monstrous horrible shrimp! I can't survive!"

him, and warmth crawled through his belly and outward as he exhaled, and the pressure across his skin released. Another breath, another pulse of pressure across his entire body, and hot fire pulsed in his belly, hotter as it spread out. Another body breath, and he ceased to feel his stomach, the heat that he felt there now rushing across his skin. The city around him became obscured as if he were looking at it through a shallow crystal-clear waterfall. An impossible pressure overcame him, and as he ceased to feel his insides, the pressure from outside increased as if air were hugging him, suffocating him. Waves of blue-and-white fire washed around him, just beyond the veil that had surrounded him and obscured his vision earlier. Then he felt the world just beyond the fire, as if his skin were twenty feet thick instead.

Lee looked out the window toward the park. He knew it was the park because it was the only barren swath in the skyline, devoid of new construction and the glow of LEDs. Then he saw it, a hole in the night.

His husband.

"Have you thought about the place in Málaga?" Lee asked. Hermod could feel his excitement. He had thought about it. He'd thought about how much calmer it would be to spend his evenings by the sea, drinking Txaikolina, eating fresh, sweet razor clams, making love with his awesome husband on the beach.

<I mean—> Hermod paused for a moment. The twinkling skyline signaled the millions of worries and traumas and issues that he burdened himself with daily. <You said your dad's friends will drop the price for us?>

"Yes, babe." Lee was unsure of what to say next. He'd anticipated at least two more weeks of stubborn back and forth before making any headroom with Hermod about a potential move. "Yes, the price, they can lower it. We wouldn't even have to sell."

<It's time, Mina. Just jump.>

Hermod was jolted by urgency of the woman's destructive thought.

<Mina. Jump.>

Hermod flew to the high-rise along the south side of the park. The woman fell into his arms at the twentieth floor. Trembling, her wide, wild eyes locked onto his as they descended.

<I'm in,> Hermod replied to Lee as he laid Mina on the ground in front of her building. He forced her mind to sleep and soared back out over the park. <Let's talk about it tonight.>

<Love you, babe. Bring some Haribos!> Lee thought, elated. He watched Hermod flicker twice for "OK." <Make sure they don't melt!>

## APARTMENT BUILDING ON BEDFORD & LINCOLN – FLATBUSH, NEW YORK CITY, NY

Heat radiated in Myron's mouth, and smoke scraped the back of his throat. He inhaled deeper, and the burning cigarette hissed. The corner of his mouth curled up, and he drew the smoke in even more. He flicked his fingers, and the glowing butt arced away from him and over the roof's edge. It landed on the fire escape and briefly burned an orange hole into the shaft shadows. Smoke swirled out of his nose and gathered around his head for a moment. He cleared phlegm from his throat and turned around to face the park. Moonlight sliced between the edge of the treetops and the night sky.

He knew Hermod was there. He always lit up somewhere around this side of the park. At least for the last ten months. Ten months, two weeks, and four days, to be exact.

He smiled in the semi dark on his roof and fished in his left pants pockets for his pack of cigarettes and in the right pocket for his lighter. It was windy, which made the heat bearable, even pleasant. He struck his thumb against the flint of his lighter, to no avail. He did it again as he walked toward the edge of the roof. Pedestrians on Bedford Avenue gripped their garments to their chests. Trees flailed, and branch tips stabbed into the white globes at the end of the street lampposts. Their rustling leaves roared.

He held the cigarette by the butt between his lips and the tip dipped into the shadow of his cupped left hand. He listened for the frequency of that whoosh in his ears. It picked up. He felt the wind rush in and out of his mouth through the spaces where his molars would have been. The whistling tickled the back of his mouth. He'd never get it lit with this wind. He stood fast, stared harder into the cup, and suddenly the stinging stopped, his earlobes throbbed, and the whooshing left his ears. He flicked the flint, and the lighter ignited. Wind slapped at his legs and chest. He smiled, huffed, and tried not to laugh or else he'd choke on the smoke. He stood upright and smiled. He exhaled the smoke, and it swirled around his head, some of it creeping along the edges of his neck and down before it was snatched and dispersed by the wind. His force field trapped the rest. The wind couldn't take it away, and there was no whoosh in his ear, not even when he reached up to take the cigarette from his lips and place it back. His smile tightened for a moment, and he looked toward the south. He was getting much better at controlling his fields. He had not been "hunting" in the park in a week, but he'd trapped three people in place in the subway earlier that evening.

"I'm ready for you. You faggots think you're better than God."

His phone buzzed in his pocket, rattling his concentration. He watched as the wind tore his smoke cloud to nothing and imagined himself in the basement of his apartment building, standing over Lee who was naked, bound, and gagged. Myron held his erection in one hand and a plunger in the other. Both were bloody, where they had been forcibly inserted into Lee. He wondered whether he could use his force field to penetrate in the same way he used it to punch and suffocate animals in the park. He imagined Hermod flying into the dank room, catching him in the act. These fantasies always ended with Hermod catching him having his way with the little faggot conquistador. He wanted Hermod to watch. Sometimes he caught them in the basement. Sometimes in Lee's office. Sometimes they were in what he imagined was Lee and Hermod's fancy faggot apartment.

His phone buzzed again. The message was small enough to fit into the SMS notification bubble.

*Ronny? U still on the roof blowin?*

*Shit, ain't you high already? It's time to go!*

Myron grabbed his right butt cheek and felt his wallet there. He switched the phone to his other hand and jiggled the back of his left pant leg. He heard the keys. Smoke rushed into his mouth and back out his nostrils a moment later. The cloud formed, wider this time. There was less wind, but he was safe either way.

*B down in a sec,* he typed into the phone.

He chuckled and then took a drag.

"Keep it up, Ronny," he said. Hermod's orb of blue fire extinguished. He huffed more smoke into a much larger cloud than he'd smoked before. "You'll come watch me one night while I fuck your bitch in the eye." His phone buzzed in his hand. "You wait and see." His lower lip curled under his teeth then released. "Faggot."

His phone vibrated again, tickling the calluses on his palm.

# PART 2 – CHAIN REACTION

# AN INTERVIEW

## RSVP TELEVISION RECORDING STUDIO – MANHATTAN – 44TH STREET & 6TH AVENUE, NEW YORK CITY, NY

"Good evening, ladies and gentlemen. Welcome to RSVP. I'm your host, Yusef Droitkin. Tonight, our guest is Hermod Vincent, the strongest man . . ."

As Yusef continued, Hermod was aware that he was on camera, and he tried to keep his face still.

"Most recently, Hermod testified as part of the congressional investigation of SPASE, its contracts and various operational failures. Hermod is a successful entrepreneur, founder of the Interactive Agency FACE, Inc., which he sold last year for a previously undisclosed amount." Yusef paused and winked at Hermod. "But you all probably know him best as the most powerful demi on Earth."

Hermod chuckled and smiled into the camera as Yusef continued speaking. It would be his turn in a moment. He'd never spoken on live broadcast, outside of his federal hearings. There'd been too many sightings and fighting clips to count over in the years since he outed himself and his abilities but never face time, never his own camera to talk to.

Yusef stopped talking and smiled and nodded at Hermod. They were sitting in a small set with two chairs on either side of a wooden conference table.

A pitcher and two glasses of water rested on top of a painted centerpiece made of black straw. Yusef reached out his hand, and Hermod shook it.

"Thank you for having me, Yusef," Hermod said. "It's a pleasure to meet you."

"Yes, thank you for agreeing to come," Yusef replied, his eyes wide. He was gleeful that this interview might land him some award nomination, maybe even an Emmy. Maybe they would finally open a category for independent streaming! Already, though, he was filled with pride, having snared the coveted interview.

"As you're aware, this may just end up being as tough as some of the scuffles," Yusef held up his fists and shifted his shoulders left and right, smiling, "that you get yourself into these days. Fair warning."

Hermod played along, gritting his teeth but still smiling. "I'll hold you to it, just in case."

"So," Yusef clapped his hands and leaned in, "down to business. Your powers." Yusef's eyelids pulsed. He smiled. "At first we thought you were some sort of living fusion reaction, right?"

"Yes, that's right," Hermod replied, nodding.

"Now, a little bird told me that it goes a bit deeper than that though. According to the Raven, you can do a whole lot more than burn things."

"What's the Raven talking about?" Hermod replied. He cursed the day he had ever gotten himself involved in SPASE, but it was the only way out to stay out of the Hole.

"The Raven says you could read my mind and figure that out, that you can even make me tell you by using your brainwaves to control me. The Raven says you have achieved interplanetary travel." Yusef paused and widened his eyes, looking for Hermod to return his gaze. Hermod nodded and looked at the table, waiting for Yusef to finish. "With passengers, even?"

"What else?" Hermod asked.

"Well, can you confirm any of that?" Yusef asked, his smile fading slightly.

"What else?" Hermod looked up and found Yusef's dog eyes wide, silently begging for goodies. Whoever spilled that bit about the brainwaves was definitely involved in the SPASE leaks. That topic hadn't even come up in his Senate committee deposition. He would consider thoroughly probing Yusef after the interview using his "brainwaves," but for now he would comply with the line of questioning.

<Don't be a dick!> Hermod said to Yusef in Yusef's own voice.

"Yes." Yusef coughed then and paused. "Yes. What else? Well, how about you tell me how all this happened. So, one day you woke up, and the next day—"

"I woke up in a SPASE holding cell, after apparently spending eight months in a coma."

"You were burning in a magnetically sealed nuclear chamber for approximately three of those months, I understand," Yusef said, wanting to push even further but thinking better of it. His source had given specific details about a 200,000-degree black skeleton complete with its own gravitational and magnetic fields. His source said there'd been talk of dark matter to explain some of the gravitational lensing and quantum movement phenomena they witnessed during his coma. They'd seen nothing like it before, not outside of an experimental particle reactor, or deep in the violent cosmos.

"The last thing I remember before waking up was feeling like I was having night sweats again. I was so hot," Hermod tugged at his shirt. "My body, the room was really hot too, heavy hot."

"And you woke up at SPASE?" Yusef looked fascinated for the camera's sake.

"Yes. There, at SPASE, I think somewhere off the Delaware coast." Censors quickly obscured the last two words of the sentence from the audience. "They told me they almost had to put me in orbit. But I came to, and I was rehabilitated and groomed for my return to the normal world." Hermod paused. "I'm very grateful for what they did for me there. I might have destroyed myself and a lot more."

"You host a memorial service every year?" Yusef asked, nodding.

"Yes, a service for the people who died. That night in my apartment building..." He paused and hung his head. "You never forget stuff like that. Politicians and reporters never forget either." He took a sip of water. "I get called 'murderer' a lot. It hurts. But it also makes me consider human frailty every second and how different I am now. I have to monitor my actions to a much greater degree. I'm proud to say that my capacity to inflict pain on others hasn't increased with my ability to do so. But sometimes, on the job, you know, it's a constant fear."

"Innocent people die. There are casualties in war."

"And warfare has changed." Hermod looked into the camera. "Just ask that crew out over the Pacific. Strategy and negotiation can fly out the window faster than I can!"

"Yes. Such a tragedy."

"But they got their target."

"At what cost?"

"Exactly." Hermod shrugged. "Two hundred and thirty-four people killed in a plane or twenty-three million new infections and casualties. They got the bug though."

"Killed her, you mean." Yusef's face soured. "And is this your official response as a demi?"

"I don't represent all demis. Just giving my personal opinion as a demi in the field. What would you have done?"

"Touché, my friend," Yusef said, backing down.

"Theo should be commended, in my opinion, along with everyone on that plane," Hermod said. "They were all heroes."

"Do you consider yourself a hero?" Yusef asked. Judging from Hermod's impassioned responses, Yusef thought it was time to excavate.

"I mean, I started those patrols for representation, really. I thought of it as a better way to expand the work that I'd done with my agency before all this happened to me."

"So, this was all a social media strategy for FACE?"

"I suppose," Hermod said, grinning, "which I'm not mad at really. FACE helped to breathe life into a lot of Black-owned brands that most agencies would have ignored completely. However, it was more about continuing the work, changing the way people like me are looked at and engaged by others. It all starts with being strong and present. Fags fighting back. The Black Panthers wouldn't have been able to make any changes on the scale that they did if they hadn't shown up with guns and good deeds and represented their community and their right to organize. Without these powers I would be made a target just as easily as any other chocolate-skinned man in this country. Even now I'm a bigger target. I'm the biggest. It's just that bullets don't work on me." Hermod smiled. "Shit, I needed a hero." He paused and took another sip.

"There are a lot of people who would call you their hero anyway."

"I have saved a couple lives here and there, but to be honest, I don't want to be anyone's hero. I'm a weirdo black queer man. I mean, I sort of looked up to myself my entire life. Not that I didn't have influences, but it's been uncharted territory, especially now." His eyes flared, as did his smile. He shrugged and shook his head, still smiling.

Yusef remained silent as he stared at him, wondering what would spill out of his mouth next.

"I'm not a hero," Hermod insisted. "I'm self-righteous and insecure just like most humans. I just have a big stick." He flared his eyes again. He wasn't smiling anymore.

"But you do acknowledge that you have become an icon within the black and LGBTQ communities, correct?"

"Of course. I draw strength from the heritage of my communities," Hermod continued with renewed enthusiasm. "Growing up the way I did and living in this demi generation, all of this forces me to realize that I can only be me. I hold myself accountable for my actions and for the most part try not to offend others or encroach on anyone else's peace. But that's just me. And I mean, if I decided not to, who could stop me?"

"Someone could. I'm sure," Yusef said.

"I'm never ever on that tip," Hermod continued, ignoring the response. "That 'I'm invincible' tip. But for the sake of this interview . . ." Hermod paused and sipped more of his water.

"With that in mind," Yusef pivoted, "tell me, how would an invincible black man end white supremacy?"

"Come on now," Hermod said.

"No, just entertain me for a second. You've written about all manner of diplomatic and social solutions. What would the demi-man do to end white supremacy?"

"I don't think he could." Hermod shook his head and frowned in confusion. "I mean, he'd have to kill them all or at least start."

"All of whom?"

"They do kill each other though," Hermod said, "all the white people, I mean."

"But that obviously is impossible. You're thinking about an eye-for-an-eye type of scenario."

"Oh, of course." Hermod's face blossomed with excitement. "I mean, the killing and terror is how it started. That's the only way it could really end. Kill and enslave enough whites. Scare the hell out of them."

"Ouch."

"You asked!" Hermod's smile spread from ear to ear. He laughed and clapped his hands, the sound echoing throughout the studio. Yusef flinched slightly.

"I did ask," Yusef agreed. "So, violence? That's your solution?"

"Not mine, but it is a solution. I started my agency as a means to try to fix things. The only thing I can do as a demi is keep doing what I'm doing. Inspire by example. Save a few lives where I can. I want all people to be as free as I am, to understand the real burden of freedom and to cherish it and yearn for even more freedom, for everyone else."

"But as far as being a black hero," Yusef continued with this irksome line of questioning, "a true champion for blackness, how does that make you feel? You're a face for black power now."

"No, I'm not really." Hermod paused. He'd had many visions of crushing millions of people at once. Some of them he'd enjoyed too much. Some of them were quite feasible. None of them really involved words though. He paused in awe that words could be as powerful as any other weapon in his new arsenal.

"I'm just a black man. I don't own blackness. I wouldn't want it. It's unwieldy." He shook his head and closed his eyes for a moment. "It's weird, really. Without these powers I could get beat up and potentially killed pretty easily. And I'd have an even greater chance of being beat up as a faggot. Black people beat me up and called me 'faggot' before any white people called me anything. Black people kicked me out years ago, and then kinda let me back in when I got powerful and scary, I can come back." Hermod chuckled. Yusef sighed. "Without these powers I'd be on the hellfire end of the sermon, you feel me? I can't own that from niggas or faggots. And now faggots call me more awful things than anyone else." He rolled his eyes.

Yusef looked at Hermod with an eagerness that could have been interpreted as flirtatious or devious. Yusef remained silent. Hermod could see on the monitor that the camera still had him in close up.

"To your original point, I'm not the face of black power," Hermod continued, rolling his eyes in distaste and shrugging as he looked at the side. "Not now. I'm not rich enough or hood enough. No disrespect to those out there who are mobilizing, teaching, leading, dying, fighting, changing policy, and saving lives. But I feel like the community sorta stopped climbing up the rough side of the mountain at some point and just decided to camp out at the plateau."

"I don't follow."

Hermod began clapping. "I'm climbing up . . . on the rough side . . . . of the mountaaaaiin," he sang and then stopped clapping afterwards. "It's an old gospel song that the ladies sang at church."

"Yes. You have a nice voice."

"Thanks." Hermod smiled. "Demis out there know how I feel about topics like this. I'm just as outcast as I would be without these powers, just as I was the moment before they found me."

Yusef struggled to keep his smile contained, the soundbites roaring in his head.

"How do you respond to criticism about your interracial relationship?" Yusef asked.

"I don't. I'm in love. I met the most awesome man in the world who made me feel like I was worthy of him. He's not black, and I'm fine with that."

"Have you ever dated a black man?"

"Yes," Hermod replied, flustered. This question had not been presented beforehand for approval. "It's complicated, but I've only had the opportunity to explore one other relationship in depth, with a Mexican man. I had a black lover, whom I was falling in love with. It was really complicated, though it could have been nice. It was for a while, the three of us. But you can't shit where you eat in my line of work. I've had other black and brown lovers, yes. Did any of them make me feel as special as the two men whom

I fell in love with? No. Could that have happened? Yes, but it didn't. The door is closed now. A little." He chuckled. "But yeah, I mean, I can't be any clearer than that, maybe a little less wordy though."

"But there is a fierce online backlash against you and comments made public by previous suitors regarding your seeking out non-African-American lovers exclusively," Yusef said. "Can you speak to this?"

Hermod shrugged. "People are bored. You like what you like. For the record, I have only been dating foreign men for the past seven years, not by choice. It's just who I meet. Y'all can misunderstand me at your own peril. Just because I want to fuck and live in harmony with some white dudes doesn't mean that I don't have a deep and thorough understanding of—generalization alert—white Americans' willingness and capacity to do and say hellish shit for their own gain. Especially the gays." Hermod smiled.

"Especially the gays, huh?" Yusef smiled back at him.

"You've been with men of different races, right, Yusef?"

"I suppose I'll play along seeing as it's after eleven," Yusef replied. "Yes."

"Like brown, yellow, red, freckly, pale, chocolate skinned, dark brown, all kinds of hair and eye colors?"

"Yes." Yusef looked at his sun-kissed, sand-colored hands.

"So . . . how do I keep this PG? So, you know how that feels when you can see yourself touching and having intercourse with someone who isn't the same color as you?"

"Yes, I do." Yusef squinted and smiled, "As in being aroused by the actual visual appearance of interracial sex?"

"Yes."

"Yes, I know that sensation completely. It's hot!"

"Exactly! I like holding hands, making out, and being inside olive, yellow, white, red, freckled, sandy-brown men. . . I like how that looks. It gets me hard. As far as the reality of love and human relationships or the visceral interactions that supersede visual arousal, I mean, this can happen with a man of any color. But it usually means a lot more if it happens with the man you're inside—or who's inside you. And usually I'm involved in those situations with lighter men."

"I see," Yusef said.

"I don't want to be the author of any dialogue that would downplay black masculinity or the reality that we are among the most beautiful men on the planet. I'm black no matter what I do or whom I fuck. For me, where I'm at it sucks that 'being black for everybody' has to mean something to you people still. That someone has to own it for you. As if having the skin and ancestry isn't enough. Being is enough."

"But can you just wipe your hands of it all though?" Yusef asked. "You are complicit, no? You mentioned that this demi-protector thing all started with a need to represent. So, are you a representative or aren't you?"

"I suppose you're partially right. I am a representative no matter what I do. As long as race means something to people. Do I want to be? I think I already answered this, but no, no I don't. Why does nobody ever ask me about the state of queer foodie relations? Or guys who are five feet nine inches tall? How about us?" Hermod shook his head and squinted in frustration. "I bet you'd kill me if I told you race was a social construct. Tell me I'm lying."

Hermod winked and smiled broadly. "My—I'm so far removed from this thinking now. You know what I think about during the day?" Hermod leaned a bit closer in his chair. The camera zoomed in on him in response. "Like, last Valentine's Day, you know what Lee and I did? We went to the moon to see the eruptions on the far side. He just wanted to do something wild. Live, you know? With his demi husband. Just last Tuesday we had dinner slash breakfast in Singapore. I could take us there right now! Lee likes the Berlin Philharmonic, so we'll check them out periodically. We try to hike somewhere in South America at least twice a month. It's our thing."

"The moon? Really?"

"Yeah! It was Lee's idea. Everybody got all afraid to visit the far side after the Rain, and we kind of grew up thinking the far side was this scary place. You know you see all the images of the eruptions and lava spewing everywhere. Lee kept talking about it, and I got just as excited about it as he did, so we said, fuck it."

"So, how does that work with your passports and . . . spacesuits?"

"Well, I'm in space every other day damn near, but I make sure to drop by the embassy or phone ahead to NASA and the Space Force first, so Lee can get his clearances taken care of. It's never a hassle. And believe it or not, we have a few proof-of-concept suits on loan from a few friends. I mean, I don't need one, but I gotta keep my man safe."

"Indeed. He sounds like a truly special guy. How was the moon, by the way?"

"Gorgeous! No words. You have to go."

"For our audience we're displaying a few photos from the trip now. It must have been the trip of a lifetime."

"I mean, it was nice!" Hermod smiled. "Lee had to go through flight readiness and zero-gravity training for a month beforehand."

"What was that like?"

"He enjoyed it, but he's pretty tough. It can be pretty grueling."

"Where do you see yourself in twenty years? "

"Oooh, that's tough. I mean, the dreamer in me wants to get off this damn rock. Just come home, grab Lee, and fly away and never come back. But we'd have to plan that. You need more than love to exist in the void, you know." Hermod smiled. "But yeah, somewhere kicking it with Lee. If I'm not dead."

Yusef nodded and took a long sip of his water. He loosened his tie, then took another sip. Sweat dripped from his jaw to his shirt collar. "Can you talk to us about the comment you made during the Senate deposition . . ."

As Yusef continued, Hermod nodded, his face stern, as he'd done throughout the interview. He was notorious for the brown of his eyes and their piercing, attentive gaze. As he sat there, blackness closed in on his peripheral vision. He sat up straight in his chair, put his hands on his knees, and looked beyond the camera. Yusef's forehead was covered in glistening drops of sweat.

"Yes, the hearings. What about them exactly?" Hermod squinted in a look of bewilderment as Yusef swiped his forearm across his brow. There was a large wet spot under his arm. His mouth moved, but no words came out. Then everything went dark.

"Unbelievable!" Hermod huffed, his voice deep and raspy. "Squandered!" The table and floor vibrated, and the metallic set pieces jingled under the reverberation of his voice. Hermod whipped his head away from the camera.

"These coons are useless! Wasted! Generations! Millions! Trillions! Wasted!" He snarled at the camera. "It was a mistake!" He looked at the floor and shook his head, then tossed it around wildly. "You hear me, Crown Moon? A mistake!" He quieted down, almost mumbling. "I've been gone far too long. It can't be too late though. We can set some of it right. It can't be this way. It can't stay this way." He stopped shaking his head and looked up into Yusef's face. "I don't know if I can even save them." His face was sunken, his lips drooping in a look of failure. The backdrop fell down behind him, and his water glass rattled. It had inched its way toward the edge of the table. Cell phones began ringing throughout the soundstage. Yusef's own phone started to vibrate, causing the fabric of his pants to chafe his thigh. It stopped suddenly, but it was getting very warm. He pulled it out, not taking his eyes off Hermod, and set it on the table.

"Save who?" Yusef suddenly felt terribly sad for whatever failure was written on Hermod's face just then.

"It was so simple," Hermod continued, hissing the "s's" and ignoring the question. His voice echoed throughout the soundstage from the speakers of everyone's phones. "Just kill 'em back. It worked! They wouldn't listen. Fucking fools! Now look!" He was almost screaming now, rage masking his handsomeness. "Kill them! Simple! Nobody ever kills them!" The word "them" shot out of his mouth like unpleasant, half-chewed pork fat. His water glass fell to the set floor and shattered. The crew fled, the echo of Hermod's words fading in their minds the farther they ran. "It would have worked!" His fists and jaw clenched, and his arms and neck trembled. "This here boy figured it out. Yes, he did!" Hermod grinned, and his eyes sunk deep into his brow.

A thin man was standing behind camera two. No one else remained in the sound stage, though the producer and his editor were still in the production booth. Yusef was standing with one foot on set and one foot off. He held out a hand toward Hermod, who was looking at the floor, his head between his hands. He looked up. Yusef sniffed the air and searched around. On the monitor smoke was rising from behind the set where the backdrop pieces had fallen, a few flames flickering. Yusef stepped off the set and took two paces back. He smelled something else that tickled the back of his throat and scraped at his nostrils, begging him to gag. His iPhone hissed, and smoke rose from it. The glass screen cracked, and sparks erupted from the fissure, becoming a small cluster of flames.

"Nobody kills the white people," Hermod said in the same manner in which one might object to the toilet being left unflushed. "But they kill all of us."

He looked up and then rose from out of the seat. His mouth and his eyes were sullen. "Nobody kills the white people," he said again, slower, sneering. Yusef, the cameraman, producer, and editor were weeping now. Viewers abroad were as well, the sadness spreading with the sound of his voice.

"But when you start the bleeding, things change, remember?" Hermod's frown dissolved a bit as he began pacing back and forth along the set. Flames danced behind him, clinging to anything not yet ablaze. The air twinkled where light reflected from water spewing out of the sprinklers. Mist rose from around Hermod as the water evaporated near him. "They need to be broken. Yesssssss, break them all into pieces."

The cameraman rushed up behind Yusef, grabbed his shoulders, and pulled him off screen.

"Gary?" Yusef asked, huffing and sobbing. Together they ran to the door of the soundstage. Gary flung it open and gasped at the large young man standing in their way. Yusef crashed into Gary's back, and they both almost fell into Mingo. The two of them stared at him. Yusef was frozen in place on his knees. His heart beat wildly, his body dripping sweat from obscure places like his upper lip and behind his knees. He wiped tears from his cheeks. Ian wore a dark suit of plasticky armor with the SPASE emblem positioned near his neck: a ringed planet resting on an open hand, an eagle spreading its wings behind the planet, and five stars in the distance. Mingo stepped into the soundstage and looked down at them. He had the bluest eyes for someone so dark, Yusef thought.

"¡Corre!"(1) He shooed them away. Gary, still weeping, was ten paces down the hall before looking back for Yusef, who was standing in the doorway looking back into the soundstage. Yusef coughed due to the smoke that

---

1 "Run!"

poured through the door behind him. Farther down the hall, another door opened, and firemen filed through it, their equipment clanging and their footsteps thundering through the hall.

<Doctor,> Mingo said, staring at the stage. <I'm in.>

<And Davi?> Dr. Gaskill inquired.

<Davi here in the production booth, sir,> Davi replied. <He's really not himself, is he?>

<No,> Gaskill replied. <He would have acknowledged you by now.>

<We've been made?> Mingo asked.

<Oh, of course you have. You two don't matter at all though.> Dr. Gaskill was honest. <It's me he wants.>

<I feel like I'm about to get the spins,> Davi thought as he leaned over onto the back of a chair in the production booth. <Doc, he's full-on raging bull today, and you know I can barely cap this off when he's a snowflake.>

<Just try, Davi. Cyral and I are standing by.>

Hermod frowned and took a deep breath. "How was that so hard for these ignorant coons to see?"

Ian stepped closer to the stage and placed his pinkies in the corners of his mouth. He whistled loudly and Hermod looked offstage at the source.

"How is that so hard?" Hermod asked. He craned his neck for several seconds then turned in place, looking for something. He stopped, then looked at the studio door. "Show yourself, Crown Moon!"

The conference table rose a few inches and then cracked in half. The water pitcher shattered, and droplets evaporated almost immediately. The straw centerpiece was consumed in the haze just as quickly. Hermod launched the pieces of the table at the camera, toppling the world's window into the scene.

In his war room in Delaware, Gaskill froze in his seat. He felt like Vincent was in the room with him, groping in darkness and trying to find him and wring him again.

## HERMOD AND LEE'S APARTMENT – DUMBO, NEW YORK CITY, NY

"It was so simple."

Lee placed his wine glass on the glass table and jumped up from the couch. He grazed his shin while rounding it, and Tig started at the hollow sound of the collision.

"It's him," Lee whispered, walking closer to the television.

"Who?" Tig asked, standing now too.

"That voice, that's the voice," Lee said, looking back and forth between Tig and the TV. "That's what he sounded like, when this happened." Lee pointed to his forearm as he recalled that night with Hermod in the dress. That love session had imprinted on him deep like Hermod's burning grip.

Tig placed his hands on his waist and drew a deep breath. Lee looked at the floor and then back up to Tig and tears fell down his face.

"What's wrong?" Tig moved toward Lee with his arms open, but Lee backed away.

"I don't know. It's—I'm no bitch. This is something else." He shook his head and let out a loud breath, then rubbed his sleeve across his face to remove his tears.

Tig found it hard to breathe, and his chest felt heavy as he thought of Darren. It had been five years since he fell. The corner of his left eye was wet, and he watched Lee scrape his index fingers beneath his respective eyes. Lee scanned the couch for the remote and then pointed at it. "Mute it!" he demanded.

Tig looked at the TV. It silenced, and the mute icon appeared in the lower-right corner. They both stood and watched Hermod pace the stage, his mouth moving. Yusef stood near the edge of the screen, flames growing taller backstage. Lee stepped back from the television, his eyes widening with realization.

"I can stop this."

"How?" Tig asked, incredulous.

"I have to talk to him. Can you—"

"Can *you*?" Tig countered.

"I'm getting a bit better." Lee looked down and scratched the back of his head. Then he began walking around the room. He retrieved his wine from the table on the third lap and walked closer to the windows overlooking downtown Manhattan. He caught his reflection in the glass and met his own green-eyed gaze. He watched his tongue line his lips and the glass splash a gulp of wine into his mouth. His face moved in and out of obscurity, competing in the glass with the glistening seaport, the lights in the Gehry building, and the stream of taillights on the bridges.

"I'll be fine, Tig. We have to do this. I think hearing my voice will bring him back."

Tig approached Lee at the window and glanced at the television. The camera, now unmanned, was tilted strangely, and Yusef was gone. Flames danced throughout the background. The table was gone. Hermod's head was out of frame due to the shifted camera angle. Tig turned back to the window. Now standing beside Lee, he clasped Lee's right hand with his left.

"You ready?"

"Yes." Lee's left hand began to tingle as if falling asleep, and the sensation spread throughout his body. His skull throbbed pleasantly, and he felt like a song was playing in his ears due to the pressure there. He faltered slightly. His head was heavy.

<Hermod,> he thought as loudly as he could. That's how it had happened the last time. Thinking as if he were screaming. <Hermod!>

He saw the city in the window, but he felt blind in his mind. There was only darkness there.

<*Hermod!*> This time it echoed in his own head over and over. In his mind a spark illuminated the blackness, and shadow spread away from the dim light. Lee could not see the city through the balcony windows. As the blackness dissipated, the city was revealed, and he met his own gaze in his mind just as he had done while standing in front of the window in his living room moments ago.

<Hermod!> He called again and scanned the cityscape, now fully visible in his mind's eye, along with the wine glass, Tig, the financial district, the South Street Seaport, and the two bridges. He fell to his knees, and the

wine glass shattered on the floor. He ignored it and the spilled wine. Lee coughed. He felt hot, and his throat felt heavy with smoke.

<Hermod! It's Lee!>

Dr. Gaskill's presence flitted on the edge of Lee and Tig's energies, dabbing and soaking them up like a bee having at a tulip's pollen. Lee had a steely resolve about him. Gaskill was pleased, relieved that he didn't have to step in.

## RSVP TELEVISION RECORDING STUDIO – MANHATTAN – 46TH STREET & 9TH AVENUE, NEW YORK CITY, NY

Hermod watched the camera crash to the floor and sparks fly from its base. The wall of the soundstage behind Hermod was now fully engulfed in flames. He looked at the next camera and saw the handsome boy.

"The handlers are here, huh?" he snarled, rising a bit higher in the air.

<Hermod!>

"Who is that?" he asked.

Mingo stepped one foot closer to the stage. He held his right hand up and balled his left hand into a fist, his arm hanging next to his leg. "I'm going to give you one chance to stand down, Hermod."

<Hermod! It's Lee!>

"Lee," Vincent said. His eyes were like quarters briefly, and his lips fought a smile. "What an exquisite man. I'm truly sorry about the other night, my love."

<Ian, be still,> Gaskill told him.

<Sir?> Mingo heard a noise behind him and turned to see Yusef and several firemen huddled in the doorway. He brought his eyes back to Hermod and waved behind him with his left hand for the firemen to stay put. <Wait,> Gaskill replied to Mingo. <Give this a moment.>

<Hermod, listen to me. You're not that man, this Vincent,> Lee's voice whispered to Hermod.

"I am Vincent, boy," Hermod said defiantly. He shook his head, and his body lowered to the set floor.

In their apartment, Lee sank to his knees and clutched the sides of his head. Stinging pain raced through his burned forearm. Vincent's voice sent waves of heat, pain, and confusion through his brain. His stomach bubbled, and hot gas stung inside it.

<No! You are Hermod. You are a lover and a giver,> Lee said. <I love you, and you need to come back before someone dies.>

"But," Hermod said. "Lee?" He looked at the ceiling and then down at his hands and then back up again. Lee's voice was loud and clear, more than a whisper in his ear. Hermod knelt on the floor and stared at his hands.

<Sir?> Mingo demanded.

<Wait.>

<I've got the shot.>

<Wait.>

Hermod lifted his head and scanned the room. His eyes met Mingo's.

"Mingo?" he asked, completely bewildered. His voice was normal and no longer shook the soundstage. He sniffed and then sprang to his feet, whirling around to get a view of the set.

"What happened?" Hermod asked. "Where's Yusef? What happened?" he demanded, rushing toward Mingo. Mingo stepped back and raised his right fist, tightened his left one in front of him, and bit his lower lip. Wisps of green and black smoke were leaking from between his fingers. It swirled in small, dissipating clouds around his hands. Craggy green lines of electricity jumped from one fist to the other.

Hermod stopped about six feet short of Mingo, just outside of his reach. He stared into the young, smooth face, Mingo's aura was bright red, burning with the psychic impressions of anger and hatred. Hermod looked around him again, surveying the damage, then turned back to Mingo, who remained in a fighting stance, his breathing heavier now.

<Hermod?> Lee called to him.

<Baby.> Hermod exhaled heavily and landed on his feet. <I'm here.>

<Let me pop that fucking mono!> Mingo thought, unmasked. He relaxed his stance and stood up straight, then spit on the floor just shy of Hermod's foot.

"Come again," Hermod said. Fire leapt between his eyes, and his jaw and fists clamped simultaneously. He rose into the air, which refracted around him as the temperature shot up. He was inching toward Mingo.

<You have to calm down, Mingo, or you'll reignite the situation,> Gaskill advised. He broadcast his thoughts to Hermod as well. <Stand down.>

"All clear." Mingo turned to the firemen in the doorway and waved for them to come in. "What happened?" he asked condescendingly as he rose into the air, staring at Hermod as he moved away slowly. "You happened." He sped out into the hallway to meet Davi in the production booth. <Algún día pronto, Super Mono,> [(1)]Mingo warned.

Hermod's tension eased as Mingo moved away. He pondered non-lethal ways to silence Mingo. Few came to mind. He held up his hands then, and the fire extinguished. The firemen all stood still and looked around and then at him for a moment.

<At least no one died,> one of the firemen thought.

<Thanks for nothing, faggot,> another thought while staring at Hermod.

---

1 *<One day soon› Super Monkey·>*

# LEAN ON ME

## DOWNTOWN MANHATTAN – OVER THE HUDSON RIVER

Hermod was floating some 1,200 feet above the river and 800 feet from the pier near the Borough of Manhattan Community College. Tig approached him in an aircraft that resembled a bubble, its aluminum/titanium surface reflecting the city and the river below.

The orb approached, and a portion of its surface became transparent. "So, what's the deal Hermod?" Tig asked, his voice broadcasting from speakers on the aircraft's small wings.

"You know I hear them every time I'm around here?" Hermod replied. He shrugged, having been afraid the conversation would end up here.

"Who?" Tig asked.

Hermod turned around and pointed east and down.

"Downtown. All of it, really, but mainly the East Side, near Foley Square."

"The African Burial Ground?"

Hermod nodded and smiled.

"Singing and shouting, stomping, like the folks used to at church, back home, when they would catch the spirit." Hermod's smile spread across his face as he remembered those joyous church moments. Everyone, from the eighty-year-old grandmothers to the day-labor-hardened deacons would succumb to ecstatic frenzy. Fueled by a roaring choir and the pianist, drummer, organist, and bass guitarist weaving a rapturous harmony, they would all rave for God. The sanctuary became a space where even Aunt Bea was allowed to flail and stomp and scream and wail away the oppression that each of them shared, written in their skin. Hermod took a deep breath. He used to hang out at the Burial Ground some days, before he met Lee. Before the patrolling and SPASE obligations picked up. It felt good to remember with those old souls. As his patrolling in the hood increased, and he started to dive into black oppression on a completely new level, the trips to the Burial Ground only made him angrier and more hopeless. But mostly angry. He stopped smiling and stared at Tig.

Tig looked at Hermod with a poker face. He was worried now. Was it too late? Too late for what? He had no idea how he might help, especially given all of the cryptic messages Gaskill had been feeding him over the last several days. From Tig's perspective, Hermod's possession was inevitable, and they were wasting valuable "run and hide" time.

"Are you OK, Hermod?" Tig asked.

"I think so."

"I'm telling you as your former SPASE-appointed therapist, they're looking for your ass right now."

"Former?" Hermod said. "What happened?"

"You! Gaskill's pulled the plug on rehabilitative therapies."

"I don't give a shit," Hermod replied. "That was all just to keep the Pentagon calm anyway. I haven't received any official contact. Those handlers are still trailing me everywhere, though." Parole had been one of the worst experiences of his life, and yet in that moment he'd expected it, in light of the events on RSVP.

"Gaskill hasn't reached out to you?" Tig asked.

Hermod shook his head. "No."

"Shit, it's back to Rehoboth, Jack!"

"I'll burn Rehoboth before I go back."

"You need some help, Hermod. That shit back there at RSVP was not normal. And Lee." Tig shook his head and took a deep breath. "What's going on with you?"

"I don't know, Tig." Hermod closed his eyes for several seconds and then opened them and looked at Tig. "I don't know."

"Is it the dreams you're having?"

"I don't know, Tig."

"Who is Vincent, Hermod?" Tig asked.

Hermod's nostrils flared. He was silent for a moment.

"Hermod?"

<No one!> Hermod spoke gruffly into Tig's mind. Tig had not expected the psychic intrusion and was barely able to conceal his ulterior motives.

"I'll talk to Cyral tomorrow. He can check me out." Hermod waved his hand and crossed his arms.

"You are something else, H." Tig shook his head. "This is all about to unravel. They're going to come after all of us demis thanks to you!" He chuckled. "They've barely started the hearing about that fuck-up with the bug! After a mess like last night, DC will be definitely looking to 'address' situations like us permanently."

"You mean start them? T, I'm just as afraid as you are." Hermod looked out beyond the bridge. "I mean, I don't know what to do now." He thought about going home and the inevitable cloud of paparazzi outside his apartment. He also thought about Mingo and Davi and Tig and his stupid race baiting. He just wanted to go to sleep.

"You know, maybe it's time people got used to the fact that they're fucking fragile and not invincible. Being black, Asian, white, whatever doesn't really fucking matter." Hermod turned his back to Tig. "Maybe people should wake up now that invincibles actually exist." He pointed to Jersey City. "They're like fucking ants! They just don't realize it."

"You already know what I'm gonna say to that."

"Everything." Hermod couldn't exactly look Tig in the face.

"And you know why, right?"

"And you know what I'm going to say to that, T," Hermod spat.

"Man, you can talk big if you want to, but there are armies and demis waiting to put you down. Two of 'em are following you every day, in fact, am I right?"

"Fuck them. Fucking rape that dude, Ian."

"Mingo?" Tig exhaled smoke.

"Yeah, fucking racist bitch."

Sometimes Hermod could hear Mingo taunting him from miles away. Super Monkey. He'd picked up horrible images and memories from Mingo. Pummeling dark schoolmates as a child in the Dominican Republic. His foul way with dark-skinned Dominican women, humiliating them during sex, comparing them to "regular negras." He would play a cruel target practice game, using his strength and stealth to assault black men in the streets. The attacks were never lethal, just brutal enough to laugh about with friends over drinks.

"Really? I'm surprised but not. Wouldn't have pegged him as the type. Isn't he Dominican?"

"How long have you lived in this city, bruh?" Hermod asked derisively. Tig ignored the question.

A ray of sunlight bounced off the surface of Tig's orb and into Hermod's eye. "That thing runs on solar power?" Hermod asked, nodding at the orb.

"Yeah, it's pretty dope." Tig smiled in admiration of the pod. "But we're not talking about this. Not now. What the fuck was all that new shit? You're not a representative? You're so far removed from this?" Tig shrugged in frustration. He'd intended to keep the conversation focused on assessing his friend's well-being. He'd never seen Lee so terrified than when he picked him up off the floor after the interview last night. However, he was particularly sensitive to what he thought were Hermod's uppity moments, and this time he had him dead to rights.

"Look." Hermod gazed south, watching the cars creep along the Verrazano Bridge. "You know exactly where I'm coming from, T. Get real. That's why they brought me on there." Hermod turned back to Tig. "Are we really going here again?"

"Yeah, we are. You been runnin around acting like Black Faggot Jesus for almost two years now, but all of a sudden you're fucking Demi Emo Boy?"

"Fuck you. I had dues to pay."

"So that's what it was, dues? Are you really listening to the dead niggas down there?" Tig pointed east to the African Burial Ground National Monument.

"Fuck you! You know what I mean." Hermod shook his head and fished in his shirt pocket for a cigarette box.

"Give me one," Tig requested, having decided not to push the parole button.

"It's bud." Hermod warned, moving closer to Tig's pod. He extended his hand, the spliff in between his index and middle fingers.

"Huh?"

"Yeah."

"Shit. What kind?" Tig looked at the time on the monitor.

"Blue Dream."

"Ha. Yeah, pass me one." Hermod reached through the clear pod enclosure, and Tig grabbed the cigarette from him and placed it between his lips. Hermod winked, and the end ignited. Smoke rapidly filled Tig's pod. He pressed a button, and the pod disappeared, the smoke dissipating along with it.

"I ain't killing nobody," Hermod said. "Shit, I'm saving them, and I'll probably continue to. I just don't want people to keep looking at me as the new face of black anything 'cause I'm not." Hermod took a drag of his spliff. "Because, yes, it is very fucking hard for me to continue to think on those terms. Like . . ." Hermod paused as smoke eased out of his nostrils and mouth. He was searching for the right word to describe what race matters meant to him now. Tig was right. Hermod was the most powerful being in the world—for now, at least. Squabbling over American race politics was beneath him.

"It's so trivial, petty." Hermod shrugged, pursing his lips for a moment. "And frankly, I would invite you to let go of some of that shit too before you'll catch a heart problem too. How's that ulcer, hoe?"

"Healing." Tig clipped the spliff in the palm of his hand and placed it on the dashboard ashtray.

"Funny how you can't hook that up for yourself as well as you can for others."

"In due time."

"But isn't that a clue to where I'm coming from?" Hermod shook his head. "Our power. Your vulnerability. My invulnerability. That doesn't reinforce your independence? Make you want to shrug off some weight?"

"I hear some of what you're saying, yes. But I'm still vulnerable, and not just my body. My soul is vulnerable too as long as people still hate and kill us and as long as brothas are still hating each other and homos and women and on and on. If I can do something for the community from this pedestal, then I will."

"And that's on you. So, why me?" Hermod had watched the RSVP interview six times, the outburst, and he still could not remember any of it. "I will respond as professionally as I can about that interview, and I will stand accountable, but as far as what I said, I meant all of that, the things that I remember saying, at least."

"It's your attitude." Tig shook his head. "You come across like—"

"Like what?" Hermod could sense where this was going. They'd had similar conversations many times, which was why he was perplexed that Tig would go on about it at length now, as opposed to trying to help him figure out what had happened to him during his "seizure" on set or helping him figure out how to reconcile being such a tax on his lover.

"Answer me this." Tig tilted his head back a bit. "Why have you never dated a Black man?"

Hermod's upper lip jumped a bit near the left corner, but he remained silent.

"Well?" Tig demanded, shaking slightly.

Hermod looked him in the eye. "Why are you asking me this right now, Tig?" His eyelids flared, and the muscles in his upper-right arm flexed.

"Answer me, dammit!" Tig screamed. "I want to know!"

Hermod grimaced and glared at Tig, his fists clenched.

"Fuck you. You can burn me to a crisp; I don't give a shit. I just asked a question." Tig closed his eyes and turned away from Hermod.

"And I'm a keep askin' until I get an answer."

"I don't know, Tig."

"Fuck you."

"I don't want to talk about this with you right now."

"Why? 'Cause you're big and bad and don't have to worry about anything now? Well, you're still Black, nigga."

"Fuck you," Hermod whispered. Fire filled the air. Inside his vehicle Tig shielded himself from the flames licking at him. He flew away several yards.

"You thought I forgot?" Hermod squeezed his eyes shut and shook his head. "Tell me, what does that mean? Was it supposed to hurt?" Hermod said to the fire. It was diminishing a bit, but a massive flame still swaddled him entirely. "Who are you to tell me who I am or whom I should date or love? Just because of my skin color."

Tig did not approach, his heart racing.

"Maybe after years and years of being treated like shit for being yourself you just figure it's safer to stay away from people who don't like you." Hermod's volume increased gradually. "Maybe I didn't want to dig through post-lock-up Pentecostal PTSD victims and DL losers calling me white and shit. Maybe I didn't want to have to teach some dude how to respect me as a fucking faggot. Maybe I needed to protect the shred of confidence I had against all that bullshit that made me want to kill myself!" he yelled. "Maybe I don't want to join some queer militant cancel army or . . . or be treated like shit cause I'm not from an island." He shrugged, though Tig could not see him through the flames. "Why don't I fuck with niggas? Shit, you're fucking enough niggas for the both of us!"

Hermod was silent for several seconds. He noticed his body was heaving, and his jaw was clenched tight and squeaking slightly. He loosened his fists, and the flames around him dissipated enough for him to see the blue sky and clouds. Tig was hovering farther away than he had been when they started talking. Hermod shook his head and took a deep breath, then let it out.

"Or maybe I was just too afraid." He looked at Tig and rolled his eyes, then shrugged his right shoulder. "Happy?"

"Are you?"

"Not without Lee. That's the whole fucking point. None of this," Hermod swirled both arms around him and then squinted and frowned, "none of this matters."

"Are you afraid?" Tig asked, clarifying his line of questioning. "Of blackness? That's my question."

Hermod was silent for several seconds. "Fuck you. What kinda question is that?"

"You're still Black, Hermod."

"I'm more than Black. Fuck you."

*I'm beyond all of this,* Hermod thought. *Better than Black or white or anything on Earth. I'm not obligated to struggle with you or anyone else and you aren't obligated to struggle with me. You couldn't.* He wanted to tell him this, but Tig would just call him an uppity nihilist again. Hermod would defend his integrity and "do unto others" philosophy. His anger would seesaw some more. He wanted the conversation to end, almost bad enough to make it so.

He and Tig had grown to be like brothers since they met in the Hole. Hermod had never been locked up before. He'd spent the entirety of his life avoiding it, but that was before the power.

Tig was initially brought into Hermod's containment team as a therapist intern. Over time the combination of his neuroscience training, engineering skills, and supernatural ability to communicate with and breed machines provided the Hole with psychic and technological safeguards against Hermod's violent tantrums. His flesh-healing abilities also came in handy, although he'd never had to use them on account of Hermod. It was their conversations that eventually led to the success of Hermod's containment. Dr. Gaskill, then the Hole's only warden, had marveled at the success of Tig's psychotherapeutic approach, and within three months of their first session, Gaskill was confident that Hermod was ready for probationary release.

No one else on the rehab team could grasp Hermod's fear of being contained, detained, or incarcerated in the way that Tig could. He'd escaped many of the same hood traps that Hermod had: drugs, guns, gangs, sex work, jail, unplanned fatherhood, addiction, and death. They shared a pedigree for the most part, and both had known the triumphs and pitfalls of being a "successful" African American man, having risen from the hood to professional esteem and wealth. Both were demi Black men, a prospect that the history of their native land had loathed since its founding. What was once a vicious myth that brought brutal suffering and death to millions of their kind was now their living truth and had brought them and others esteem and adoration, the likes of which no American had ever seen. The notoriety, though, was not new. Few people understood that, but Tig did.

Where they differed then and probably would forever was in their understanding of responsibility to the community. Millions of people, millions of Black people even, didn't reach out and love Hermod and make him a better person. Only a select few did. And these people were going to love and nurture him despite his or their skin color. Hermod argued that this was ultimately the case for all individuals, and given the history of hatred toward his body prior to becoming a demi, he was even less inclined to join hands with a community that hated him now that he didn't really need them. Years earlier it had become apparent to him that he would need to pick a side, and he had picked the fags, homos, lesbians, transgenders, and queerdos. For a while, this community accepted him without expectations. But then the expectations came, and he found himself being purposefully misunderstood and fetishized in all sorts of new ways. He'd searched tirelessly for emotional maturity, expecting to find many who shared this morality once he had reached the mark. He found one: Eliot "Lee" Sánchez. Hermod would be responsible for him. If true love made him elitist then he would gladly accept that.

"If we're going there, I got a spade for you." Hermod closed his eyes and his body tensed, his hands clenched into fists once again. *Let's change the subject,* he thought.

There was a flash, and Tig covered his eyes, unable to see for a few seconds after. Suddenly, the pod's interior felt like it had been parked in direct sunlight for several hours. His vision was still blurred, but he could tell there was something different about Hermod. The blurred silhouette was thinner than it should have been.

"H?" Tig closed his eyes, as if his eyelids lids would erase the blurriness. "You there? You OK?"

"Yeah, I'm here."

"What's with your voice?" Tig opened his eyes again, and things were clearer. "Jesus Christ!" Tig screamed. The pod reversed and reared as if it were preparing to charge. "H?"

"Who's Black now? Whaddaya think?"

Tig gasped. He was looking at a black skeleton. He could see the Financial District refracted in between black rib bones. The rest of the city flowed around the skeleton's haze. The black bones appeared flat like the paper decorations that Halloween revelers would adhere to their front doors, only these bones were not flat, and they were as black as space. Nothing reflected from them. Every so often a flicker of blue flame would worm around the skull's eye socket or peek from around the skeleton's hip bones or a phalanx tip. Sweat dripped down the side of Tig's brow, and a thin sheet of condensation gathered on the monitors inside his craft. He looked at them and began punching his fingers into the keyboard, shaking his head.

"How? Like, how did this happen?" Tig said, staring at the screen. "Are your handlers here?" He was alarmed by the data displayed. His eyes darted toward Hermod, who looked like a skeleton-shaped hole in the ground. Tig cut his eyes back to the data display, wiping his brow and huffing out hot air. His pod reversed about fifteen feet, the air conditioner fans screaming. "Dude, your core is almost fifty thousand degrees right now. How did this happen?"

"I suppose that's too high?"

"I'm serious!" Tig hissed.

"IDK they told me this is how they found me in that crater in Jersey. So I kind of let loose on yesterday morning's solar storm run, and it happened again." Hermod's bones started to glow bright white, too bright to look at. The light dissipated, and he was flesh again, nude. He hung his head. "I can turn into a skeleton!"

"Wow," Tig said, still glued to the monitors. "You maxed two hundred and fifty thousand right there." He glanced at Hermod, and their eyes met. "Just don't kill me, man." He was only half joking.

Hermod's body slumped. "Something's going on, T." Hermod's voice was quieter, heavier, and lacked the jovial tone he'd had during his reveal to Tig. He looked down at a ship passing them in the marina below, a few gulls flying beneath them. A blinding flash was followed by a thin coat of mist that thickened into fabric next to Hermod's skin, slowly solidifying into the outfit he'd worn before. "I hurt Lee," Hermod said. "I hurt him, and I . . . it's tearing me up." Their eyes met. "Help."

"I'm here, man." Tig picked up the clipped spliff, lit it, and took a pull. "So, this is what happened the night you exploded?"

"Yes. I think I had another nightmare where I was like this too." He tried to recall what he could of his recent blackouts and nightmares. "You know, it's like, when it's happening I can't remember anything, but I feel like, this malice, this anger, but it feels good. Like being avenged."

"Against whom?" Tig asked. The thought of Hermod out for blood sent a chill through him.

"Against everyone. Like . . . humanity." Hermod laughed softly. "I sound crazy, right?"

"This isn't you, Hermod." Tig had never heard him speak like this. "You're still human, H."

"I mean, not really, Tig."

"Lee is."

"I know. That may be about the only thing that keeps me human still." Hermod looked at their high-rise in Dumbo. "And I'm trying to kill him."

"Stop it!" Tig chided, then looked at the time on his monitor. "Shit, I got a proposal to present in twenty."

"All good."

Tig could sense that he didn't want him to leave just yet. "You guys will be fine. I mean, honestly, I'm a bit worried, H." Tig shrugged. "But I doubt it's anything that some *rest*, love, relaxation, and healing won't help. "

"Well, we're off to Morocco in three days so . . ."

"Good. You know, I'm actually going to agree with you and suggest you take your advice for a bit. Hell, we're all new to this. And neither of us should have to bear more than we want to."

"Hmm . . ." Hermod chuckled

"I mean, go be all high and mighty with Lee. Maybe you're right—about the responsibility. I mean, listen to you. Look at you, H."

Hermod hung his head for a moment. He smiled, remembering the days when he was thinking with thousands of people at a time. *It could be worse,* he thought. There were days when he was certain he would lose his mind to a sea of others, not just one. Cyral had quieted them. Sly bitch that he was, he had shown Hermod how to mute the voices rather than shut them out entirely. That made for more efficient access to them later on.

"Well, we see eye to eye on that at least. I need a fucking break, man."

"It's coming, brother."

"You're out with Lee tonight?"

"Yeah. It's whatever he wants. He said there's some gallery openings tonight. Free drinks. Thursday nights."

"Thanks, Tig."

"Of course, man."

Hermod smiled. "Maybe I'll see you later tonight."

"Peace, man," Tig said.

Hermod turned and sped away. Tig watched his handlers, Mingo and Davi, pursue him and the three of them disappeared between the buildings near Hudson and Canal.

"Call, Cyral," Tig said.

A single phone ring buzzed through the pod.

"Tig, what's crackin'?" the pod sounded again.

"Cyral," Tig replied, "we've got a problem."

"Tell me something I don't already know, Tig."

# ACQUITTAL

## FOLEY SQUARE, MANHATTAN, NEW YORK CITY, NY

Hard leather shoe soles chopped down onto the marble on the outside of the courthouse threshold. Dr. Gaskill looked out onto Foley Square as he continued down the sprawling staircase. A phalanx of cameramen advanced toward him. Journalists, packed behind and in between them, roared and rushed at Gaskill as he continued his descent. Cameras and microphones flailed, and strobes flashed in a wild anti-rhythm. Faces and bodies registered last. He had already seen them, though, while seated during the hearing. He had watched all of them arrive. He'd heard the questions they would scream, though only moments ago. He couldn't see too far ahead anymore. He hadn't been able to do so for a long time. Pascal Divino from the *LA Times*. Sally Gallagher from the *Wall Street Journal*. Naomi Turrell from CNN. Karen Black was absent, and he was slightly disappointed. She was a latent healer. Her purity always invigorated him during these types of press struggles. He didn't want to struggle without her this morning, though. He could have silenced them all even before exiting the courthouse and been on his way. That would not have been kind or wise for his recovery strategy though, not now.

"Doctor? Can you tell us about the hearing?"

"Do you think Hermod will stand trial for murdering municipal and federal law enforcement officers?"

"Are your defense contracts in jeopardy after the recent events at RSVP?"

"Can you talk about the unexplained deaths of several police officers who were acquitted for the murders of Black people? There's speculation that a demi is involved!"

Dr. Gaskill kept a moderate pace as he descended the stairs. He looked straight ahead and not into any lens or eye in particular but out onto the square, at the buildings along Lafayette, and the cranes farther west, hugging the skyscraper spawn in Tribeca. His height spared him from a great deal of intrusion. But the flashing. He wanted to swat at the strobes every time they fired. He maintained his stride, Ade and Sean right behind him. Reporters, cameramen, policemen, and gawkers tightened their cloud around them as they reached the bottom of the staircase.

"Doesn't SPASE have a responsibility to own up to the loss of those policemen and federal agents killed in Austin?"

Gaskill stopped walking, and the cloud tightened.

"SPASE also lost ten brave associates in that battle," Gaskill said. He was calm and still had not looked directly at a single person or device. "Three of these men were killed by federal agents. So, if you want to play the culpability and tragedy game then—"

In an instant, the sun was eclipsed, and all of the commotion around him froze. Strobe flashes shone continuously, frozen in time.

"Ninixetlau SiqT' Qkar. Hraqk Sisvumm. Qihvumm SiqT' Qkar," Gaskill said.

The words were forced from his mouth, and his awe quickly exploded into rage. He tightened his fists and his jaw and then the muscles in his arms and legs and abdomen all tensed. Small cracks spread across the granite beneath his feet. No authority had forced him to do anything in centuries. The spell echoed in his head, and his rage softened to something a bit more obscure than uncertainty. He felt like he was being watched as he fell back into time.

Sunlight filled his eyes once more, and everything was silent. Even inside him.

"Doctor?" A woman asked from behind him.

Gaskill looked out at the reporters and cameramen, now strewn about, rolling around the stairs and sidewalk. Some people were groaning and trying to stand. Others were still unconscious. Several policemen were converging on the grand staircase from across the square. More were pouring out of the courthouse.

He couldn't help but glimpse the burial mounds at the African Burial Ground National Monument across the plaza. He could hear them. They were singing and shouting. What joy. What pain.

Gaskill turned around. "We have to go," he said, looking up at Sean and Ade standing behind him.

Gaskill closed his eyes and continued walking. Four policemen approached and were almost upon them when Gaskill, Sean, and Ade disappeared into an invisible door opening into the doctor's war room some 190 miles away deep beneath Cape Henlopen, Delaware.

"Find Cyral," Gaskill said through clenched teeth.

Ade and Sean stood still for a moment.

<Now!>

They were both jolted by the word. Ade sighed in distress and sweat crept down her brow. Sean tensed the muscles in his arms, chest, and right fist for several seconds as he knelt on one knee. Ade took a deep breath and shook her head, then staggered toward the door.

Sean finally found his way to the nearest conference chair. Something told him that Cyral was already on his way.

## GRANITE FOREST, GEORGIA

Sunlight fell through holes in the Granite Forest canopy, casting bright speckles into the air between the rocks, roots, and saplings. One ray ended on a doe as it grazed near two more and a fawn. A buck approached them, standing straight and still in the shadow of the large stone where they lingered. Some crows hopped along the top of the rock. Rapid knocking echoed through the trees from a woodpecker hunting nearby. Cardinals sang to each other in the distance.

A tremor brought the grazing heads up from the ground. The crows lifted into flight, cawing, and several others sprang up from nearby trees.

The ground near the buck liquified and poured into a sinkhole. The buck hopped away to more stable ground. On the other side of the hole, the does charged into the trees, the fawn struggling to catch up. The buck leapt into the air over the sinkhole and landed on the other side.

A shadow, as large and as heavy as a bear, raced up from the sinkhole. Its large fist grabbed the buck's antlers and pulled, breaking the animal's stride and its neck. The shadow flung the buck into the air and then slammed its head against the ground. Its antlers and skull shattered, and the animal's brain sprayed across the forest floor. Impossibly black, the creature crawled out of the hole, still clutching the buck, and stretched its long arms out into the air.

<!>

A normal creature would have made a fearsome sound, but this one called out fear itself, deep in the viscera of birds, men, deer, and forest creatures near and far. It crouched over the broken buck and took large mouthfuls of the warm flesh in a vain attempt to satisfy a centuries-old hunger. It would have preferred man flesh, but until it could find some, the buck would have to suffice.

## SPASE HEADQUARTERS – WAR ROOM A – CAPE HENLOPEN, DE

<He looks just like her,> Gaskill thought. Juno and Hermod's resemblance exasperated him, made it harder for him to divine winning scenarios.

"Like who?" Cyral replied, concerned. The thought was laced with all sorts of emotions that he had never received from Dr. Gaskill. He and Ade were seated at the conference table. Gaskill was standing next to an empty seat at the table.

Ade kept her eyes fixed on the LED screens at the far end of the room. One of them was Mingo's POV on Hermod. Sean was standing in front of the screens in silhouette.

"Nyhemaa's Star is here," Gaskill said. "It's starting."

"When?" Ade asked.

"Right now."

"What was that spell?" Ade asked. "At the courthouse?"

Gaskill was silent for a moment.

"Yeah!" Sean said. "What the fuck was that?" He approached the others at the table.

Dr. Gaskill remained motionless. He looked at Sean and then at the other three.

"Juno and Vincent have an ally," Gaskill said. "And now it's free. We . . . I cast a spell to bind it and send it back to the void in order to end them."

"So, you decided to let him free today?" Cyral asked.

"It . . . has liberated itself under the light of merciful Nyhemaa's Star."

"It?" Ade asked.

Cyral squinted at Gaskill, who remained immobile, his eyes fixed on the wall ahead of him. He could feel their confusion and frustration. Cyral's doubt stung him the most.

"Why now?" Cyral asked.

"Does that need answering?" Ade said.

"What are we aiming at here?" Sean asked.

"Remus," Gaskill replied. "The Void King. A formidable shadow creature from a place . . . We never figured out where they went, into that rock. Juno called it the void."

"Remus," Ade said softly.

"You will know it when you see it," Gaskill said, "and if you survive, you will never forget it."

"It will be looking for Hermod?" Ade asked.

"It will feed," Gaskill said, "and then meet its master, yes. It will obey and protect him." He looked at the LED screens along the wall opposite them.

"Then we should find it now," Ade said.

"One doesn't find Remus," Gaskill replied. "It will only reveal itself to destroy you or in service to its master. Either meeting will be a decisive one."

"I don't like when you talk like this," Sean said.

"I won't waste SPASE resources pursuing it," Gaskill said. "Sean, Cyral, we will preserve our manpower in preparation for confronting Vincent and Juno. Ade, feel free to investigate on your own terms, with your own personnel."

Ade nodded and then returned her attention to the screen that showed Mingo's view of Hermod hovering over downtown Brooklyn.

"We are wasting an opportunity," she said.

"If you want to go be devoured right now, then have at it," Gaskill replied. "All of you will understand the peril at hand very soon."

# LET'S DANCE

## LONNIE'S – WEST BROADWAY & READE STREET – MANHATTAN NEW YORK CITY, NY

"Baby, I'll be right back," Nino said. He grabbed Carl's shoulders and looked into his eyes. Red fluorescent lights and rays from the disco ball danced in them. Nino swayed and gently guided Carl's body with him, then smiled and leaned in and kissed him. He felt Carl's mouth curl into a smile against his own. It was contagious. Nino backed away, still holding Carl's shoulders. "Hurry up and pee, baby. Let's get out of here. "Carl pushed Nino away gently. Nino danced backwards a few steps, then whirled around and headed to the bathroom.

Carl backed away from the crowd and stood near the bar. The wood in it rattled in time with the beat. He smiled and let the bass course through the floor and up into his body. Large hands grabbed his waist and tugged at his belt loops. He was pulled into a contoured chest, and he felt a few sweat drop onto his shoulders, followed by a heavy exhale on the back of his neck as a long, hard pressure poked into his left buttock. The man pulled Carl even closer. He watched the lights dance above the shadow of the throng of people bobbing and throwing their bodies around to the infectious, heavy bass beat. Carl stepped away from the man and grabbed his hands, then lifted them from his waist.

He turned around, reclasped hands with the stranger, and looked into the handsome mustached face.

"Hello," Carl said. He smiled and grabbed the boy's waist and stepped toward him, moving his own hips from side to side. He guided one of the boy's hands to the back of his waist. The other moved on its own, its fingers crawling up Carl's shirt. The boy smiled at him, and Carl looked into his dark eyes. His strong, firm hands gripped Carl's butt, one palm over each cheek, the fingertips digging in between them. Carl arched his back and hiked himself up a bit to fit in the man's palms. They pressed their hips together, and their dicks collided and rolled around each other beneath their clothing.

Carl wondered where Nino was.

The man's eyes were wide and filled with the neon light. Carl felt his fingers stop digging and his palms slowly loosen from his butt. The man's face flattened, and his hands fell to Carl's thighs and held his jeans loosely for a second and then he stepped away. Disappointed, Carl turned around to determine what had caused him to do so. Three people were lying on the floor just ten feet from him. One was lying still. The two others were convulsing.

A scream cut through the beat, and Carl saw a shadow speeding across the floor about fifty feet away from him, just to the right of the DJ booth. The hot man turned and fled.

Lasers scanned the dark dance floor. Red and purple slivers of light struck a heap near the booth, showing black pants, a yellow security guard emblem embroidered into an oxford shirt, and the man's light-brown hand. Carl looked toward the doorway beside the guard and saw another clump of shadow lying in the middle of the dimly lit hallway.

Where was Nino? Carl thought. Frightened he knelt low and continued scanning the floor.

A strobe light hit the disco ball, and rays shot out across the room, illuminating another young man near the booth. He had fallen on his knees, his head propped up against a nearby speaker. Lasers shone on the man, removing the shadows. He moved his hands and arms around him and then clenched his hands together so hard that the veins in his arms and hands bulged from his skin. Then the man's body completely relaxed, and he folded to the floor and farted.

There were more screams, and Carl saw three more people from the throng drop to the floor before the strobe light died, and the room plunged into darkness. He was jostled by bodies flying in fear around him. Thin slices of green, purple, and red neon light cut through the room, sweeping over the fallen bodies. Carl turned to the bar and saw the bartender slumped over it, his face blue with veins stretching across his neck and around his eyes.

Lee stopped shaking off the last drips of urine from his dick and stood still for a moment. A man started screaming, and in the next second, a dozen more were yelling. He heard feet scuffling and voices and then a din filled the bathroom. The stalls rattled and then someone pounded his stall door three times. He tucked his dick back in and zipped up.

"Lee, it's me!" Tig shouted. He pounded on the door again.

Lee unlatched the door. It flung open, and Tig rushed in, knocking Lee against the toilet. He shuffled his feet and braced himself on the rattling stall wall.

"What's goin' on?"

"I don't know." Tig pushed Lee's head down and peeked above the stall door. Eyes stared back at him. He nodded. "In here."

The song playing in the main dance floor ended, and with no other following, the club fell silent.

Tig opened the door, and three men pushed into the stall.

"What the fuck, man?" One of them said with a French accent. He closed his eyes, pushed his back against the stall door, and crouched.

"Like, where are the cops?" another man said. He was thin and muscular, and his arm looked like it could have been chiseled out of milk chocolate. He rubbed his hands frantically in the direction of the waves in his fade and then stared into his phone as his thumbs flitted across its glass surface. His sharp elbow flew around just an inch from Lee's nose.

Tig caught Lee's eye. "Any word?"

"No, I . . ." Lee shook his head, then noticed the third guy was crouched with his arms clutching his knees. He was holding his phone in front of his face and was talking into it. Lee couldn't hear what he was saying. "What the fuck is happening?"

"I don't know," Tig said, his voice tinged with frustration. He closed his eyes. The word was out. "Someone's sending a text now that says people were suffocating. They saw a man walking around, and everyone he looked at or touched fell down and just . . ." Tig shook his head and closed his eyes. "There are a lot of people outside and a few cops now."

"Comment savez-vous tout cela?" the Frenchman asked. "How can you know this? You are demi?"

The crouching man looked up from his phone. "Save us, man!"

Lee stood up and ducked under the chocolate boy's arms, then pushed him into the corner where he had just been standing. Lee stood and stared into Tig's eyes.

"Help me a sec."

Tig nodded and then grabbed Lee's shoulders. "Guys, stay quiet for a sec."

"What do you mean stay quiet?" The Frenchman stood a bit taller than Tig's shoulder. He reached up to grab Tig's jaw, but the instant his fingers made contact, he gasped and fell back against the stall door. Startled, the crouching man hopped to his feet and backed into the corner near the door hinge, stepping around the sprawling Frenchman.

"He'll be fine in about ten seconds," Tig said.

Lee felt warm. His skin was tingling, and his chest felt heavy, like it did when he took his pre-workout drink. He tried to concentrate amidst the panic rattling the walls and bodies in the room.

"Ignore it, Lee," Tig said. The tall Frenchman began to stir near Tig's feet. The other two men stared at Lee. Tig grabbed Lee's hands and flinched due to the violent pounding on the stall behind him.

They all heard a scream and then a deep gagging sound coming from the bathroom entrance. Voices in the bathroom quieted.

The Frenchman was on his knees now. His friend held his phone to the space in between the stall partitions. His chocolate- skinned friend crouched so that his head was below the top of the stall. He leaned against the brick wall with one foot on the back of the toilet, his fists balled tight.

"Hermod!" Lee said.

"Eliot Sánchez!" Myron yelled.

## DOWNTOWN BROOKLYN, NEW YORK CITY, NY

Hermod was perched on the roof of the Ashland condominium tower. He didn't want to leave Brooklyn, so he had gone there. He watched the red-and-blue lights flashing at the foot of the Manhattan Bridge. His head pounded due to a strange spike in the anxious noise in Tribeca. It wasn't a dead spirit flare up either. Tribeca, Battery Park, and FiDi were good for those. The discomfort was big and hot like gas, but it was in his head.

<What the fuck is happening now?>

<Niggas are up to no good. I gotta get to work!>

<¡Aye Dios! ¿Cuándo empieza la fiesta?>

He felt someone choking to death around Tribeca. A young man. A sister. His heart rate quickened for a moment. There were more. Ten. Maybe more. His eyes fixed on the shining new high-rise on Church Street near—

<Hermod!>

He jumped up. Any normal man would have fallen to his death. <Lee?> he thought, moving toward the bridge, Tribeca. <Where are you?>

<Lonnie's.>

Tribeca. His eyes fixed on the small dark building a block away from the shiny new high-rise on Church Street. He could see their bodies huddled in the back corner of the building where the bathrooms were. He saw them in the stall. The other stalls were packed as well. Men knelt near the bathroom door, peering into the dark club. One of them was brandishing a knife. About fifty feet away from them, a man was being choked by something that Hermod could not see. People around the dying boy were also in terrible fear of this thing. This man? Hermod ground his teeth as the man's life was extinguished. Immediately another began suffocating. Hermod could feel the anxious people reacting to someone. He had only received a silhouette from the crowd, until, in a dying effort to identify his killer, the suffocating young man flung himself onto his attacker. Hermod saw the boy's last vision: a would-be handsome, addiction-worn Puerto Rican man smiling, enticing even when murderous, with dark shadows where his molars should have been.

"That motherfucker!"

Hermod was off. In seconds he was approaching 5,000 miles per hour without even realizing it. He twirled his body to the left just in time, or else he would have destroyed a shiny new high-rise near Adams Street.

## LONNIE'S – WEST BROADWAY & READE STREET – MANHATTAN NEW YORK CITY, NY

Inside Lonnie's, Myron shook his head as he brought his right foot over a dying young man and advanced toward the bathrooms. He approached another body and kicked it. It winced and cried a bit and then the crying locked up into a gag. The body flattened back to the floor, going still. White light glimmered in the man's eyes as they bulged out of the sockets in his skull. A dry, gurgling sound issued from his throat; he dropped his knife and fell to one knee, clutching his neck with both hands.

Myron uncurled the fingers on his left hand and let his right hand fall to his side, and the dying man fell face first to the floor. Myron smiled as he continued walking toward the bathrooms.

"Eliot Sánchez!" Myron said, quieter than he thought he should have. He looked back at the man he had just strangled. "I know you're in here!"

Gasping and cursing echoed through the bathroom. The wall to Myron's right was lined with sinks and mirrors. To his left was a stainless-steel well. The floor beneath it was slick with piss. Its scent irritated him until he became accustomed to it. Stalls ran along the rest of the wall. He stepped toward the first one and then turned toward the mirror at his right. He noticed that his forehead wasn't sweating, not as much as his feet and underarms were. The stall wall shimmied in front of him. Men were cursing and shushing each other. He heard whimpers.

"Don't cry," he said, his regular voice returning. "I'm only here for one person."

In their stall Tig shook Lee a few times.

"I'm OK," Lee said.

The three strangers all stared at Lee.

Myron approached the first stall door and looked into the partition between the door and the stall wall. He saw a sweaty shoulder and a bicep. The man had brown hair. He couldn't distinguish his face. He looked at the latch on the door and balled his right hand into a fist. The door shimmied as the men moved about inside.

"He's right outside. I see him," one of them said. More shifting and shimmying from the stall in response. Groans and whispers in the other stalls grew louder. Stall doors farther down rattled. There was a retching sound, but a flushing toilet drowned it out.

Myron's eyes remained fixed on the latch. He'd practiced this. He'd broken into three cars just that morning. He clenched his fist harder until he felt his nails digging into his palm. He punched the air just inches short of the latch. The impact resounded through the bathroom, and a man roared in protest. He punched again and watched the stall door shake violently. He slammed his hand down like a gavel, and the men responded as the stall door shook, and the latch began to detach.

"Fuck this!" one of the men in the stall yelled.

Myron watched as the exposed latch turned. The door flung open, and he jumped back. In his peripheral vision he saw a tight-jawed, wide-eyed, muscled blond man in a black T-shirt rush out the door. Myron fell onto his buttocks and then flipped his lower body around to rest on his knees. He locked his eyes on the mirror and held his hand up, watching the boy's eyes narrow.

"Yes!" Myron whispered.

The boy fell forward and cleared the door, locking eyes with Myron. One of his hands caught the sink in front of him, and the other clutched his throat before he fell to his knees. Another young man leapt out of the stall and landed on his side, then rolled away toward the bathroom exit. Myron whipped his head around just in time to watch the boy scamper out the door. Myron stood quickly and looked down at the boy. He was gagging louder. Satisfied, Myron moved past him toward the next stall.

## LONNIE'S (OUTSIDE) – WEST BROADWAY & READE STREET – MANHATTAN, NEW YORK CITY, NY

<Ian,> Dr. Gaskill called to him. He looked across the table at Cyral and nodded.

<Yes, Doctor, I'm here.> Mingo hovered just above the streetlight at the corner of Reade Street and Church Ave. He looked down at Davi, who was standing several feet west.

"I'm approaching the entrance," Davi said, his voice sounding in Ian's earpiece. "I see Sergeant Trevisan."

Mingo watched as the army of officers parted around Davi. He stopped next to Sergeant Trevisan.

"Sergeant." Mingo watched Davi and Trevisan shake hands. "I'm here with my colleague—"

<He is close,> Dr. Gaskill Interrupted. <Hurry.>

<By any means necessary?> Mingo's vision blurred for a moment. He focused inward, heard his heart rate quickening. He punched his fists together, sending sparks into the air around him.

<You have to neutralize Myron, and make sure—>

<Seriously? He's begging for an ass whooping, Doc!> Mingo looked uptown as if the doctor was there.

<Not this time.> Gaskill looked at Cyral as he turned his chair around. <Davi will deal with Hermod. He is in violation of his federal parole, and there are far too many civilians within the immediate vicinity to leave this to his passions.>

<He called you?> Mingo asked. <Asked you for help? I'm tired of babysitting Super Mono! Why risk my neck? Let him save his own man. Then when that's done, let me take him down a notch.> He pounded his fists again.

<I'll remind you, Ian, that you are also under federal mandate.> Gaskill's teeth ground in his head as he spoke. <As a ward of SPASE, you will do as you're told.>

White burned in Mingo's eyes, and he clenched them shut. His ears roared for a moment, and the air burned. His nose filled with a thick, burnt, sour odor. He'd smelled it dozens of times, and each time it made him want to spit. The white had gone, but everything he saw was blurred, silhouetted for a moment. Something orange glowed in front of him where Davi had been standing. The orange blob disappeared, and Ian clenched his eyes for a moment again, then reopened them. Hermod was standing near the entrance to the club.

"Mr. Vincent," Sgt. Trevisan said, trembling and beginning to perspire. "I've . . . dammit, Hermod, I've got to ask you to stand down." He wiped his brow with his sleeve.

"Sergeant." Hermod had discerned that the seven officers around him were friendlies, even Trevisan, despite his fear. Four more officers were exiting their vehicles. Sirens screamed in the distance, and he had passed two helicopters on their way just a second ago. He was just a stone's throw from the African Burial Ground. He cringed, and a flare of anger rushed through him. He could hear the singing and shouting.

"My . . . my husband is in there."

"I'm afraid . . ." Sgt. Trevisan looked down at his shoes and back up again into Hermod's eyes and then advanced. "I'm afraid I can't let you do that, Hermod. It's the feds. I—"

Hermod turned toward the door.

"Hermod." Davi stepped forward. Hermod turned and faced him. "Per your federally mandated parole, you need to stand down." He pointed to Ian above.

"Fuck you!" Hermod turned back around to the entrance to Lonnie's. "We're wasting time." He jumped into the air and fell back down to his knees, winded. Davi moaned and knelt as well. Hermod turned around, and locked eyes with him. Davi gasped for air through his open mouth. He stood up slowly and held out his palm, the other hand balled into a fist.

"Fuck off, Davi." Hermod felt like he was being pressed in between two buildings. Sadness called at him from just a few blocks away, and dread coursed through him, permeating from the scene inside Lonnie's, and fucking Davi had been putting in some work with training his dampening ability.

<Davi, continue to hold him,> Gaskill ordered. <Ian, find Myron.> He could feel Davi's strain. His blood pressure pounded in his skull, and his

shoulders and knees ached. Davi was the most powerful enlisted nullifier. Gaskill stared at the wall where he was projecting Davi's thoughts and vantage onto a large rectangular area. He did the same for Mingo on the adjacent wall. Hermod looked patient, kneeling there. He would crush Davi if he needed to. Gaskill thought about Lee and wondered with how great a fury the inevitable would lash out. Had he delayed it longer than he should have? Would Vincent recognize him? Was it too late?

"Doctor, he's too much," Davi said.

Hermod continued to kneel, his breathing calm. Panic and dread from the living and the dead yelled in his brain, coursing hot anguish through him. Policemen gathered around him, their SPT-grade demi assault weapons drawn. He was flattered by their resilience. The SPT weapons line was powerful and surprisingly effective. Only a handful of officers were selected by SPASE to be trained with them.

Davi held his hand out to keep from collapsing. He stared Hermod down from between his fingers. He was trembling. Sweat was running down the sides of his head. Crowds started to gather on the corners nearby, and several officers left the flank to secure a perimeter around the confrontation.

"Davi, let go. I can deal with this." Transfixed on Hermod, Mingo barely noticed that he had descended to the sidewalk. He approached Davi and Hermod on foot and stopped just six feet shy of them. His lower arms and fists were completely black, lost in the silky clouds swirling around them and gathering around his torso and neck.

<Ian, no!> Gaskill slammed his fist on the table in front of him as he watched Mingo's broadcast. Deep within he felt the fates shifting wildly in response to Mingo's stubbornness. Reality was aligning with the riddle he had seen in the night five years ago. He abhorred the thought that his foresight might have returned after all these years to reveal what it had. He would have preferred not to know. But there was still time to influence fate. He brought his focus back to the present to see what he might be able to salvage.

Mingo's hatred was palpable, stealing Hermod's attention. Feeling Mingo take aim, Hermod looked up and then rose into the air. Davi tried to stand as Hermod ascended, but he fell to the ground, unconscious. Hermod clenched his fists.

Mingo moved in the blink of an eye. Hermod had just enough time to lock eyes with him before they collided. Thunder clapped right there on the street. Policemen dropped their weapons and gripped the sides of their heads, some ducking to the ground. Glass rained from windows high and low and splashed from buildings and cars all along the block. Alarms sounded in a cacophony. They were gone. Mingo's small black cloud lingered where he'd tarried.

## LONNIE'S (INSIDE) – WEST BROADWAY & READE STREET – MANHATTAN

Everyone in the bathroom was completely still, their ears ringing from the force of the blast outside. Myron took a deep breath and tried to stand. His head hurt. The mirrors behind him had shattered outward, startling him. He had been protected from any dangerous shards, but his body was rattling, and his head was aching and throbbing.

"Now," the brown-haired man said. He stared at Myron and pushed his nearest friend forwards. Three of them darted around their dead friend and Myron and ran to the exit.

The brown-haired man stopped in the doorway and looked back as Myron rose to his feet. "Fight, guys! Run!" He ducked out of sight before Myron could get a fix on him.

Two more stall doors opened. Tig peered out of one of them and saw two more men running toward Myron. Two other's hung back in the stall door. One of the fleeing men swung at Myron, and his fist crashed into something invisible covering Myron's face. The second man charged Myron and pushed him back. His effort was more effective. Myron tumbled into the corner on top of the man who'd broken his hand on Myron's unseen face shield. The other man stood there, stunned, not believing that he'd been able to knock Myron down. He backed away and then turned to the door and ran. Myron jumped to his feet and reached out. The man beneath him clambered away and darted through the door before Myron could catch him.

One of the young men who had remained in the stall closed his eyes and took a deep breath. He exhaled quickly and then darted from the stall toward the exit. Myron locked onto him, and the young man immediately fell to his knees, gagging.

Tig ducked back into his stall, holding his index finger to his lips. Lee looked at him, wide-eyed. The Frenchman approached, but Tig held out his hand, and the Frenchman crashed into it. The chocolate-skinned man stepped toward the two of them.

"Just give me a sec. He's got a phone. Lee, hand me yours." Tig pulled out his own. He made eye contact with each of the other three men individually. "When I throw these," he said, holding up his and Lee's iPhones, "run. Got it?" The three men nodded. Tig turned around and braced his back against the open stall door. He peeked his head out and saw Myron standing over the man he'd just killed. He made eye contact with the man in the stall next to his, who had stayed behind. He nodded and waved one of the phones in front of him, then extended his chin toward Myron, who was approaching them. Tig ducked back into the stall and closed his eyes.

Myron could see their legs and feet beneath the small stalls. *I bet they make the walls so tall so they can go in there and fuck*, he thought. His head was still buzzing from the explosion outside, and the edges on the surfaces in the room were still vibrating.

Suddenly, his right pocket was very warm. His phone began to vibrate and buzz. He reached to grab it but then dropped it back into his pocket. It was so hot, it started to burn his thigh. He reached back in to grab the phone and throw it away. His fingertips grabbed the corner just as the corner of Lee's phone smashed into Myron's eyeball. He instinctively caught the fragile device, and it too was burning. He flung it away. Another phone landed at his feet. The burning and aching in his thigh forced him to his knees. He tried to pull the phone out of his pocket again.

All three phones exploded. Myron's vision turned white, and a thin black cloud of smoke rose around him. He heard the stall rattle, followed by slick footsteps running toward him. He shot out his arm but just missed the person who passed him. Myron groaned due to the pain in his thigh. It was badly burned and bleeding from the phone shrapnel lodged in his flesh.

He fell to the floor. He wanted to just shut his eyes and vomit due to the acrid smoke crawling into his nose and down his throat. He wheezed and tried to stand again. Two men passed him on either side. He ignored them, still unable to breathe.

Tig pushed Lee as they approached Myron.

Myron gasped and then coughed. He heard footsteps approaching and looked up. His vision was returning, and he could see a silhouette.

"Lee!" Myron said, relieved. "I found you." He smiled and tried to stand straighter, bracing himself on the sink beside him. His smile widened for a moment and then his lips curled in pain. He leaned even harder on the sink. Tig grabbed Lee and pulled him back just as Myron shot out his hand.

"Get out of sight!" Tig tossed Lee behind him, and he ducked back into the nearest stall.

Tig kept his chest and back away from Myron and held his chin down into his neck. He felt a pressure on his forearm and another trying to wrap around his neck and chin from behind.

"Two . . . one!" Tig said.

A police cruiser crashed through the wall behind the first three stalls directly beside Myron. He snarled and flailed his arms to shield himself. The stall structure and crumbling brick smashed down on them. The porcelain sink dug into Myron's hip bone. He heard a cracking sound and realized it was the sink and not his hip. His shield was growing more reflexive, though it had not spared his ribs. Tig ducked to shield himself. Red-and-blue lights dispelled the darkness, and water poured out of the mangled pipes. Broken tiles and toilet pieces clinked and clanked as they bounced across the floor.

Lee crouched near the front corner of the stall, completely still. He was in the last stall. It and the wall behind were pretty much intact. The toilet and pipes had protruded from the wall and broken a bit of the tiles there. He could see Tig's leg beneath the stall wall. The room started to reek, and his pants were soaking up water. The entire floor was slick with it, and he heard it trickling along with the sound of traffic outside.

<Lee?> Gaskill knew it was a great risk, but he had to make sure that Lee was still alive.

Lee looked around to see if there was anyone else in the bathroom. He didn't recognize the voice in his head.

<Lee?> This time Lee was able to recall the voice, the presence.

<Doctor Gaskill?>

<Yes. Are you alright?>

<Yes. I'm OK, I guess.> Lee stood up and grabbed his left shoulder. He'd landed on it when Tig threw him. <What's happening? I thought we were—>

<Never mind that. We will be safe,> Gaskill assured him. <Listen very carefully. I know you're there with Myron but I can't see him like I can see you. Neither can Cyral or Hermod. No one can. It's his power. Can you see him?>

<No. No one else is moving. He may have been hurt by the crash. I'm with Tig.> Lee tried to peer beneath the stall door, but all he saw was rubble. He stood as still as he could. His shoulders and hands were trembling slightly, and his throat was drying out. Hermod had mentioned his unease with Myron before, and even Lee had picked up a strange vibe from him, not unlike the sensations he had picked up from other demis. He'd never imagined that Myron was harboring such violence. His skin crawled as he recounted Myron's rude flirtations a few days earlier. He wondered how many people had died this evening. He decided to feel guilty about it later.

He listened between the gurgling water for any signs of movement or breathing. Hearing nothing, he pushed the half-open stall door fully agape.

<Lee, I need you to stay put until someone arrives,> Gaskill advised.

<But Tig,> Lee said, his palm resting on the door. He could see Tig's leg moving slightly. <I see Tig, and he's moving now.>

<Lee, stay put,> Gaskill said. <The officers are entering the building now.>

Lee pushed the stall door open and crouched to assist Tig. The moment his knee hit the wet floor, he felt something grip his neck and something else in his throat. He looked up instinctively and locked eyes with Myron. The left side of Myron's face was swollen, a line of blood dribbled from his mouth, and his eyes were blood red. He held out his left hand and gnarled his fingers in a tight grip. His right arm was held fast, pinned awkwardly between the crooked pieces of the stall partition, bricks, and the police cruiser. His lower body was hidden beneath the rubble and the vehicle. A wide streak of blood washed down the surface of the twisted stall wall, gushing every so often. A cloud of blood spread through the water pooling on the floor.

“Qué guapo,” Myron whispered.[1]

Mingo held Hermod with incredible strength. His body was impossibly hard, and Mingo increased the force of his grip. His hands and Hermod's face were shrouded in his black clouds. Their smoky wisps streamed from the corners of his mouth and eyes. Mingo's teeth mashed into each other, and his gums and jaw were throbbing. He dragged Hermod up far beyond any of the city's towers and then released him for a moment. Glowing, meandering orange lines and twinkling lights spread across the surface below. Dark and glistening, the rivers snaked along either side of Manhattan Island. Buildings rose from the gloom in the distance.

<Mingo!> Gaskill called.

Mingo smashed his fist into Hermod's face and then landed a powerful kick in Hermod's side. He punched Hermod in the stomach and then tossed him up into the air. Mingo had never punched anything harder. Each blow popped and resounded in his own body.

“¡Te odio!“ Mingo said, stiff jawed. “¡Maldito mono!” He clapped his hands in front of him, and several bolts of green light struck Hermod's body. Hermod shook violently and his body contorted as the lightning crawled over him[2].

<Mingo!> Dr. Gaskill called again. He crept further into Mingo's mind. Immense black clouds were everywhere. A blue sun burned beyond them. Bulging clouds swirled and stormed over an abyss in the distance. Legs of green lighting arced down into the hole. Thousands of flashes crisscrossed in bright sprints of energy. Gaskill receded from Mingo's tempest. He looked at Mingo's projection on the wall and breathed deeply. He looked down at the aluminum-and-leather office chair he was standing next to. It rose

---

1 “So handsome.”

2 “I hate you!” “Fucking monkey”

several inches into the air, and the swivel bottom broke away from the seat as it tore in half. The three chair parts fell back to the floor in a neat pile.

Hermod was still shaking, trying to set himself upright. He could sense Mingo lunging at him. Davi's nullifying hex was powerful though. Hermod threw out his jittery arm, and a massive burst of blue-white fire issued from his hand. Mingo growled, spun out of his attack, and rolled with the flames.

"Back in business," Hermod said, his eyes locked on Mingo rushing toward him. He coughed and shook his body to help alleviate the effects of Mingo's lightning. He opened his hand in front of him, and another burst of fire shot out at Mingo. Mingo dodged it and then steadied himself, his torso hidden behind his clouds. Inky black obscured his face for a moment before it appeared again, riven with fury. Hermod threw out a line of flame. Mingo quickly aligned his body behind his fists and charged through it. Hermod dodged too slowly, and Mingo clipped his waist and knocked him into a spin. Mingo stopped himself, then turned to charge again. Hermod swatted his hand in front of him, and his unseen force sent Mingo spinning away. Hermod pursued and caught him in his gravitational pull. He ignited, flames enveloping them, and then smashed his fist into Mingo and held his body in place in front of him. Mingo slouched and moaned and held his arms up, summoning his cloud to shield him from the flames.

"I'll show you burnt pussy," Hermod said, using slang he'd plucked from Mingo's thoughts days earlier.

"¡Muere, maricón," Mingo growled[(1)]. Lightning shot out of his mouth and snaked around his body and his arms. He spun around and launched his fist at Hermod, nearly landing the blow to his face. Hermod grabbed Mingo's forearms and intensified the flames encompassing them both. Mingo winced and ground his teeth. He shut his eyes and bowed his head away from Hermod's to shield his mind. Hermod was just about to force his way in when Mingo looked up into his eyes. Lightning flared from his hands, and several bolts shot into Hermod's face. Mingo tried to turn his body but could not move. He gasped. He had blown off the right half of Hermod's face, revealing a black skull beneath the skin. Exposed sinews singed away. Then

---

[1] Die· faggot!

the intact skin and flesh sparked up in a hiss and burned away as well. Hermod's jaw lowered, and the left half of his face opened into a wide-eyed smile.

"Filth!" Hermod said. "Such a vile-minded boy."

Mingo screamed as the pain beneath Hermod's grip became unbearable. Hermod's black skull and jaw bones were fully exposed now. Mingo had heard that voice, that drawl, that reverberating depth, at the RSVP studio.

Hermod looked into Mingo's green eyes. "Beautiful," he said, marveling. "I might just take one of those for myself. That way you will see black all the time." His jaw dropped, and fire burst from his mouth. "You'll love it! What do you say?"

Mingo squealed in pain. His body shook as thin bolts struck between their parallel bodies.

Hundreds of miles away, Gaskill cringed and looked away from Mingo's thought projection. He held his fist so tightly in front of him that it shook. Fates swirled and burned inside him, making him sick to his stomach. Centuries ago, divining had been one of his greatest gifts. Futures screamed at him. Now only precedent and vague fates spoke, always drowning out the future's whispers.

<¡Adiós, bebe!>[1]

Hermod looked away from Mingo and tossed him hundreds of yards aside. His flaming blue orb extinguished, and black night surrounded him again. He looked directly toward the Freedom Tower, then slightly to the left of it. The voice, the word, echoed in his head, and his largest muscles tensed up and quivered.

<¡Adiós, bebe! ¡Adiós, bebe! ¡Adiós, bebe! ¡ ¡Adiós, bebe! ¡Adiós, bebe! ¡Adiós, bebe! ¡Adiós, bebe!>

Lee's voice echoed in his head. Hermod took a deep breath. His weight fell to his knees, and he descended about one hundred feet and then stopped. He grabbed his head and looked down at the place where the red-and-blue lights were flashing near City Hall. His chest heaved twice, and he slowly exhaled, then descended. He felt the last four years draining out of him like his intestines were being pulled out through his navel.

---

1 "Goodbye, babe."

<Babe.> Hermod felt nothing on Lee's end.

"Lee!" Hermod screamed. Pressure in the corner of his eyes made him grab his face again. His fingertips dabbed the corners and came back wet. He looked down at the ground below, trying to orient himself, trying to find the building so he could jump down and—tears blurred it all. He heaved again three times and breathed out. His throat felt full.

"Eliot. ¡Di algo!"[1] Hermod's mouth moved, but only cracked whispers issued from him. He felt nothing.

Heaviness pulled at his chest, and he toppled over in a freefall. Mingo charged in pursuit, raging, furious. A chill spread over him just before he smashed into Hermod and sent him tumbling faster to the ground. Mingo steadied himself and clapped his hands, and a bolt of lightning shot down into Hermod's back, speeding up his descent. Thunder roared as Mingo charged after Hermod and then stopped briefly. He held out both hands to discharge more massive green bolts. One of them struck Hermod, and Mingo charged and smashed his fist into him, sending Hermod crashing to the surface. Mingo held his hands together in the air high above his head, and several bolts shot down into the small crater where Hermod lay in Lincoln Park in Jersey City.

Mingo had paid no attention to their location during the fight. As he approached the smoldering hole in the park knoll, he was thankful they hadn't landed in the middle of an apartment building or a highway.

Hermod was naked and lying on his stomach. He looked calm and unblemished like he might have just taken off his clothes and fallen asleep there.

"The target is down," Mingo said. Thick plumes of smoke and steam rose up, obscuring his vision.

<Sean should be arriving,> Dr. Gaskill replied.

A quiet whistling sound changed to loud throbbing in Mingo's ears. Lights bathed the crater, casting Mingo's long shadow against the screen of rising smoke. MASS landed behind him. Mingo looked up at it and nodded. He felt it suppressing him, dampening his powers just in case. He rubbed his left hand around his right forearm as he stood admiring the fallen body.

---

1 Eliot· Say something!

"You alright?" Sean asked, the machine broadcasting his voice to Mingo.

"I got him! How's Davi?"

"He's OK. Just a slight headache, which is good 'cause we're gonna need him."

MASS stepped over Mingo and knelt down near the edge of the hole. It reached in and pulled Hermod out, holding him by the waist in its palm. A thin film crept around Hermod's body. It adhered close to his skin and clung around every fold. Mingo could see his sleeping face through the film. A second later, the film turned opaque and took on the color of the humanoid.

"What does that mean?" Mingo asked, regarding needing Davi. He rose to near MASS's head.

"We'll see when he wakes up." Sean nodded, and MASS's humanoid head nodded at Hermod's body.

"Yeah, we'll see." Mingo poked out his chest and drew in a deep breath, then sneered at Hermod.

Sean shook his head several times while MASS continued collecting Hermod. Hermod's body lifted from MASS's palm and levitated beside it. It and Hermod rose higher and then sped away to SPASE headquarters.

Mingo followed. He wasn't worried. Even if Hermod did wake up, it wouldn't matter. He'd smashed him once, and he would do it again.

# IT WAS ALL A DREAM

## SPASE HEADQUARTERS – WAR ROOM A – CAPE HENLOPEN, DE

Ade had been staring at the screen in silence for several minutes now. Her chocolate-brown skin glowed blue in the screen's light. It reflected a ridge along the top of her head and down her neck to her collar.

"Captain, we've got an unidentified . . ."

*Unidentified. How?* she'd asked herself. Decades later she was still asking. Jeff Binders' last words echoed in her head. The meteor that he had been trying to report smashed through his cargo rig, scattering him and his shuttle pod into the mesosphere.

Though her eyes were fixed on the screen, her head was filled with the distant memories of May 4, 1990, the day the Rain had started. The day she had failed, and what a thrilling failure it had been.

"Look at this, will you?" Carl had said, excited about the rocks they had brought back to the spacecraft for analysis. He turned from the shimmering specimen under his microscope and looked at her. "This is part of the original rock."

"What am I looking at?" Ade asked. "It's just a rock. It's pretty."

"It's not just a rock, Ade." Carl placed his eyes back against the black ocular lenses and marveled at the specimen from the original asteroid that had smashed into the moon. "It's a fungus. It's alive." He turned his thin, oak-skinned, bearded face from the ocular lens, and his eyes met hers. "You're looking at an alien."

His enthusiasm had brought her such joy. In the eight years he had been with Seku Labs, she had not seen him as ecstatic as when he woke her up that night to tell her that the specimens they were collecting were actively consuming the silicate rock that they were fused with. They were growing more even as they were collecting it! Though this news had given her great misgivings, she was happy that her friend was happy.

Carl Beesley had also died in the accident. Over time she would have made him a partner, most certainly. Maybe if they hadn't brought so much of it back. Did they really need four cargo containers? She could have designed a stabilized rig with just two. How many times had she asked herself these questions and sat staring as she redesigned the cargo rig in her mind, over and over?

It had been thrilling hearing those words, though, "It's alive!" The entire crew had been buzzing off of Gaskill's excitement. The views: green glowing mountains against a backdrop of golden spewing lava. She gasped at the splendorous memory as she stood in the glow of the screen.

Her awe decayed into dread as she recalled the sight of the container, cracked like a baker's egg, its massive, viscous, alien, fungal yolk oozing out into the world. Gaskill had exited the shuttle in a vain attempt to do something, but all he could do was watch helplessly as the Ojun spores merged with the atmosphere. The sparkling silvery-green clouds moved across the globe and rained down invisibly on it for a month afterwards. Within days there were reports from all over the globe of strange medical phenomena: miracle cures and advanced cancers.

The first demi-being, a shapeshifter, Sarah Neilstrom, was reported three years later, in the spring of 1993. Four months later, a mob killed her.

Three years later, Ade herself was admitted into the SPASE headquarters ER for observation of acute osteochondroma. Small bone tumors were developing rapidly around her joints and along her rib cage. Subsequent CT scans and X-rays showed Ade's bones growing and shifting and her internal organs shrinking and morphing around them in real time. She grew a third arm that evening, and it had retracted back into her by the morning. She had felt no pain throughout it all. Since then she could taste and smell emotions, and she hadn't been sick. She didn't realize the full extent of her healing power until six years ago when Sean shot her in the heart twice. It was her idea, to test her powers. She remembered he was as white as a bedsheet looking down on her bleeding body, begging her not to die.

Ade sighed. She'd had enough time to replay the story right down to the last detail of her game of demi-roulette. Sometimes she didn't. Her weekly penance. It was her fault. The Rain was her fault.

"When do you think he'll wake up?" Sean asked.

Startled, Ade turned around.

"Calm down. Just me." Sean smiled at her. He was standing just three feet behind her, though she had not heard or sensed his approach.

"We won't know until he does," Ade said. "The only readings we're getting are radioactive and gravitational. No brainwaves, no vital signs, nothing."

"So, this fusion is his only sign of life?" Sean looked past the massive braid reflecting blue, draping across her smooth, dark shoulder. He watched the graphics and visualizations on the screen beyond her. Hermod was indeed flatlined across the board, except for the visualizations near the top left of the wall screen. One of them, an electromagnetic particle monitor, was circular, its circumference ringed and spiked like the silhouette of an eclipsed sun.

"He's literally off the charts. And the containment vacuum is holding?"

"For now."

Sean approached her, and she tensed up. He eased his hands to rest on her hips. He held himself just a few inches away, keeping his rock-hard penis from resting against her ass. She was shivering slightly. He leaned in and felt her warmth against his chest without even touching her. He sniffed her fragrant braid, inhaling her fear.

"It's OK."

"Says who?" Ade asked. Sean felt her hips relax in his hands and watched her shoulders fall as she leaned back. Ade's soft braid rested on Sean's chest, and his right hand rose to cup her smooth shoulder, the dark brown contrasting with his pink, ruddy fingers. He rested his chin on her head, his stubble scratched her scalp where it was bald. She moved her left hand to rest on his.

"I wonder what Vincent would have to say about this," Sean said as he looked at the screen. He felt her body against his, her heat radiating into him. On the screen, Hermod's black skeleton was a tiny dot in the midst of a great white glow. Arms of white and blue flame whipped around and through the shining light. He kissed her neck, and she stepped forward.

"He might get hard. Or wet. Vincent's lover was part Irish." Ade smelled blood. "They're coming." She heard their hearts beating, their lungs drawing in air and pushing it back out. Davi was afraid.

She turned around without looking into Sean's eyes and tiptoed forward until her lips met his. She went to a seat at the table behind Sean and stood near it, looking at the readings on the left of the LED wall screen. Ade shuddered at the thought of Juno and her brother, Vincent. Initially, she thought she might have been able to empathize with them. They were both powerful Black demis, lovers and adversaries of white people, queer in their identities—or so Ade thought. For Ade, Vincent and Juno seemed much more than demi, man, woman. Ade wasn't capable of emoting in their way. The doctor had shown her a glimpse of his death during one of their first briefings regarding Vincent's return. Ade had been given just a moment of the battle, but it had still tainted her. The psychic replay of their demise fueled her nightmares. She watched the screen. Hermod's readings never dipped.

Juno, Vincent, Sister, Crown Moon, they were far beyond Ade and most other demis. Besides Hermod. And maybe Cyral. Thoughts of Cyral rarely brought her relief, but this one did.

"They bear a striking resemblance." Gaskill's voice interrupted her silent querying. She and Sean turned away from the screen as Gaskill, Cyral, and Tig entered the room.

"And his gravity is steady?" Gaskill asked. He was at Ade's side now. He looked down as she looked up. He nodded, and she nodded back, then watched as his ruby-and-gold pupils rolled back toward the screen.

"Yes," Ade began, "and his internal temperature has increased by eighty thousand degrees."

"All this in a coma?" Cyral said, shaking his head. His arms unfolded from his chest. He read the left side of the LED wall screen as he sat. At that moment, Davi and Mingo entered the room.

"You might do the same if you could," Gaskill said, turning slightly to face Cyral.

Cyral was unsure how to take the remark, but given Gaskill's penchant for riddles, he decided to ignore it.

Ade eyed Cyral as she took the seat nearest the screen. Sean sat in the chair next to her and leaned onto the table. Tig sat next to Sean.

"What's he doing here?" Sean asked. He nodded his chin up at Mingo, then looked at Gaskill.

<I want him here,> Gaskill replied. <I've seen something, and he has been exposed to Vincent's sorcery. I'm monitoring him.>

"Front line, huh?" Sean said as he leaned back in his chair and Mingo and Davi took a seat.

Gaskill turned away from the screen and waved his hand. The door slid closed and locked. He approached the empty seat between Ade and Cyral. "People," he said, looking toward the back wall near the door. "I'm not going to lie to you. This is going to be tough."

Mingo shrugged and rolled his eyes. "How tough?"

"Well, for starters," Sean began, "suppose 'bony legs' wakes up right now, just like that." He leaned over the table and looked to his right, beyond Davi and into Mingo's faces. "You gonna stop him? Something tells me he's got you pegged."

"Fuck him," Mingo said. Cyral's lip upturned slightly at the vulgarity. "Faggot. Let him come," Mingo finished.

"He will disintegrate you," Cyral replied. He'd grown used to Mingo's offensive mouth. "He will enslave you first." He said it without affect, like he was reading a recipe.

"Enslave all of us, right?" Ade said, straightening her back. Cyral shook his head in disagreement. "I fear this may be the battle we have all been training for," she continued.

"Alright now, Athena," Tig mocked. Sean smiled, leaning way back in his chair.

"Ade is right." Gaskill waved his hand in an arc and then faced them all from the head of the table. On the LED wall, the visualizations monitoring Hermod's internal temperature, the corresponding live body scan, and radiation and particle radiation infographics all enlarged and took up most of the viewing space. "This isn't going away. This wild sort of cocoon is a test of limits. That's not Hermod in there. He's never burned that hot. And his gravitational field is equally off the charts. I bet he might emit gravitational waves to some degree if we let him loose."

Gaskill turned and pointed to the other portion of the LED wall. It filled the room with a bright light. Sean turned to follow the doctor's hand motion and squinted at the black skeleton asleep in a bed of cosmic fire. He was exhilarated by the thought of Hermod let loose, burning uncontrollably in the wild. He could fuel worlds or just as easily destroy them.

"Who is it then?" Davi asked.

Cyral looked at him for about ten seconds. He was brave; his fear masked it well. "You'd never faced anyone that heavy before, had you?" Cyral asked. "Outside Lonnie's. He was heavy, right?"

Davi peeled his gaze away from the screen to look at him.

"You're afraid of me?" Cyral laughed. "I'm flattered."

Davi was one of the world's strongest dampeners and had been assigned to handle Hermod indefinitely. All of SPASE was aware. And yet Cyral could feel the fear emanating from him. Cyral was truly flattered and fascinated. He smiled thinly at Davi. "You think you could hold him like that again?"

"I . . . I . . ." Davi stammered. Cyral was right. It was heavy; that's how Davi had described it to Flor the morning after. She'd fed him and rubbed his aching body with Tiger Balm, massaging his back as they shared a joint. Hermod was so heavy that he'd nearly crushed Davi. He hadn't mentioned it to anyone else. "I could do it," he said finally. He was compelled to tell the truth in front of Cyral. Even more so than when he spoke with Gaskill.

Cyral nodded. "Your courage will reward itself," he said, smiling.

"Are you done?" Ade asked, turning to Cyral. Her question was followed by silence. The white LED light illuminated their bodies and faces.

"I presume," Gaskill said, "that when he does wake up, he'll be lucid, compliant for a time."

“For how long,” Sean asked.

“Not long,” Gaskill replied. He waved his hand in front of him. The pixels dimmed, and the infographics faded, piece by piece. LEDs slowly turned back on again, illuminating in puzzle chunks. Sean recognized the peninsula, Florida. The puzzle pieces filled in a map of the Caribbean. Davi and Tig noticed the catastrophe first. It was in the same spot as yesterday. White clouds spiraled in a massive, nearly perfect circle around a black hurricane eye. The storm obscured most of the Dominican Republic. A red dot was labeled “Santo Domingo” just outside the northeast edge of the black storm eye.

“¡Super Mono!” Mingo whispered. “¡Maldito!”

Tig sat up straight. He was not strong enough to pick a fight with Mingo, a renowned hothead and alleged racist. He was perplexed by the idea of a racist Dominican person and also wondering how Gaskill had come to be in league with one.

<Power,> Cyral replied to Tig’s vague inquiry. Tig looked at him, and they exchanged smiles across the table.

Sean was also unnerved by Mingo’s insult. Ade smelled the tension wafting between the three men.

“It hasn’t moved,” Davi said.

“No, it hasn’t,” Gaskill agreed. He turned away from the screen, and in his silhouette the ruby-and-gold circles twinkled at Mingo. Cyral was rarely ever wrong with his declarations, Gaskill thought. God help them if Hermod did enslave him. He smiled and turned back to the screen.

“Hurricane Faust,” Gaskill began.

“You’re shitting me,” Sean exclaimed, understanding the translation.

“Hurricane Faust,” Gaskill continued, “was supposed to officially make landfall this morning. But it strengthened into a much larger category-five storm and made landfall a day early. I’ve negotiated an open contract with Dara Brentwood and Tracy Ford. Bruja Hanuri is accompanying them.”

“Hanuri’s elemental sorcery is barricading the storm surge and inland flooding,” Cyral said. "Tracy’s wormhole prowess has been a true lifesaver, enabling more efficient mass evacuation of citizens to safety. Hanuri reports that the winds have shadows, and the clouds are swirling like tar.”

"They are doing this, right?" Ade asked, pointing at Hermod. "Juno and Vincent, I mean."

Mingo stood up suddenly.

"¿Tienes algo que decir?"[1] Sean asked.

"Nada." Mingo balled his hands into fists.

"Not here, bro," Davi pleaded. He turned to Mingo and held out his hand. Davi rocked his head on his shoulder. He was not yet nullifying either of them.

"You'll need your strength for greater tasks," Gaskill said, looking at Mingo and then sweeping a pacifying thought suggestion across the room.

"Of course," Mingo said. "Doctor, if you'll excuse me."

"Yes, of course," Gaskill replied. "Ford is expecting you at the hangar." He waved his hand, and the conference room door opened. Mingo shot a grimace at Sean before exiting the room.

"As we were," Gaskill continued. "To answer your question, Ade, yes, Juno, Vincent, and Hermod are all responsible. When he wakes up, we won't have long. Losing his lover was exactly what we didn't want to happen. My apologies, Alexander, Tig." He nodded at each of them. "But here we are."

"You alone brought us here, and we need to stop it," Sean said. "So, which side of the street does the rain fall on this time?"

"Ask her." Gaskill glared at Ade.

"Sean, please?" Ade begged. "This isn't the time."

"Isn't it?" Sean asked. "I mean, you're right; he's potentially asking us to prepare for the battle of our lives. Scott, you've been telling us about you and your ancient posse for years, and now the biggest and baddest . . . Excuse me, the *second*-biggest and baddest is back from the grave with a big fucking stick, and he's ready to swing it."

"They are ready to swing it," Gaskill corrected him.

Tig's face tightened as he looked at his friend on the screen.

"Who are they?" Davi asked. "What are we talking about exactly? They? I mean, you guys are being pretty vague, and I'm kinda new here."

"My apologies—"

---

1 "You have something to say?"

"I don't need apologies; I need answers, Doctor," Davi interrupted, looking at Gaskill's ruby-and-gold eyes as the doctor turned to face him.

"Vincent, Davi," Gaskill began, "and Juno. They're coming for us." He smiled at Davi and held his hand out, signaling for them all to be still for a moment.

Davi relaxed in his chair and focused on Gaskill's smile. Everything went black and then he felt like he was flying through a cloud. Then he was in a shack. It was dark and hot, and he began to sweat and cough. Through the smoke he saw a thin young, brown-skinned man laughing and floating in the doorway. The flames had engulfed the building, but he was unscathed. He wore a white dress with hand-stitched sequin flowers all over it. It was beautiful and somehow untouched in the midst of the roaring blaze.

In the shack a small group of young men and women were huddled in the corner in a tight ball. They were throwing off layers of clothing in a vain effort to find relief from the heat. The young brown man laughed horribly. Burning beams had fallen on a few of the young men and women cowering, and they were cooking beneath them. Davi had never smelled burning humans before. The charred, musky odor was acrid and scratched the back of his throat, pressing up into his nostrils and down on his tongue.

"The future burning bright," the young brown man said through his laughter.

Davi was flying again. He landed in a great field. The night was pitch black, the jagged grass illuminated in the stark moonlight. A forest was a hundred feet ahead of him. Treetops rustled, and several branches cracked, breaking the silence of the night. A haze of startled birds emerged and then dispersed above the treetops.

A black figure bounded out of the forest and charged toward Davi. A tall, smooth boulder broke through the wall of thick tree trunks behind the creature. Splinters flew out into the night, the moonlight reflecting off the tree flesh.

As the figure bounded toward him, Davi could not tell whether it was man or a beast, but he feared it more than anything he'd ever encountered. Despite the cold night air, he broke into a sweat as the being and the boulder rushed toward him.

As the figure neared, he was certain it was no man. He saw lines of spit stretching between its fangs. It was black with striped fur. He wanted to scream and piss his pants, but at the same time he wanted to stay and admire and submit to the beautiful, alluring beast. It leapt into the air, and the dark fur, eyes, and claw tips glistened for a moment before the boulder, as large as a barn, obscured the moon.

Davi was flying through clouds again. Then he was standing in the middle of a dirt road. People were lying all around, dead. Dead for days, weeks perhaps. Some were slumped over horses. Some hung outside of their carriages, their horses decaying before them. Some were slumped over each other in the doorways of the stores, the bank, the church. Others hung and oozed over railings. Some clutched decomposing babies. Still others held green, peeling children's hands. There was so much hair. It looked grotesquely long for anyone, especially dead people. Blond, brown, yellow, red, growing even along the sunken skinless cheeks of the rotting well-dressed men. Maggots and raptors had their way with all of them, grazing leisurely on the bounty.

In the parlor window to his left, he saw shadows creeping behind the bar inside, swirling slowly like mist. Something was standing in them. It had followed him. He turned just in time to gasp before a black palm closed around his head.

Davi gasped again and jumped up to his feet in the war room. His eyes locked with Gaskill's eyes at the head of the table. Horrors continued dancing in Davi's head. He felt almost ecstatic, enlightened, having witnessed the justice. But the justice was carnage, and that made the rest of him want to weep and retch. He struggled with the dissonance as he sat back down and tried to settle his breathing.

"So, what do we do?"

"We get ready," Gaskill said. "Sean and Tig and I have been designing some autonomous MASS prototypes over the past few years, and with your combined approval, I'd like the protocols to bring that project back online."

"Seriously?" Tig asked. "Do you realize how dangerous that is?"

"Hey!" Sean responded, holding his hands up in self-defense.

"One or two may be fine," Tig continued, "but a gang of these things could potentially go online. Then who knows what? We discussed this eventuality and decided to squash the AI prototypes, or so I thought."

Silence filled the room. They were all aware that the fungus was, in fact, alive. They had never been able to gauge its degree of sentience. Even considering its mass infection of humans, with their superpowers, and miracle cures, it had remained a cooperative parasite. The new cancers that were attributed to its introduction into human DNA had been incredibly rare in the decades since the first demi sightings, and even US Army scientists still were unsure whether the alien Ojun fungus was the cause of these novel cancer infections.

Sean shook his head and raised his hands again.

"Do we even know if this Ojun alloy—"

"Fungus," Gaskill interrupted.

"Whatever," Tig continued. "We don't know if it's toxic in higher concentrations than what we have tested in the MASS formula."

"Well, it's all a moot point, right?" Cyral said. "We're out of raw Ojun to continue testing."

"There's more," Gaskill assured him, looking at Sean. All eyes turned to him.

"Where?" Tig asked, incredulous. "The Atlantic reserves are off limits." He glared at Ade for a moment and then Sean caught his attention. He pointed his index finger at the ceiling and jabbed it up a few times.

"Where we got it last time," Gaskill said. "I can go."

Cyral frowned at Gaskill. Tig squinted at Sean and laid his hands on the table, his fingers interlaced.

"Yeah, but when are we going?" Sean asked. "Before or after this battle?" He scooted toward the edge of his seat.

"We have two mining engines online," Ade said, "and two more coming online next quarter."

"You're in on this?" Sean smiled at her. "Go on."

"I can get there and back in less than two weeks," Gaskill said. "If I leave immediately."

"C'mon, Doc," Tig said, slapping his palms on the table. "We don't have two weeks. Plus months of testing and fabrication."

"I'm with Tig," Cyral said.

"We know," Ade replied in annoyance. Cyral had always been a naysayer. Even when she'd tried to reintroduce the space-mining initiative, he would have no part of it and made every effort he could to block it all while rubbing the Rain catastrophe in her face. And rightfully so, which annoyed her even more. It was her failed cargo rig and her misguided astronomers who had caused it, her failed crew. Cyral, the eager ass kisser, had pulled all these bits from her head and dangled them gleefully over her every chance that he could. She had used Gaskill's direct involvement as captain to shield her from the fallout, and he resented her for it. He was so self-righteous, that fucking mind reader. Nothing could shield her from him—not yet at least.

"You're in on this too, huh?" Sean pointed a thumb at Cyral. His smile was wide and toothy now. "Was anyone gonna deal me in?"

"You're in now," Cyral said.

"So, what if we start mining more of the raw Ojun fungus *again*," Tig asked, "and it contaminates us all, *again*?" He was on the edge of his chair now too. Ade smiled at him and then turned back to Gaskill and shrugged.

"We're fucked," she said.

"I'll grow another eye next time," Davi muttered.

"This guy," Sean said, chuckling.

Davi was warmed by their inclusion. Aside from Sean, who was intimidating enough in his own right, everyone in the room was incredibly powerful. It was literally giving him a headache. Normally, he could see a demi's power as an aura of some kind. He could not tell exactly what property determined the aura's color. Sometimes it was mood, sometimes it was hunger, sometimes it was sexual arousal, and sometimes it was seasonal. It differed for everyone. Most demi auras had a roughly twelve-foot radius. Anger, rage, excitement, orgasms, and passion increased a demi's aura and made it even more unwieldy. All of his partners on this SPASE battle team had big auras with a fifteen- to twenty-foot radius. Cyral's was pretty big. Hermod and Gaskill's were immense and heavy. The conference room would have been large enough for maybe twenty humans with normal auras, but with these four plus Sean's weird human aura, it was quite a lot for him to pay attention to any one of them even in silence.

"But what if H doesn't wig out?" Sean asked, looking at the LED wall.

"Exactly," Gaskill said. "It's a grand chance but one we may need to take. I presume that if Hermod is going to crack, it will happen soon. He will wake up soon and then crack soon. Faust isn't enough. So, I propose we monitor him once he wakes up. We assess him, and I assess him to determine where we are on this . . ." He paused. He'd had trouble speaking the possibility of his demise into existence in front of his followers. "This countdown. Or even if it exists." *That's better,* he thought.

"And you'll be able to tell if it's Vincent or not?" Sean asked.

"Or Juno," Cyral added.

"The lot of you should be able to, no?" Ade said.

Tig nodded. "I know my friend."

"And they know everyone," Sean said as he pointed his left pinky at Dr. Gaskill and his right one at Cyral. Ade smirked at Sean. Cyral raised his head on his long neck and looked at Gaskill with his pensive light-brown eyes.

"Yes, we could make an immediate assessment of Hermod if we really needed to," Cyral replied, though he was skeptical. "Might he be triggered during the process?"

"We would have to be very careful—"

"Not to pull the trigger," Tig said, finishing Ade's thought.

"Ha!" Sean said. "The gun is smoking! Are you kidding? This is all damage control. Look here, how much Ojun do we have left? Is there anything I can work with?"

"There's a little, but it would be a waste," Ade replied, squinting. She was struggling not to think about how their failed mission had cost them access to the greatest treasure that humankind had ever discovered. More than twenty years later, she wondered if she would ever be able to claim her prize. "You could make maybe another smaller MASS. Its systems and weaponry would not be as extensive as the original, and it could not be manned internally. Some things would scale, but it would still be a waste of our last supplies."

"How about we stay put and kick his ass?" Davi asked. "If he wakes up right now and decides to stay Hermod forever, and we start that thing growing, we'll be SOL, and it'll be our fault."

Everyone looked at Davi. He stopped talking and couldn't continue for several seconds after he'd captivated them.

"If he wakes up," Davi said, speaking slowly, "and it's Vincent, and he decides to kill us, then we'll have to just win, right? All of us right here!" He looked squarely at Gaskill. "You're the only one here who has killed this guy before. You can't leave. Not now."

Everyone was silent for several seconds.

"Well said, Davi," Cyral said, clapping his hairy, heavy, manicured hands.

Gaskill looked around the table, then turned back to the LED screen and waved his hand. The hurricane disappeared pixel by pixel and then the infographics speckled their way back up.

"He's that bright, huh?" Tig said, his eyes on the screen.

"Huh?" Sean asked, turning to him.

"No, the processor," Tig said, pointing at the screen. "He's so bright that the GPU can't handle it, and it's slowing down the other visualizations and transitions."

They all saw the blip on the flatlined monitor near the doctor's head. The stark lighting softened as the LED wall dimmed on the right side for the first time in a week. Sean's eyes throbbed slightly in sudden relief. Tig stood up and watched the line blip again. Only a faint glow shone from within the vacuum chamber now. The war room lighting, as designed, seemed like barely enough now that the screen had diminished. In the center of that screen, where the black skeleton had been, a small blue flame flickered in the vast darkness.

## SANTO DOMINGO, DOMINICAN REPUBLIC

Hanuri stood on the edge of Playa Sansouci at the mouth of the Rio Ozama, whispering a prayer to Guabancex, Taino goddess of catastrophe. She held her hands up to the sky, the left one balled into a fist around a small snake skull.

She'd arrived thirty-six hours ago. Immediately, she started whispering her prayer, and she hadn't moved since. Hurricane Faust had slowed to three miles per hour and strengthened to a category-five storm just five miles off the coast of Bajos de Haina in the San Cristobal province of the Dominican Republic. She would remain there in supplication until it diminished. Her people depended on it.

Twenty-four hours ago, while the sea was still barely manageable, a Coast Guard boat had approached her. Two men had crawled up the embankment to her against the wind and waves lashing at them. She remained inert, her eyes closed, unmoved by the tumult and the men screaming at her. She continued to pray, beseeching the Lady of the Winds.

One of the men touched her. He'd grabbed her shoulders in each of his large hands and was about to try to hoist her into the air when she opened her eyes and looked into his, and he screamed and let her go. He was still screaming when the Coast Guard boat left. She had paid him no mind. The protection hex would not kill him, depending on the fortitude of his character. Instead, she continued to concern herself with prayer and the swirling gray-blue storm clouds towering in the distance.

Hurricane Faust had made landfall officially within the last hour. Hanuri lowered her hands to her sides and looked along the coast, watching the surge crashing and breaking against an unseen wall. She was still dry, and her dark robe fell to her sides, undisturbed, though the maelstrom raged all around her. She was five feet from the barrier, staring at a wall of swirling, gnashing water two dozen feet high. Guabancex had heard her prayer. The protection extended the length of the river mouth and a few thousand meters beyond in both directions along the coast. Thunder exploded, and lightning tore through the sky and into the buildings along the Port of Santo Domingo on the other side of Rio Ozama just to her right. Though the winds lashed and roiled its waters, the river itself had not swelled. Gubancex had spared thousands of lives so far, and Hanuri was grateful. Broken trees, boats, people, and all manner of debris accumulated against the barrier in front of her. Unbothered by Faust's defiant, macabre display, Hanuri gathered the tail of her robe and wrapped it around her left arm, the snake skull still clutched in her left hand. Its smooth dome gently caressed the top of her palm beneath the first knuckle.

She walked inland.

"Bruja."

She heard the whisper through the cacophony of the storm: winds screeching, debris crashing against the buildings around the port, themselves coming apart, their steel panels crashing like cymbals. The voice had not come from the nano-comm device nestled inside her ears. Even if it had, the name would have been foreign to her. She was known as Hanuri to her comrades at SPASE.

"Bruja."

Some 500 feet from the barrier, she stopped her chant.

"Gracias por protegernos, Guabancex, Madre Cosmica." She wrapped her right hand over her left fist and lifted them both to the sky. "Sabemos que esto no es tu culpa."[(1)] She let her hands fall back to her sides and turned to face the barrier. Rocks, water, sand, and tree limbs were all thrown at her, but she remained unscathed. The boats in the port behind her crashed against each other. Two ships had been torn from their anchors and were drifting up the river, on a collision course with several more crafts near Puerto Sansouci. A violent gust of wind ripped two palm trees from the beach just twenty feet away from her. They spun through the air toward her, their fronds scratching at the sand. A web of lighting arced down toward her, several bolts striking the beach just a few paces away from her. She closed her eyes against the blinding flash. Though any other person might have been incinerated, Hanuri was unharmed.

"Gracias, mi reina," Hanuri said as she scanned the storm for her pursuer.[(2)]

Lightning struck the naval building behind her, igniting it. Thunder roared and shook the ground beneath her. A car door and sheets of steel sliced through the air, crashing into the naval building.

"Bruja." The wind was not a whisper but a low man's voice this time. "What can you do?"

---

1 "Thank you for protecting us· Guabancex· Cosmic Mother· We know that this is not your fault·"

2 "Thank you· my queen·"

Across the river a swirling wall of the black-and-blue storm cloud stretched down. Pieces of the cloud broke away and whirled around each other. Lightning crawled through the cloud, illuminating its dance. For a moment the cloud wisps lingered in place, and the lightning and shadows brought life to the formation. Two identical orbs near the cloud ceiling, a wisp extending down and ending in a knob and a long, spreading symmetrical mass of clouds near the bottom of the form.

Hanuri, matrixing, gasped and clutched her left fist to her chest.

"Demonio!" she whispered. She felt at once the curiosity of a first sighting of an attractive person and the revulsion from having overturned a rock with creatures beneath it. "It's him!"

As the form began to swirl faster and gather, the bottom wisps spread and parted in the center. One of the eyes had returned to the swirling funnel, but the other remained briefly, a wink and a smile.

"What can you do, Bruja?" a voice asked, a woman this time.

The swirling of the funnel increased in speed, and the face was swept away. It was replaced by the wide cyclone completing its touchdown. The port hangars near it offered their steel walls and panels to the winds. Several trucks, dumpsters, cars, and everything else less weighty were accelerated up and away. The ships there rocked back and forth, offering some of their constitution to the tornado as well. One of the hangars imploded, its remains immediately scattering into the funnel.

Fire erupted from a demolished building next to the ravaged hangar. Sheets of metal soared through the air and were carried even farther by Faust. Intermodal containers rolled along the port and into the river, crashing into each other. Hanuri gasped as she watched the tornado race upriver.

"Hanuri!" a voice yelled over the winds.

Thunder clapped and rolled through everything around her, and a tremor shook the ground. Hanuri flung out her left arm, releasing her robe. It fell straight to her feet, unmoved by the winds. She turned to face the caller and held her left fist out in front of her. Bright orange sparks around her knuckles spread into a roiling flame around her fist, its bright light sweeping away the storm's shadow and revealing the wind-scoured beach.

"Quién me llamó?"[1] Hanuri demanded.

"It's me, girl," Dara said from behind her. Hanuri turned around to face her, standing in Tracy Ford's doorway to San Cristobal, 15 miles away. "Are you done here? Ford can't keep this door open for long." Ford, Dara's lover and their transportation, was exhausting most of his energy on the dozen "highway" doors that he had opened throughout Santo Domingo, San Cristobal, and San Pedro de Macoris to transport evacuees to safety.

Dara looked upriver. All she saw was darkness at first. Then several bolts of lightning illuminated the tornado, which was now half a mile away from them. She gasped and extended her hand to Hanuri.

"Hanuri!" Dara said, exasperated. She stepped her other foot onto the beach in Santo Domingo, transfixed by the cyclone. Ford's door closed behind her. Lighting struck the beach just ten feet away. She winced and glared at the spot where it hit and then up at the clouds racing through the air as fast as water flows. An uprooted palm tree spun toward her. She kicked her foot into it, and it splintered.

"Dara, beware," Hanuri warned. She held her left fist higher, and the green flames illuminated much of the area around them. She smiled at the sight of her comrade. "I don't like the way you look with your hair tied back."

"Me neither," Dara said. "Bitch. Now come on. Tracy—" Dara had turned back to reenter the doorway and was startled by its absence.

"Baby, what's the holdup?" Dara looked at Hanuri and shrugged.

"I told you not to step out of the doorway," Ford replied. "I've got thirteen highways open still. Give me another ten minutes."

"Fuck," Dara said. "You don't have an Ojun suit on, do you, Hanuri?"

"Of course not," Hanuri replied. She was not a demi and was not required to register with or have any affiliation with SPASE. A descendant of Caribbean and Native Central American sorcerers, Hanuri kept a reasonable distance between herself and Gaskill and his machinations. Gaskill had sought her allegiance decades ago, long before the Rain. Hanuri's familiars had warned her earnestly about the Double, Ninexetlau, after

---

1 "Who called me?"

she'd looked into his fortune on her own. She'd had half a mind to destroy him for the greed and manipulation that she saw. Dara had briefed her on Vincent and Juno's threat to her people and her world. She was more than willing to partner with Dara and Tracy and the other demi contractors in her network. She had great respect for them, and she pitied them for having to live under the eye of SPASE. However, she knew that her power ran much deeper than theirs, and she would not have it manipulated or cataloged by Dr. Gaskill.

"Fuck! Well, hurry up, babe," Dara said as she swatted a flying sheet of steel away from her.

"Make yourselves useful," Ford replied.

"No, you hurry up!" Dara put her hands on her hips and looked around her at the ravaged beach. "Mingo? What's your status?"

"Ocupado."(1) Mingo had been focusing his attention on the mouth of the Haina River approximately nine miles down the coast.

"Mingo," Hanuri said. "¿Guabancex ha protegido el rio, sí?"(2)

"Sí," Mingo replied. "El rio esta bien pero hay algo en los tornados."(3)

"Claro," Hanuri said. "Lo vi también. Mantente seguro y buena suerte, hijo."(4)

Lighting struck near Dara, closer this time.

"Fuck!" she shouted. "That actually scared me." She probed her abdomen and left thigh to see if there was any damage to her protective suit. It was still intact. Her body could withstand far more than the suit could. "Don't wanna mess up my new umbrella," she quipped.

An explosion drew their attention upstream. A fireball rolled up into the racing clouds, and in its light, they could see the tornado funnel and the swirling cloud of mangled city that it carried back toward them.

"Hanuri!" Dara said. "We should take cover somewhere."

"I will be fine." Hanuri stood still, her flaming fist still raised in the air. She remained as dry as she had been back in Miami three days earlier.

---

1 "Busy·"

2 "Guabancex has protected the river· yes?

3 "Yes· the river is fine but there is something in the tornados·"

4 "I also saw it· Stay safe and good luck· child·"

"Alright, girl," Dara said, smirking. "Mascara still dry and everything. I'll learn how to do that one day!"

Hanuri smiled. She was happy for the moment of joy. She had seen the man in the storm and was worried. Though Faust would end, what would the man do afterwards?

Another explosion ripped through the air, audible over the roaring storm. The tornado was much closer now, just a few hundred yards away, and Dara had to knock away much larger, heavier debris, like scooters and small cars, whole sections of buildings, and shipping containers.

Hanuri looked at the black wall of storm surge sloshing against the unseen barrier. It was about twenty-five feet higher now.

"Hurry, Tracy."

## SPASE HOLE – MAXIMUM SECURITY SUBAQUATIC DETENTION CENTER – 280 MILES OFF THE COAST OF DELAWARE

Sean opened his hands, splayed his fingers, and aligned his fingertips with ten small orange swirls projecting onto the air in front of him.

"Welcome to Globe Two, Agent Sean Porter Mathers," MASS said.

Sean nodded, and the airlock opened. He moved into the chamber, and the door closed behind him. He heard the heavy clicking sounds of the locks securing and then a prolonged hiss as the water receded around him, sucked back into the sea. A blue orb burned about fifty yards ahead of him. Once the chamber was completely drained, the foot-thick glass doors parted before him. MASS cleared the door and approached Hermod in the darkness. The doors closed silently behind him. He glanced above him and saw, on the other side of the barrier, a school of fish gliding through the sea, glistening erratically in the red lights that lined the vacuum globe's perimeter. He turned back to Hermod. "He's still unconscious, sir."

"Is he cool enough to handle?" Ade replied from the war room.

Sean pressed a few keys on the small keyboard in front of him, and the white, yellow, green, and red lights morphed and changed in front of his face. Graphs, programming code, video images, seismographic readings, his own vitals, all of it a glowing repository at his fingertips and in his mind. Connected directly to his brain was a second spine and body and sensations, WMDs, secrets, and abilities untold. Sometimes he felt like it was driving him instead. "Your powerful disease," Ade had once chided him. Whenever he was outside of the machine, he yearned to be in it. While inside of it, they were one and the same.

"You want me to handle him seriously?" Sean asked. They were about 1,000 feet away from each other. Hermod was slumped over, his body limp and his lips hanging away from his skull. He spun slowly on an axis, his limbs flopping around him and swinging with every rotation of his body. Sean chuckled.

"What is it?" Cyral asked.

"I mean, he's fine down here for now, isn't he?" Sean said, ignoring Cyral.

"Are you afraid?" Gaskill asked. "Yes, I do want you to handle him. We have no time to waste. We have to save the Caribbean."

"Bullshit," Sean replied.

Davi looked across the table at Gaskill as if a man like him would flinch at Sean's rebuke. He wondered how little the doctor cared for those people dying in the sea.

"Engaging him is the only way," Gaskill said, then turned away from the screens to look at Davi.

"Sean," Tig chimed in, speaking to the ceiling as if there were

microphones up there. "Gaskill's right. Faust could be the high he needs to really go under."

Sean took a deep breath and watched Hermod's body complete the axial rotation. His arms and legs flapped around him in a spiral before dangling limply beneath him. His left foot wiggled at the ankle as if he were having a spasm.

Sean laughed. He'd always been told not to disturb a sleepwalker. "So, I'll reel him in then," he said.

He approached Hermod, stopping a hundred feet away from him.

In the war room, all of them, save Dr. Gaskill, shielded or shut their eyes against the glaring light.

Sean could see him clearly with the help of MASS's enhanced machine vision. His fingers flew across the keyboard and then he held his hands out. MASS copied his motions and spread out its hands, secreting a thick black cloud from its fingers. As the cloud collected around MASS and Hermod, it swallowed up the bright bluish white of Hermod's light. Hermod diminished in the black substance and was moved upright from his axis. His head hung to the right as he spun in a circle.

"I have completed the particle suppression container," MASS said to Sean. He nodded, and the machine turned toward the exit, its hands held out to its sides. The infinite blackness still surrounded them. Sean hesitated to look directly into the "dark, icky space," as he called it. They could not figure out another name for it yet. He and Tig, and Gaskill had produced all kinds of unknown weapons prototypes with their Ojun samples. Samples like this one that had yet to be tested. There was still so much about it—the fungus, its true strength, that he didn't know.

He looked into the dark, icky space. "At least I can take it off," he said. Ade laughed heartily at his response.

"You can try!"

"Sean!" Cyral yelled. Static crawled over the screen in the war room, and it went blank for two seconds.

Sean heard a cough echoing. The sound had come from within the chamber. Suddenly, Hermod screamed.

"The container has been compromised," MASS said. Lights dimmed to total darkness inside the machine. "Motor functions and host life support are still operational. I'll have the lights and electronics up shortly."

"Turn on the backup—" Sean stopped talking and squeezed his eyes shut. Everything above his neck was vibrating and pounding. Blood dripped out of his left nostril. He gripped the sides of his head and clenched his jaw.

"Sean, hang on." Cyral could feel Sean's intense pain and was working to block his receptors.

Sean felt himself whirling toward the perimeter. Through squinted eyes, he could make out the suppression container. He saw it break apart and swirl and trail behind him as he spun away from Hermod.

"S-start the backup generators," Sean said and then shut his eyes completely. His brain roared with pain, and the sides of his skull throbbed. Blood trickled from his left ear as well.

"Where's Lee?" the voice roared throughout the chamber. Sean heard it in his skull and screamed. He was still spinning out of control and just feet from crashing into the perimeter. He glimpsed the blue flame and the black body at its center, struggling not to vomit.

"The backup engines are online," MASS said.

Sean clenched his fists, and MASS jerked to a stop five feet from the wall of the globe. A large black shadow with small shining round eyes moved beneath him and continued along the underside of the globe. Sean looked up at Hermod.

"Are you alright?" Cyral asked. He had risen from his chair and was floating a few inches from the floor. He'd absorbed a great deal of the wild psychic energy tearing at Sean. Most of it was still grief. Ade was literally on the edge of her seat, and Davi was leaning back deep in his. Gaskill stood near the head of the table adjacent to the screen, his eyes glued to it. His shadow stretched down the length of the table.

"Fine," Sean replied. "Is it him?"

"Yes," Cyral said. "It's Hermod. He's hysterical, but it's still him. Hang on."

"Who are you?" Hermod asked. "Where's Lee?" MASS's arms and chest reflected in Hermod's light. The large shadow was back and completely surrounded MASS for several moments as it moved outside the glass.

"You have to calm down," Sean said.

Hermod clenched his teeth. "Where is he?"

"Activate the container," Sean said. He watched the blue flame intensify and heard the explosion propel him.

"Activating," MASS replied.

"Hurry!" Sean screamed. He held up his hands and watched the machine hands disappear as the black container amassed again. He steadied himself and stared at the ball of flame hurtling toward him. He would have only a moment to secure Hermod, or they would destroy the glass globe.

"Now!" Sean said. A wide beam of blackness reached out, and the great blue ball disappeared into it.

"You have to calm down," Sean said to Hermod. He spoke slowly, though he knew he had little time. He could not see or hear Hermod through the envelope of the dark, icky space, but he could feel him and speak into it.

"Backup generators are at eighty-five percent," MASS said.

"Where's Lee?" Hermod screamed.

Sean winced as his guts jostled around inside him. He licked his lips and tasted the salty mix of blood and sweat dripping over them. He'd never taken MASS this far. This was typically Gaskill's territory.

"I'm sorry, Hermod," Sean said.

Hermod whirled around in the great black particle suppression cocoon but could not free himself. The thick blackness surrounded him, and suddenly he could not see the machine anymore or the shadows at the edges of the globe and those swimming beyond it. He was dizzy and weak. As much as he wanted to smash the machine, he could barely feel or move his body. Even the light of his raging flames had been devoured in the blackness. He could barely sustain his ignition. It was as if he had been cut out from reality. He could hear a voice begging him to calm down, but how could he? He had to find Lee.

"Where is my husband?" Hermod pleaded. "I couldn't hear him anymore. He's not gone; I just can't hear him. What did you do to me?"

"Sir?" Sean asked.

"Convince him to calm down," Gaskill replied. "Tell him Tig is here." He nodded at Tig in the war room. "Tig will talk to him if he calms down."

Tig nodded in affirmation.

"Listen, Hermod," Sean said, "you don't know me. We've only met a few times briefly. So, you may not remember me right now, but I'm Sean Mathers. MASS and I are here to help."

"SPASE only helps itself," Hermod said, looking around in the dark for any clue as to where the voice was coming from, so he could lash out at its source. "Where's Lee?"

"I'll help you out if you calm down," Sean said.

"I am calm!" Hermod screamed. "Stop saying that."

"No. You're about six hundred and eighty thousand degrees right now, and I need you to turn it down a bit. That's the only way I can let you talk to Tig."

"Tig is my friend," Hermod said. He was motionless now. Tig. Yes, Tig. He folded to his knees as the previous weeks' events replayed in his mind. Even Sean's voice sounded familiar.

"He's my friend too," Sean said. "He wants to reach out to you, but you have to calm down first."

"Tig is there?"

"Well, not here, but he can speak with you, if you like."

"Yes. Yes, l-let me s-speak with him, p-please." Hermod stammered. His throat was full, and the words would barely come out. The sound he wanted to make stayed inside and swelled, filling his upper belly.

"If I lift the container, you have to promise not to blow me up, OK?" Sean asked.

For several seconds there was no response.

In the conference room watching MASS's broadcast, Gaskill was exasperated by Hermod's resemblance to his ancestor.

<He looks just like her,> he thought.

<Like whom?> Cyral replied, concerned. Gaskill's thought was not only unguarded but also laced with all sorts of emotions—guilt and remorse, feelings Cyral had never ever received from Dr. Gaskill.

"Never mind," Gaskill replied.

"Hermod?" Sean looked into the dark container for some sign of a response.

"OK," Hermod said. His voice was feeble. He remembered. The swelling in his chest started to hurt and dry out his throat.

"You promise?"

"I promise."

"OK," Sean said. "Suppress the container," he told MASS.

Solid sparkling blackness flowed like the waters outside the globe. It softened and then dissipated into a fine gray mist, revealing Hermod beneath it.

No longer burning, he lifted his head and turned to face the giant faceless humanoid. Sean noticed Hermod's moist cheeks. The grimace crept over him. Feeling emptiness in his own chest, Sean looked away. The misty remains of the particle container swirled around and gradually reintegrated with MASS.

"Tig?" Hermod said, looking around the globe.

"H," came Tig's reply.

"Lee?" Hermod whispered. His throat loosened, the painful pressure there was released, and he huffed out heavy breaths. Sean frowned and continued to look away as the man heaved and made a sound that only grief could produce. It issued from deep within his loins with more power than anything his vocal chords alone could accomplish.

"I'm so sorry, H." Tig's voice broke, and he struggled to keep himself composed as he remembered waking up outside of the club, begging to know where Eliot Sánchez was. Screaming in defiance at the responses that he was given. Struggling against the police officers, even incapacitating three of them as they tried to restrain him from reentering the club to see for himself.

In the war room, Gaskill watched the screen, and Ade watched Cyral and Tig both stare at the table. Davi took a long, deep breath and tried to ignore the anguished cries broadcasting from the vacuum globe ninety miles away.

## SANTO DOMINGO, DOMINICAN REPUBLIC

Lightning struck the river and illuminated the dark tornado and the swirling cloud of debris at its base. A neat web of lightning imprinted on the cloud ceiling behind the storm. Dara could see more of the funnel's volume in the web's glow.

"Fuck," she said. She estimated they had ten minutes. "Tracy?" She swatted away a tree that was flying at her and then ran up the beach to stand beside Hanuri. A shipping container was rolling toward them. Dara prepared to punch the container away, but it bounced off to their right, as if something had pushed it. The same thing happened to the trees and boat pieces that followed. Dara noticed that it wasn't raining on her right breast and arm, the side of her closest to Hanuri.

"Can I have some of that?" Dara asked.

"I don't understand?"

"You're as dry as a damn bone," Dara said, "and unharmed."

"You are almost indestructible."

"Yeah, but I'm not wind proof yet!" Dara lamented. "Look at you!"

Dara reached for Hanuri's robe and had almost grabbed a part of it when Hanuri vanished and reappeared a foot from where she had been standing.

"¡No me toques!" Hanuri snapped.[(1)] She gathered her robe around her left arm, still clutching the skull. "I'm . . . it's not personal, D."

Dara nodded. She opened her mouth, but before she could speak, a high wave of water splashed at her back. She felt something much larger approaching her from behind. She clenched her fist and whirled around just as a shipping container smashed into her, sweeping her into the air. She felt inhuman hands grab her arm and watched the beach fly away as she was carried up into the twister. Lightning struck the beach near Hanuri, and deafening thunder shook the ground beneath her.

Hanuri stood fast against the tornado and its maelstrom. She felt herself sinking as the wind pulled the sand from under her.

"Llevamé," Hanuri said.[(2)] She rose into the air some five feet from the eroding beach. Her robe hem dropped down past her feet. Cars, concrete rubble, bodies, street signs, and more departed from her.

"Guys!" Ford called over their satellite communication channel. "Are y'all alright?"

"I'm fine," Mingo replied.

"The storm has Dara," Hanuri said.

"I'm fine!" Dara said.

"Stay away from here, Ford," Hanuri warned. "For now."

"Copy," Ford replied.

---

1 "Don't touch me!"

2 "Carry me."

Hanuri was at the base of the tornado now. Unharmed by the maelstrom, she merely stared into it, unable to find anything to say. She had seen Hermod's face in the storm. These were not Guabancex's winds to command. Dare she beseech SiqT' Qkar? She shamed herself for the thought of abandoning her goddess for the Void.

"¡Maldito, Hermod!" Hanuri spat. "Solo eres hombre."[1]

Swirling debris bounced along what was left of the beach. Half of a car rolled several times and then stopped. Rio Haina appeared in front of her between the haze of shingles, sheets of metal, paper, leaves, and tree limbs, all of which were now coasting in the wind. The twister unscrewed itself from the ground and retracted into the diminishing black-violet wall of clouds that had spawned it. Rain fell straight down again, both water and decelerated debris.

Dara launched from the river, and a geyser shot up in her wake. She landed next to Hanuri and immediately began swatting things away from her, much smaller debris this time, pieces of the larger debris the storm had carried earlier.

Dara put her hands on her hips and took several deep breaths. "You did it!" she said as she smiled up at Hanuri.

"No," Hanuri said. "It wasn't me; it was him. Something else has his attention now." Hanuri turned to the sea. It still sloshed violently, and waves licked the top of Guabancex's protective wall even though the winds had quelled. Guabancex would protect them until the entire sea had settled. Hanuri was sure of it.

Hanuri saw shimmering in the air, and her vision began to ripple like the seawater around the raindrops. Ford's mustached yellow-brown face poked out of the ripples.

"Could use some help here," Ford said. Dara and Hanuri could see and hear cars honking behind him, people carrying luggage and baggage, and children filing in between the jammed traffic.

Dara huffed and kicked a tree trunk at him. He stepped back through the door and closed it.

---

1 "Damn you· Hermod·" "You are only a man·"

# LAID TO REST

## MALASAÑA, MADRID, SPAIN

"And he's still fine?" Cyral said to the nurse.

"Yeah I mean . . ." Dr. Tedi stopped talking for a moment and looked behind her into the house. "He's up cooking, exercising, and reading and handling a bit of business too . . . emails. He went on and on about checking his stocks and crypto as soon as we got here. Something about the hurricane. He found that laptop as soon as we got here."

"You're done for today?"

"Yeah, Tig just got here. I'm headed back home. There's a thing in North Philly I gotta get to."

"You're back in tomorrow morning?" Cyral asked. "Ambitious."

"Gotta get paid," Tedi said. "Be safe, Cyral."

"We'll try," Cyral replied. He watched Tedi walk down the path and then disappear behind a tall hedge bush. He knocked on the door, and Tig opened it immediately.

"Good evening, Tig. Ade can't make it."

"Where is she?" Tig asked.

"Ask her."

That was Tig's cue to drop it. Cyral followed Tig into the living room.

"He's here." Tig motioned Cyral into the double doors of the living room. Cyral entered and closed them, and several locks clicked automatically.

South-facing windows allowed the sun to bathe the large room completely. Hermod sat near the largest window on a low couch staring out the door that led into the small yard.

"Hermod," Cyral said.

He didn't answer. He continued to recline on the low couch and stare out the open door. A breeze fluttered his unbuttoned dress shirt.

"You ready?" Cyral asked.

Hermod turned his head toward Cyral. "No."

"Well, whenever you're ready."

Hermod turned back to the window and reclined.

Cyral walked toward the foyer and into the lounge adjacent to it. He found Tig tightening a Windsor knot around his neck. He was seated on the far side of the room at a small table near the south-facing window, glued to a laptop screen.

"Nice tie," Cyral said.

<Respond however you wish; this channel is secure.>

Tig stood up and looked at Cyral as he closed in. <You're getting good?>

<I am good,> Cyral said. <Are you sure he can handle this?> He placed his hands in his pockets and closed his eyes, then took a deep breath. The warming light was pleasant against his face. He removed his jacket and threw it on a dark leather loveseat nearby.

<He needs to mourn,> Tig said. <Hell, I need to.>

<Me too,> Cyral replied.

<Davi and Mingo will be on standby.>

<So, will the Spanish, French, and Portuguese armed forces.>

<They pulled the plug.> Tig's face was drawn as he sat on the edge of the table and crossed his arms.

<The Pentagon is pissed. Ade is in DC right now pampering the Joint Chiefs of Staff this morning or else she would be here. Do you know what I had to do to get them to agree to this Ruins of Isidro business?>

<They're not having it then,> Tig said.

<Boy, it's wartime. It's like fucking us versus Hermod versus them versus God. They want him back in the globe the minute the last tear drops.>

<Are they hip to the Ojun harvesting mission?> Tig's face was blank.

<No.>

<Good,> Tig replied. <That can't stop. We're gonna need it. I've put a good deal of the Ojun stores to use.>

Cyral smiled. <Ade mentioned this.>

<What if—>

<Shh!>

"I'm ready," Hermod said. He was in the entranceway standing in the only shadow big enough to fit him on that side of the house. In the center of his thigh, his pants crease caught a stray beam of light from the polished floor.

"Let's do it then," Cyral said as he floated over to Hermod, and the two embraced.

"Thank you," Hermod whispered.

"Anything for Lee."

## ATOCHA, MADRID, SPAIN

Lee was eulogized in the Basílica of Nuestra Señora de Atocha in Madrid, where he used to sing as a boy. Protesters, reporters, cameramen, and gawkers packed Calle Julian Gallare and Av de la Ciudad de Barcelona and were surrounding the basilica. Traffic had been blocked on the avenue, and helicopters, having been forbidden to fly anywhere near the basilica or the nearby trainyard, hovered from afar, near the park, capturing the spectacle at a distance. A combination of Spanish policia and SPASE magistrates held tight lines on the ground.

Hermod had not noticed the commotion. Not during the drive to the church. Not even when he exited the limo, and the frenzy around him intensified. He hadn't even paid attention to anything that was being said or done during the service or after, for that matter. He remembered greeting

Lee's mother, father, and two sisters and then walking with them to the front pew in the sanctuary. So many people, planes, and helicopters were flying around outside, watching him. He was angry and wanted to make them leave Lee alone.

Lee's mom, Sofía, grabbed his hands several times during the service as people spoke. He loved her. She would periodically send them Hermod's favorite gordal olives, Vicens turron, conservas, and olive oils. She always prepared a special paella with extra pulpo for Hermod whenever he and Lee were in town. Lee's youngest sister began wailing during the final prayer, and the grief radiated from her, pulling tears and cries from everyone in the row except Hermod.

They all stood as the casket was carried out of the church and placed in the hearse. Lee had always expressed his desire to be cremated. Mourners exited behind the body, starting with the family. Cyral and Tig met Hermod near the entrance door. They escorted him to the hearse. Cyral was wearing a nice tie, Hermod noticed.

Lee's parents, Sofía and Franco Torrente Sánchez, approached and said something to him that he couldn't really remember. Then they grabbed him and held him between them for several seconds. He had cried briefly, hidden in their embrace. Lee's father squeezed his shoulder, saying something that almost made him cry again. Finally, Hermod stepped away and wiped the tears from his face as Lee's parents walked to their car.

A caravan of mourners drove to the Ruins of San Isidoro at the northeast corner of El Retiro, not far from the basilica. Hermod flew above the hearse. Once it parked, Tig and Cyral emerged from it and met him at the back end. Three sets of eyes bounced between each other. No thoughts were projected or read, and no words were spoken. Cyral closed his eyes and took a deep breath before opening them again. Tig nodded at Hermod. The back hatch of the hearse opened, and the casket slowly emerged.

He wished there weren't so many helicopters, planes, and spies in the air. It's my own fault, he thought. It was his fault that his husband was dead, his fault that Lee could not have a quiet funeral.

The mourners left their vehicles and meandered into the park, making their way to the ruins. Hermod moved the casket from out of the compartment and it settled in front of him in the air. He carried it to the ruins and settled himself about ten feet above the remains of the Romanesque apse. Lee's casket hovered several inches in front of him. Hermod rested his hand on it and bowed his head as mourners gathered beneath him around the apse. He exchanged nods with the minister who had spoken the most during Lee's service. The minister turned to the crowd and opened a book and read from it. Hermod and Lee's body were one hundred feet above the apse now. Three helicopters hovered dozens of feet above them. He could feel several men with scopes and ADS weapons in the trees and in the windows of the buildings along the northern and western edges of the park and beyond.

Hermod closed his eyes for several seconds, and transparent clouds moved in the dark undersides of his lids. He opened them again and jolted in surprise. A figure blacker than the shadows was moving in between the trees some forty yards away from the ruins.

Hermod reached out with his mind but encountered only cold. The figure vanished behind the trees, and he strained to see through them. A bright red-and-white soccer ball flew out of the brush not far from where the shadow had appeared. It rolled onto the adjacent path, followed by three boys. Hermod relaxed and turned back to the crowd of mourners.

He closed his eyes and ignited and then moved the casket closer to him. Several mourners yelped in awe. Sofía and Lee's sisters, Belen and Veronica, covered their faces and started to cry before moving in closer to huddle together in tears. Hermod watched the casket melt and warp around the edges. He intensified his fire, and the casket's surface and handles rippled even more, flaking away into ash and smoke. Flames whipped up into the sky. Free of the coffin, Lee was briefly exposed, swaddled in Hermod's fire. Hermod closed his eyes as Lee burned and crumbled and vaporized in three seconds. He reopened them and then extinguished himself.

Yelling filled Hermod's ears. He turned toward the commotion and watched the three boys play just 200 feet south of him. One of them held the soccer ball in his hands as he ran away from the other two.

The large shadow creature was standing beneath the trees near the spot where the boys had emerged. Hermod had barely noticed it at first and gasped again once he did. He knew instantly that it was the creature from his dreams. Was it a shadow or a man? Hermod could see it, but then its features would disappear as the shadow, blacker than any other, washed over its form. Bristly black fur on its arms and shoulders waved in the wind gusts. It was striped, deep midnight blue. Long clawed fingers hung at its sides. Its head remained obscured, but the silhouette betrayed the smooth dome, its pointed ears, and mane. The being had not revealed this much of itself to Hermod when it visited his dreams. He wished today was just another dream.

<Hermod.>

His eyes caught and followed the ball. The boys charged after it toward the shadow. Hermod started to move toward them but stopped when he saw the boys run past the creature, laughing as they headed down the path chasing the ball. The creature hunched down on all fours and crawled back into the trees. Before it disappeared, it stopped and looked back, its eyes piercing the shadow and meeting Hermod's. Then it turned and crawled into the small patch of trees. Its silhouette lightened and blended with the shadows that the sun cast. A large group of tourists crowded the path then, obscuring Hermod's view of the trees. He knelt in midair and held his face in his hands. Warmth spread through him, a feeling typically associated with his happiness.

<Hermod!>

"What?" Hermod said. <Tig?>

<You alright?> Tig asked.

<Umm . . . Yeah. Yeah. I just need a moment.>

<I spoke with Cyral, and they've OK'd you to fly back on your own.>

<No handcuffs?> Hermod asked. He spotted Tig in the crowd gathered in the park. Tig smiled at him from afar. <Who's my escort?>

<MASS.>

<Alright.> Hermod turned away from him. <Can I just have a minute?>

<Come down here and get a hug, man.>

<I don't need a fucking hug!> Hermod replied.

Tig groaned, and his left knee buckled. He wheezed and sweat pooled in his chest and seeped from his forehead and underarms. Cyral grabbed him to prop him up.

<What's happening?> Cyral asked.

<Nothing,> Hermod replied. They stared each other down.

"I'm fine," Tig said, still catching his breath.

"Good." Cyral said. <MASS will meet you at Torrejón.>

<Fine,> Hermod replied. <I'll leave this evening after my goodbyes with my family.>

He stayed in that spot for three more hours under the sun and one under the moon before heading to Lee's parents' house in Moncloa.

The creature did not return.

## LEE'S PARENTS' HOUSE, MONCLOA, MADRID, SPAIN

Hermod stood on the porch of the three-bedroom apartment where Lee's parents had lived for the past fifteen years. He watched stars sparkling in the black sky beyond them. He couldn't remember the last time he had looked up at the night sky and let the thoughts disappear into it. He sipped the gin in his hand. He could barely remember the last time he'd seen so many stars. And then he did. That time with Lee.

Something invisible and heavy pushed into his chest. His face soured, and he squeezed his eyes shut for a moment. A hand landed on his shoulder.

"¿Volverás a visitarnos y quedarte un tiempo, ¿sí?" Franco wrapped his arm around Hermod's back as he stepped up beside him. "Son solo dos horas de vuelo para ti, ¿cierto?"(1) He kept his hand on Hermod's shoulder and squeezed it twice before turning to face him. He nodded and held his own gin out, his face wet. Their glasses kissed, and they both took a sip.

"Uno y medio, esta viaje."(2)

"¡Ay! Mas rápido que antes?"(3)

---

1 "You will return to visit us and stay a while, yes?" "The flight is two hours for you, right?"

2 "One and a half this trip."

3 "Faster than before?"

Hermod smiled.

"¡Ahí está!" Franco said. "¡No pierdas esa sonrisa, precioso!"(1) Franco squeezed Hermod's shoulder three more times, shaking him. Hermod's smile widened, and Franco smiled too.

"Esa hijo," Franco began. "Lo crees o no, yo me preocupaba, pero no Sofía. Lee me dijo, '¡Me casaré cone Superman! Pero con la piel como chocolate.'" Franco shook his head and winked at Hermod. "Esas fueron exactamente sus palabras."(2)

"Sánchez!" Hermod smiled and looked up at the sky. The pressure in his chest came again, pressing down into his gut and diaphragm this time. He lowered his head as he exhaled, deep and long.

Franco laughed and shook him again on cue. "¡No pierdas esa sonrisa, hijo!" He said it again louder, authoritative, as if a spanking might have depended on it. "Levántate, Superman de Chocolate." He coughed out a loud laugh and continued to jostle Hermod until he did indeed lift his shoulders and head again. "Es de Eliot, esa sonrisa. No te sorprendas si te pide verlo de nuevo."(3)

Hermod turned to look at Franco, who was now staring up into the sky. He let his hand fall from Hermod's shoulder.

"Hijo!" Sofía called from the kitchen. "¿Estás seguro de que te irás? Hay una habitación cómoda."(4)

Small arms suddenly grasped Hermod's waist, and a tiny head pressed against his thigh. He reached down and ran his brown fingers through Timoteo's smooth head of almond-brown hair. The boy's green eyes look up at him.

"Quédate, tío Hermod."(5)

"Vale, Timo." Veronica, Lee's eldest sister, came onto the porch with them. She and Hermod exchanged smiles before she knelt to speak with Tim.

---

1 "Don't lose that smile, son."

2 "Believe it or not, it was me who was worried, not Sofía. Lee told me, 'I'm gonna marry Superman, but one with skin like chocolate.'" "Those were his exact words."

3 "Don't lose that smile, son. Stand up, Chocolate Superman." "That's Eliot's smile. Don't be surprised if he asks to see it again."

4 "Son, are you sure you have to go? There's a comfy bed for you."

5 "Stay, Uncle Hermod."

"¿Que te dije?" she scolded him, pulling him away from Hermod and into an embrace. "Tío Hermod está muy ocupado y debe regresar pronto a Nueva York."[1]

Hermod turned around and looked down at the two of them, then took another sip of gin. Franco sipped his gin as well, still looking into the night sky.

"Deja de molestar al tío Hermod." Veronica patted Timo on the butt and then pushed him into the house. "No te preocupes," Veronica said to Hermod. "Ven, y cámbiate la ropa, Timo!" She pointed through the door and into the house. "Benicio!" she yelled. "Ayuda a tu hermano con sus PJs."[2]

Veronica turned around and threw herself into Hermod. He felt her shaking as he tightened his arms around her.

<No llores. No llores. No llores. No llores.>[3]

Still holding her, he turned around. Standing taller than her, she was not visible from inside the house.

<Esta bien,> he told her.[4]

Her shaking intensified. Franco, still staring at the night sky, grabbed her hand and held it as she sobbed into Hermod's shoulder.

She stepped away from him, and her hand slipped from her father's grasp. She leaned against the porch railing.

"Siempre estara contigo, Hermod," Veronica told him. She hugged him and then stepped behind him. "¿Timo? ¿Te pusiste los PJs?"[5]

"¡Sí, mamá!" Timoteo yelled from the guest room on the second floor. Veronica disappeared inside, and Hermod turned back to stare at the sky.

Headlights in the distance scanned the horizon and then cast the shadow of the property's perimeter fence onto the lawn. The shadow danced and vanished and appeared again, smeared this time, as the car stopped some 500 feet down the road adjacent to the house and then turned and approached

---

1 "What did I tell you? Uncle Hermod is very busy and has to get back to New York·"

2 "Stop bothering Uncle Hermod·""Don't worry·" "Come and change your clothes’ Timo!" "Benicio! Help your brother with his PJ's·"

3 <Don't cry· Don't cry· Don't cry· Don't cry·>

4 <It's alright·>

5 "He will always be with you’ Hermod· Timo? Did you put on your PJs?"

them. Its headlight beams swung across the lawn and then directly into Hermod's line of sight. When the car was about 200 feet away, the beams snagged on something larger than a man standing on the sidewalk. Its shadow cast on the lawn and spread closer to them as the car slowed briefly. The silhouette stood still and straight, and its edges fluttered like smoke moving through the wind.

A hand gently grabbed Hermod's shoulder. He jumped into the air and stayed there floating a foot off the porch floor. Franco gasped as well and jerked his body away from Hermod. Hermod settled back to the floor, and the wood slats groaned beneath him. The headlight beams rose up their bodies.

"Solo soy yo, hijo," Franco said. "Voy para otro trago." He nodded at his glass and then at Hermod's. "¿Tu quieres uno?"[(1)]

The headlights washed over the yard, blinding them for a moment before diminishing again as the car rolled away. Hermod turned to see the spot where the shadow had been, but the night was dark, and not even the red glow of the vehicle's taillights could penetrate enough for him to see.

Hermod smiled at Franco. "Gracias, Franco. Solo un momento más y te veré adentro."[(2)]

"Cuando estes listo, hijo," Franco said.[(3)] He stepped into the house and disappeared into the kitchen.

Hermod's eyes quickly returned to the spot where the creature had been, but the dark was too efficient. He could not tell whether the shadow was still there. He turned behind him and scanned the house. Veronica was busy with Benicio and Timoteo. Her husband, Pablo, was asleep on the sofa. Sofía and Franco were embraced in mourning. He closed the door to the porch, rose into the air, and floated toward the spot where he'd seen the shadow. He stopped thirty feet shy of it, the lights from the house no longer of use. His stomach tightened at the thought of scanning the area with his mind.

---

1 "It's just me· I'm getting another drink· Do you want one?"

2 "Thanks· Franco· Just a little longer and I'll join you inside·"

3 "Take your time· son·"

<¡Muestraté! I mean . . . show yourself!> His thoughts rang out violently into the yard. Any person in hiding would have been jostled from it.

Floating there in the dark, he turned around and scanned the house again, then whipped his head back to the darkness in the yard. A few dozen feet away, the shadow moved, and something white tried to shine on the ground. Hermod tossed a burst of fire into the air just in time to see the legs and back of the hulking black creature as it dove into the darkness at the edge of his light. On the ground the white mound of cloth sparkled briefly in the diminishing light.

He approached the thing and then descended, continuing toward it on foot. Black and white orchids, pink rhododendrons, and red roses were vibrant against the white cloth. He picked up the dress and held it aloft in front of him. How? He thought for a moment. Surely this was some illusion or trick . . . from that creature!

He whirled around to examine the house and then turned back to the spot where the creature had escaped, also glancing around at the neighboring properties. He stood still for a moment, the garment swaying in the breeze. He pulled it closer and fussed with it until he could see the hem on the back. It was there, a stain. He closed his eyes and clutched the dress in his fist and moaned. His jaw clenched, just as it had that morning after he awoke to find that Lee had cum all over his new dress.

His phone buzzed in his pocket. He retrieved it, and the notification read one word: MASS. His escort was ready. He darted back toward the house, folding the dress along the way.

Everything was still inside. Veronica had fallen asleep with Timoteo in her arms. In the darkened den, Benicio had bootstrapped the television with his video game system and was seated inches away from the screen, haloed by its glow. Franco and Sofía were asleep on the sofa in their den.

He set the dress on a chair on the porch and then entered the house. One by one hugged them and said goodbye. He returned to the porch and picked up the dress. He was to meet MASS at the Base Aerea Conjunta Torrejón.

"Wear it."

Hermod turned, thinking he saw a pair of pale green eyes and that beaming smile in his sharp, chiseled jaw. Hermod's heart skipped, and he rushed to the spot, only to find no one there.

"Wear it, chile!" the voice said again.

He fell to his knees and buried his face and tears in the garment, which muffled his cries.

## BASE AEREA CONJUNTA TORREJÓN – MADRID, SPAIN

"You're wearing a dress?" Sean asked, his voice broadcasting from MASS.

"Yes," Hermod said. He wiped his palms down the front of his body, smoothing the dress down his ribs, abs, and thighs. "I'm wearing a dress." He was floating several feet away from MASS. Something about the machine made him nauseous. He whipped his head away from it and closed his eyes.

Sean tapped the black microphone icon on the hologram interface. It turned green. "Are we seeing this?"

Back in Delaware, Cyral refrained from responding and turned his head slightly toward Ade. She looked back at him and then at Gaskill, who was standing near the screen they were watching.

"Just bring him back," Gaskill said. He turned to Cyral. "What are you getting?"

Cyral shook his head and squinted. "Nothing. Grieving . . . nostalgia . . . rage."

"Typical, eh?" Ade laughed before turning back to the screen.

"He's quite stable, in fact," Cyral said.

On the Torrejón runway, Sean watched Hermod. An airliner's engines roared above them, and they were covered in the plane's shadow briefly as it approached its runway. Hermod turned his head to follow the plane. Its wheels bounced twice on the runway as it reconnected with the surface. Wind whipped the dress around and between his thighs. The fabric clung to his chest like a second skin, his sinewy chest and nipples visible beneath it.

Sean tapped the microphone icon again. "We're almost up for take-off," he said.

Hermod whirled around from watching the planes and faced MASS. He blinked rapidly and then rose into the air.

"Are you good?" Sean asked, staring up at him, though MASS made no movement.

"You act like you've never seen a faggot in a dress before," Hermod said. His face was set in a grimace as he stared at MASS, and Sean felt a tingle in his spine as if he'd made real eye contact. Hermod's face suddenly broke into a wide smile, and he shook his head and closed his eyes. "Don't mind me. I just cremated my husband, but don't mind me." Hermod looked back at MASS, at Sean. "I bet Gaskill's loving this, huh? I'm fine guys! Did they hear that?"

"Yes," MASS replied, chuckling.

"Where's his other luggage?" Cyral asked.

"You brought nothing else with you?" MASS broadcast.

"N-no," Hermod stammered. "Well, I only had the suit and some toiletries. Lee's parents are sending it and some other stuff to me." He smoothed his hands over the front of the dress. "I found this and . . . and I wanted to wear it. Forgot I packed it."

Hermod closed his eyes and took a deep breath. He opened them again and looked up into the blank, featureless, smooth face.

"That's enough for me," Sean replied. "Glad you're feeling OK, buddy."

"We're not buddies."

"Well, we are for at least the three hours or so."

"Three hours?"

"Yeah," Sean replied, mirroring Hermod's frustration. "We have to abide by upgraded flight regulations. No quantum jumping or light speed or anything like that on an escort."

"Fuck that." Hermod bowed his head. He'd rather not have this breeder looking up his skirt the whole time.

"Follow the law."

"Well, I guess that's that." Hermod smiled.

"Don't worry, I'll stay beside you to give you some privacy." The machine nodded as Sean did in reference to the dress. "It really is quite pretty."

Hermod laughed. "Thank you."

"Is that a smile there? We buddies yet?"

"You're pretty personable for a giant, faceless robot. To think that SPASE would actually hire a real human being."

Sean pressed one of the microphone buttons projecting in front of him to switch the comm line to the SPASE team. "You guys taking notes?"

"You keep this up, and we might avert a catastrophe," Cyral replied.

"Doubt that," Sean said. "I just want my raise."

Hermod hovered off the ground. A large jet rolled directly in front of them. The engines roared, and with a great rush the thing soared into the air.

"You're all clear, Sean," Cyral said.

"That's us," MASS broadcast. It rose straight into the air, and Hermod followed. They stopped. "Match my speed on three . . ."

Hermod nodded and smiled.

"Two . . ."

Sean looked at him and shuddered as he remembered what Dara and Bruja Hanuri had told him about the smile in the storm.

"It was crooked and handsome," Hanuri had said. "Just like his."

"One . . . zero."

MASS accelerated first and then Hermod took the lead, and they moved from hovering to soaring.

Moving at such speeds was as easy as walking for both of them, though Sean required the might of his machine to do so.

They flew for thirty minutes in silence, without disturbance.

"Sean?" Ade asked.

"Yeah?"

"How are you feeling?" Ade was sitting at a desk in her office at SPASE headquarters. An LED wall shone brightly some twenty feet away from her. Sean was looking at her from one side of the screen, and MASS's view was broadcast on the other side.

"Tired," Sean replied. "What's up?"

"Just wanted to fill you in on Mingo's status. He and Davi will meet you here at Rehoboth and escort you and Hermod back to Brooklyn."

"You're not keeping him at HQ?"

"Well, no. He's not under arrest, and there are no federal orders to detain him. And he's behaving, or so it seems."

"So, we're just gonna sit around until the world catches fire?"

"Would you rather poke the bear?"

"Sweetie, we're already running from the bear."

Ade laughed, and Sean joined her.

"I miss your smile," he said.

Inside the war room in Delaware, Sean's face disappeared from the LED wall. MASS's broadcast also disappeared.

"Your camera just died," Ade said.

Sean stopped smiling. Hermod was twenty miles behind on the radar and not moving. MASS halted its acceleration and did an about-face.

"Fuck!" Sean said. "He must have heard us."

He could still see Ade on the screen, but his neural link with the outside world had died. He was deaf and blind except for his radar.

"MASS," Sean said. "I can't see."

"Understood," MASS replied. "I will triangulate an external signal between the nearest satellites and broadcast back to you."

"I'll need some auto-evasion backup until then."

"Of course."

Sean watched his radar and jabbed his fingers into the keyboard in the holographic panel. The display changed, and Hermod's vital statistics appeared beside the radar. He still wasn't moving, but he was much heavier, 1,000 times heavier, and hot.

"I'm gonna need that feed, MASS, now!" Sean commanded. "Ade, are you getting this?"

"Nothing," Ade replied. "What's happening?"

"These stats."

Another square appeared in the holographic panel, and Cyral came online.

"Sean," Cyral said in a low voice.

"I know. Just send backup."

"There's no time. If it gets bad, take it upstairs. He'll be disoriented outside of the atmosphere."

"Or unbound," Sean said.

"At least you'll be alive," Ade said. "And you'll have more immediate assistance from satellite defense systems nearby."

"Sir," MASS said. "You should have visuals."

On his radar, Hermod was moving quickly toward him.

"Yes," Sean said. "Thanks."

MASS readied itself, one hand balled into a fist, the other positioned near the machine's shoulder. A hole opened in the palm, and wisps of black smoke crept out of it. Though the neural networks were still malfunctioning, Sean could hear and see again.

On the large viewport, clouds shone dully beneath him in the moonlight. In the darkness in front of him, a soft, shining wisp of something approached him, and he soon realized it was the dress. The body wearing it though was still too dark to discern, and it appeared that the dress was flying on its own.

When it was about a mile away from him, blue fire exploded around the dress. A bolt of something, dark and glistening, shot out from the hole in MASS's hand. It missed, though the green glare illuminated the exposed skull, humerus, and outstretched digits.

Sean had not noticed, but Cyral and Ade's screens disappeared from his holographic panel.

MASS discharged another glittering dark bolt. It connected with the skull, and the skeleton was sent spinning several yards back. MASS rushed after it and wrapped its massive hand around Hermod's core. The other hand fired another of its dark energy bolts into the skeleton. Hermod endured the assault and put up no struggle, clamped in MASS's palm. His skull directly facing MASS's featureless face. Inside the machine, Sean watched the temperature continue to rise past 800,000°F. He felt short of breath, and his pulse quickened.

"Sir," MASS said, "you will not be able to free yourself from his gravitational pull if you hold on.

The temperature went to 1,000,000°F.

"Ade!" Sean screamed. "Cyral! Dammit!" The frustration crept down his arms from his white knuckles into his neck and deep down to draw his scrotum up in front of him. The skeleton in MASS's hand began to stir. Sean opened the machine's palm and smashed his fist into it.

"Gaskill! Dammit, come through!" Sean screamed.

"MASS has reached a critical altitude of one hundred thousand feet, Sean," MASS said. "Should I engage the gravity ladder?"

"Not yet."

"Gaskill," Vincent whispered. "Traitor." Wind whipped into his skull as he felt the pressure of the massive hand and the crushing power of the atmosphere, but he was unfazed.

"MASS, let me know when the satellite is in range," Sean said as he punched to the space in front of him with his index finger in a strategic pattern. A three-dimensional map of the satellites orbiting the planet appeared in front of him.

"Sir," MASS said.

"I'm aware, MASS," Sean replied. He let his head fall forward and took a deep breath. "Just do this please."

They slowed their ascent.

"The Epsilon Satellite is not responding, sir."

"Of course it's not," Sean said.

He chomped his jaw down and bit off a sizable amount of gum tissue inside his mouth. Its tangy chalkiness lingered on his tongue.

"Doc?" Sean pleaded. Then MASS pounded its fist into the skeleton in its other hand.

Hermod felt nothing. He remained inert. He and MASS were wrapped in a swaddling blaze. He was nearing 2,000,000°F .

"I need that satellite online or else we're fucked," Sean said. "MASS."

Sean watched the inert skeleton on his screen. The hem of the white dress fluttered in the wind near the heel of MASS's palm. It remained intact in the inferno, though the glittery Ojun disintegrated and flaked away its mystic embers.

Sweat poured down Sean's forehead.

"Dr. Gaskill has stored the initiation protocols in a discrete signal in that satellite," MASS said. "We cannot attain particle autonomy without the protocol. Danger! Defense precognition fields have primed the secondary—"Everything went dark inside the machine.

"Fuck me," Sean said into the pitch black, punching the screen that enveloped him. MASS tilted and fell backwards, head first into freefall. Sean felt a flushing sensation, the fluids and organs inside making him hallucinate an even more terrifying freefall. Vomit was pulled back down from his back teeth. Sweat poured in rivers down his hairline and around his ears. He disregarded the sensitivity of his connective wiring and unplugged himself from the lumbar node. The hip braces were warm to the touch. He thrust his triceps and propelled himself toward MASS's left hip. A ladder to the emergency drone was stored in the machine's left leg. He climbed down it and looked up, only to see the command bubble burst. A bright light shone behind it and the circuit glass screens. Thousands of micro projectors burst in quick succession.

Sean reached up and slid a plank from within the machine's interior, closing off the ladder from the smoldering control core. He closed the escape exit and sealed it, then continued climbing. He was two rungs from the drone hatch when the escape ladder door began to hiss and glow in the center. Molten and glowing, it dripped down onto Sean, who wriggled his leg and shoulder clear of the falling molten alloy. It would soon melt the drone door. He reached down to pull the escape drone hatch open, and the orange glowing metal seeped inside, wrecking the interior.

"Damn you!" Snarling, he punched the side of the corridor and broke three knuckles. He wiped sweat off of his brow. His eyes were burning. "MASS? Do something."

He held his hand up to shield himself from the light and the molten Ojun pressing down into the corridor. It rolled closer, and Sean tried to sink away. His tailbone banged against the escape hatch door, and he closed his eyes tight as the molten metal washed down farther.

Frantic, he tried to thrust his head down near the hatch, away from the flow of molten Ojun. It splashed on his back and ate away the sensory armor covering it. He winced at the intense heat there. Molten Ojun began to pool around him in the small space, covering his legs. Sweat flowed between the neurosuit and his skin. He felt it squishing in his armpits and groin folds. He smelled his skin cooking and relaxed into the world of hot pain. He refused to scream. In the final moment, he took a deep breath before noticing that the air had become sparkling and green like a cloud from a dream.

There was unfathomable pain, and he could no longer keep his cries at bay. Just as the sound might have issued from him, the pain disappeared, and everything went black. For an instant, he felt like he was raining.

## SPASE HEADQUARTERS – WAR ROOM A – CAPE HENLOPEN, DE

Ade's hand was a black gnarled claw for three seconds. Then it was her soft, dark chocolate-skinned hand again. Then gnarled.

"He just . . . melted it?" Ade finally asked.

"Yes." Cyral hung his head as grief and empathy had their way with him. Ade couldn't tell. She noticed very little about the others around her these days. The one she did think about had just been killed.

Cyral lifted his head and watched her hand change into the claw, then back to her normal hand. Claw again. Hand again. She let it remain and then wrapped both arms around herself for a moment in front of the large LED wall. She let her hands grip the opposite triceps and squeezed herself, trying to press out the knot that was forming in her belly.

Cyral stood next to the chair he'd been sitting in. His eyes were fixed on the screen, the word "SPASE" in big, bold white letters crawling, transforming, and morphing and bouncing across the screen according to a generative algorithm.

"Vincent is here," Gaskill said.

Tig stared down at the war room table.

"We must find him and engage," Gaskill continued.

"What about Sean?" Ade asked. She turned away from the screen and faced Gaskill, who was standing near the far end of the table.

"Sean knew what he was doing," Gaskill said. "I'm certain of it. There are Ojun battle suits tailored for each of you. I will brief Dara's team and dispatch them to New York."

"And how do you know he's there?" Tig asked.

"Where else would he be, Tig?" Cyral asked.

# VINCENT'S REVENGE

## BROADWAY JUNCTION MTA STATION, BROOKLYN, NEW YORK CITY, NY

Hermod stood still on the train platform and looked to either side. His eyes hopped from one person to the next and then back to the off-white sequin orchid near his left thigh.

<It's so pretty!>

He spotted the stairway at the platform exit and headed towards it.

He'd seen Lee earlier. He was standing on the terrace when Hermod arrived back at the apartment. Lee shooed him away, just before he was about to land on it, just before the door opened, and Mingo stepped out of it. He had not scanned the apartment before arriving and was just a split-second shy of being detected. Lee had saved him. Afterwards, he flew to the High Street MTA station and caught the Far Rockaway bound A train. His car had remained pretty much empty for most of the ride up to the junction. He had gotten off to transfer to the J train at Broadway Junction.

People were staring at him. He didn't care. He mounted the stairs to the street level headed towards the escalator to the elevated J and L trains.

Much to his surprise, despite the morning traffic, he'd been able to ignore the psychic commotion concerning the hot man in the pretty dress. Several children looked at him admiringly while their mothers and caretakers' responses varied. Some stared in awe while others' faces quickly turned to scowls. A handsome policeman nodded politely.

Hermod stepped onto the escalator to the J train platform and lifted his dress slightly to keep the hem from being sullied or snagged. At the top he stepped off the escalator and was greeted by a throng of brown schoolchildren who immediately burst into an uproar upon seeing him.

"Where's her shoes?"

"He needs your hooker shoes, Shayla!"

Some of them admonished the others for their ignorance.

"Don't you know who that is?"

A rotund, handsome MTA worker nodded in passing, defying the other who sneered at the sight. The older black ladies were quite kind. And, as always, the Jehovah's Witnesses near the J platform smiled and said hello.

"Good morning."

<Sorry for your loss, Hermod,> a young schoolboy had projected to him as he passed.

Another young man graciously smiled at him and wished him well as he stood holding his Japanese boyfriend's hand.

It had all been relatively calm until he finally reached the J platform.

<Dammit. I hate it. I can't even look at those faggot motherfuckers . . . >

The intruding thought had surprised him, dragging his attention away from his dress. It was so pretty and fit so nice today. It made him feel good. He was admiring one of the tulips near his hip. The intrusion had come from a breadcrust-brown woman standing about three car lengths away from him. She had large brown eyes, and the thin, meticulous line of her eyebrows cut a wide V in her face. Her mouth was tight, and her shiny, purple lips rippled as she pulled them into her teeth. Her mental voice was coarse and ragged though, like an old smoker's with a tired throat.

<Oh God, he's hot!>

<I have those earrings. They look way better on me.>

<Isn't that lovely? Why is he looking at me?>

<Where are his shoes? Her shoes?>

<Shit. I missed Shetia's birthday.>

<Barbera. Yes! I'll pick up a nice one before. She likes that one with pork.>

<Ba da ba ba bweee, Dwa dop bop bop boo.>

<Mmm. Her ConEd share. Venmo Ho!>

<My titties are too big?>

<I mean, I should have fucked her. No one else was there either.>

<Griffin and Kala should be there early.>

<Jesus, how am I gonna pay that ConEd bill?>

<Fuck that. He must have paid two thousand for that easily. I'm putting that up tonight. I could probably make five hundred dollars on this train right now!>

<He's not that cute in person at all.>

<I would think her feet would be much dirtier than that!>

<What a waste. Like, school is free if you apply. I mean, you're Black!>

<These MTA ads are so bizarre.>

<I'm *not* spending that much money unless there's a pool.>

<How is it down fifteen percent? He said that was a good coin!>

<Ooohh she's got a *fat* ass! Wow.>

<Ain't that some shit? It's gonna be ninety-five degrees tonight.>

<Oooh, I don't want to sit in this fucking discovery meeting with Kellum. He's too dark for that dress. It's so pretty.>

<Those titties are tasty looking.>

<It's not polite to Instagram strangers, but that dress is hot.>

<That's that guy! I'll wait for the next one.>

<I'm horny. I'm sleeping over at Petra's tonight.>

<Uhhh, I look so fat in this thing.>

<It's either overpaid hipsters or strollers around here now.>

<Why is that guy looking at me?>

<I should have stayed in bed.>

<That jukebox was cute last night. I haven't danced to good Pink in ages!>

<This lab report doesn't really . . . no, we'll have to rewrite this.>

<I bet that guy's dick is huge. He would never sleep with me.>

<Goddammit! If he doesn't call me back today he's fired. Fuckin' Spics! Fuckin' Jews!>

<I haven't gotten a text from Darren in two days!>

<That's the boy from the liquor store! Is this his morning train too? He's hot.>

<Isn't that that guy from RSVP?>

<You sit and smoke dro on mah livin' room flo. Play Nintendo wit Ceez a Leo! Get money niggaz! Damn Kim used to be fine. I'd still hit tho.>

<If she pokes me with that bag one more time . . .>

<He's got the right idea. Shit. My balls are *so* sweaty right now.>

<He's gonna flake on me.>

<You really are a fucking shit bag, Alex.>

<Oh, she's getting married, she's getting married, she's getting married!>

<That picture is terrible. It must be why she blocked the comments.>

<That *is* that Hermod guy!>

Hermod looked around, swinging his head from side to side much faster now and darting his eyes every which way. He couldn't turn them off.

<Poor guy.>

<They better have scones today, assholes.>

<Chives! Yes! Chives!>

Why was the human noise so loud now?

He was hearing and interpreting these thoughts, and he couldn't ignore them. There was so much worry and angst and self-absorbed drivel. Why weren't the higher machines, supercomputers, and satellites drowning it out? Their white noise was usually a safe haven from this.

He quivered ever so slightly and straightened his back, his arms hanging stiffly at his sides. He took a deep breath as he stared around, trying to understand the people around him but growing increasingly perplexed. His brow ruffled, and he felt disoriented like he had upon first traversing the cramped, unapologetic streets of China. He'd muted these people every day for years! Why was today so different? He looked around the platform and noticed there were few brown people. This was also a daily ritual, counting the spots. Fewer and fewer each year. It was normal.

Not today.

The train arrived.

<Thank God!>

<Dios mi amor.>

<Oh, God, there's *never* a seat>

<Fuck, it's Sylvia! Shit!>

Hermod inched toward the door in file with the other passengers. Stragglers tried to squeeze past the large Italian woman in front of him. She giggled as they pressed between her belly and the tall Dominican lad who had also boarded the train. On board, there was a reasonable crowd of people, but there was a little room to move. He leaned against the door and waited for the frail ones to sit down. Chivalry had always been second nature. Love thy neighbor as thyself, Granny had told him. Some things did stick.

He heard their hearts beating, though he could not hear his own. He didn't need one. Not anymore. He looked down at the Italian woman as she situated herself in her seat. The Dominican man ended up right across from her. Her legs dangled, and she kicked them excitedly and looked into his eyes. Her smile grew wider, and her shoulders bounced. The Dominican man smiled and nodded bashfully. Hermod looked at both of them and their moment of pleasantry.

Hermod's head shot up, and he stared at the window in the door across from him. He had always been warmed by this type of interaction in the past. There were myriad occasions where strangers had opened themselves and shared a brief, amiable moment. Such occasions used to thrill him. His body would tingle, and he would delight in the civility of others and the goodness of his species. Those moments had assured him that they were pleasing in the sight of God despite the horrors that he had seen in his lifetime. He smiled slightly to try to will the warm fuzzies to life within him. He failed. Over the past two weeks, so much had been taken from him, but standing on the J and failing to empathize with the fat Italian woman, he felt what was missing so much more. He should have died with Lee.

He had waited for the others to sit. That was kind. Nice. An honest display of human decency. He stared at his reflection in the window.

*I'm a lady today,* he thought. *I should have sat down.*

His reflection rippled as the apartment façades and side streets along Broadway passed behind the window. Granny had taught him that being polite and chivalrous were the easiest ways to stay out of trouble.

"Don't give them the stick to beat you with," she had said. And he hadn't—ever. He had been constantly aware of the ever-present critical eye of those around him. "They don't want the Black man to have nothing! Crackers."

At the Halsey Stop, he noticed several young professional men occupying more than their share of seating on the opposite end of the train car. Two luxurious-looking Black women stood across from the loud men in suits. The frailest of the two Black ladies shimmied back and forth until the train doors, her resting spot, closed. She relaxed her shoulders and let her purse strap fall from her shoulder to the pit of her elbow. The two women, both Ghanaian, flew off into heavily accented conversation. Hermod divined that these two ladies were actually trading operations supervisors at the same bank as the bull suits who had so callously neglected to offer up the seats they were hoarding.

His hands tingled as fury brewed within him.

As the train pulled into the Myrtle Avenue stop, the dozing Mexican man standing next to him almost collapsed to the floor. The train stopped suddenly, and Hermod bent to scoop the man just before he hit the floor.

"Muchas gracias amigo! Thank you, friend."

He laughed, and Hermod helped him to his feet as the train doors opened. Passengers boarding the train huffed with annoyance that the two of them took up so much room. Hermod was alarmed that the people were so upset. He had just saved the man from breaking his nose off into his brain. He had prevented a minor catastrophe in this man's life, but vicious eyes and grimacing faces glared at him as a handful of white passengers boarded the train.

<Why is this faggot in a dress this early?>

<I thought this was the express! Is it going to Chambers at least?>

<Jesus, why is this train so packed?>

<I need to grab some rugelach before that flight, or she'll kill me.>

<This must be what PMS is like. In pain on a packed train.>

Hermod burst into uproarious laughter. He reached out to the young Dominican man.

<Good one,> he told him, tickled by the pretty Dominican man's wit.

The man's head jerked about suddenly. His eyes were wide, and they darted around as he huffed out each breath.

The Italian woman furrowed her brow, perplexed by the sudden and alarming change in the man's demeanor. She looked at Hermod, who was still laughing. The Mexican man awoke again due to the sound. He was just in time to catch himself as the train stopped suddenly.

"Why are there no Black men going to work with you on this train?" Hermod asked quietly as his laughter subsided. The young white woman next to him looked at him quickly and squinted and then walked farther into the train. Hermod immediately doubled over. He had tried to quell it in him, but it poured out, uproarious and painful in his diaphragm.

More people boarded the train with more grimaces. They shoved Hermod, almost knocking him to the floor.

"There's, like, two," Hermod said. He held up his right index and middle fingers and twisted them around in the air, laughing.

<Fucking pretty bastard. Get out of the way. How is that dress fitting him?>

<Why is this train local today? Fuck!>

<I don't have time for this. First, he's in the way, and now he's as loud as all hell.>

<That big Black guy is scary.>

<Wow, what happened to him? I want some!>

Hermod recognized the tones of their thoughts and laughed even harder. He was supposed to be embarrassed, and yet he was not. It had taken the collapse of his world for him to fully shed the chains of his human self-consciousness.

As they departed the Flushing stop, Hermod noticed that still, no one in the car looked like him except for the two Ghanaian women, who were now eclipsed by an ever-growing crowd of commuters.

He laughed and laughed as he held the pole near the entrance, the train moving toward Lorimer now. More white people and then a few Asians boarded. But this was Bed-Stuy, right? Where were the Black people going to work in the morning?

The door opened, and those who could, exited the train. The passengers on the platform looked around at each other. So many people had just exited the train at rush hour.

<Somebody must have farted.>

<Yo, that fucking homo is wigging out.>

<Fucking MTA.>

<I'll wait for the M.>

"They took a shit?" he heard someone ask from the platform. He watched through the windows as people moved from his car to the next one. Some waited on the platform, the car was far too packed already.

"Why are there no Black men going to work with you on this train?" Hermod yelled between his guffaws. Passengers moved away from him, though the seats nearest to him remained occupied. He was kempt and freshly shaven from Lee's funeral the day before, and he smelled pleasant. There was no need to flee from him like the pungent, soiled, and repugnant ones. Instead, they looked at him with upturned mouths and snarling lips.

"Why?" Hermod yelled. His laughter had quieted, but his mouth and eyes were wide with the sarcastic glee still bubbling out of him.

The Ghanaian women had found a place to sit. Both of them were hysterical. One laughed openly while the slight one shielded her mouth with her head hanging down. Her shoulders bounced up and down as her body shook. One of them looked at him while they were laughing and stared at his dress at length, then shot her eyes back to his and then to her friends. The businessmen had straightened up to crane their necks toward the commotion near Hermod's end of the train. One of them rolled his eyes and huffed, then folded his arms.

<Fucking dirty... uggghhh! Now *there's* a nigger if there ever was one.> He was the cockiest of the bunch. Hermod turned to look at the man. The words shot out of the dirty blond man like electricity. <. . . if there ever was one.>

There it is.

<How many are there?> Hermod probed. He caught the man's eyes from across the train. <You hate us. Why?>

He stared at the young man, who was standing now, his eyes wide and his face turning red. The man's leg was shaking, and his friends looked up into his face with alarm.

"What's got you, Frank?" his stocky Korean friend inquired as he rose to his feet. Hermod looked on, delighted. Frank clung to the rail and tossed his head every which way, his eyes bulging. The passengers near him were all staring at him now.

"Someone . . . who said that?" he said between panting breaths. "He heard me!"

"Who?" his Korean friend asked.

Frank drew in a deep breath and then blew it out. His shoulders relaxed as he sank back into his seat. His Korean friend shrugged. Hermod stood absolutely still, leaning on the pole, staring at Frank from the other side of the train. The lights in the car dimmed, and a shadow grew around Franklin.

The train stopped and filled with more people. They huddled around him, trying to find their footing. Franklin sat up straight in his seat and looked at the ceiling. He began trembling and drew in a long, deep breath through his nose.

"Frank?" his Korean friend asked.

"Why are there no Black men going to work on this train this morning?"

"Frank, are you OK?"

The train chugged away from Marcy Avenue on its way to cross the bridge.

*They don't see it,* Franklin thought. They would be shaking too. He couldn't hear them anymore. His ears started ringing, and the shadow spread through the train like smoke, covering more and more of it in darkness. Franklin felt himself gasping and coughing, but he couldn't hear it. His vision blurred, and the skirts and pants and hands and arms and bags around him all blended together. Though he knew he was in the train car, he could only see a smattering of multicolored blobs fading in and out of the shadow that filled most of his view. The colored blobs moved around, blending, and disappearing. His body jerked back and forth in his seat when the train curved and jostled as it mounted the bridge.

As Franklin watched the shadow withdraw, the colored blobs moved around quickly, suddenly, some of them melting into each other. Hard lines, reflections, colors, and textures formed in all of the blobs again. Bright blues and grays became windows. The multicolored ones became people. They were moving away, panicked. He wanted to join them, but he couldn't move, and his head hurt like there was hot blood caught in a migraine in there. The ringing in his ears diminished into screaming and then the shadow swarmed. He felt it this time as it engulfed him. A large hot hand lifted him into the air. He felt a short pinch, and his tension and trembling ceased as his spinal cord severed. Screaming passengers hurried toward the middle of the train, away from Franklin and the thing that had attacked him.

"There are no Black men going to work on this goddamn train this morning?" Hermod screamed from the opposite side of the car. "Why?"

Remus held Franklin, who was still alive, pinned to the ceiling of the train. Blood poured from the holes in Franklin's neck and collar where Remus had gripped him. Streaks of blood flowed down the beast's arm and splattered on its chest and thighs, a red Pollockian nightmare on the blackest of canvases. Franklin's eyes bulged and stared at Remus as it lowered him to the train floor. Franklin watched the creature's mouth open as it exhaled wisps of shadow into his face. Black fangs plunged into Franklin's meaty neck. Remus took several mouthfuls of flesh and gulped them down, then dropped Franklin's carcass to the floor. It stood as tall as it could, hunching over where the ceiling met its neck.

<!>

Cries of desperation filled the train at the creature's psychic bellow.

"Feast, my friend." Vincent looked into Hermod's hands and then pressed them down the length of his body. He admired the roses, orchids, marigolds, and tulips in his dress. He'd missed this garment. It was his favorite.

He turned his attention to the other end of the train and then out the window to the city spreading uptown and beyond. He'd only dreamed of such a vision, a city where the buildings overpowered the people and reached up toward the stars. Such prosperity, such industry.

His smile faded as marvel collapsed to dismay. He looked around the train car, through the window near him into the white faces of those standing in the adjacent car. He opened the door and crossed into it. The door slid shut behind him, and he heard the latch click into place. People backed away from him. He grabbed a young white man near him by the neck. Screams roared through the car.

"Hey, man," the young man protested, grabbing Vincent's wrists. His eyes widened in fear, and he screamed in pain at the burning flesh of his hands and neck.

"Why are there no Black people on this train?" Vincent yelled as he dragged the young man down to the floor.

"I don't . . . I don't know, man. Please!" The young man's brown eyes watered. He waved his blistering palms up at Vincent. "Please don't kill me."

"No!" Vincent replied. He released the boy and stepped down into his chest, as if into thick mud, through the flesh and to the train floor. Blood boiled and hissed around his leg and out of the wound and seeped from the boy's mouth. He made a gurgling sound, and his arms and legs beat wildly against the floor and seat near him as he convulsed. Vincent stepped out of him and looked into the train car. Blood and flesh burned away from his skin. Passengers screamed hysterically and climbed over one another to get away from Vincent and the dead young man. Some of them held their noses and gagged at the smell.

"Only the crackers can earn, huh? Still?" Vincent yelled. "We'll fix it this time."

As he approached the crowd, passengers scrambled in vain to get away from him. A tall young man in a gray suit swung his small rolling suitcase into the window behind him. A middle-aged brunette had torn her stockings along the outside of her thigh while trying to maneuver herself in a position beside him. She grabbed the horizontal railing above her and swung herself forward, kicking at the window with her chunky platform heels. Other people rushed into the adjacent car. A few clung to the train's perimeter and assisted those feverishly bashing shoes and bags and bodies into the train's windows. Others collected themselves behind Vincent to start the journey to the car there. They mingled with frightened passengers who had taken refuge in the partition to escape from Remus. Two men had already fallen and were crushed beneath the train. Another was working his way to the same fate, trying desperately to grab onto one of the girders of the Williamsburg bridge just a few feet beyond his reach.

"I'll fix it this time," Vincent said.

<Fuck this,> a mind whispered.

"Yes, come!" Vincent said.

A young Asian man stopped punching the window and jumped down from the train seat. He elbowed his way against the few people in his way and faced Vincent. He reached behind him and drew a Glock. He fired into the train ceiling. Two women yelped louder than the crowd in response.

"Fuck you!" the young man yelled. He tightened his jaw and fired three shots at Vincent. Though his aim was precise, all three bullets exploded just before they would have entered Vincent's sternum. The young man held the pistol firm and advanced slowly as he pulled the trigger five more times.

"You don't want to run out," Vincent said. He pushed his palm out in front of him as he approached the young man. The man fired again, and the bullet broke in front of Vincent's hand.

Shaking, the young man stood with both hands on the gun.

"I might have spared you," Vincent said, looking the man up and down. He frowned. "Interloper. Only a dying man would greet me with violence."

The boy moaned briefly and then fell to his knees, never breaking eye contact with Vincent. The young man's face softened, and Vincent winked at him. The man put the gun into his own mouth and pulled the trigger. Blood and bone and brains sprayed into the air and fell to the floor after his body.

*I have returned just in time,* Vincent thought, *to set right the injustice.* He felt a pleasant warmth in his bosom. He was proud of the chaos that he had wrought in the train. He felt Hermod's ignition and reveled in it for the first time. He shuddered as the vacuum formed in him, and a great gravitational field enveloped him. He steadied himself, and his body rose off of the floor of the train. It and the railings and the door near him disintegrated. Then he felt hollow, as light as air, like everything and nothing. Tears filled his eyes, threatening to stream down his face. He quelled them and remembered another time when he would go to the void in the rock and enjoy the same sensations.

The train came to a stop just past the halfway point on the bridge. All of the frightened worlds in his car fed into him, and he was ecstatic. Hermod had not allowed this body the true freedom that it deserved. Hermod, in all his learning and all his life experiences, had retained the belief that he must commit himself to morality, civility. Morality was a choice, one that this body did not have to make anymore. One that Vincent had never made and never intended to. Hermod, had not yet realized what Vincent and Juno held to be true. Only the strongest *and* most unscrupulous men had risen above the law, had subverted it and performed whatever self-aggrandizing and atrocious acts that they could fathom. And they alone had brought wealth and prosperity to their kind. They would not fail again.

"You are beyond it all now, boy," Vincent said.

He swooned at all of Hermod's memories. He assumed not only his body but also his pleasures, pains, loathing, and rage.

"Mmmmm . . ." Vincent moaned. "Relax. Let me make it right."

Vincent could feel Hermod's pent-up anguish, the burden of being Black. Being queer. It was time to cast it aside. So many times in Hermod's thirty-eight years had he wanted to have his way with racist teachers, fellow students, publishers, politicians, gays . . . how many gays? So many times he had wished he could force people to respect and even acknowledge him and all the other Black people and queers like him. Hermod had yearned to raze the Friar school the night they had locked him under it. How many interns had he wanted to throttle? How many Franklins had he wanted to end before today? How many Black people had he wanted to throttle as well? How many homophobic Black men had he wanted to purge from the ranks? How many hateful breeders? How many crusades could he have already waged and won all over the world? Vincent felt for his nephew. Though he sensed the boy had found some relief in "meditating," as he called it, there was a much more efficient pressure release.

"We'll set it right together, child," Vincent said. "Today. We will show you how."

Vincent looked around and smelled burning flesh. The commute had aroused everyone else beyond anything they could have imagined.

<It's happening again!>

<We're going to die!>

<Aren't there any demis on this train?>

<That smell!>

<He's coming this way . . .>

He hovered toward a group of people who had thrashed at the window opposite him. They quickly scattered, but one woman remained, frozen in fear.

"Please don't kill me!" she screamed.

"Good morning, Koral," he said kindly to her.

She cringed and tightened her eyes. He held out his hand, and she was raised from her seat, which melted away. She was unscathed. He looked into her and saw her body flashing brightly with neuro signals and impulses spreading from her brain, down into her center, and out through her appendages. Her spine was like a giant tendril of lightning. He wondered if this was what fear looked like.

"You are a good mother, Koral. And this may sound strange, but you're also a good white person." He moved her to the seat across from them, which was not molten and bubbling. "But," he paused. "Goodbye Koral . . ."

"No!" she screamed. Her body ignited even as she turned and ran. The scream tore through the train, and passengers cowered and whimpered and cried and pissed themselves. The flaming lump fell and burned in the center of the train car, filling it with rancid smoke.

A group of four was huddled near the door ahead. One of them was a brown-haired male with large shoulders. He stood pressing his fingertips in between the partition of the train door. His fingers strained as he tried to pull the door open, far enough to wedge them in. He looked up suddenly and froze, turning to face Vincent. Two girls were clinging to the young man's legs. The girls wore loose-fitting monochromatic pants and tops. Each had yellow lipstick, sharp fake nails, and buzz-cut, black-dyed hair. A few inches from them, their other friend, a young brown man, huddled near the seat with his body tucked into a ball, his head between his legs, and his hands interlaced around the back of his neck.

Vincent pointed at the brown-haired boy's shoes, and one of them caught fire. The boy danced out of his shoes and kicked them down the opposite side of the train. He stood in stocking feet with his back flush against the train door. He wet himself and the girls beneath him. They coughed and squirmed away from his leg and clasped each other with such force that their earrings shook. They whimpered as the judgment began, and Vincent plucked the thinnest of the two girls from the arms of her doppelganger. He drew her close to him. Her face was wet, and her makeup ran yellow and black. The huddle on the floor was quickly renegotiated. Her friends did not even look to see what had become of her.

"Dora." Vincent smiled at her as she floated before him. "I'm offended. What have you to say?"

She was well aware of what he meant. He rifled through her most private memories and impulses. When he found the picture she had drawn after her contemporary literature class had finished reading Richard Wright's *Black Boy* three years ago, she had forfeited any defense for her life. Her black friend, Jordan, the one cowering on the floor, had been in that class with her. He had been the subject of her creative work.

"Fuck you." Dora spat at him, the wad of spittle hissing and evaporating in between them.

Vincent looked at the brown-haired boy. He flew away from the door, and his head and arms snapped backwards, the bones in his shoulders and neck cracking loudly.

"Oh, look, I ruined it," Vincent said, admiring the dead young man floating in front of him. "I wanted him alive. I wanted to see if he could stick his cock in the ground and spin around like a top!" Vincent yelled into Dora's face. She screamed and whimpered. He let the boy's body fall to the floor "He didn't have to die. That was your fault, Dora."

Dora yelped, and snot poured from her nose to her mouth. She was still floating and unable to move. He wouldn't let her speak. He'd heard her brand of sniveling countless times. "Literature?" Vincent asked. "He should never have had to write that book." He forced the girl around to face her friend. The body flopped around on the floor to face her as well. The head fell at an awkward angle, almost upside down. A tear streaked the dead young man's face.

Dora wept loudly, and her sobs turned into a wrenching scream as her body burst into flames. It was not a wild inferno that consumed her but a succinct, intense heat. Four seconds later, she was nothing but vapor and ash.

"Stick your nigger dick in the ground and spin around like a top?" Vincent asked, incredulous, remembering.

He advanced through the train car, burning and glowing white with fire beneath his dress. Passengers cowered away from him and shielded their eyes. The extreme gravitational fields that he manipulated had begun to warp the train, and the windows shattered into millions of pieces. The flying glass fatally wounded at least one of the passengers instantly.

Passengers throughout the train made their way to the first and last cars. Those between Vincent and Remus risked their lives trying to find either end. His car was nearly empty except for a handful of leftovers, like the woman he just passed. She was face down on the floor, bleeding to death from her left side. Then there were the three old ladies holding hands and praying on the bench farthest ahead of him. Vincent read them quickly. In one of them, the most infirm of the three, he saw a bloody newborn baby lying in a field. Its arm was mangled, and the dark red blood shone like slick oil in the moonlight. Several yards away a group of people were tossing beer cans and blowing cigarette smoke into the air. Several of them were holding guns in their hands. Their white skin glowed even whiter in the moonlight, which was the only light source in the vast expanse of a wheat field. A man in the crowd lit a match and tossed it into a heap near where the crowd lingered. Flames jumped high into the air, the fire's light outshone the moon. The burning heap came to life. A brown hand shot out from beneath what appeared to be another body. Screams erupted from the pile of burning people. A young white man jumped down from the bed of a pickup truck parked nearby. He loaded his shotgun and then fired at the burning bodies. Three of the brown man's fingers flew off into the night, and the flames leapt higher as the hand fell limp at the wrist. The crowd cheered, and the young shooter spat into the fire.

Marsha also remembered how they had cheered and cursed as loud as they could to try to drown out the screams. She remembered gagging from the smell of cooking men and the taste of Jamie Sullivan's semen, which had lingered on her saliva. Marsha had managed to speak through the reflex, "Y'all got that lil niglet right?" She had doubled over in laughter, tickled by the new word she had invented. Seventy-five-year-old Marsha Tinsley was nineteen then, and had coined a phrase for baby niggers that evening with her friends out on Emory's Uncle's farm outside of Mobile, Alabama.

From across the train, Vincent pulled Marsha from her seat and held her upright. She smelled sweet with perfume and diabetes as her prosthetic foot started to melt. She had been a rotund girl in the memory that he had found, but now she was thin and frail. Ovarian cancer had eaten her like she might have devoured a sumptuous cake, in her youth. She closed her eyes and continued in prayer with her friends. He hovered there staring at Marsha, intercepting her supplication for grace and forgiveness. He had an overwhelming urge to spit on her. He wondered if his spittle would have eaten away at her slowly like acid, or if he would have breathed out a ray of white fire with which to consume her. His being filled with such loathing that he almost ignited fully right there in front of them.

Then he calmed himself. He did not want to hurt her friends right now; one of them shared his birthday. He stared at the women as they continued to pray.

The door opened behind him, and a black woman in a blue uniform and MTA baseball cap stepped into the train. She covered her mouth and thrust her head down into her chest and coughed for several seconds before looking up to survey the damage.

Vincent whipped himself around at the sound of her coughing and threw his hand in her direction. The woman screamed as fire rose up from the ground beneath her. She jumped back and fell to the floor on her buttocks. Her hat fell off, and she began rolling around, trying to extinguish the flames that burned her.

"Sister." He held out his hand again, and the flames diminished, leaving the woman lying on the floor of the train, panting. Her leg kicked about, and glass crunched beneath her body as she writhed around. She had been badly burned, and her screams had quieted to a throaty moan.

Vincent turned back to Marsha and glared at her. He could feel the conductor's pain. She had three children, and her husband was a local restauranteur. He heard the screams of the burning man again, the father of Marsha's "niglet." The memory still lingered in him and was a strange parallel to the screams of the burned conductor and the image of her smiling, rambunctious young boys. His eyes widened as he glared at Marsha.

"Devil," she said, looking up at him from her prayer. Suddenly, her cancerous body flew from the spot where he had held her and through the car toward him. She smashed into a pole along the way, the collision silencing her scream. Once she reached Vincent, her body cremated almost instantly, her hot, heavy remains falling in a heap on the floor. A cloud rose from the settling ashes.

He ascended, and the train car's roof dispersed as if he were moving through a mist. He looked down through the hole and saw Marsha's old, pious friends looking up at him. They clung to one rosary and continued to mouth their prayer as they watched him rise higher.

Remus stopped eating and watched its master float away, flesh still hanging from its jaw as blood was absorbed into its shadow. Remus let the meat fall from its mouth, the cowering passengers in his car whimpering as he moved. Remus threw itself into the window, which shattered easily. It clung to one of the girders and swung nimbly between the steel beams before landing in the traffic on the bridge.

Tires squealed and horns roared as Remus leapt from the nearest car to the highest truck and then back toward the train and up onto the bridge walking path. It snatched up a woman running on the path and impaled her on its claw. Clutching its meal, it bounded several yards and then leapt onto the bridge tower. It scaled the height and came to rest at its peak, staring out at its master floating high above the river. Yellow, purple, red, orange, blue, green, and black flowers sparkled vibrantly against white rippling fabric. Hermod's chocolate-skinned body contrasted with the garment and the vibrant flowers' dazzling effect.

Finished with the muscular young brunette who had been out for her morning run, Remus crawled to the edge of the bridge tower roof and scanned the bridge. A woman appeared and stood on the road not far from the tower. A second woman in dark robes stepped out of the thin air next to the first. Remus felt something approaching from behind. It turned to the south side of the river and watched as a green streak raced from up and around the bridge and several of its interlacing beams before landing in front of the two women who had appeared out of thin air.

<Crown Moon's servants are here,> Vincent said.

## SPASE HANGAR #8, SPASE HQ, CAPE HENLOPEN, DE

"Y'all ready?" Ford asked as rocket engines roared in the testing space on the third level.

"What?" Dara yelled.

"Y'all ready?"

"Is that your battle cry?" Dara replied. "You better put some bass in it." She stopped chewing her gum and smiled at him, then pursed her supple lips as if she were kissing something. "I'm just playing, sweetie. We're gonna go get this bitch for Sean. Right?"

Ford frowned and looked up to his left. Sean had a workspace just above Hangar 3. In the last year, he and Dara hadn't gotten many commissions that included Sean, but they often kept in touch. He and Sean would often sneak away to Vegas on weekends to watch fights, get wasted, and bitch about common woes, like how cheap and oppressive Gaskill was. They also shared quite a bit about their respective love lives with Dara and Ade.

"For Sean," Ford replied. He hated grieving. He was grateful that Dara was there to keep him from climbing into one of his holes and never returning. This one was going to be rough.

Ade overheard the conversation through her battle comm link. She grimaced, and her stomach churned. She opened her mouth to reply but could not voice a response. She had delayed processing the fact that Sean was dead. She would mourn after the battle, as she always had.

"Agreed," Cyral said. Though he was still in his workspace above Hangar 2, he was part of the battle comm link. He and Ade and Tig would join the second trip.

Hanuri stood next to Dara and remained silent. Ford nodded at Dara, then turned around and extended his arm. He waved his hand, and a rippling reflective plane spread out in front of him. In it he saw himself, Dara, and Hanuri standing behind him, workers servicing a manned drone twenty yards in the distance at Hangar 4, and sparks flying farther beyond at Hangar 7. The reflection dissolved as daylight poured through the door he had created to the northbound lanes of the Williamsburg Bridge in between Brooklyn and Manhattan. Dara stepped through first.

"Be safe," Ford said as he watched Dara step into the sunlight. He caught a whiff of coconut and lavender from her hair, and he inhaled it deeply.

Hanuri passed through the door next. Once she was on the other side, she drew in a long, deep breath and then exhaled it slowly. She sniffed the air several times. "A Void King is near," she whispered.

Only Dara heard this, and the title made her diaphragm tighten. She stopped and watched Hanuri walk and scan the bridge road, her robe snaking behind her like a long, dark, velvety tail. Dara often forgot that Hanuri's robes were actually violet. They'd spent so much time in the field over the last ten months that those details had become commonplace. The tightness in her diaphragm loosened, and she felt increasingly relaxed. Hanuri's presence was always a balm for her. Though she was still a bit leery of this Void King, she had faith in whatever Hanuri had faith in that they would be alright.

Mingo hovered over the bridge road just a few feet away from the door.

"Bienvenidos a Brooklyn, guapas," Mingo said, smiling at them. Dara did not smile back. Neither did Hanuri. She could see Ian's toxic "insides," corroded with self-loathing. *There are so many other bright, intelligent, kind, deserving Dominican brothers,* she thought. She wondered why such power had chosen this boy. Dara looked north at the midtown and uptown Manhattan skyline. Vehicles were creeping along in a large block on the southbound East River highway. Towers on Billionaire's Row jabbed at heaven. The Chrysler Building was dwarfed by its neighbors, glass giants glowing as blue as the sky. One of them obscured the view of the Empire State Building.

"Beautiful morning to try to die, huh?" Dara said.

"I'll see you on the other side," Ford said. He winked at Dara and closed the door.

"I have spoken with the police captain," Mingo said. "They have their orders to remain and respond as necessary, but they have been warned."

"Fuck them," Dara said. "Bruja, what's a Void King?"

Hanuri did not respond.

"Doc," Dara said, then frowned at Hanuri. "What's—"

<Remus,> Gaskill said, speaking directly into all of their minds. <We may never again have enough time for me to explain how dangerous it is. Do not underestimate it.>

"Well, that helps," Dara said, frowning as her eyes rolled around their sockets.

About twenty yards ahead of them in the center of the bridge was the stalled train. Half a dozen policemen and eight MTA engineers were helping passengers out of the rear entrance and down onto the tracks. About a dozen more officers lined along the track, ushering passengers away from the dangerous third rail and toward the service exit in the bridge scaffolding. Twirling red-and-blue lights were still approaching from the Manhattan end of the bridge in the northbound lanes. A blockade had formed on the Brooklyn side.

Dara squinted as she looked out and over the river. "There," she said. She pointed at the white dress shining in the morning light. She could barely see any part of Hermod himself.

"We have eyes on the target, Doc," Dara said.

"But not the Void King," Hanuri added. "It's watching us."

Mingo rose a bit higher into the air and looked around the bridge and its scaffolding. He spotted blood smears on the gray scaffolding just a few yards ahead of him. A trail of blood led up the bridge tower.

"I've got a trail," Mingo said. He continued to drift farther up and into the scaffolding, examining it.

"Heads up, Mingo," Dara said. "Don't wander too far."

"I'm a big boy," Mingo replied.

Hanuri stepped closer to the bridge railing.

"Too much for one body," Hanuri observed. She could not look away from Hermod, unable to decide whether she was feeling pity or admiration. Her stomach tightened, and she shuddered. Despair and death radiated from the stalled J train, manifesting in her as hot pressure in her sinuses and around her eyeballs.

"Guíame, reina," Hanuri whispered. She turned to Dara, behind her. "Cover me," she said. "I will need a moment to conjure my familiars."

Dara nodded in reply.

Hanuri opened her mouth and then hesitated for a moment. Even if SiqT' Qkar answered her and did not smite her, she would still have to seal the spell with a touch. Risks dueled in her mind as she took a deep breath.

"Hanuri SiqT' Qkar. SiqT' Qkar T'len T'len Quiox," Hanuri chanted, repeating the words over and over. Her shadow spread along the ground and engulfed her entirely, transforming her into a swirling wisp of shadow.

"SiqT' Qkar T'len T'len Quiox. Hanuri SiqT' Qkar."

## WILLIAMSBURG BRIDGE, NEW YORK CITY, NY

Mingo stopped his ascent and examined the smear of blood on the scaffolding just two feet ahead of him. The trail was wider, fresher. He was close. He looked up and could almost see the top of the bridge tower just fifty feet away. Beneath the cap of the bridge tower, where the cables joined, he thought he saw something move. Darkness spread down from the shadow beneath the cable joints. Steel and cables and the clouds and sky beyond disappeared in the shadow. Mingo recoiled and gasped.

A bloody corpse flew out of the shadow at him. He barely dodged it, drops of blood splattering on his face. As he watched it fall, Remus lunged out of the shadow next.

<!>

Its psychic roar obliterated Mingo's resolve. Remus gripped his throat and held fast, dragging Mingo down into freefall. They plunged several yards before colliding with a steel tower beam. Remus gripped the beam with its free arm and both feet to stop their descent. The creature squeezed Mingo's neck as hard as he could. Its claws dug deep into his skin but did not break it. Mingo gasped and punched at the creature, but his fists passed through its shadow flesh just as they did the air. Green electric currents crawled out of Mingo's eyes and mouth as he gasped through the creature's impossible chokehold. Remus drew Mingo to within inches of its gaping jaws and then threw him down. Mingo struck the bridge tower, bending the steel beams where he collided with them. He bounced away and struck a police cruiser on the southbound bridge road. It crunched beneath him, flames erupting from one side of the hood.

Remus landed on the northbound road near a blockade of policemen. Several officers opened fire. It approached them and locked eyes with the nearest man, Officer Louis Kolbeggan. He immediately dropped his gun. The muscles in his arms, legs, back, and neck all tensed, and he started trembling and sweating. Warm urine spread down his leg as Remus approached and then pushed its open hand deep into the officer's abdomen. It grabbed the officer's intestines, stomach, and liver and pulled the handful out of him, throwing it onto the road. The steaming carnage oozed next to the rest of Officer Kolbeggan's trembling, dying body. The other officers scattered and hid behind a nearby cruiser. Officer Wellesley was next.

Remus's call echoed in Vincent's mind. Something must have really upset it. The psychic bellow roused him like the cries of the host used to, when they would ride beside him and the Rock on their way to break white men. Back then they were all filled with a zeal for justice. "Nigger justice" was what the white preachers used to call it back then in their sermons, which denounced slave life and encouraged slave murder.

Vincent blinked several times and broke his reverie. He remained fixated on One World Trade Center, the Freedom Tower. He'd never dreamed he might see something so beautiful. His awe at the structure melted as he wondered who owned this marvel and all the others. Who didn't own them?

"Crackers!" Vincent spat out the word and clenched Hermod's jaw as tight as he could. "They won! Look at this kingdom. Where's ours? Where's mine?" He smiled Hermod's smile, and Hermod's eyes lit up and shone. Only Lee and Granny had seen this face.

"We'll ask Crown Moon," Juno whispered.

"Yes, dear," Vincent replied. "They will take us to Ninixetlau." He looked at Dara and Hanuri assembled on the bridge. "And we will ask them ourselves."

Vincent broke his fixation with the tower and then turned to the bridge. The beauty of battle enthralled him, Dara in particular. She reminded them of Josephine, one of the seamstresses they'd saved near Nashville. Josephine had ridden with them for three breakings and then decided to make her home at the Macintosh Plantation in Virginia. Caramel-reddish skin and hips contoured like a river. A sight to behold such a Black woman.

The tedium and spontaneity of battle dismayed him though, especially surprise developments like the shadow on the bridge that he did not recognize. Though it was only a shade, a simple weapon in SiqT' Qkar's arsenal, whoever had conjured it was powerful. There were always surprises in battle, but a foe in league with SiqT' Qkar in any capacity could make a battle far more troublesome. He didn't want to have to destroy this beautiful, powerful girl because of Ninixetlau. SiqT' Qkar must have blessed her for a reason.

He traversed the 500 feet he'd drifted away from the bridge in three seconds and then stopped a dozen feet above Remus and Officer Wellesley on the bridge.

Green lightning streaked from the southbound side of the bridge and struck a police cruiser next to Remus. Windows exploded from the cruiser, and flames raced through the interior and crawled out and sped along the exterior. Mingo flew from the southbound side of the bridge and steadied himself a few yards away from Remus and Vincent. A small black cloud gathered behind him and swirled its wisps around his fists. Lightning danced from fist to fist. Remus tore off Officer Wellesley's arm and threw it at Mingo. It launched Wellesley's remains at the three officers surrounding it, firing rounds in vain. Remus leapt into the air and hopped from the bridge tower to the road. Mingo twirled his body in midair to lock onto Remus and in doing so locked eyes with Vincent. His impulse to chase Remus diminished, and he stopped short.

<I've got this,> Vincent told Remus, still staring at Mingo. The creature turned and galloped toward Dara and Hanuri some twenty yards away.

Vincent descended to the road. A police helicopter flew above him, and he watched it perform a U-turn around the bridge tower and hover there.

Mingo charged at Vincent. Vincent dodged and watched him ascend and reposition himself to charge again. His dark cloud appeared deep navy in the hot, bright morning light.

"Of course, it's you," Vincent said. "Hermod has shown me a lot about you."

Blue flames ignited around Vincent and crawled over his shoulders and arms and along the hems and folds of his dress. Mingo tightened his fists and raised them, and a thick green lightning bolt sliced down at Vincent. Vincent jumped aside and then looked at the smoldering hole where the lightning struck the road.

Mingo accelerated down toward Vincent, but four writhing pillars of blue flame shot up from Vincent's scorching aura. Each was twice as thick as the beams in the bridge, swirling and writhing through and around each other. Mingo halted his advance and watched the pillars of flames dance. Heat pushed into his eyes and mouth as the writhing arms reached out at him. He could smell his Ojun battle suit smoldering. Small cables on the bridge's suspension network melted and snapped.

"Freeze!" Vincent heard an officer scream from about twenty feet away. He turned to face the officer while the blue flame pillars danced with Mingo above and behind him. NYPD cruisers were parked haphazardly along the bridge. Officers were peeking out from behind the vehicles and pointing their weapons at Vincent. Sirens were screaming and flashing red-and-blue lights were approaching from Manhattan in the distance.

"I said freeze!" Officer Thomas shouted again.

"I'm not moving," Vincent replied.

Officer Thomas fired two rounds and then the eleven officers nearby joined him. Bullets exploded in the air just inches from Hermod's skin. It had been ages since Vincent had faced a bullet, and they were just as boring today as they had been hundreds of years ago. The officers' blitz would not avail them. Vincent could feel the mortal dread in all of them, but four of them radiated murderous hatred. Even a young chocolate-skinned boy could have felt it, but Vincent was far beyond boyhood; he could see it in them.

Screams cracked the air even before the threat was visible. White-hot fire spread around Officers Tuni, Yee, Thomas, and Bruckley. The other officers immediately stopped firing and abandoned their burning colleagues, retreating behind some parked cruisers farther away. Officers Tuni, Yee, Thomas, and Bruckley were reduced to piles of clumpy ash, and the roar of flames filled the air again.

Dara had been watching Remus from afar as it maimed several of the officers farther down the road. The Void King. Though she could see Remus moving and bodies around it responding to its movements, it appeared to be without depth, as if it were only the shape of a monster. It was as dark as the shadows she'd seen in outer space, the only void she'd ever known, and that one had scared the piss out of her. Infinite uncertainty at every turn. No thanks. This one was alive, or was it undead? Dara struggled with this.

It bounded toward her, and she felt tightness deep in her abdomen. She stopped breathing and looked at her feet. Her leg muscles tensed as if they might cause her to turn and run. She allowed herself to breathe again and faced the foe approaching her. She'd seen a *lot* of shit since she had started contracting with Ade and then Gaskill, but a living void was new for her. She fought her fear as she wondered if she would be impervious to it too.

"Only one way to find out," Dara whispered. "Team Two, you guys comin'?" she asked much louder. She took another deep breath and then slowly closed the gap between herself and the cloud that Hanuri occupied.

"Deploying in three," Tig responded. "Two . . ."

Remus stopped its advance and crouched low to the ground. Dara watched the creature, awestruck. It was staring at her and Hanuri. She could feel it.

<Dara,> Gaskill called to her. Dara remained inert, transfixed by the creature, unable to move. He used her own cerebral cortex to shake her body. <Snap out of it.>

Dara steadied herself and shook her head. Surely the death awe was one of the creature's simplest tricks, and she had fallen for it head over heels.

"I see you, Remus," Dara said. She felt ashamed for having faltered. The cold, hard sensation melted into vengeful anger and spread through her body. She punched her right fist into her left palm.

Flickering ahead caught her attention. Dara saw the bridge and train tracks and downtown Brooklyn reflecting in a large circle. Then a doorway opened over the reflection, and she saw Ade standing in the SPASE hangar. Ade stepped through the door and onto the bridge, and Cyral floated through behind her. Tig, armored in an Ojun flight suit of his own design, flew out over the river. He was accompanied by four drones. As they flew up above the road, Tig swept his head to get a better view of the engagement.

Ford stepped through the door last, and it closed behind him. He pressed his left index finger into four places on his right breast. The suit morphed around his arm, and what was once a solid cuff liquified and flowed around his right forearm. His eye swept the bridge until he found Dara. Before he could smile at her, he saw the shadow moving just ahead of her. He froze and dropped his right arm to his side. It was heavier now that the Ojun cuff had completed its arm-cannon modification.

"Jesus," Ford said. "What is that?"

Remus turned its attention from Hanuri to the newcomers and then back to Hanuri. Then it launched itself into the air and lunged at the shade.

"The Void King," Dara replied. She turned around, and her eyes met Ford's. "Thought you knew."

"No, I did not," Ford replied as he approached her.

Ade had not moved. As she watched the creature approach, the impossibility of its formlessness made her skin crawl. Cyral was standing behind her, still absorbing the scene around him, scanning the minds of all the attendants: the officers just a few yards behind them, the frightened officers confronting Vincent farther down the bridge, Mingo frustrated and growing angrier, maimed passengers in agony dying in the subway car, and the anxious first responders trying in vain to save them.

"Are you ready?" Ade asked. She did not turn to look at him. She pressed her left index finger into her right breast three times. Her Ojun battle suit collar flowed around her face, and the substance crept up around her entire head and solidified into a helmet.

"I can taste the chaos," Cyral whispered. It was then that he registered Ade's question. "I am ready, yes," he replied. His Ojun collar responded to his thoughts and prepared a helmet for him. "Besides, I need a good fight. I'm low on kills this year."

"That doesn't surprise me," Ade said. "Scott never lets you out to play."

"I play," Cyral said. "Just not on the field. It gets boring."

"Oh, I don't doubt it," Ade said. "The smell of fresh death is invigorating."

"You kiss your mom with that mouth?" Ford asked.

"I ate her," Ade replied.

Ade laughed, and Ford did as well.

"Guys!" Dara said. "Battle faces."

Above the bridge Tig watched the police helicopter fly closer.

"Go," he said. The chopper immediately rose a little higher, the pilot inside struggling in vain to regain control. The helicopter made a U-turn and flew away on Tig's command until it reached 23rd Street. He turned to Remus and Hanuri and then to his right where Mingo was zipping around a flurry of swirling fiery tentacles. Hermod was standing on the bridge at the gentle end of the flailing blue flames.

"Hey, you!" Dara yelled, pounding her right fist into her left hand. Remus looked at her and then spread its arms down at its sides and splayed its claw-tipped fingers. She felt that it might have roared at her if it were a beast. And then it did, directly into her mind and soul. Its white eyes glared at her, causing her stomach to coil and all of her muscles to tense. She fell to one knee and took a deep breath.

"I'm not afraid of you," Dara said.

Ford approached Dara, aimed his fusion arm cannon at Remus, and fired. The fusion bolt passed right through it. The creature briefly turned its attention to Ford before it swung its large arm into the air at Hanuri. It grabbed the shade of SiqT' Qkar and pulled it away from her like a sheet from a bed. Exposed, Hanuri fell and collapsed onto the bridge.

"Bruja!" Dara screamed. She lunged at Remus. It dodged her charge and tossed Hanuri's shade aside, then dove at her. Dara landed some ten feet away and turned around to double back. Remus hulked over Hanuri and brought its claw down into her abdomen, tearing a large piece of it away. Blood misted around them as Hanuri's entrails spread out onto the road, her shade drifting up and away.

"No!" Dara screamed.

Ford fired several more bolts at the creature, knowing they would not avail much but hoping perhaps he might get its attention.

Dara charged at Remus again, both fists extended in front of her. This time she pummeled its abdomen, and Remus was knocked away. It rolled several feet and then regained its footing and stood upright. Dara ran to face it.

Tig hovered above the bridge, surveying the scene. He nodded at the two drones to his right, and they darted to Dara's side. The three of them and Ford surrounded Remus. Ade and Cyral rounded the perimeter of their huddle and ran to Hanuri's side. Tig dove down toward the river, flew beneath the bridge, and emerged on the southbound side, approaching Hanuri from there.

"Tig," Hanuri said. "I . . . I need—"

"I'm here," Tig said. He was kneeling beside Hanuri. His drones were close, two hovering above and the others standing guard near Ade. Ojun gloves flowed away from his hands. He placed his bare hands on Hanuri's forehead. Her eyes were still bright and brown like almonds, though her skin was pale, and her black robe was thick with blood. She covered the open wound with her hands as blood spurted around her.

"Is it bad?" Ade asked. Tig turned toward her and nodded. She stepped closer and knelt on the other side of Hanuri.

"We have you, Hanuri," Ade said. Through the hole in Hanuri's body, Ade could see the bruja's blood-soaked robe on the ground. "We must hurry," she said to Tig.

Ade tapped her fingers into her left breast this time, and the waist of her suit peeled away, exposing her abdomen. Her gloves had also removed themselves. She took a deep breath and dug the fingers of her left hand into her body. The bones in her hand hardened and elongated, and her nails became hard, like a shovel. Blood spurted from her lower-right side, causing her to groan.

"You OK?" Tig asked.

"I'm fine," Ade said. She huffed out a deep breath and continued to dig her fused hand into her own flesh. She sharpened the bone on each side and sawed away a large chunk of her own abdomen. Even as she did, her flesh quickly regenerated, the angiogenesis beginning the moment she broke her skin.

Ade held the piece of her own flesh before her and then placed it over Hanuri's wound. Tig had been able to stop the excessive bleeding and had primed her immune system to accept Ade's flesh, lest Hanuri reject it before he and Ade could merge the women's DNA. Ade held the transplant in place and rubbed her hands over it, smearing their mixed blood all over the wound. Tig moved his hands from Hanuri's forehead to her abdomen and swirled his hands around Ade's. Hanuri closed her eyes, and her attempt to draw air into her lungs was successful this time. She had a diaphragm again.

"Maldito, maricon!" Mingo said. He was facing a wall of flame far too hot to penetrate. He flew straight up into the air and then dove beneath the south side of the bridge, stopping a few yards above the surface of the East River in the shadow of the bridge. He tightened his fists, and green lighting flew out of his eyes, extending several feet ahead of him. He charged up at the bridge and punched through the road just beneath Vincent.

Mingo stopped his charge and watched Vincent tumble through the air with the rubble. Then he charged at Vincent and gripped his neck, carrying them both out over the bridge and farther south out over Chinatown.

Vincent kicked at Mingo and winded him. Mingo released him and took a deep breath. Vincent steadied himself. He could hear people crying somewhere behind. Some were also shouting and singing a song he used to know:

Pray a little longer, O Lord!
Pray a little longer, Yes, my Lord!
Patrol aroun' me.
Patrol aroun' me, Yes, my Lord!
Tank God he no ketch me.
Tank God he no ketch me, Yes, my Lord!

Vincent felt a heavy pressure deep inside. He tossed Hermod's head to the left and right and scanned the city. It was coming from the south, near the building that looked like the obelisk in Egypt. Hermod's face sunk in and frowned.

"Who—"

"Putita," Mingo said, interrupting Vincent, who was clearly upset. "Look at you in a fucking dress. You gonna cry now too?"

"You have it in for my nephew, do you?" Vincent said.

"Fuck the both of you!" Mingo replied, spitting at Vincent. He clapped his hands, and lighting flared at Vincent. Vincent consumed the bolt in his hand. "You will pay for DR . . . .maldito Cocolo."

"Tank God he no ketch me!" Vincent sang and clapped to the line of the song. Hermod's eyes were moistening.

"Tank God he no ketch me, yes, my Lord!" Vincent sang and clapped again, and an explosive flash lit up the sky. Mingo shielded his eyes and closed them. He felt like fainting due to the heat in Vincent's wake. Heavy, burning phalanges dug into Mingo's neck and blistered his skin where they gripped it. Vincent smashed his other skeletal fist into Mingo's face, and blood exploded from his nose. Vincent reduced his flames then and wiped his left hand across Mingo's mouth, dabbing at his blood. He smashed his fist into Mingo's face again. Blood splattered along his left wrist bones and tibia.

"SiqT' Qkar Qaha!" Vincent whispered, drawing a figure eight in the air with his right index phalange.

"Qaha K'lir Syaow SiqT' Qaha!" Vincent said, these last words echoing several times.

Mingo shuddered. His head began throbbing and burning, a strange language echoing in his thoughts. He felt burning around both of his wrists, and his skin tingled all over his body. His vision blurred and faded, and he felt like he might swallow his tongue. He remembered Cyral's warning to him in the war room the day he left to defend his homeland against Hurricane Faust: "He will disintegrate you," Cyral had told him. "He will enslave you first."

Vincent pulled Mingo's face close to his black shiny skull. "Be a good boy," Vincent said. "Protect me."

Hanuri braced herself on one knee, Tig held her right arm and shoulder and assisted her as she stood up. Cyral and Ade backed away to give her room.

"Thank you, my friends," Hanuri said.

"Think nothing of it," Tig replied as he ascended. He saw Remus surrounded by Ford, Dara, and two of his Ojun drones. The creature hunched down on all fours and turned in a circle, its attention bouncing between the four of them as it swiped at them with its claws.

Hanuri's shade was hovering above the road, wafting in and out of the area where the train tracks lived in the center of the bridge. She approached it and raised her hand, and the shadow moved toward her and consumed her once again.

A swirling, rippling shade approached the group encircling Remus. Remus stopped thrashing and stared at the black mass approaching and then Remus pounced on the nearest drone and tore at it with its jaws. Remus ripped the arm out of the drone and flung the body at Hanuri's shade. Dara and Ford and the remaining drone dispersed as the shade approached Remus.

The black cloud diminished, exposing Hanuri's body. Much smaller now, the black shade swirled around her right hand. She threw that arm into the air and closed her fist, then whipped her arm back down to the road. A whiplash cracked the air, and Hanuri faced Remus, the shade manifested as a long black whip. She lashed it at Remus, and the creature hopped away. Hanuri cracked the whip again and a bright flash exploded where it lashed the void flesh on the creature's thigh. Remus growled and lunged at her, and she threw her left hand out, fingers splayed. A shadow wall rose from the ground in between them, and Remus crashed into it and rolled away. Hanuri stepped through the wall, and it disappeared. She lashed the black whip at Remus again, and it caught the creature's right arm and wrapped around it. They engaged in a tug of war until Hanuri dropped to the ground and leveraged her momentum to pull on the whip with all her strength. Remus lost its footing and was thrown across the road.

"Get him, girl," Dara said. She reared on her hind legs and charged at Remus. Thunder exploded above, and green lighting struck her down mid-stride. She screamed and crouched on the road as another bolt struck her. Several more bolts struck the bridge and cracked the road near Ford and Ade and the drone accompanying them. Hanuri stood fast and looked up at the source of the maelstrom. Tig and the two drones accompanying him flew south over the train tracks and the southbound side of the bridge. Cyral rose above the road and caught a bolt in his hand, then tossed it back up into the air and sped away from the bridge, out over the river. Ford appeared in the air a few feet above him. He hovered there and watched the bolts striking down, destroying much of the bridge where they had been standing.

"He's got Mingo?" Ade asked. Cyral saw her ducking and rolling toward cover at the edge of the road and the train tracks.

Hanuri was standing not far from Ade. Remus a few feet in front of her. She raised her whip into the air to lash it down at Remus, but before she could, a bolt of lightning struck her. Remus vanished in the same instant. Though Hanuri was unscathed, she was startled, and in the brightness of the flash, she had not noticed Remus swarming in a black cloud. Its void spread quickly at her and obscured its presence. A claw emerged from near the edge and grabbed Hanuri's left leg and flung her out over the river. From above, Ford watched Hanuri fly over the bridge. He opened a door, and she exited above the walking path on the bridge.

Disoriented, Hanuri fell onto the walking path. She stood up and watched Remus creep from the shade of the bridge. It lunged at her, and she swirled her whip around it. She felt it lash the creature's chest. It recoiled and glared at her.

"Bruja!" Dara said from the road. "You good?"

Hanuri locked eyes with Remus as it flew toward her. Unblessed eyes would only have seen shadow, formless void racing through the air. She could see the Void King in all its accursed detail, its gaping jaw with fangs bared, its claws just inches from stabbing into her flesh, and the faint swirls of blue in its fine fur, details that only a few had seen and lived to tell of. Hanuri closed her eyes, and Remus passed through her and landed on the road behind her. She spun around and cracked the shade whip in the air.

Remus stood inert and stared at Hanuri for several seconds. She could feel the creature's fury tearing at her mind as it prepared a second attempt to rend her body. Her flesh was defiant. Remus stooped and scraped its claws into the road again and again. Shadow swarmed around it and spread around the bridge corridor.

"I'll be fine," Hanuri said.

"Never had a doubt," Dara replied. She instinctively rolled to her right just in time to dodge another bolt of lightning. She stood and looked up at the sky, using her right hand as a visor. She could see the dark navy looking cloud above. Green flashes dazzled the sky as she jumped toward the train tracks. She stepped into the shaded area and pressed her back against the steel beams that separated the two lanes of bridge road. She turned to her left and made eye contact with Ade, who was just fifteen feet away huddled with one of Tig's Ojun drones. Ade and Dara each took a deep breath.

"I saw this," Cyral said. "I told you all." He was still hovering above the river with Ford.

"You sure didn't do anything about it!" Tig replied. He and the two drones accompanying him were above them all now and moving toward Manhattan.

"I don't think it would be wise to try now," Cyral said.

<You doubt yourself yet again,> Gaskill told him.

"I've killed Mingo's incoming comm," he said to the team.

"Can you stop him, Scott?" Cyral asked.

"Vincent and Juno are friends of SiqT' Qkar," Gaskill replied. "I am not."

<Who are your friends, Winston?> Gaskill spoke directly to him.

<Not now, Scott,> Cyral replied. He stared at the spot where Hanuri had nearly bled out on the bridge and thought about how impossible it was to make human friends. Even the friends he had might die at any moment. He chuckled silently.

"Hell, maybe I should go fuck some demons too, huh?" Cyral said.

"I thought you were already," Ade replied. Dara laughed.

"Guys!" Ford said.

"Where is Hermod?" Tig demanded. He and his drones were hovering slowly above the highway. He was not registering anything unusual on his radar. The hologram projecting in front of him was showing several dozen demis scattered throughout the Lower Manhattan and Hoboken New Jersey areas. Each of them was marked with a green square. None of the signatures were Hermod.

"Tig, find him," Dara said. "We'll handle Mingo. Ford will be on your tail eventually."

"I'll follow you, Tig," Cyral said. He rose above the bridge tower and flew toward the Manhattan end of the bridge where he met Tig and his drones.

"Dammit!" Tig said. He decided it was time to take a closer look. He closed his eyes and focused on the sight of Hermod, burning on the bridge. Focusing harder, he broadcast this memory of Hermod to as many of the millions of cameras and microphones and receivers that he could. He felt his grip on his drones slipping and eventually lost complete control of the one accompanying Ade, and it reverted to autonomous AI mode. He felt like a balloon was filling up in his head. Half of the circuits in downtown Manhattan were searching frantically for Hermod.

"Are you getting anything, Doc?" Tig asked.

"On Vincent?" Cyral asked.

"Hermod," Tig said, sounding curt. "I can usually grab him on the gravity scale, but it's giving me nothing. I just pinged every camera, phone, computer, and receiver in the downtown area, and I've got fucking nothing."

"I've got a faint signal," Cyral said. "He's close, but . . ." He squinted his left eye and twisted the same corner of his mouth and shook his head. "Downtown. It's always like this." Cyral had always attributed it to the density of people below Canal Street in Manhattan. "Lot of noise to sift through."

"Hermod used to tell me the same thing," Tig said. "Says it's haunted down here."

"Hermod is in Chinatown, heading south," Gaskill said. They both looked southwest past the Manhattan Bridge and flew toward it.

"Where is he going, Scott?" Tig asked.

"The singing and shouting," Gaskill said. "The brothers and sisters."

Gaskill was silent for several seconds. Tig and Cyral heard an explosion behind them. Cyral turned and saw smoke rising from the Williamsburg Bridge.

"Scott, it's no time to be vague," Tig said. "What's—"

<You still can't hear them?> Gaskill asked Cyral, frustrated. <Even now?>

<Sir, I—> Cyral paused. The scolding tone in Gaskill's voice was destabilizing. <Can this wait?>

<Such a waste, Winston,> Gaskill said.

Cyral frowned. Several things were going wrong. He didn't like being disarmed during combat, he didn't like being called Winston, and he didn't like being called an underachiever.

"Who am I listening for, sir?" Cyral asked, his voice lower and the words coming out sharp.

"Hermod was right," Gaskill said. "They're singing and shouting on Duane and Broadway. They always do. He'll join them."

Cyral felt a hardness in his throat. It was as if Gaskill were speaking in riddles. The thoughts were scattered and unsure, afraid even. Cyral struggled not to be angry and unnerved. In the past fifteen years he'd not known the doctor to fear anything. Neither had the doctor ever upbraided him in such a way while in the field. Gaskill had repeatedly chided him in private for "squandering his omniscience."

"One day you'll speak with the dead," Gaskill had told him, a few times. Cyral had always assumed the doctor was kidding in his cryptic way about mortality or some other macabre aspect of life. And yet it made sense to him. There was a density of souls in downtown, many of them tortured. Between the African Burial Ground and 9/11. Lonnie's. How many others were screaming and shouting right now? Then it occurred to him that this was probably why he couldn't hear any of the living.

Tig was beginning to accept the reality of the coming confrontation with his friend. He'd been unable to sleep since the events at Lonnie's. Hermod had told him about the shouting and crying at the African Burial Ground on Duane many times. Hermod routinely avoided that part of town because of it. It enraged him, is what he had told Tig a few months ago. He described it as the feeling one got after watching a civil rights documentary and wanting to smack a bunch of white people. In reality, neither of them had been in fear of their lives from white people for some years, but the feeling, the burden, was still clear. What disturbed him even more was that the African Burial Ground was just a few blocks away from Lonnie's. It had barely been two weeks since Lee's murder. Tig felt waves of grief wash over him, and he struggled to repress the events of that night as he and Cyral slowed and hovered for a bit and scanned the area.

"There," Cyral said. He pointed to a train of screaming police cars racing down Center Street and Broadway.

## ATLANTIC OCEAN, 1,000 MILES FROM THE US COAST

Sean could discern motion and depth and light, although everything was still pitch black. He'd been awake for about ten seconds. It was a strange waking state, though; he couldn't really remember anything. And he was not afraid. He felt weightless and yet he could tell that he had a body, that he was separate from the dark world that surrounded him. But he couldn't feel himself, the weight of his head, the pulse in his fingertips, his toes knocking against each other. Nothing. But he could feel. He felt like he was being pulled down, slowly. He was drifting on something. He felt a familiar pressure all over, and he thought he might be underwater, but something about the sensation was off. He struggled to distinguish whether he was dreaming or awake.

*Why isn't it cold?* he wondered. *I don't feel wet.*

His mind raced, and he tried to take a deep breath, only to realize that he was not breathing. Panic swept over him then. He wanted to thrash his body around, but it wouldn't move. He couldn't feel his diaphragm pulling, his chest expanding, or his arms or legs, floating or laying. He could not orient himself in space, but he could feel that he was separate from it. He wanted to look down at his chest but could not. He could not feel his neck or his head and yet he knew he was there. Falling? Floating? Both?

A small light approached him in the darkness. As it drew closer, he saw a form around it and several other sparkling spots orbiting the brighter light. Then he saw sharp teeth aligned in small menacing gaping jaws just beneath the light. Tendrils wafted around the creature, their tips twinkling. Sean recognized it was an anglerfish approaching him and was relieved despite its grotesque appearance. He felt relaxed, but he couldn't exhale, couldn't feel his shoulders drooping or his stomach loosening. The fish swam up close to him and remained in place. He felt the water shifting around him but couldn't place the sensation on any particular body part. In the light that the fish's tendrils provided, he could barely see its fins wafting beside its round, smooth body, the pitch-black ocean swallowing its hind parts in shadow.

Sean yearned to touch the anglerfish. He needed proof that he wasn't dead, or worse, undead. He focused hard on the fish and stared into its jaw. He wanted his hand to appear and to stroke the fish and scare it away. But nothing.

"Fuck!" He heard his voice, and it startled him. He was sure he had not opened his mouth, and yet he could hear his own voice as if he had done so.

What happened? Was he paralyzed? If so, how had he ended up so deep in the ocean? He knew that his flight suit had a day's worth of oxygen storage and could also protect him from deadly climates and extreme-pressure environments, but it could also float.

*Where is MASS? Yes! MASS!*

They were flying and then . . . there was excruciating pain, unlike anything he'd ever experienced. He'd been shot, stabbed, bludgeoned, awake during intensive surgery, twice, and he'd endured psychic pain-center attacks and even third-degree burns. But nothing like that. He was unsettled even recalling it. Had he managed to eject the escape pod? If so, where was it? Had he ejected the escape pod and then ejected himself from it? That would explain its absence, but . . .

The anglerfish turned and swam back into the shadows. Its movement distracted Sean. His thoughts unchained, and his mind went quiet. He followed the fish through the ocean. For now it was his only proof of life. He was beside it for a moment and then beneath it, looking up into its belly, and then above it suddenly, and then he was in front of it looking into its maw. Something tickled him, and a moment later he was watching a giant squid as well as the anglerfish. Its enormity startled him, and he was aggravated by the darkness. He surveyed them both with the same focus and intensity, yet the two creatures were fifty yards apart. It was so dark! He wanted so badly to see a little better.

*Fuck!*

He felt what he might have described as being shaken awake by an ejaculation. Head, arms, chest, loins, feet, hands, he felt whole again. Glistening wisps of Ojun floated around him and then disappeared into the sea. The squid's tentacles no longer tickled him but instead wafted just a dozen feet away from him. A bright light shone from near his left shoulder, exposing the creature completely. In the distance shadows large and small swam in and out of the beam of light. He was captivated by the squid. Suddenly, he could see its vital signs and a variety of metadata about the squid's scientific classification, all of the information that might have appeared in the holograms inside MASS. The squid appeared in infrared now, and the shadows in the distance turned into orange, yellow, and red balls. There were many more outside of the beam of light as well, all floating in nothing, though he could feel the water on his body.

He raised his hand in front of his eyes, and its black silhouette obscured the green, red, and orange infrared signatures of sea life. At his thought, his vision reverted back to the human spectrum. He pulled his hand into the light beaming from his chest and shoulder. He could see the creases in his palm and the halo of his fingernails peeking above his fingertips, veins snaking down his wrist and forearm. All of him was sparkling dark Ojun. He realized he was not breathing, and he felt as alive as he had just hours ago.

*09:58:45 AM EST* flashed in his mind.

*"Fuck, Mingo, give me a break!"* Dara said.

*"We need an offensive, immediately,"* Ade said.

*"Dammit, Dee,"* Ford yelled. *"Just fly!"*

The squid was about twenty yards away now, enveloped by the beam.

There was a battle, and his colleagues needed him. He needed an emergency slide to join them. He opened his mouth to voice the command and then stopped. He brought both hands to his head and felt his face, his eyes, his nose, his lips, even the fine hairs of his buzzed head. How could this be? Everything was there, soft and fleshy and fuzzy and prickly where it needed to be, even in this extreme subaquatic pressure and freezing cold. He did not doubt that the attributes were the result of the Ojun's atomic sorcery. Yet, he was not afraid. He felt like something had been set right.

Ford's last command was still fresh in his memory. He replayed it, the exact recording, once more in his mind.

*"Just fly! Dammit!"*

He empathized with Dara's fear of flying and darkness. He had also been lost in space but not nearly as long as she had been.

*"Just fly! Dammit!"*

A bright satellite map of the Atlantic seaboard overlaid the deep black ocean. It was as seamless and perfect as his thoughts would allow. His coordinates were marked by a pulsing green icon. In the open Atlantic. The map disappeared, and he saw the map with the satellites as his eyes, the smoke billowing from the Williamsburg Bridge. Six pulsing green icons indicated his colleagues' positions on the bridge. Four more were in Chinatown. They were approaching a red pulsing icon on Duane Street. Red-and-blue lights twinkled in a line extending up Center Street.

"Ford," Sean said. "I need you to do exactly as I say."

## SPASE HEADQUARTERS – WAR ROOM A – CAPE HENLOPEN, DE

In the war room, Gaskill watched the battle unfold from all of their perspectives except Sean's. Each one played out on the LED wall in front of him.

Gaskill smiled even as fear clawed at his insides. He had seen Sean's fall and assimilation with the Ojun in a vision five years ago, one so peculiar and frightening that he had dismissed it as nonsense, a riddle in the night, but he had not forgotten it. It had gnawed at him all those years and today had finally totally eaten its way through the reality that Gaskill had been trying to orchestrate. The horrid vision was the only reality now. He had stopped guessing since Hermod's infernal RSVP interview. Lee's death, Hurricane Faust, and now this resurrection had aligned perfectly with his vision. He had seen Mingo's corruption as well, even before his brave pupil, Cyral, had foretold it.

Another warrior would be tested, the boy would face his kin, and then the end. The end.

Gaskill closed his eyes and then turned away from the battle broadcasts. He kept his smile and clenched his eyes harder.

He was glad the Ojun had chosen Sean. Such a bright mind and now with such strength. Perhaps the vision would remain folly. Perhaps reality would yield to Gaskill again and not the chaos afoot.

## WILLIAMSBURG BRIDGE, NEW YORK CITY, NY

"Get . . . the . . . fuck . . . out!" Dara said. "Sean, is that actually you?" She stood up from her crouching position, and a bolt of lightning struck her right arm. Her body was thrown to the ground. "Fuck, this," Dara said as she stood up and massaged her right bicep.

Ford uncurled himself from his huddle and leaped to his feet. One of Tig's drones was rising from the ground to his right. It was hard to see anything beyond the drone. He looked up and struggled to see the sky through the cloud of smoke and dust rising around them.

"Sean?" Ford asked, incredulous.

"At my coordinates," Sean said. "In three . . ."

Mingo's lightning flashes blinded Ford for a moment as he launched himself into the air with the aid of his battle suit. Clear from the dust cloud on the bridge, he could see Mingo hovering a few yards farther away, lightning discharging from his clenched fists.

"Two . . . one. Now!" Sean shouted.

Ford winked. The air above and below Mingo shimmered, and Mingo's back briefly reflected in the portal above him. That door opened first, and from thin air, a cascade of the ocean swept over Mingo. He braced himself in the impossibly heavy torrent, much of which was falling into the door just a few feet below him, which he had not seen. Ford watched the door like a hawk.

Deep in the ocean hundreds of miles away, a whirlpool twisted rapidly in the door in front of Sean. Using infrared vision, he could see Mingo on the other side. He reared his right fist and jet propelled himself through the door and into the Manhattan morning light.

Sean smashed his fist into Mingo's collar, sending him hurtling into the door beneath him. Ford had opened the exit just immediately above, and Mingo flew out of it and then back into the entry door. Sean moved several feet away from the trap and watched Mingo fall over and over through the set of doors.

"Nice work, Ford," Sean said.

Ford hovered not far away. He chuckled at the sight of Mingo flailing and tumbling between the portals. He was hesitant to face Sean. Then he braced himself and turned his full attention to him. Sean appeared without a face. His body was also smooth and without any distinguishing features in the same way that MASS had been. He looked like a man-sized version of the machine.

"Dude!" Ford yelled. "What's—" He struggled to determine which question to ask first. He was elated, confused, and dismayed all at once. MASS was usually much larger than the humanoid that he was looking at now. Had it reconstructed itself after the attack into this, a new suit for him? It had Sean's voice and not that weird baritone AI that all of their Ojun equipment used.

"How?" Ford asked. "You . . . it's really you, right?"

"Yes," Sean said. "We've got tickets to UFC 300 next month right?" he said, though his tone lacked certainty.

"My man," Ford said. He smiled and tried his best to keep his eyes dry.

Sean descended to the road not far from Ade. Ford remained in the air a few yards away from Mingo, who was still flailing in his trap.

"Guys, I won't be able to hold this for long," Ford said.

Ade watched Sean's helmet morph into his face and his gloves morph into his large, rough, manicured hands. It looked like Sean but Ojun Sean. His skin and eyes were shimmery navy, black, green, and gray, like the fungus. His pupils were still gray-blue. She looked into them and welled up, tears teetering on her eyelids. She struggled not to let them spill. Sean smiled at her with shimmery black-green lips and stepped closer, their eyes still locked. His Ojun hair shifted gently in the air. He grabbed her hand. His felt rough and human, almost like his old ones, just heavier and stronger. He tugged at her, and she flinched against his pull. He persisted in his gaze, pull, and smile, and finally, a tear escaped and fell down her cheek. She dropped his hand.

"Welcome, back," Ade said. She wiped her arm across her face and then tapped her fingers into her arm console. Her helmet flowed around her face, and she turned and began marching away from him. Sean was grinning, the hand she had released still dangling at his side. Tig's drone was marching behind Ade. Sean hovered to catch up with them.

From a few yards away, Dara saw three silhouettes through the smoke and dust still lingering from Mingo's lightning blitz. One of them was shimmery and larger than the others. She knew it was Sean.

"What did you do?" Dara asked.

"We don't have time for questions," Ade said. "Hanuri needs assistance."

"Agreed," Dara replied. Her smile faded, and her jaw went slack. She could not take her eyes off of Sean. "What did you do, Sean?" she whispered. She shook her head, her open hand approaching her mouth. "I'll go—"

"No," Ade said. They all turned to look at her. "I'll go. You need to knock some sense into Mingo."

Dara nodded and then looked up at the trap that Ford had set. Mingo's silhouette was flashing green as it passed through Ford's doorways.

"We don't have long," Ford warned.

Dara walked out into the middle of the road, and Ford descended to stand with her.

"Come," Ade said to the drone. She ran to the steel beams separating the bridge lanes and climbed up the scaffolding and hopped the fence, landing on the walking path.

"Tracy!" Dara yelled. Ford was still airborne but close enough to hear her in person. "Straight ahead on three."

Ford nodded.

Sean lifted himself into the air, his sights set on Mingo. Something was shining in the middle of the road. He was instinctively drawn to it. As he neared the mass of the broken Ojun drone lying in the road, it melted and vaporized into a shimmering thick cloud. Sean floated into the Ojun cloud, and it receded into him.

"Two."

An explosion of thunder drew Sean's attention back to the sky. His eyes were immune to the brightness emanating from Mingo's flurry of lightning. A moment later a blast sent him flying away.

"One," Dara said. Shimmering revealed the door, and she thrust herself through it.

Sean steadied himself and braced for more lightning, but it did not come. He looked up and saw Dara gripping Mingo's torso with her thighs and pounding her fists into his head. A fusion cannon emerged from Sean's shoulder and locked onto Mingo.

"Dara," Sean said. "Heads up."

He fired, and with his integrated sight, he sent it directly to Mingo. Dara punched Mingo's collar, and he released her. She rolled away from him a moment before Sean's fusion missile exploded. Stunned, Mingo plummeted to the bridge. Dara pounced on him and smashed her fists into his back. Sean approached them as they writhed around each other. Dara held Mingo in a bear grip and tried to lace her arms in a figure four around Mingo's shoulder and head.

"Go!" She yelled at Sean as she and Mingo flopped around the road. "I got this."

On the pedestrian walkway above the main roads, Ade and the drone were crouched some twenty yards away from Remus. They watched it try in vain to maim Hanuri with its claws.

The Ojun drone unsheathed a battle staff and brandished the fusion cannon on its arm. It rose into the air and prepared to charge the Void King.

"Wait," Ade said. "Cover me."

The drone obeyed and moved in front of Ade, placing itself between her and Hanuri and Remus's fight. She struggled to continue to watch them. Their shadow dance was unlike anything she had seen before. She wondered what she might add to the choreography. The crunching sound inside her body grew louder and louder. The Ojun around her abdomen began to dissolve, revealing her skin on her back and obliques. Gross protrusions were rippling beneath her flesh as if something was crawling inside her. With a loud pop, portions of her back burst open on the left and right sides, and in the gush of blood, arms extended from each of the bloody holes. Ade knelt and held her face in her arms the new ones grew from the bloody wounds in her back. The hand on the new left arm melded into a claw with three thick fingers tipped with long, sharp bone talons. The second right arm was identical to the first and set in a new shoulder grown on top of the original. Ojun spread quickly around the two new appendages, sheathing and fortifying the claw and arming the second right arm with an Ojun battle staff. Ade stood and aimed her fusion cannon and fired it at Remus. The blast melted the pedestrian path barrier fence behind the creature. Remus stopped and stood tall and faced her. Hanuri was still for a moment. She looked at Ade and smiled.

"Welcome, sister," Hanuri said. Then she lashed her whip at Remus and charged.

Ade fired her cannon again and then sprinted toward Hanuri. The Ojun drone sped out in front of her and struck at Remus with its staff.

# JUNO'S REVENGE

## AFRICAN BURIAL GROUND NATIONAL MONUMENT, NEW YORK CITY, NY

A choir of voices echoed in Hermod's body. Juno danced it around the yard and entryway of the African Burial Ground. Strangers ignored her as they walked by. She hiked up her dress and tossed it around as she bumped and scooted her way across the African Burial Ground plaza, singing:

> I don't feel weary and noways tired,
> O glory hallelujah.
> Jest let me in the kingdom
> While the world is all on fire.
> O glory hallelujah.
> I don't feel weary and noways tired,
> O glory hallelujah.
> Gwine to live with God forever
> While the world is all on fire.
> O glory hallelujah.

She dropped her dress and sang and clapped in rhythm with the brothers and sisters. Slowly, some of them began to emerge from the wall near the burial mounds in the plaza. Some were coming from out of the federal building across the street. Others were rounding the corner from Elk Street.

Hermod stopped dancing and looked around the plaza as more brothers and sisters and sons and daughters gathered around. Most of them were singing with joy. Hermod's smile opened across his face as everyone gathered. Everyone looked so sharp, outfitted like kings and queens, some of them in western clothing with tight bodices and flowing lacy skirts and fine satin shoes. Men and boys were outfitted in perfectly tailored suits. Some wore the clothing that they used to wear before they were enslaved, before America. Beautiful tapestries fabricated from bark and animal skins and hand painted with plant pigments, embellished with gold, and gems. They wore fine leather and animal-skin sandals along with gold and gems draped on their arms and dangling from their ears and necks. A small crowd was gathering around Hermod now. She closed her eyes and felt them embracing her. Voices laughing and cheering. Bodies moving, shuffling around in circles, shouting and dancing. Brown faces smiling from ear to ear.

"Is it her?"

"No, it can't be."

"Has she come again?"

"Is it really?"

"Vincent and Juno done came?"

"They rose on up like Jesus did!"

"An' came on up to shout wit' us!"

"Jus' like Jesus did!"

"Not jus' Jesus but Juno too!"

"And Vincent too?"

"Let 'em shout wit' us!"

"Where is he?"

"They don came up north!"

"Yes," Juno said. "Yes, I came."

"Sir."

"I'm late," Juno whispered. "But I came."

"Is it done, Juno? Did you set it all right?"

"Did you and Vincent fix 'em?"

"I tried, young un," Juno replied. "We tried." Juno hung Hermod's head and clenched his trembling eyelids shut and frowned.

"You can stop tryin', girl."

"We's all free already!"

"Fix 'em Juno."

"Sir!"

"Hush now. We already free!"

"Amen."

"No ways tired, ya hear? No ways!"

"I'll try again," Juno said. "Live with God forever," she sang. "While the world is all on fire."

She whirled around, and the brothers and sisters dispersed. She couldn't feel them anymore. She watched as they carried their joyous song back into the burial mounds. Singing and shouting continued, as it always had.

Heaviness filled Hermod's chest, and he stumbled. Wind cooled the tears on his face. She stopped twirling, and the beautiful dress fell still around Hermod's muscly chocolate-skinned body. She knelt down on the sidewalk a few feet from the burial mounds and began to cry.

"Sir," the police officer said again, even louder. He gripped Hermod's shoulder. "I'm gonna need you to leave."

Juno continued to cry her tears to the ground.

"Sir!" the officer said as he shook Hermod. "Can you hear me?"

Juno heard a strange crackling noise and then the man was speaking to someone else about her. The officer shook her again, and she grabbed the officer's hand and crushed it, bones and all, in her grip. He screamed. She held the officer's hand as she stood up and twisted his arm around, crushing the radius and ulna inside. She stared into his eyes as pain brought him to his knees.

"Wheeler, you alright? Wheeler?" a voice from Officer Wheeler's walkie asked.

A few yards away, near the federal courthouse barricade, an officer hurried out of the small station booth he was manning and craned his neck around to find the source of the agonized cries. He approached three more officers as they were exiting the US Court of International Trade building.

"Over there!" he yelled, pointing at Juno and Officer Wheeler. They all drew their firearms and rushed across the street to the African Burial Ground memorial.

"Freeze!" one of them yelled as five more officers rushed out of the court building now.

"Wheeler!"

The voice over the walkie-talkie grew more frantic as Officer Wheeler's cries increased.

"Don't call me 'sir,'" Juno said to the officer. "Dammit! I'm not him!" She stared down into the man's eyes as flames licked around Hermod's. Wheeler stopped screaming, and his body trembled as sweat ran in rivers down his face and neck.

"I said, 'freeze!'" One of the officers surrounding Juno yelled.

Officer Wheeler's body burst into flames, and his cries roared through the narrow corridor nestled on Elk Street in Federal Plaza. The city tumult quieted as people nearby stopped to listen. In seconds the cries were no more.

Their hive just a five-minute walk away, the NYPD swarmed. Juno stepped away from Wheeler's body and looked around at the phalanx of officers and police vehicles pouring into Federal Plaza and Center and Duane Streets. More officers filed out of the courthouse across the street, and more and more were rushing from every corner of the plaza.

"Freeze!" the same office yelled at her again, shriller this time.

Juno clapped her hands. In an instant she was upon the nearest officer, Owen Peoples. She passed her hand through Peoples' protective body vest and the flesh beneath and pulverized his pectorals and ribcage. Juno pushed Hermod's hand farther until she felt Peoples' innards, hot and mushy. The hand lingered inside for a moment, and Peoples' body convulsed around it. Blood spurted out of Peoples' mouth and flowed heavily from it. Smoke issued from the wound in his chest, and his eyes caught fire. Juno removed the hand from Peoples' chest and let him fall to the ground, his boiling blood bubbling out of the wound, his ears, and his mouth. Viscous and dark like molasses, it pooled on the ground.

Thirty officers had cornered her now. Those at the front of their line opened fire. Some of them were firing handguns while a handful were also firing from their SPT-grade demi assault weapons. In the maelstrom Juno remained unfazed, the bullets exploding within inches of Hermod's skin and the SPT rounds, low-grade fusion bolts, evaporating into nothing.

Juno formed a circle in the air with Hermod's bloody hand. "SiqT' Qkar Qaha," she whispered. "Qaha K'lir Syaow SiqT' Qkar Qaha."

Peoples' blood spread down Hermod's wrist and over his forearm. Juno clapped twice. The gunfire ceased immediately.

In the morning sky, the pale crescent moon resembled a nail clipping before glowing yellow and then saturating to deep blood red.

Juno approached the line of officers and grabbed Officer Illig's hand and held it tight. Their fingers interlaced, his white ones with Hermod's brown ones, slick with Officer Peoples' red blood.

"Hermod!" Tig shouted.

Still holding officer Illig's hand, Juno looked around for the source of the call.

"Are they bothering you, ma'am?" Officer Illig asked.

"Hermod!" Tig yelled. "You have to stop this!"

"Yes," Juno said. She locked eyes with Tig. "Protect me, Officer Illig."

He raised his walkie-talkie to his mouth and activated the receiver. The radio issued a scratching noise in response.

"All Units," Illig said. The sound of his voice echoed from several radios in the line of policemen. "All Units, 10-13, 10-48. 10-13, 10-48." When Officer Illig was finished, he moved the receiver to Hermod's mouth.

<Vincent!> Juno heard the strange voice in her head just as she spotted Tig and Cyral and two pretend men floating above the crowd of police officers.

<I am *not* Vincent!>

Cyral gripped both sides of his head and plunged five feet before catching himself in the air and curling into a ball. White fire exploded over and over again deep inside his mind. The inferno expanded as far as his mind's vision, and void creatures of all sizes crept in and out of it. A sharp hiss scraped at his eardrums.

<Why don't you ride with us, beautiful?> a man and a woman and Hermod asked him.

"Get out of my head!" Cyral screamed. A small fissure tore through the ground just beside Juno and webbed away from her in several directions.

<I am Juno.> She clenched Illig's hand tighter and looked up at Tig and Cyral. "Nobody kills them," she said into Illig's radio. "Set it right!" She released Illig's hand and clapped twice.

The blood-red crescent moon slowly desaturated back to a pale cosmic nail clipping.

Illig and several of the officers in the crowd opened fire on Cyral and Tig. The other officers broke away and scattered onto Elk Street and farther up Duane Street. Tig told all of the SPT demi-Assault grade rifles to power down. They complied, to the astonishment of the officers wielding them. Their pistols were still functional, though, the hail of bullets continued.

One of Tig's drones reached out its hand, and all of the officers immediately collapsed due to the supersonic audio burst that it emitted.

Gunfire erupted from within the federal courthouse building adjacent to the African Burial Ground, followed by screams. More gunfire exploded from around the corner on Chambers Street. Sirens began wailing all around downtown Manhattan as the gunshots and screams echoed through the narrow streets.

The gunfire and screaming in Foley Square startled Cyral. Still shaken from Juno's psychic attack, he shook his head and took a deep breath. He turned and saw a group of people running from the Supreme Court building into Foley Square. They were being chased out of the building by police officers and into gunfire from officers gathered in the square. Cyral watched three officers chasing and firing at a group of people running in between the traffic on Center Street. A brown-haired white woman was hit in the head, and her blood sprayed across the windshield of the car that she collided with as she fell. An officer ran up to her and shot her again twice and then shot the bald white man in the car. The officer walked around the car and fired into the one behind it, killing the white driver. The backseat passenger doors opened on either side of the car. A rotund Asian American man fell to the ground on one side and a slim older white man scrambled from the other side. The officer jumped onto the car's hood and fired on the slim man. It was then that Cyral noticed something that sent a chill through him.

The officer stood on the car hood for a moment, scanning the car's interior. Then he hopped off the car and reached to open the front passenger-side door, but it would not budge. Cyral heard a woman's high-pitched muffled screams from inside the car. The officer pulled with all his might on the door, to no avail. He smashed his elbow into the window, and it shattered, freeing the woman's cries for help. He reached into the car and opened the door, then stepped back and held out his hand.

"You're safe now, ma'am," Cyral heard him say. "Please step out of the car now."

Slowly, the small dark-brown hand reached out of the car and took the officer's white one, and he knelt and pulled the trembling chocolate-skinned woman from the floor of the car and set her on the hood of it.

A white man with chestnut hair jumped out of a car some twenty feet away.

"Excuse me, ma'am," the officer said. He ran to the back of the car and then stopped. He raised his firearm and fired twice. A spray of blood exploded from the fleeing man's shoulder, and he fell to the ground. A nearby officer approached the bleeding man and fired three shots into the back of his head.

"Go," Tig said to his drones. "Stop them." One of the drones backed away and flew out over Foley Square. Using its sonic concussive blasts, it began nullifying every possessed officer that it could find. The other sped up and out over City Hall park to find and incapacitate murderous officers elsewhere. The third drone that accompanied Ade abandoned the fight with Remus to do the same. Gunfire, sporadic and incessant, like popping corn, sounded from all over the plaza and beyond.

Tig shuddered as he wondered how many officers had heard that call. "Team, be on the lookout," he said. "She's got the cops."

He descended to the ground and stood among the unconscious officers. Cyral rounded the corner from Foley Square and approached Tig and the pile of fallen officers.

Juno was transfixed by the peak of the Freedom Tower and the buildings adjacent to it. She'd seen marvelous things in the void but none like these. They enthralled her and repulsed her.

"Shrines to crackers!" Juno said, the last word louder than the rest. "It shouldn't have been this way," she whispered. "We were going to set it right! Traitors! It should have been ours!" She grimaced and threw her gaze at the burial mounds just a few yards away.

"Vincent," Tig said. "You have to stop this."

Juno flinched and slowly turned around. She gripped the front of her dress in her left hand near her chest.

"You are a fine man," Juno said. "Please do not call me by that name again."

"I won't let you harm my friend," Tig replied. He stepped closer to her and raised his arm. Listening to Juno up close, he shuddered at the sound of Hermod's voice. It was clearly Hermod's baritone but also very clearly not Hermod speaking. Tig could hear the undertones of what he imagined was Juno's soft, almost raspy alto. She spoke slower and with more conviction than Hermod. *This is what a killer sounds like,* he thought.

"I would never harm my kin," Juno said. "These crackers harmed him. I bet you Crown Moon harmed him." Juno raised Hermod's hand, and she could feel Tig's face in the palm, though he was two yards away from her. She closed her hand around his jaw, and Tig fell to his knees. "He's been harmed enough. My poor baby."

Cyral could feel the impressions of Juno's hold on Tig. He cast himself into Hermod's mind—a world of white-hot fire. He was engulfed, and the heat was almost unbearable, but he stood his ground, and the fire receded a few yards beyond him. Creatures, blacker than night, crawled and slithered and flew around him. The ground trembled beneath him as something large moved unseen in the fire.

<Stop this!> Cyral said to the inferno.

<What can you do, Alex?> Juno, Vincent, and Hermod said in unison. <You have Crown Moon's magic all over you. Do you even think your own thoughts anymore? Would you even know?>

<I'm not afraid of you,> Cyral replied.

<No?> They asked. <You should be. Aren't you mulatto?>

A bright flash pressed into Cyral's eyeballs and lingered even after he shut them. A wall of flames rushed him and scorched the left side of his body.

He closed his eyes as the fire washed over him, and he was expelled from Hermod's mind.

Juno released her hold on Tig, and he began coughing. Cyral was kneeling not far from him. Pain lingered over the left side of his body as if he'd just walked into a scalding shower. He could barely see, and a loud hiss was still scraping through his ears.

"This here boy is fond of you," Juno said, "or else I would have popped your traitor heads like grapes. Do you hear me?" she shouted, her voice echoing off the walls and buildings around her. "Ninixetlau! Your league is weak! Traitor! Show yourself!"

"Guys," Sean said. "I'll be at six o' clock in fifteen."

Glistening and almost translucent, Sean drove closer to them.

"MASS," Sean began, "Load up some quantum flares." It had not immediately occurred to him that they were already loading before he completed the sentence. He would have to learn to break the habit of dictating his commands.

He steadied himself in the air a hundred feet above Foley Square and then locked onto Juno standing at the African Burial Grounds.

"Fuck," Sean said. "Can you get her away from the sacred ground?"

Tig stood up and looked behind him. Cyral was standing not too far behind.

"Dammit, Sean," Tig said. "Just do what you're gonna do."

Juno grimaced at the glimmer above Foley Square.

"Weak, Ninixetlau!" Juno said. "I'll bring you their hearts and then you can tell me why you failed us!" She shot up into the air.

"I think you got your wish, Sean," Tig replied as he watched Hermod fly away from the African Burial Ground directly toward him.

Sean held out his palm, and from it, a small grenade flew out and away. At the same time, a larger missile, approximately ten inches long, emerged from a cavity in his shoulder and launched at Juno.

Juno charged through the missile's explosion and reached out her hands eager to throttle the meddlesome glimmering man. A much larger explosion went off behind her. A thick dark-green substance lashed through the air, and a tendril wrapped around Hermod's foot. Having found a target, the rest of the heavy taffy-like substance flung itself around Hermod until he was fully enveloped. The dark quantum polymer continued to whip small tendrils around itself for a moment and then it was still. Juno struggled beneath the cocoon, using all of her might to stretch the thing wherever she could, like a flailing child caught in an immense blanket.

Sean approached the polymer and hovered a few feet away from it. He could feel his Ojun body synching with the polymer's center of gravity. He ascended, and the polymer followed him.

"Have we talked about how we put this guy down?" Sean asked. "'Cause this surely ain't gonna hold."

"Bring him here," Gaskill replied.

"Ford, can you assist?" Sean asked. "I'm still kinda reeling from our last date, if you catch me."

"I hear you, Sean," Ford said. "I've got your coordinates. Give me—"

"Oh shit," Sean said. What would have been a vocal message and simultaneous onscreen message display from MASS were now just thoughts and sensations.

Sean stopped his ascent and began to head south in the hope of clearing Manhattan and taking the battle out to sea before . . .

"Fuck!" he exclaimed. "Polymer's disrupted."

An eruption sent him tumbling several yards off course. Almost immediately he could feel the heat against him. He steadied himself and, just by chance, dodged the gripping black phalanges.

"Is frustration your only defense, Ninixetlau?" Juno yelled. "You send buzzing flies instead of an army."

Juno turned about face and lunged at Sean again. The sight of the black skull disturbed him, though this new body did not startle or feel anxiety or pain in the same way as the old one. He grabbed the wrist bones and propelled himself into a spin and threw the skeleton away from him. Juno whipped out her arm, and a ray of atomic plasma flew out at Sean. He held his ground as the wave of plasma and fire washed over him. He felt the same sensation that he'd felt in the deep ocean. Being and not being, being here and there at once, incorporeality. Then, as the fire passed, and his matter reassociated, he felt whole again.

He charged at her, his fist growing to three times its size, he smashed it into the black skull. He gripped the skull in both hands, and a fusion beam issued from his chest, blasting Juno several yards away.

Juno steadied herself and ignited a brilliant aura of fire around her. She set herself to strike but looked down first. A hundred feet below them the beacon at the spire of the Freedom Tower blinked on and off. Sunshine glowed across the height of the building's southern and eastern façades and from above the square foundation was almost wreathed by daylight.

Juno remained still. The lower jaw descended and remained agape for several seconds before closing. Flesh and skin would have displayed Hermod's elated smile.

Sean rushed at her.

"Enough," she said. She held out her hand and swatted it down. Sean toppled to the harbor and steadied himself just barely in time to avoid crashing through the mall at Brookfield Place.

<Friend,> Juno called as she began her descent to the corner of Vesey and West Street. <Bring me your void.>

She had discerned that there were 1,058 African Americans still in the One World Trade Center building.

<Leave now,> she'd told them.

By the time she reached the street, one hundred of them had already exited.

## WILLIAMSBURG BRIDGE, NEW YORK CITY, NY

"Vanished?" Ford asked, incredulous. He stepped through a door onto the elevated pedestrian path on the Williamsburg Bridge and immediately threw his head around searching for Ade and Hanuri. They were directly behind him. He ran toward them.

"What do you mean Remus vanished?" Ford asked, dumbfounded.

"I mean just what I said," Ade replied. "We were fighting the thing, something weird happened, everything went black for a second, and then it was gone." She was kneeling, resting her two original arms on her knee, the other two holding onto her staff. Hanuri stood beside her with her arms folded over each other, the whip neatly coiled in her right fist.

"We've lost Remus?" Ford asked.

"I've got eyes on him," Sean said over comms. "Need all hands at One World Trade."

"What?" Ade replied.

"Now!" Sean screamed. He was hovering over West Street near the entrance to Brookfield Place mall.

"On it, Sean," Tig said.

"What was all of that gunfire earlier?" Ade asked.

"You don't want to know," Cyral replied. "Just put down any cops that you see."

"What?" Ade asked.

"Just do it," Cyral said.

"And then what?" she replied impatiently. "What's the endgame, Doctor?"

Gaskill remained silent. Suddenly, it occurred to Cyral that Gaskill had no plan.

"Can someone give me a hand, please?" Dara yelled and then groaned. "While y'all are yapping."

"We're on it," Ford said. He nodded at Ade and Hanuri. "Put on your smiley faces, ladies."

Ford's door opened onto the road level. He stepped through it after Ade and Hanuri.

"Guys! Ford!" Sean screamed. "All hands!"

"Heads up!" Dara screamed from behind them. "Why?" she whispered to herself.

A police cruiser was hurtling through the air at them. Dara sprinted at her comrades and shoved them to the ground as gently as she could. She rooted herself and caught the cruiser, then pivoted on her left heel and slung the car back at Mingo, who had launched it.

"Thanks for joining!" Dara said, turning around to face her teammates. She briefly rested her hands on her knees and took a deep breath, wiping her forearm across her brow.

"You're welcome," Hanuri replied, smiling at her. "We're delighted to be here."

Ford opened his mouth to reply, but the sound was cut short by a clap of thunder. An explosion of green light blinded him and sent them all flying.

"Is he still at it?" Ford asked. He rolled over from his back to his chest and lifted himself up on his hands and knees. "Have we figured out how to neutralize him?" He saw Dara charging down the road, Hanuri not far behind.

"This magic is strong," Hanuri replied. "I can break this spell, but I can't do it from afar."

"Sean needs y'all," Dara said. "Tracy, go. You have to take this to HQ. Let the doc take this on before more people die." She sighed. "I gotta stay here and take care of Mingo."

"Copy," Ford said. "He's all yours, babe." He stood up and looked at Ade, and they nodded at each other.

"He's *ours*!" Hanuri said, correcting Ford. "He needs a good spanking."

"Don't enjoy yourselves too much," Ford replied. He opened a door in between them, and he and Ade sprinted toward it and stepped through.

Dara was comforted by Hanuri's voice. She smiled and jumped into the air and balled her fists, raising them above her head. She locked eyes with Mingo just as she began to descend, and her smile tightened into a grimace. Mingo raised his hands, and the green glow surrounding his fists was just set to discharge when Hanuri's shade whip lashed out and wrapped tight around his head. Hanuri dragged him to the ground an instant before Dara smashed into his back. She growled at him and pounded her fists into his head and back repeatedly. The collision echoed in the bridge corridor. Dara snaked her arms and legs around Mingo's and pulled them away from his body as she rolled onto her side. With Mingo restrained, Hanuri wound the whip around his neck and shoulders.

"Snap out of it, Ian!" Dara said. "Fuck!" She struggled to keep her hold on him. "What the fuck? He's stronger than I thought."

"You are invincible, girl," Hanuri said through strained breath as she tightened the whip around Mingo's head and shoulders. "And I am a priestess of the Dark God, this blood spell will be broken."

"Make it quick, Bruja," Dara said, sweating a river.

"I will try," Hanuri replied. She closed her eyes and pulled tighter on the whip. "Hanuri SiqT' Qkar," she began. Green light shone through the partitions of the coiled whip around Mingo's head. "Qi'visu Qi'vu Qtkiin SiqT' Qkar. Hanuri SiqT' Qkar—"

Mingo whirled around violently despite Dara's restraint, shoving Hanuri several yards away. Hanuri stood up and continued her chant. "Qi'visu Qi'vu Qtkiin SiqT' Qkar."

Mingo, his head still wrapped in Hanuri's whip and his body still wrapped up in Dara's, rose into the air and smashed the two of them into the ground several times until Dara loosened her grip. He writhed free of her and kicked her in the sternum. Dara rolled on the ground and came to halt, coughing. Mingo hovered in the air, pulling at the whip wrapped around his head.

"Qi'visu Qi'vu Qtkiin SiqT' Qkar," Hanuri repeated. "Hanuri SiqT' Qkar." She clapped her hands twice, and Mingo stopped thrashing and fell to the ground, unconscious.

Hanuri ran to Mingo and gently unwrapped the whip from his head and then wrapped it around her own torso. She knelt down next to Mingo and held his head in her lap.

"We've got Ian back," Hanuri said. She turned and saw Dara several yards away, sitting cross legged on the ground propping her back up with her arms behind her.

"Fuck you, Ian," Dara said.

## ONE WORLD TRADE CENTER, NEW YORK CITY, NY

Cyral and Tig neared the Freedom Tower from West Broadway. When they cleared the corner of Vesey Street, they immediately noticed Hermod's dazzling dress on the corner of Vesey and West streets. People were running away from him in every direction, screaming. Some were being chased and hunted by police officers. A few civilians had managed to subdue a handful of officers and steal their weapons and then barricade themselves near the tower's park-side entrance. They were engaged in a shootout with several officers who were lined up outside in Memorial Park, adjacent to the building.

Policemen crouching near the Vesey Street entrance were being fired on by civilians inside the tower. Some of the officers were periodically firing rounds into the windows of the building across Vesey Street. Several people had walled themselves up in the Duane Reade pharmacy at the corner of Washington and Vesey just across from the tower. Freezers, pieces of the cashier's counter, and storage containers lined the windows and doorways.

Traffic had crawled to parking on every corner south of Houston Street as many people had abandoned their cars to try to find shelter from the NYPD onslaught. Police had set up barricades in Battery Park and Uptown at Canal Street prohibiting the flow anywhere. More officers were filing down West Broadway and clogging up Washington Street, hunting.

Tig lowered himself to the ground near Vesey Street. Cyral reached out his mind and put all of the officers surrounding the building to sleep.

Tig approached Juno. "Hermod!" Tig yelled. "Stop this."

"Or what?" Juno replied. A shadow spread from beneath her into a large puddle. It rose up into a pillar beside her and became the foe, Remus. The creature bounded at Tig, but just inches away from him, it disappeared into one of Ford's doors. The creature reappeared out over the Hudson River and fell into it without making a splash.

"He'll be back," Ford said as he stepped up beside Tig. Ade held back and stood still, deciding where to strike.

"Damn all of you!" Juno screamed. "If you knew whose battle you were really fighting. It was supposed to be a world for us!" She threw a ray of fire at Tig, Ade, and Ford, but it was cut short as one of Sean's missiles exploded at the base of Hermod's neck. Sean fired another polymer grenade and landed a hard kick in Hermod's ribs. Juno ignited at the sight of the grenade, and it was burned up in her aura before it could explode.

Cyral was still surveying the scene from above Vesey Street. He was startled by the woman's voice that had just screamed out. He'd been hearing Hermod's voice this entire time, as all of him was being commandeered by his selfish kin. But now he had heard a woman's voice, a sultry alto: Juno's voice

"You damnable coons are just like him!" Juno screamed. "You squander your souls for that weak liar. What service are you to your people?"

It was her. Cyral forced himself to remain present and not to dive too far into his amazement.

"I can show you how to fix it! How to bring our people to our rightful place in these states. I can level the field and plant new seed. Bring our people what is ours!"

"Behind you, Sean," Cyral said.

Sean turned around to see Remus's claw pass into him. The creature recoiled and pulled away. It clapped its hands and pushed them palms down, and Sean was flung to the ground and pinned down in the spot.

"You can still join me and enjoy your lives and the spoils. Stand down now, and bring me the traitor, Crown Moon."

Tig knelt and braced his right arm on his left and aimed. Ojun flowed around his right arm into a gamma burst cannon. "Heads up, guys!" He fired once and struck Juno and Remus, blotting out a section of the creature's torso and right arm. Remus knelt on the ground and bounded at Tig even as its dark countenance was reformed. Ade flanked the creature, using her staff to vault into it. Sean flew in from behind to tackle the beast, and the three of them rolled several yards into West Street.

Juno knelt on all fours, stunned by the gamma blast. She looked down at the black phalanges on the ground.

"I'll take it myself," Juno said. Kneeling in the middle of West Street, she looked up and saw the tower, a single-plane triangle extending high up into the air. She could barely see the tip from her position. She waited a moment and reared up on all fours and then launched into the air. She pushed with all the strength she could gather, and the pull of the building held her at 200 feet above the ground.

Tig and Ford were shaken to their knees. Sean was wrestling with Remus not too far away from them. Ade, also recoiling, paid close attention to Sean and Remus's struggle. Several car alarms sounded. So did many alarms within the Freedom Tower and the office building across the street.

Cyral could no longer see Hermod from his side of the tower, but he could see the water in the 9/11 Memorial reflecting pools splashing and jostling unusually. One of the pools' foundations was starting to crack. There was a loud squealing and wrenching noise, and the glass façade of the tower's lower floors purged their windows to the street. People in the lobby darted from the building. Some were crushed by falling fixtures and unable to escape. Crevices began to crawl around the street and sidewalks. Window and façade fixtures high up in the brick building across Vesey Street began to crumble to the ground. Several fissures opened up beneath Tig and Ford. They both hovered in the air and watched the tower's foundation crack and crumble.

"Fuck," Ford said. "You think?"

"Yes," Tig replied. He ascended about one hundred feet in the air and neared the corner of West Street. Cyral was right behind him. They saw the skeleton slowly inching its way up, its arms held out, palms up. Ford remained near the ground and watched the building's foundation crumble away, revealing the steel innards stretching and pulling beneath. A pane of glass sliced down in front of him and shattered on the ground. He instinctively ascended and hovered with Cyral and Tig.

They were all silent.

The American Express Tower across West Street purged its lower floor windows also. Alarms inside the building were sounding out of unison in a cacophony. Large portions of West Street buckled and crumbled into the subterranean spaces beneath the city.

Juno had risen ninety feet higher and was ascending with greater ease. The street behind her was refracting in her atomic aura. Blue flames exploded in a ring around her. More glass exploded from the American Express and Freedom towers, and millions of shards swirled in the air.

Cyral became nauseous. He was hearing voices. New voices. Dead voices and their thoughts. He felt full and heavy. Their woe and vengeance sent shivers through his shoulders and neck. Louder and louder the voices grew as more and more became audible to him. So many voices. So much pain. The psychic burden pushed at the insides of his skull, like needles behind his eyes. He gripped his head and clamped his jaw shut. Then he heard *her* voice, clearer than all the others.

<Meddler!> It was a sultry, seemingly kind alto that almost made the insult sound flattering. <You would make a fine partner. Do you remember

what I asked you, boy?> The words slinked into Cyral's head, and for a moment he caught a glimpse of her beautiful, round milk-chocolate face with curtains of sheeny, crinkly hair flowing down either side, partially hiding her enthralling eyes. <Whose thoughts are these? Are they yours? Really now?> Her voice was seductive and taunting in his mind. <You think you're special, don't you?>

The adjective stung him.

<Crown Moon lost that powerful double mind when we brought them together.>

"My head is closed for business today," Cyral said. "My head is closed for business today!"

<Why do you think he keeps you around, darling? You're just a puppet. You and your friends.>

<My head is closed for business today,> Cyral told her.

<Is that you?> she asked <Did you do that?>

<My head is closed for business today,> Cyral repeated the elementary psychic training mantra that Gaskill had taught him.

<Good boy,> Juno said.

"Cyral?" Tig asked. "You OK?"

<Good jo—>

"Closed," Cyral said. Her voice was gone. His ears stopped throbbing, and the pain in his skull stopped radiating. Slowly, the voices quieted to a tolerable psychic vibration, though he could still hear them, and more were speaking every moment. He knew he didn't have time to comprehend, let alone explore, this galvanizing expansion of his mind. For a moment he was afraid of himself and of the uncertainty. He had so many questions. His anxiety exploded into anger. Why had Gaskill kept this from him? Was it hubris? Envy? What could have become of this had Gaskill not dangled it beyond him so cryptically for all this time? Juno's quip stabbed fresh into his mind, *"Do you even think your own thoughts anymore*?" He couldn't answer it with certainty.

"I . . ." Cyral began. "I'm fine, Tig."

In fact, he was still straining to keep the peace in his mind. All of those who remained from the Trade Center's previous tragedies were screaming at him.

Their rage and despair clawed his heart up into his throat. As strange as it was, he found solace gazing at the marvelous sight of the skeleton, blacker than night in the midst of a great white fire. The flowers in the skeleton's garment sparkled in the inferno light, the white linen dress barely distinguishable from the white-hot inferno. It was all beautiful out of context. It was freedom, something the world had forbidden brown people like him, Hermod, Tig, Ford, Mingo, Dara, Hanuri, Davi, Gaskill, and scores of others to have. A basic right that Gaskill, too, had stolen from others with glee. At that moment Cyral understood something about himself that Gaskill had seen for some time.

At SPASE Headquarters, Gaskill felt Cyral exit his mind completely.

<Cyral?> Gaskill asked.

<You're afraid of me, aren't you?> Cyral said.

Gaskill tried to respond but could not. Cyral's connection was gone.

From the naked windows in the tower, people, girders, paperclips, computers, and floors and walls poured out toward Juno and were burnt up in the air as they joined her infernal aura. Streets and sidewalks buckled, and geysers sprang up out of the broken ground from the cracked and exposed pipes beneath. Explosions erupted from the sinkholes forming along Vesey, West, Barclays, Washington streets.

"Cyral you're—"

<Your spell is broken, Crown Moon,> Cyral said, interrupting Gaskill.

"Very well, Winston," Gaskill replied.

"Be sharp, team," Cyral said.

Remus, Sean, and Ade were locked in a struggle in a deep crevice at the corner of Vesey Street. Remus smashed Ade into the side of the crevice and threw her at Sean. It crawled out of the hole and crouched and saw its master.

Juno, straining with all her effort, watched her friend emerge from the hole on West Street. As they locked eyes, Juno remembered the old days when Remus had appeared to them in Virginia. When she had vowed to see her people thrive by all means necessary, Remus aided her. She remembered when she first communed with her birthright under the rock. Hundreds of years later, in that moment, gripping One World Trade Center, she understood the power of her bloodline like never before. Her own sorcery and might were enhanced by her very own blood in Hermod. She could feel herself in his veins. They were kin. His magic was unlike anything she had ever felt or heard of in the void. She had never felt the planet in its entirety before let alone been aware of how distinct she was from it, even to the point where she might up and leave it at will.

Where she had joined with the void, Hermod was joined with the mysteries of the stars and the universe! Vincent's blood had borne this. Her blood. How had he held it together? How had he not smashed them all over and over? Surely, he had learned the special gifts—peace, love, kindness—those that she had never had the fortune to keep, nor the interest. He was a Vincent's Vincent. He would be a Juno's Vincent. She felt every living creature on the ground and in the sea and air around the planet, as if they were living and being in her instead. She was assured now more than ever that Hermod could set everything right. *They* would set it right.

At this, Juno relaxed, and the building wasn't nearly as heavy as it was moments ago. So, like a frivolous child at the seashore, she plucked it up like a cockle shell and flung it into the air.

## WILLIAMSBURG BRIDGE, NEW YORK CITY, NY

"Oh fuck!" Dara yelled, incredulous.

"It's about the people outside now," Cyral said.

"I'm powering down the interior," Tig said.

She, Hanuri, and Mingo watched the Freedom Tower ascend above the skyline, leaving a trail of debris beneath it.

"Gods avail us," Hanuri said.

"Open it!" Cyral yelled.

"Doc, I'm headed to HQ!" Mingo said.

"While it still has momentum!"

"Take me with you," Dara said, still transfixed by the happening.

"You will fly there, girl?" Hanuri asked, looking at Dara with wide eyes. Her fear of flying was as characteristic as her might and beauty.

"I'ma have to," Dara said, shaking her head. "I want a piece of this fucking bitch."

"I will be more useful here," Hanuri said. "Undoing what was done."

## ONE WORLD TRADE CENTER, NEW YORK CITY, NY

Astonished, Cyral soared up with the building without even realizing that he had telekinetically grabbed Ford and was pulling him up faster than Ford's own Ojun suit was propelling him.

<We can't let that thing come back down!> Cyral screamed his thoughts at Ford and Tig.

Tig hurried to catch up to them as they all raced to catch up to the tower, now its own height off the ground and climbing.

"It's about the people outside now," Cyral said.

"I'm powering down the interior," Tig replied. He was speaking with the boiler systems, HVAC, gas and fuel reservoirs, sprinkler systems, power grid, electrical systems, and backup generators, making sure that any and all preventable explosions would be minimized whenever and wherever the building finally broke apart. "I may only get thirty percent complete."

Ford struggled to concentrate enough ahead of the building to find a place to open the door. He was still not propelling himself, caught in Cyral's telekinetic flight. They were all racing so fast that he could not yet see the spire to know where the building began.

"Open it!" Cyral said.

Ford opened a door ahead of them, and they were immediately at the top of the building. Five thousand feet in the air now, their Ojun suits autonomously spread over their heads as helmets to shield them from the extreme cold in the upper atmosphere.

"Now!" Cyral screamed. "While it still has momentum!"

The three of them watched the city beneath them reflect in the sky in the moment before the door opened wide above them.

Juno burst from the tower façade and gripped Ford by the neck. "Now," she said. "Take me to him, Tracy."

Ford gasped as Juno's touch electrified him, and he reflexively and unknowingly closed the exit door. The four of them along with the tower flew through the entrance and then it closed as well. Large chunks of the building that did not make it—lower floors, elevators, and parts of the façade—fell thousands of feet back to the sea and land below.

Stuck in between his doors, Ford felt three hands gripping his neck. He was not in pain anymore and was no longer screaming. He drifted silently above a shimmering ocean with Hermod, Juno, and Vincent surrounding him. Each of them was wearing the same beautiful dress. He could only recognize Hermod from inference. He appeared in void flesh, without substance. Vincent was gritting his teeth and squinting. Juno's eyes and mouth were wide with excitement.

Tig was not far from him. He could not see Cyral due to an unusual blinding light that was concealing him. One World Trade Center was drifting above him at the same speed. They all lingered for several seconds in the still air beneath a blue sunless sky. Ford, fully aware of the effects of this place, the All Realm, swarmed his focus and opened the exit door again.

"Jesus," Ade said. She scrambled on all four limbs away from the crumbling pavement surrounding the tower. The ground beneath her was shaking apart, and it was hard to get her footing and watch the sight at the same time.

"It's about the people outside now."

She decided that her safety was more important and grounded herself so that her suit could propel her away across West Street. She tarried there stupefied, her head craning up as the building rose and Ford, Cyral, and Tig flew away with it.

"Open it!" Cyral yelled.

Juno stayed behind for a moment and then raced up through the center of the building.

"While it still has momentum!"

The air high above shimmered and then Ford's door opened, and Ade watched it swallow the Freedom Tower.

## CAPE HENLOPEN, DE

Gaskill stood on the beach watching gulls circle over the Atlantic, which glistened a morning yellow. Davi stood just ten feet ahead of him, closer to the waves. His head was down as he watched the waves lap against a rock jutting out of the sand near his foot. He wanted to be at home. He wanted to die there instead.

"Stay close to me," Gaskill said.

Davi felt safer where he was.

"Open it!" Cyral yelled over their comm link.

"You will do fine," Gaskill said.

"While it still has momentum!"

Gaskill raised his eyes to the sky and watched as a section of it was blotted out. He saw the tower falling at them and New York City above them, upside down. The doorway closed, and the sky returned. Gaskill's eyelids widened, and he held his breath for a moment. A second later the sky shimmered, and the broken building reappeared.

A loud wrenching and crunching sound drew Davi's attention up. Immediately, he recognized the spire and triangular façade despite its wrecked state. He screamed and fell to his buttocks.

Nearly lateral, the Freedom Tower fell, twisting in the middle as if it were being wrung out. The bottom side of the building bulged and broke open as the edifice spewed out its innards. Glass, concrete, steel, office furniture, fire, electronics, and people sprayed into the morning in an ugly cloud around the tattered building.

Davi took a long, deep breath and then scrambled to stand up. He was knee deep in the ocean before he realized he'd been backing away from the sight. Gaskill remained where he was, watching silently.

The first of the wreckage landed before the bulk of the building itself, about one hundred feet away from them in the ocean. The building spire remained intact throughout the ordeal until it finally splintered on the sandy earth as it crashed into the beach, followed by the rest of the building. A roar filled the air, and Cape Henlopen rumbled. Mangled edifice and seashore exploded into the air and rose up in a cloud that would rain down new destruction.

Gaskill raised his hands, and he and Davi were cocooned from the maelstrom of torn earth, engineering, technology, and flesh washing over them. Davi cowered in the sand and covered his ears due to the skull-rattling crashing and banging.

After several moments the largest chunks of debris had settled, and the air glittered orange from the haze that lingered. Particles in it were large and sparkly, like bugs. Paper and cloth and strips of aluminum and plastic were tossed in the wind. The sound of splashing waves signaled the end of the maelstrom. Small fires were burning all over the beach and in the ocean not far from the shore. The smell of the burning world of One World Trade Center raided Davi's nose and coated his mouth. Ojun flowed around his neck and materialized an oxygen mask.

Gaskill was thankful there were no souls suffering. He'd found that they could be loud and bothersome in their slow dying. He couldn't afford to lose focus over such trifles, not right now.

"Davi," Gaskill said. "Up now."

Gaskill, with his will, brought Davi closer and then released him. Davi rooted himself in the sand and took a deep breath, then looked around at the shadowy crags of debris jutting up from the sand.

"Doctor," Tig said. He was descending from directly above them.

"Tig!" Gaskill exclaimed in relief. He found himself smiling. It had been days since he'd been moved to do so.

"Where's Cyral?" Gaskill asked him.

"We were split up," Tig said. He looked around at the torn beach and building and shook his head. He focused on Davi, who was visibly frightened. Davi had spent most of his SPASE career in containment centers and on probation details. This level of engagement was far beyond all of their experience, let alone Davi's. "Be sharp, Davi. You're the secret sauce right now."

Cyral and Ford stepped out of a doorway just ahead of Davi. Cyral immediately rose several feet into the air.

A clump of torn steel beams and other debris exploded from the sand several yards in front of them. Juno's approach was lightning fast. She threw them all to the ground in the wake of her presence and then approached Gaskill, gripped his head, and pulled it close.

"Ninixetlau," the black skull rasped at him. "I hate to say it, but you look good, brother. Traitor." A slender cyclone of fire rose up, and the debris around them was whipped into the air and thrown around with the fire.

Davi clambered to his feet and approached her from behind. He raised his hand and tried to turn her off. He could barely see all of her aura. It filled his view like Hermod's, but it was black, blue, and gray where Hermod's was purple, red, and blue most days. Hermod's aura was normally still and calm, but Juno's was a swirling tempest of midnight colors. Davi's eyes spread wide open, and every inch of him was as tense and as hard as his muscles could flex. He felt like he did in the gym when he needed to call a spotter while doing bench press but was too afraid.

The swirling fire cyclone extinguished and spun out, and Juno released Gaskill and stepped back a few steps. Davi welcomed a bit of relief as Juno lessened her exertion, and he backed away from her as she turned to face him. The black jawbone lowered, and where she would have burned his flesh away reflexively, she had not the strength.

Davi fell to one knee and breathed in deeply.

"You are a prize, Davi," Juno said. "I will most certainly spare you if you make the wise choice today."

Tig and Ford approached her on foot and Cyral from the air. She was still strong enough to wield Hermod's gravity and smite the three of them back to the ground.

"You won't have me, Crown Moon," Juno rasped at him.

"Are you certain?" Gaskill said from behind her. He stepped around her and stood next to Davi.

"I will finish what I started, traitor," Juno said. "I won't let my people down again. Your men will grow tired, but my fury won't."

"Yes, indeed," Gaskill said. "You have held this mighty grudge for hundreds of years and even brought it back from the grave."

"You belittle our destiny even today?" Juno said. "Even with all the evidence of its inevitability? A wrong left unamended cannot linger. Rot can never be hidden."

"You are still a grandiose bitch," Gaskill said. "Inevitable? The nerve of you. Such small-minded carnage. Inevitable?"

"Rot can *never*," she spat out the word as if it had spoiled in her mouth, "be hidden. Justice will spring from the void, Ninixetlau."

Fire crawled around the holes in the black skull. She perched up a bit and folded her dress beneath her knees and relaxed on the sand. A small atomic fire spread out around her. Sand and debris beneath her burned away, and she remained in place in her kneeling position. From the fire, Hermod's flesh grew over his black bones.

"Where's Vincent?" Gaskill mocked. "We're done."

"Doctor," Davi said. He took a deep breath and clenched his fists, beating one of them into his chest.

"Hold on, Davi," Gaskill said, "you've got this." His tone was uncharacteristically warm. It was a pleasant and much needed surprise for Davi. Part of him wanted this act to add to his faith in Gaskill, but another part of him had gleaned that it was most certainly a tactic of the master strategist and manipulator.

<Always learning the right lessons,> Gaskill replied to Davi's discernment of his character.

"Can any of you move?" Tig asked.

"Uggh," Ford replied. "No. I mean, I could open a door beneath us, and we could jet out of here."

"It would release us from Vincent's restraint," Tig replied, "but let's think this through for a moment. Plan's gotta be tight."

"I'm actually quite enjoying the time to breathe," Cyral said. His thoughts were still wrapped around his fresh understanding of his all mind back in Manhattan. "Shit."

They were silent for a moment staring up into the orange-and-pinkish haze still lingering around the cape. Tig turned to Cyral, who started laughing. Tig and Ford looked on in silence.

"We're gonna have to move HQ," Cyral said. "These souls will never rest. I can't work like that."

"You never quit, do you, Cyral?" Tig asked.

"What?" Cyral said. "I'm Operations. Ask any psychic. For you it'd be like you trying to talk to every phone in Brooklyn at once and fuck at the same time."

Tig considered the task and silently agreed to its tedium and unpleasantness.

"Ford, what is in between your doorways?" Cyral asked.

"Huh?" Ford asked.

"When we were stuck there, I've never felt so . . . I don't know."

"Oh," Ford said. "Yeah." He was silent for a few seconds. "It's . . ." He could not find the words to describe the state of being in between space and thought and perhaps even time and life. "It's just weird." He shook his head and shrugged. "I sleep there sometimes."

"Doc says it's not like Remus's void, right?" Cyral asked.

"Did you hear anything I just said?" Ford replied. "I couldn't sleep in a void! He calls it the All Realm. It's a pretty chill place, but I don't like to spend too much time there when I'm awake. It can get weird. It's like a drug."

"You know, when Hermod grabbed me, it shocked me. I think he was trying to dig into my mind, to force us to come here. I closed the door as a reflex. And then when we were in the All Realm, I was really out of it, but I saw all three of them separately. She's beautiful!"

"Who?" Tig asked. "Juno?"

"Yeah! I mean, damn."

"Yes!" Cyral said. "That makes sense." He had been completely lucid when they were trapped in the All Realm. His thinking had been clearer than ever, in fact, and he could hear billions of voices. They all felt so good, echoing inside him. His body had been buzzing the entire time, almost like he'd been having a prostate orgasm. He'd seen his deceased mother. He'd heard her voice call him by her nickname for him, "Winnie." She had approached him with open arms, and then she disappeared when the exit opened again, and they were falling to the Cape Henlopen beach. What felt like several minutes was, in fact, just a second or two. He wanted to go back and was suddenly more than a little jealous that he'd never been there.

"We're going back," Cyral said to Ford. He locked eyes with him and winked and then turned and pointed his head toward Hermod. "The five of us." Cyral looked at Tig. "Six of us," he said.

"Why?" Tig asked.

"You can stay here if you want," Cyral said.

<I would suggest you go, Tig,> Gaskill said. He'd heard their plan over the commlink. <Hermod will need a trusted anchor between Earth and the All Realm.>

"I won't risk it," Tig said. "If something happens in there, I'll be more of an asset on this side."

"Agreed." Cyral's mind was racing thinking about exploring the sensations he'd felt during that brief moment in the All Realm. "But right now we gotta get Hermod back there. That's the only way we can bring him back here."

"Do you remember that night that we took the Thomlinsons?" Juno asked. "I had seen it all under the rock. All of it."

"And here I thought you were just weak and impotent that evening," Gaskill replied.

"Worm," Juno said, dismissing the insult regarding her demise.

Gaskill stood in front of her as she knelt in the sand.

"There really was nothing we could have done that wouldn't have led to chaos in our ranks. I begged Vincent to end you all, but he stayed his hand. We were all too young, the new gods, and not yet harmonious enough to not destroy each other. I could only hope that someone would continue what we'd started for the prosperity of our people. I knew your remnants would survive, but I could not see the selfish fiend that you would become. We needed a hammer strike, and you all wouldn't let me deliver it. Now look."

"Astronaut, ambassador, senator, diplomat," Gaskill said. "Scholar, billionaire, pre-eminent authority on supernatural beings and physics. I've shaped this world—"

"For crackers!" Juno hissed. "Turncoat!" She spat at him. Gaskill waved his hand, and the phlegm was carried up and away from him.

"And what of the Carters, who we left at Potters' Grove? The Whitlock Riders outside of Louisiana? Sister's kin," Juno said. "And Mo' Jo. Mo' Jo must be alive!" Hermod's eyes were bright and wild as Juno remembered Mo' Jo. "Yes?" she pleaded, knowing she wouldn't hear what she wanted. Knowing she wouldn't believe Mo' Jo had perished.

Gaskill shook his head slowly. Juno looked at him and cringed. His flesh fully renewed, she coiled Hermod's fingers in front of his face, and his eyelids crushed together briefly.

"There's nothing? No one?" Incredulous, she rubbed Hermod's hands down his thighs several times, smoothing the dress over them. "I mean, Ruben Carter was going to Congress. They had an independent chamber of commerce and sheriff. In that there town. I—"

"They were all wiped away," Gaskill said.

"Liar!" Juno screamed, refusing to believe him. "How?" Her breast was electrified as she listened to Gaskill spin his truth. She wouldn't believe it. Mo' Jo was also kin to SiqT' Qkar; surely, he must be alive somewhere. Hermod's frown dragged down his cheeks and jowls. "Y'all didn't protect 'em?"

"Would you have?" Gaskill countered.

"Yes!" Juno screamed. "By Nyemhaa, yes! If what this boy has been telling me is true, then—"

"What has he said?" Gaskill asked.

"Failure," Juno replied. "That's all I see. All I hear. You all failed us." Juno remembered the song that she had sung just minutes earlier in downtown Manhattan with the brothers and sisters and babies. No ways tired.

"He told you that?" Gaskill asked. He huffed out a laugh. "Hermod tried to shame me about being responsible?"

"No, he didn't. He didn't need to tell me." Vincent was speaking now. Davi groaned under the increased weight of Hermod, Vincent, and Juno's combined might. His nose was starting to bleed. "The history speaks loud and clear. Though she may be surprised, I am not." Vincent paused and stood. "Ninixetlau, the twin glass temples. I knew your legend. We all did. I saw the self-loathing. You toppled yourself long before we did, Crown Moon."

Gaskill looked down at his two different colored hands and remembered the day Juno brought him together.

Vincent closed Hermod's eyes and lifted his head to the sky. "You are more like the whip crackers anyway. It was a hard lesson for you, fighting your own battles. Even with two bodies you had to manipulate others to do your dirt."

Vincent looked at Davi, who was kneeling and trembling with both hands extended to the sky. His eyes were squeezed shut, tears trickled from the left one. "Even now!" Vincent continued. "You let this poor boy die just for a few more seconds to gloat. As soon as he's done," he nodded at Davi, "I will kill you and get on with my business."

"What is your business?" Gaskill asked. "Steal away the life of your offspring, Hermod? Destroy his home and relationships? Exact your revenge on whom? Who has harmed you, Vincent?"

"Crackers did!" Vincent rasped. "You did. My people need retribution. Black men and women and babies. Everyone you offered up for power!" Vincent closed his eyes and turned his head away from Gaskill.

"Rot can never be hidden," Vincent said after several seconds of silence. "It must be burned away."

Davi screamed in pain and fell over onto his hands. He breathed heavily into the sand, blood and spittle dripping into the sand.

"HQ!" Sean yelled over the commlink. "Heads ups."

Hermod stood up. Fire swirled around the sand and debris near his feet and stretched up dozens of feet into a new infernal funnel.

"Enough talk," Vincent said.

"We've lost Remus," Sean remarked.

"Now, Tig!" Cyral said. He gripped Ford's hand, and the two of them rose into the air and approached Vincent from behind.

Vincent turned around and was immediately startled by their proximity. Ford opened the door behind Vincent and Cyral, using his telekinetic power, thrust the three of them into it.

# THE ALL REALM

"This feels amazing." Cyral was unsure whether he'd said this aloud. He was floating but also lying on something. It was a strange sensation. His body started to hum. The vibrations were low and almost ticklish at first and then the song he'd felt before, when they had been trapped there with the Freedom Tower, began singing through him again. Billions of voices strong. Buzzing, ecstatic, and unraveling, he was full of the harmonious echo. It was a splendid feeling, like being in love. He didn't want it to end.

"Cyral?" Hermod called to him. "Is that you?"

Cyral's smile was unseen as he only appeared as a bright pillar of light rising from the ground, a surface that was hard and solid like concrete but as shimmery and silky as a cenote.

Hermod glided toward the pillar of light and stopped a few feet in front of it. Ford was sitting crossed legged on the shimmering ground beside Cyral.

"Wow!" Ford said, his eyes and mouth growing. "You and that thing have matching outfits?"

Hermod looked down. His body appeared as Remus did, without form and substance, void flesh. Despite what he was seeing, he did not feel any different, and he was not afraid. Ford turned away from Hermod.

"Ma'am," Ford began, "you are really, really beautiful, and I'm not just staying that to save my life." He winked and extended his arms behind him on the ground, propping himself up.

"Clever, handsome boy," Vincent said. "We can't harm you now. That's why you brought us here."

Hermod looked to his right and was startled by the round-faced, almond-eyed woman standing next to him. As he turned to face her, he was surprised again by the taller, slightly darker man standing next to her. He looked at Cyral and then Ford and then back at the pair as he backed away from all of them.

"Uncle Cissy?" Hermod asked slowly.

Vincent and Juno stood side by side watching the void man step away. The three of them were wearing the same dress. Juno was just a few inches shorter than Vincent but still tall for a woman. Her hair was thick and shiny. It was twirled in a beautiful thick pretzel braid that snaked around her head and shoulders.

"Come and rest, child," Juno said. "Let me hold you."

"Cyral?" Hermod asked. Where were they? How did they get there? Was he dead? If so, how did that happen? Why did he feel completely normal? Where was his body? Where *were* they? Why was Cyral a sun? How did he know it was Cyral? What was wrong with Ford? Why was this woman so familiar? Where were they?

"Stay calm, Hermod," Cyral told him.

"We are in between everything right now," Ford said, "life, time, space probably some other dimensions too."

"You wear it well, boy," Vincent said to him, "the void."

"What the fuck is going on?" Hermod yelled. "Where am I?" he asked, referring to his body. "Where are we?"

Juno stepped up to him, but Hermod recoiled as she reached out to touch his face. She frowned and then stepped back to stand beside Vincent.

"Don't touch me."

"Jaqueline would be proud," Juno said.

"Who are you?" Hermod yelled. A stone thrown into the cenote. The ground beneath them began to ripple gently.

"We are in the All Realm," Cyral said. "It is indeed a place between time, space, mind, soul, life, and death. You all brought your discord, and the realm cured it with harmony. This is divine reality.

"This isn't SiqT' Qkar's reality," Juno said, sneering.

"Only truth can exist here," Cyral replied. "You feel it, don't you, Hermod?"

In fact, he did. He was smoldering inside, and yet he wanted to lie down with all of them and stare up at the sky and never leave.

"What is SiqT' Qkar?" Hermod shook his head. "Why are we here?"

"Isn't it obvious, boy?" Vincent said. "Crown Moon's league is indeed very powerful and very resourceful." Vincent flashed his eyes at Cyral and Ford.

"Am I dead?" Hermod asked.

"You are more alive than ever now," Cyral said. "You are free, Hermod. They cannot harm you here."

"Let us show you," Juno said, approaching him. "You will see that this was an act of love for you and for family, boy."

"What are you talking about?" Hermod demanded, recoiling from her. He was having a hard time remembering where he had been or how he might have gotten here. "What did you do to me?" he asked. He was looking at Vincent and Juno, his void form obscuring his twisted, anguished face. "What happened?" His last memory was of slowing down over the Atlantic and watching MASS speed away from him in the dark. "What did you do?"

"Show him," Cyral said.

Vincent and Juno approached him, and he instinctively backed away. As they came closer, though, he felt an overwhelming sense of peace come over him. The two of them embraced Hermod. He was comforted by their touch, and he wrapped his arms around them. Then he saw them, and his arms fell to his sides.

"You did it," Hermod said. Fully aware of what had transpired in the last six hours, he was unsure of how to respond. "I'm a monster now." He stepped out of their embrace and stared at them.

"You are a Vincent," Vincent told him, "a child of the void. Do not be ashamed."

"All those people are dead."

"Y'all have their ways through and through," Juno said. "Poor babies. You had no choice. No one to guide you."

"But that has all changed, boy," Vincent said. "We have broken your yoke and set the stage for you to set right the enslavers' transgressions. Now the rightful kings and queens of this land can thrive!"

"Thrive!" Juno yelled, clapping her hands. "That is the glory of SiqT' Qkar, the Container. Vanquish our foes, balance the scale, and thrive!"

"Oh, y'all niggas are on some ride *and* die shit!" Ford said. Vincent looked at him and smiled, then glided closer to him, his dress dragging in the air behind him.

"Never die," Vincent said. "Your future would be bright in our world." He looked into Ford's eyes. "Can you see it?" Vincent winked at him and then looked away and drifted back to Juno's side. "You negroes, the white man's eunuchs, gleefully eating his poison and lies and offering yourselves up for murder, objectification, and savagery."

"They call it success," Juno said. "You are whores for the enslaver."

"Had you known what real power could do for us all," Vincent said, "had it not been corrupted by the likes of Crown Moon and insidious crackers, you castrated negroes would rule this planet, and the whites would fear you and beg for their own murder instead."

"The whip is in the other hand now!" Juno said. "Be grateful, boy. We have opened your eyes."

"You are forgiven," Vincent said, "you have redeemed them."

"No!" Hermod shouted. "This is fucked up! How could you do this to me?"

"How could we not?" Vincent said, "And waste another two hundred years to harness Nyhemaa's blessed star? You needed to be shaken awake! Would that we had just a little more time with you."

"Don't you fret, boy," Juno said. "Our run is over. Your clever friends have ruined our fun for today."

"But there is something more to see and do," Vincent said.

"You will know the source of our rage," Juno added, "and your real power, and then you can decide which way is up."

"Let's take him to Mama," Vincent said. He clasped his hands and grinned at Juno.

"Yes, let's let Mama show him," Juno said. "You ever met your Granny Jaqueline?" Hermod watched her with revulsion and envy. Juno waved her hand in front of her body, and the shimmery ground changed to cloudy gray. The sky above also darkened, and soon they were standing in complete darkness. Slowly, the ground began to change, and Hermod felt crunching under foot. He was standing on hay.

Something illuminated several feet away from where they were huddled. As it shone brighter, Hermod realized it was an eighteenth-century lantern. As more of the surroundings were uncovered from the shadows, he saw hay bales aligned along the back wall of the room they were in and shelves lined with gardening tools. A large eighteenth-century hand mower was aligned with several scythes. A whip was coiled on a hook attached to one of the beams. On the wall adjacent to the door, several machetes were hanging. Closer to them a young woman was kneeling on a cot in between another woman's legs. She was sweating profusely and screaming and wheezing. It became clear what he was witnessing as the baby exited its mother, Jaqueline. Immediately, the baby began squealing. The girl, Jaqueline's nurse Whitney, raised a small knife and quickly sawed through the newborn's umbilical cord and tied it as tight as she could. Then she scurried across the barn to a table with a small basin of water prepared on top of it. Whitney began to whimper as she washed the newborn clean.

Hermod approached Jaqueline. His anger and confusion were subverted by the compulsion to assist the distressed woman.

"Hey!" he said. "We can help you." He turned to Ford and shrugged, then back to Jaqueline and Whitney.

"Hey!"

"They can't hear you," Ford said. He was standing next to Cyral, who remained a pillar of blinding white light. "We can only observe."

"Let me see it!" Jaqueline barked over the newborn's wails. "Come!"

"We—" Whitney was shaking as she stared down at the baby in her hands. She lowered it to Jaqueline's face, so she could see without needing to strain herself. "We said it all just . . . just like you . . ." Whitney paused and stooped down, and Jaqueline raised her chest and neck and head up. "Just like you say to."

Jaqueline saw the penis and screamed but then immediately silenced herself. Whitney stepped away with the baby to the other side of the small barn and wiped him clean in the basin.

He finally stopped crying, which brought false relief to Jaqueline. She groaned and shuddered as she tightened her grip on the edge of the pallet on which she was lying. Her fluids oozed out of the fabric as she squeezed it. The second child squirmed against her body's efforts to birth it, pain radiating from deep in her groin. It spread down her legs and up her abdomen and over her breasts in much the same way as waves of orgasmic pleasure might have. Also similar was the inability to make the sound that accompanied the feeling. Her back arched, and she flung her head backwards, her mouth agape. She gasped several deep breaths until finally the thrall of agony eased and allowed her to release a cry.

"Quick, Auntie," Whitney said. "Name 'im!"

"I don't understand," Hermod said. "What's wrong?"

Juno and Vincent looked at him, and his eyes leaped between them.

A thunderous pound rattled the barn door.

Jaqueline sat upright in a fright and then immediately flopped back down on the pallet and groaned.

"Girl," Jaqueline whimpered, "Come! Come pray wit' me . . ."

"Jaqueline!" a man's voice yelled from outside the barn. "I hear a baby cryin' in there. Is it mine?" The barn door rattled again, and this time the entire barn shook.

Whitney hurriedly wrapped the newborn boy in the blanket. She folded it as many times as she could around and around the boy in a tight diaper. Then she found another blanket to wrap around its body. She ran to Jaqueline and nestled the baby in her arms, then settled by her side.

"What's happening?" Hermod asked. He looked at Cyral beside him and then at Juno on the other side of Cyral's pillar of light.

"It will be clear soon enough," Vincent said. Hermod looked at him and then back to Jaqueline and Whitney.

A chill wind swept through the barn and extinguished the lanterns. Whitney shivered and moved closer to Jaqueline.

"Jaqueline SiqT' Qka—"

The barn door exploded into splinters. A blinding white light filled the barn, and Jaqueline and Whitney shielded their eyes from it. Hermod, Vincent, and Juno did as well. A tall thin man in a long snow-white duster stepped through the threshold. He wore a long pointed white hat made of the same pure white material as his duster. He held a long, knotted walking stick. Its handle was a bulb of glass with a man's eye inside of it. A monstrous albino cyclops followed him. It was taller than the man in white and looked about four times as strong. Its feet were larger than any man's, and it had only four fingers on each hand. It wore a crude pair of hemp pants, and it emitted a sour, pungent stench.

Hermod balled his hands into fists.

"There's nothing you can do but watch, boy," Juno said.

Hermod looked at her and then at Vincent, who remained inert and unblinking.

"Jaqueline," the man in white said, "we had a bargain."

Jaqueline, her face turned away from the horrid light, grimaced and shuddered due to the hot labor pains ravaging her body.

"I promised you . . . nothing!" Jaqueline groaned.

"Now, now," the man said, "we abide by the word of the good Lord here at Mueller Farm. Goes without saying, right?" He stopped smiling and glared at her as he stepped closer to Jaqueline and her pallet.

"What a beautiful little—" The man moved the tip of his staff over the baby and poked it in the belly. Jaqueline moved the baby out of the way and yelped.

"Show me!" he rasped through clenched teeth. "We had a deal. I lost my boy, Murphy, God rest his soul," he shut his eyes and shuddered, "hunting your disobedient nigger man, so now you will give me a boy in return." He opened his eyes and smiled at her again, wide and bright. "I'm happy, Jesus is happy, eye for an eye, the end."

He held the smile on his face as he leaned down and reached out to the baby. Whitney stepped around Jaqueline and grabbed the baby from her, then set it on the pallet away from Master Mueller. She retrieved the rag from the hot pail of water behind the pallet and rubbed it on Jaqueline's forehead.

"Y-you t-took my Aristotle al-already," Jaqueline stammered. "You don't need his baby too."

Mueller let the end of his staff hover over the newborn as he watched Whitney try to soothe Jaqueline, who was squealing in pain and holding her belly.

"You are mine, girl," Mueller said. "I've got the receipt." He squinted at her and then poked his staff into her belly. Jaqueline wailed out in pain as she retrieved her still unnamed boy from the edge of the pallet. "That baby is mine."

She gripped the newborn boy and tried to scramble away from the smiling man. Whitney moved across the pallet to put herself in between Mueller and Jaqueline.

"My, Whitney," Mueller said, "I would have Higgins, here string you up and lash you right now." He smiled widely, bright, and toothy at her and then nodded at the whip hanging from the post nearby. "This whole time I thought you only had one of 'em burnin' up in the oven. You didn't tell me it was a nigger giveaway!"

Jaqueline watched Mueller turn his wide smile toward Higgins. Then he brought it down on her again.

"Higgins?" Mueller called.

Higgins, stinking and hulking, lumbered closer to the pallet as Mueller stepped away. He focused his single pale pink eye on Whitney and growled. Yellow spittle flew out at her. Her nostrils flared, and she stood up and faced the brute. Higgins smashed his fist into her side, toppling her into a pile of herself. He stamped down on the pallet, and Jaqueline kicked her leg away just in time to avoid it being crushed under his weight. Higgins brought his face close to Jaqueline's, and she closed her eyes against the single-eyed stare. His odor lingered on her tongue and in her nostrils, and she gasped and struggled to quell the reflexes in her throat. Her body jerked from the pain coursing through it and again from heaving and retching. Higgins punched her face and then grabbed the baby with his four-fingered hand, wrapping it entirely around the newborn.

Hermod raised his fist and instinctively set to charge at the albino fiend, but his reaction was immediately tempered by that of the others beside him. Juno looked on, straight faced, as did Vincent. Ford had been stricken immobile since Vincent and Juno brought them into the barn. Hermod could feel him oscillating between the All Realm intoxication and the horror they were witnessing.

The newborn boy began to make a squeal that only newborns can make. Jaqueline lay on her side, shuddering and sweating. She flopped onto her back and placed her hands over her belly and her unborn child. The child had settled; it would come soon. The left side of her face was burning as hot as her vagina. She leaned to her side and spat out a tooth and a mouthful of blood. Her jaw was not broken, and the pain there was eclipsed by labor. Her vision began to blur as she watched Higgins hand the baby boy to Mueller before exiting the barn. She could not see his face, but she knew that Mueller was smiling at her. Tall, white, and blurry, he stepped through the threshold with her baby boy, whom she had not the time to name after his father, Aristotle. The boy's shrill cry scraped at her ears and heart. Whitney reignited the lanterns and approached Jaqueline. She felt Whitney's hands on her right shoulder, and she was suddenly being propped up from behind. A warm rag wiped across her head.

"Jaqueline SiqT' Qkar," Jaqueline began, "SiqT' Qkar Y'inpu Y'inpu. Qi beeeo Y'inpu beeeo Jaqueline. Aristotle SiqT 'Qkar Y'inpu Y'inpu Y'inpu."

Jaqueline whimpered, and she looked like she was having trouble breathing. Though she made no sound, her face was streaked with tears. Hermod could hear the child rounding the building. He looked at Juno and then at Vincent, who both remained unmoved. Cyral, still appearing as a luminant pillar, made no response. Ford was shaking, his eyes agape. He was as disturbed as Hermod.

"Jaqueline SiqT' Qkar, SiqT' Qkar Y'inpu Y'inpu," Jaqueline began again, and Whitney joined her this time. Jaqueline's baby boy was crying from behind the barn now. "Qi beeeo Y'inpu beeeo Jaqueline. Aristotle SiqT' Qkar—"

An explosive impact to the back wall shook the barn. Whitney gripped Jaqueline's shoulders as hard as she could.

"Y'inpu Y'inpu Y'inpu," they finished in unison.

The night was silent again save for Jaqueline's deep breathing.

"Whitneeeey!" Mueller sang out her name. She flinched at the sound of his voice. It was at the side of the barn approaching the front. "I'm gonna need you and Bea to take care of that mess out back of the barn." He stood in the doorway, leaning on his staff with his right arm, his left hand resting on his hip. Higgins stood motionless a few feet behind him. "Early now, Whitney! Don't want all that mess sittin' under the sun and bakin' into the barn or else Thomas will have to repaint it. Mind you, he's gon' be busy diggin' that mess a grave, so don't wanna over work 'im in that heat."

Jaqueline sat up on her elbows just enough to peer over her belly to get a good look at Mueller. He was approaching the barn door, his malignant smile widening as he locked eyes with her.

"Is the other'n done yet?" Mueller inquired.

"SiqT' Qkar Jaqueline," she whispered, and with all the strength she had, she threw her hands above her and clapped twice before letting herself relax into Whitney's embrace.

A shadow in the corner behind Hermod thickened and bloomed into a seemingly tangible mass. It consumed the entire corner of the barn and moved through Hermod, Vincent, Juno, Ford, and Cyral, briefly blotting out all of them. Ford jumped and cringed. Once the shadow had moved away, Hermod saw that Vincent was smiling, and Juno's face had also brightened, her eyes following the mass across the room.

Whitney, fully aware of what was happening, was nevertheless petrified and stricken immobile. Mueller stopped just shy of the barn threshold and watched the void mass approach him. As it moved over Jaqueline, she sighed and let her head roll down onto her right shoulder. It condensed slightly and settled itself along the full height and width of the barn façade. Higgins stepped up beside Mueller. They stared into the void, which now occupied the barn, preventing them from entering.

"Mercy!" Jaqueline screamed and arched her back and then began huffing in and out of her mouth. "Girl!" That was all that she could bring herself to speak.

Still staring at the black mass swarming the front of the barn, Whitney gently laid Jaqueline's upper body on the pallet and moved around and knelt between Jaqueline's legs.

Outside, Mueller prodded Higgins with the tip of his staff. "Go on!" Mueller said.

Higgins grimaced at him and then used his left hand to probe the thick shadow barricading the door. Immediately, his hand caught fire.

Higgins bellowed and dove to the ground and scraped his hand around in the dirt and grass to try to extinguish the flames. Mueller watched the cyclops work for what seemed like an excessive amount of time considering the size of the fire.

Inside, Jaqueline continued to struggle with Whitney to birth the second child. Though she loathed to offer it up to this world, life would not have her completely renegotiate the terms of its gift.

"I see the head!" Whitney said, excited. She glanced behind her to check whether or not the shadow was still there. "It's comin', Auntie."

Jaqueline let her body do its work as she drifted away into her mind. Pain numbed her, and she could only register pressure. She felt the second child pushing its way out of her, Whitney's guiding hands all around her thighs and vulva. She listened earnestly as the pressure released, and the pain pulled in from every inch of her body to just her abdomen, head, and genitals. She was less full than she had been a moment ago.

Her eyes shot open at the sound of the newborn's squeal, and they met Whitney's immediately. Whitney's face was trembling, a tear rolling down her face. She shook her head slowly.

"Nooooo, SiqT' Qkar, noooo!" Jaqueline cried.

"Quick, Auntie. Name 'im!" Whitney said, rushing to the far wall of the barn to where they stored clean pails of water. She placed the baby on a table there, poured a fresh bath, and cleaned him. She could not spare as many diapers to swaddle the baby as she had for his brother, so she wrapped him in a single sheet and then brought him back to Jaqueline. She was still crying, though her newborn was not anymore. She received the baby and let herself fall completely into woe, burying her tears in the boy. He kicked gently into her throat and pawed at her forehead.

Whitney retrieved three tattered blankets from the back of the barn and folded them neatly on top of each other behind Jaqueline's pallet.

"Auntie!"

Whitney knelt behind her and grabbed Jaqueline beneath her shoulders and dragged her back to the pallet she had made. She covered Jaqueline with the remaining tattered blanket and helped her into a new gown.

Whitney wrapped up the bloody afterbirth in the soggy pallet and dragged it to the far side of the barn.

"Whas the chile's name, Auntie?"

"Vincent," Jaqueline replied, weeping. "Vincent, like my daddy."

"Hey, Cousin Vincent," Whitney said, returning to Jaqueline's side. "He will save us, Auntie Jaqueline," Whitney whispered in her ear. "Look now, didn't he come when you called?"

Jaqueline continued to heave and cry.

"SiqT' Qkar works more mysterious than God. Ain't that what you say?"

Silence filled the barn. Jaqueline stared into the void protecting them from Mueller. That which she had asked for. Slowly, Jaqueline sat upright. Whitney retrieved the warm rag from the pail beside the pallet. She gently wiped Jaqueline's forehead and the bulbous purple bruise on the left side of her face. Jaqueline winced.

"We're done here," Mueller said, glaring at the shadow in his way. He raised his staff and pointed the handle at the door.

"Kuklos leukós Thanatos boēthóos![(1)]" he shouted. The glass handle of the staff illuminated brighter than the moon. Though its light did not penetrate the void barricading the door, blinding rays tore into the barn through the partitions in the wood planks in the ceiling and the walls. The building shook violently. Gardening tools and pots fell from the shelves affixed to the walls, and dust rained down on Whitney and Jaqueline. The small windows along the walls exploded into the night.

The void began to condense even further. As it did, the bright light around it flooded through the barn door. Dense and more compact, the void shrunk to the size and form of a tall man.

Outside, Mueller's smile grew as he watched the barricade shrink away. Then he saw a man wearing the void standing there in the doorway, and Mueller's smile faded to an indignant toothy grimace.

Light could not touch the void. Even in the wicked shine of Mueller's staff, blinding and white, the man was black like the edge of the universe, reflecting nothing, defined by that which it could never be. The void stepped

---

1 "Circle of White Death· come to my aid·" loosely translated from ancient Greek

away and into the barn. Wisps of his shadow lingered in the air around him as he moved. Whitney and Jaqueline had been shielding their eyes for the light of Mueller's staff, but as the man approached, his void cast on them, and they looked up at him and were immediately compelled to bow their heads. Newborn Vincent squealed once and cooed softly as the man in the void approached. He walked up the pallet and through the three of them and stood behind them, then placed his hand on Jaqueline's shoulder. She looked down at her newborn son and smiled. He had come. After all these years, he had come to her. SiqT' Qkar. The Dark God without image. Lord of the Void. The Container of the Universe.

Hermod stared at the man, and in this flesh that he wore in the All Realm, he could not help but feel connected to him. To it. He noticed then that Juno and Vincent had both turned around and were smiling at him, Juno, as always, smiling more so with her eyes than her lips. Then the man who wore the void disappeared.

Mueller stepped into the barn and lowered his staff, and the light diminished.

"Where is it?" Mueller said. He waved his staff, and Higgins quickly approached the pallet. Whitney hopped up onto one knee and crawled to shield Jaqueline and newborn Vincent. "And you better not have wrapped it all up like the last one. Waste o' time."

"Let him come," Jaqueline whispered. Whitney settled back onto the pallet.

Jaqueline offered up the baby just as Higgins loomed over them. He grabbed the baby and brought it back to Mueller.

"My," Mueller said as he took the baby from Higgins, and Higgins turned and faced Jaqueline and Whitney on the bed. "My, I . . ." Mueller removed the blanket from the baby and let it fall to the floor. He motioned his walking stick toward Higgins, and Higgins took it from him. Mueller held the baby out in front of him, and his lips squeezed into a new smile. His eyes closed, and he brought the baby to his breast and turned away from Jaqueline and Whitney.

Startled, Whitney hopped up to one knee again. Hermod also flinched, briefly forgetting that his efforts were futile. Jaqueline held her hand out in front of Whitney, and the girl settled near her on the pallet.

Mueller turned back around with the baby cradled in his arms. He locked his teary eyes on Jaqueline. He was moving his jaw, but his mouth did not open.

"She's beautiful," Mueller said finally. Jaqueline's eyes bulged at the word "she," and she quickly turned to Whitney, who also looked amazed. "She's a gift entirely from God," Mueller said as he shook his head and approached Jaqueline's pallet.

"Leave us now," Mueller said, and Higgins turned and exited the barn. Mueller knelt down and handed the baby to Jaqueline.

"Peace between us," Mueller said as he stood back up and took off his hat. "I want that baby girl to thrive here at Mueller Farm. What will you call her?"

"Juno," Jaqueline said immediately. "The god queen."

Mueller nodded. "Hello, Juno. My little queenie pie!" He stared his teary eyes at Jaqueline. "Peace to your little queen."

Mueller backed away from them and then stopped a few feet shy of the door. "Whitney," Mueller said, "don't you worry about the barn. I'll get Martha to clean this here place on up. And tomorrow I'll have Mark find us a doctor to come take a look here at Queen Juno and Jaqueline. We wanna make sure everything's gonna be alright for her."

Juno turned around and looked at Hermod. She waved her hand, and Jaqueline, the barn, young Juno, Whitney, all of the world they had just witnessed melted back into the shimmering endless plane they had been standing on before.

"He made opportunities to lash out at Mama whenever he could," Juno said, looking out at the horizon. The sky was a clear light blue, though in the distance it was harder to discern where the land and air began and ended. "But he loved me more than his own some days. I never knew why he hated her so. It wasn't about his son. Mama and Daddy must have crossed him some other way 'cause he was mean to Mama." She gnashed her teeth, and her pretty face twisted into an ugly grimace. "But Vincent showed him that one night." She turned toward Hermod, and her grimace softened into a loving smile. "He showed him what SiqT' Qkar's children could do."

"It's in your blood, boy," Vincent said. "The void."

"The blood of SiqT' Qkar still flows," Juno said.

"Why did you do this to me?" Hermod asked. "Why did you use me?"

"We did nothing of the sort," Juno replied. "We set you free, baby." She stepped toward him with her loving smile and reached out to grab his chin. He swatted her hand away, startled by the warmth and life in it.

"You got something we didn't get," Juno continued, rubbing her wrist where he had struck it. "A chance to understand civility, righteousness, conscience. We were born in the midst of war, and you needed to see, to taste that birthright, or else it would never have come out. You are beyond any of them—"

"A star in the void," Vincent said.

"And they've wronged you." Juno waved her arm around. "They've wronged all of us."

"There had to be another way," Hermod said. "All those people."

Vincent shrugged. "Grass in the mowers."

"What have I done?"

"Tell me another way, Hermod," Vincent demanded. "You've pondered it yourself. You've just been so timid, castrated by our foes, by the white man's law, white Jesus." He stood motionless and stared at Hermod from several yards away. "It makes no difference now." Vincent smiled. "Tell me, if someone wronged you for five hundred years, and they had no intention of stopping and only planned to make it worse for you and yours, if you finally had a chance to do something about it, to set it right for good, what would you do?"

Juno turned around and looked at Vincent and then back at Hermod.

"What did you do?" Vincent asked.

"Let the rot fester," Juno answered matter-of-factly. "Let it creep on up and choke your mama and your daddy and your granny and you and your friends and the children and your future and everything else, is that it? Huh?" Juno's almond-shaped eyes were wide, and her pupils drilled deep into him. "Rot can never be hidden, boy. I know it, and so do you." Juno flashed a wide smile at him. "You done cut out some of it already, no?" Her smile grew even more as she stared at him. "Officer George Tomicello, maybe?"

"Stop!" Hermod yelled. He balled his hands into tight knots at his sides. Ford examined Hermod with squinted eyes.

"Sergeant Carol Branchford, what about her?" Juno continued. "Officer Harold Bronders."

"My nigga," Ford said. He smirked and nodded. "Didn't think you had it in you."

"Officer Volkoski . . . Sergeant Quincy Cavanaugh," Juno continued. "There's more."

"Shut up!" Hermod yelled, then turned away from them all.

"It felt good didn't it?" Juno asked. "I know it did."

"We felt it, boy," Vincent added. "Well done!"

Even without a face, Hermod's anger radiated into Juno. Though she would never have found herself in his position, Juno tried to imagine how angry she might have been if her elders had done this to her. Not at all, she decided. She'd wished she'd had the kind of assistance that they were giving Hermod now.

"Finish the work, boy. All this cryin'." Juno approached him and set her hand on his shoulder. "You are the light. You see it plainly now." Hermod took her hand in his.

"The star in the void," Vincent repeated. He clapped his hands and held them together under his chin, projecting a wide, toothy smile. His milk-chocolate brown skin was beaming, and he looked ecstatic.

"We love you, boy," Juno said. She jabbed her index finger into his chest. "Give up the man and be a star."

Hermod let her hand go, and his fell to his thigh. Her voice was so soft and loving, like Granny Selene's had been when she would sit and listen to him complain about school, Auntie Beatrice, and the white teachers at the Friar's school. He'd never known family before, real family. Staring into her eyes, he saw the eyes of his own mother and his Aunt Beatrice. Yes! He saw it then. They had the exact same "I'm gonna get you" face. He felt safe with her for a moment, a feeling unlike anything anyone else was ever able to give him—except Lee.

"Hermod," Cyral said. "It is time."

Hermod turned to Cyral. Ford was standing next to him. He saw smoke wafting over the devastated beach in a doorway behind them. Ford turned and stepped through it.

"I'll try and keep this open as long as I can," he said.

"Baby!" Dara's voice called from the beach. Ford turned and ran toward her.

Cyral, blinding and awesome still, moved through the doorway. Immediately, the light diminished and his handsome and immaculately tailored self reappeared.

"You cannot stay here, Hermod," Cyral said from the beach. "We don't belong here." He moved away from the door and joined Tig, Gaskill, and Davi several yards away.

Vincent approached Hermod, and Juno stepped aside. Vincent raised his hands, and Hermod stepped away from him. Then they both paused briefly. Vincent stepped forward and extended his right hand. Hermod stared at it for a moment and then made eye contact with Vincent and slowly reached to take his uncle's hand. Vincent pulled him in and embraced him. "We will leave you alone now, love," Vincent said.

Hermod remained still, then slowly raised his arms and returned his uncle's embrace. He closed his eyes for a moment. The tingling feeling of familiarity and safety washed over him again, and he felt like he might cry. He opened his eyes and, in the distance, across the shimmering field, he saw a silhouette approaching.

"You should have been a king and not the savior," Vincent said, holding him at arm's length and looking into his void face. "Save them, Hermod. Save them by your means."

"We must find our way back to the void," Juno said.

"Yes, dear," Vincent replied. "Father will show us the way."

They admired Hermod in silence for several seconds and then turned around, clasped hands, and drifted away toward the horizon.

Hermod reached out his hand and took a step toward them. He had so many more questions for them. He felt as he did that day that he woke up deep in the sea when Tig told him that Lee had—

"Hey, babe."

The voice.

"Why are you wearing that?"

"Oh, I . . . Uhhh." Hermod shook his head and quickly turned around. "I . . . I couldn't take it . . . take it off."

"Sí," Lee said. "Lo puedes hacer. Muéstrame."(1) He frowned and stepped closer to Hermod.

"I can't, Lee," Hermod said. He was uncertain whether he was trembling or not. He began to cry. "It's . . . it's me."

"Quien lo dijó?" Lee asked. "Este no es mi amor."(2) He approached Hermod and reached out his hand. Hermod took it, and it felt exactly as it had the second to last time he had held it: strong and warm. The ridges and calluses on his palm were the same, and his nails were still neatly manicured.

"See?" Lee asked. He settled his other hand on Hermod's face and leaned in and kissed his lips.

Hermod looked down and saw the sparkling roses, orchids, and marigolds in his dress and his own chocolate-brown chest and arms, his hand in Lee's.

"How?"

"You had to ask, babe? I got you." Lee winked. "So, what's up?" Lee wiped a tear away from Hermod's left eye. They were silent for a moment. "You letting them drive you crazy?"

"Lee," Hermod began, then turned his head away. "I . . . I hurt a lot of people. I killed so many people." His voice trailed off into sobbing, and he closed his eyes. Lee stepped closer and hugged him. Hermod fell into him and rested his head on Lee's shoulder.

"I'm not gonna lie, babe; that's some big shit. But just start by remembering that wasn't you. That was someone else using you. Fuck. Two people using you! Two crazy, manipulative people. Process it. Push through it and get back to life." He jabbed his index finger into Hermod's chest, "You are love. You taught me that. Don't ever forget that."

"You don't get it. It's . . . it's like I don't care. Like Vincent was right. No one ever has oppressed them or killed them or terrorized them. Like at scale, like they did to us."

"I knew you shouldn't have bought this dress." Lee smirked at him and tugged on the side of the garment. "Babe, look, I'm a descendant of

---

1 "You can do it· Show me·"

2 "Says who?" "This is not my love·"

conquistadores, no? I can't weigh in on this." Lee laughed and kissed him on the cheek. "Hermod, that wasn't you. I don't even need to say it. You know how to make real change."

"Not anymore," Hermod said, shaking his head. "I've never changed anything. Ever. I made some money and got some attention, but what did I change?" He fell silent, frowning at the shimmery ground. "You didn't see what I saw, Lee. They don't know the lasting effects of the kind of oppression and genocide that they have brought on us." He jabbed his index finger into his sternum. "The . . . the shit I hear all day in my head! The subconscious, psychic terror and collective anxiety. Lee, its—"

"I know, baby," Lee said. He grabbed Hermod's head in his hands. "But you don't have to solve these problems. You can turn it all off. You can do you."

"But that's the point, right? I could turn it off."

"You're a good person, Hermod."

"I'm not good. I killed those cops, Lee." Hermod shook his head. "Willingly."

"What cops?" Lee asked. "Who killed Marshawn Butler?"

"Yeah."

"Didn't they deserve it?" Lee shrugged. Hermod looked at him and remained silent. "Fuck 'em! I mighta killed one too if I were you. Lots of us would have."

Hermod nodded. "Maybe Vincent needed to happen. Maybe you do. You just gotta cut it away. Either that or start over."

"What does your heart really tell you, Hermod?"

"Why aren't you here?" Hermod asked, his voice quivered, and there was a heaviness beneath his chest "You made me care about things . . . about us. I never cared about me or anything else, only you."

"¿Qué te dice tu corazón?"(1) Lee asked again.

Hermod started to cry. He knelt on the shimmering ground, and Lee approached and caressed his head. Hermod flinched at the unexpected pressure there and then moaned in agony.

---

1 "What does your heart tell you?"

"I'm so sorry, Lee." Hermod huffed out the words between his cries. "I should have been there." He raised his head and looked into Lee's eyes. "I should have protected you. I—" He squeezed his eyes and his left fist closed as hard as he could as he thought about that evening again and the single hurdle between himself and saving Lee's life.

"Follow your heart. Don't do what she wants you to do."

"We need to end this," Tig said from the beach. He was staring at Hermod's back through the doorway to the All Realm.

"Give him a moment," Cyral said.

"What I want to do is worse," Hermod said, struggling to speak through the impulse to bawl. "I still need you, Lee."

"Life happened, babe." Lee shook his head. "Life goes on. You got this." He hugged Hermod as hard as he could and then held him away. They locked eyes.

"Tenemos que irnos, bebe," Lee said. "No hagas algo estupido o voy a castigarte."(1)

Hermod wiped his eyes and then they kissed. It was a long, passionate, vain attempt to unite through the impossible barrier of death. Lee stepped away from him and grabbed his hand. Hermod smiled and sniffled and struggled to keep his wails in his throat. They walked to the threshold, and though they both stepped in, only Hermod stepped through. He immediately felt the humid, prickly air on the Cape replace Lee's warm, strong palm.

He stood still for several seconds, then raised his head to the sky and closed his eyes. He imagined Ford's door closing behind him and Lee standing in it waving at him. He opened his eyes and turned around but saw only the ruined beach. He slumped over and knelt on the sand.

When Vincent had taken over him during the flight home from Lee's funeral, he'd thought he had died. He had no recollection of doing some of the things popping up in his memories of this morning. Part of him was thrilled by what he was seeing. And as awful as it seemed, he felt liberated, just as Juno and Vincent had said. It was a visceral feeling that he had not felt possibly since his first ignition. He felt great! Yet, he was far from good.

---

1 "We have to go· babe·" "Don't do anything stupid· or I'm going to punish you·"

He wondered if he could ever be good again, be a good person again. Did he have the patience with himself and others to get back there again? He lowered his head even more and fixed his eyes on a broken concrete slab just a few feet away from him. He thought about the means of its wreckage and displacement over a hundred miles and told himself, *I did that.*

In the few moments he'd been back, he could already feel Earth's woes and psychic strife starting to gnaw at him. He shook his head as he realized he couldn't just go home and sleep it off. Hell, he was at SPASE Headquarters; they probably had a room waiting! He wondered which types of probes and hearings and probations and bullshit he would have to subject himself to in order to calm down a bunch of weak and useless crackers. Weak and useless everyone!

He was the victim here. Why should he have to play the hero? The villain?

He needed a lot of fucking help right now.

He needed saving!

But who had ever really saved him?

Who had ever, *ever* saved him?

Lee had saved him. Even just a moment ago.

He wanted to be gone again.

Hermod clasped his shoulders and squeezed them together as tightly as Lee might have. His teeth ground on each other in the back of his mouth. He whimpered and started perspiring. His bowels relaxed slightly, and every muscle in both of his thighs flexed.

He unwrapped his arms from his shoulders and clenched the sand in his fists.

"Please!" he groaned, his nails digging into his palms as he squeezed the grains.

He relaxed completely. His back arched forward, and his head rested on his legs a few inches above his knees. He clasped his ears and heaved.

Remus emerged from the shadow of two stories of the Trade Center ruins about ten feet ahead of Hermod. It stood and watched Gaskill, Tig, Cyral and Davi, who were about fifteen feet ahead of it. Then it turned its attention to Dara, Ford, and Mingo, who were standing together several yards to its left.

Tig started to approach, but Cyral held out his arm and blocked him.

"Wait, dammit!" Cyral said. He looked up into the air and nodded at Sean.

No one made a sound. Helicopters buzzed around the perimeter of the scene. Waves lapped against the shore. The tower ruins crunched and squealed as they continued to settle into the cape.

Ford grabbed Dara's hand and squeezed. Still stuck between the swoon of the All Realm and the horror of Juno and Vincent's birth, he could not help but think about being with her and how much she had brightened his life in the nine months they had been dating. Contemplating the joy that they shared had eclipsed the electrifying anxiety of the moment. He was optimistic that things would be alright.

"Baby," Ford said, still staring at Hermod, "make this all be done, so I can love you and lie in your hair."

He, Dara, and Mingo were silent for a moment.

"Faggot," Mingo interjected and then laughed quietly. "Let me lie on your hair," Mingo said, his voice going briefly soprano as he flitted his fingers around his head.

"Ian?" Dara said. Her attempt to scold him failed with her own laughter. "I love you, baby," she said to Ford. She squeezed his hand and, sensing his chagrin, leaned in and turned his head toward hers and kissed him softly on the lips. Mingo patted Ford on the back as he continued laughing. "That was kinda gay, though," Dara whispered. That fueled more of her and Mingo's laughter.

"Dara," Tig said, "what the fuck?"

Cyral turned to his right and glared at the three of them. He quelled his reflexive defense to the insult as the certainty of Hermod's reaction settled in his imagination. He sighed and looked up at the sky.

Hermod had felt the word "faggot" stab into his brain, as was *always* the case when spoken by a breeder. But this breeder . . . that voice! Hot salt packed deep into the wounds of his soul; it having been rent thoroughly in the last several weeks until that very moment. Still kneeling, he gripped sand in his fists, and it superheated and crunched into glass shards and then vaporized.

How many times had this scene played out in his life? Some thirty years later the script remained pretty much the same. The Black people. The word. The jolt of danger. The sting all over his body just beneath his skin. The pounding heartbeat. The numbness in his lungs. The retreat. The lingering anxiety, wondering from which "brotha" or "sista" would the assault come next.

He would not retreat today. On his hands and knees, he turned his head to the left and saw them. Dara, laughing, held Ford's hand and pulled it closer to her mouth as her lips puckered. Ford hung his head slightly and frowned. Mingo held his hands behind his back and looked down at the sand. Though he was able to silence his laughter his bouncing shoulders betrayed him.

"This is all just some 'faggot shit' to you people, isn't it?" Hermod whispered through clenched teeth. He blinked his eyelids closed, and he was upon the three of them by the time they reopened. He kicked Dara into the air, breaking three of her ribs, and then reached his right arm into Mingo's abdomen.

Dara bounced and rolled along the beach and smashed into a large section of the tower ruins. She braced herself on one knee and tried to focus. She coughed up a thick glob of blood and phlegm, spat it onto the beach, then wiped her mouth with her forearm.

Lightning crawled out of Mingo's wound and sizzled the blood spurting from it. Hermod moved him closer. Their noses might have met had Hermod still been wearing his flesh. He turned to his left and looked down at Ford, who was cowering and scooting away on his buttocks.

Hermod looked into Mingo's gorgeous face. Even in anguish, it remained so. Slowly, his burning black phalanges dug deep into the beautiful visage, bursting Mingo's right eye and pulverizing his mandible. Hermod gripped the young skull by its sinuses. Cheek flesh cooked around his digits. Lightning, smoke, and burnt carnage spewed from Mingo's broken mouth as he convulsed around Hermod's forearm.

"You . . ." Hermod's voice was soft and trembling, his black jawbone barely moving. "Todavía estaría vi—"[(1)] He flung his arms away from each other, and Mingo came apart.

---

1 "He would still be al—"

From afar, Dara watched Mingo's innards spray across the beach. Ford, shielding his face from the intense glow of Mingo's after-death, clambered away from the violence.

"Tracy!" Dara screamed.

Unbound by his flesh, Mingo's energies erupted. Its shockwave sent Dara flying again. This time she was able to steady herself without colliding with anything. She stood and, in the distance, she could barely see Hermod's silhouette standing a few yards away from Gaskill and his huddle.

"Tracy?" Dara pleaded. "Come in, babe!" She raced toward where she had seen him last.

Remus emerged from the shadow of a large steel girder jutting out of the beach and stood in her path. Dara quickened her pace and cocked her fist, then lunged at its abdomen. Her fist sunk into the creature's nothingness, and she could not pull it back out. Remus stood unflinching as Dara yanked on her arm, to no avail.

"Fuck is this?" Dara said. "Sean, need an assist." She closed her eyes as she continued to yank her arm. The dark of her eyelids sank deeper and deeper into the blackness that comprised the Void King.

"No!" Dara yelled. Her eyes burst open, and she gasped. She pulled as hard as she could and rolled a dozen feet away from Remus.

Sean descended from the ceiling of smoke and haze above their position. Dara watched Remus as she reached down to steady herself. She recognized the bright red blood contrast against its void flesh just as the stump of her left arm plunged into the sand. She screamed her agony across the beach. She had not known so much as a mosquito bite since the Rain. She had forgotten what pain was, and now her mind was made of it and the accompanying shock of dismemberment.

Sean fired a fusion blast at Remus, but it passed through its form and collided with the sand. He flew to Dara's side. Her Ojun suit was reforming over the wound, cauterizing and sterilizing it.

Remus loomed over both of them and looked down into Dara's watery eyes. She closed them tight. A tear fell from the left one and slid around her face. Remus stepped away from them. Having collected her hand, it was still wearing her blood when it walked back into the girder's shadow.

Hermod looked down into the black bones of his own hands. He recalled the images of Vincent and Juno's birth. The sounds echoed in his head, the cries of his Uncle Aristotle.

"I can't set it," Hermod whispered. "I'm ruined." He shook his head and then focused on one of the sparkling orange marigolds in his dress near his left pinky. "It's . . . I can't!“ he paused and looked over his right shoulder and focused on Gaskill, who was huddled with Cyral, and Davi several yards away. "We've ruined everything." He looked at Tig and watched him approach. Remus emerged from Hermod's bony shadow and stood tall beside him. Tig stopped immediately.

"It was always—“ Hermod interrupted himself and looked at Remus. While imprisoned in the void, Remus could only appear to Hermod in his dreams as nebulous shadow. Hermod had not interacted with it before he succumbed to Juno and Vincent's rage. He thought it was beautiful, the void alive. Its presence was soothing, and he wanted to embrace it. He looked down at his black bones and then back at Remus. He was almost certain that Remus was all he had left. It wasn't judging him.

"What would you do, friend?" Hermod asked. His black mandible and teeth clenched.

"Doc," Sean said, flying above. "What's the plan? Pentagon's got nukes coming this way in less than two if you don't speak up real loud."

"Nukes," Gaskill said, "stones, take your pick."

"What would you do?" Hermod asked again. He fell to his knees, shaking his head.

Remus turned and faced him.

<Abolish them.> Its million voices spoke a silent cacophony. Life, pain, joy, and death sounded in void tenor deep in Hermod's bones. He turned his black skull to face Remus and it stared its white glare down into his empty eye sockets.

He was a plucked harp string; the beautiful and horrid tone resounded through him.

*Abolish them.*

It did not speak again, but the sound lashed Hermod's mind over and over, joined now by the singing and shouting at the African Burial Ground, and his wailing baby Uncle Aristotle and a mighty chorus of voices from his past ridiculing him.

*Faggot!*

"Stop!" Hermod screamed, gripping his skull.

*He looks white!*

"Stop it!"

*Abolish them.*

He wanted it to end.

*Faggot!*

He wanted everything to end.

*Fucking mega nigger!*

*Why he gotta talk like a white boy?*

They had done this to him.

*This faggot ass nigga!*

*Abolish them.*

They had ruined his entire world.

*Now there's a nigger if I ever saw one!*

Even before he was here to live in it.

*Fagg—*

"Adiós, bebe," Hermod recited Lee's final living words to him, his own voice silencing the clamor in his mind.

They had ruined it all.

Now he would ruin them.

He stood and faced Tig.

<Let's see about that cliff then.> Hermod told him.

Tig took a long deep breath and exhaled slowly, then sat down on the beach.

Hermod focused on Cyral for several seconds.

"No," Cyral whispered, understanding. "You can't!"

Hermod ascended. Tig began to cry.

"Hermod?" Cyral shouted. He tried to give chase but could not. "Dammit!" Cyral said, struggling to lift off. "Let me go!"

Cyral settled on the ground and grabbed Gaskill by the shoulders, shaking him.

"Can he do this?" Cyral pleaded. His eyes were wild, gaping, his entire body shaking.

"He can do anything," Gaskill replied, ignoring Cyral as he watched Hermod fly away.

Davi stood and stared at Gaskill and Cyral. His face was blank as he watched their contrasting resolve.

"We have to stop him!" Cyral said. "Jesus, Scott, do something!"

Twenty miles from the surface, Hermod ignited completely. Unbothered by Earth's pull, he jettisoned himself away from it at nearly fifteen kilometers per second and accelerated. As he raced toward the moon, he realized he might have been wrong about Mars; he might have to jump from a bit higher.

"It is done," Gaskill said. He lowered his eyes from watching Hermod and looked at Cyral's face. His eyes were flat, tears falling from the left one.

Gaskill clenched his teeth in frustration. "Save some tears for us, Alex."

# EPILOGUE: HERMOD'S REVENGE

## SPASE HQ CAPE HENLOPEN, DE FOUR DAYS LATER

*"T-Minus ninety-eight hours, forty-five minutes, and thirty seconds until impact."*

Cyral's mind had successfully integrated with those of all fifty of the psychics who were strong enough to meet the task. His body tensed and then relaxed down into the bed in his chamber. Ade grasped his hand for a moment. It was cold, but his grip was still firm and strong. He looked distressed, and yet even his scowl was strikingly handsome, she thought. A tear streaked down the left side of his face. His eyes remained closed.

<I am ready,> Cyral told her.

Ade squeezed his hand and then withdrew hers and closed the glass hatch over Cyral. She pressed the holographic icons on the glass. The chamber began to hiss, and within it small robot arms began to place needles into Cyral's wrist veins and an oxygen mask over his face.

He felt all of it. Their fear, their hunger, their rage. Their pasts and futures. All the panic on Earth raced through him, even as Hermod raced toward them at thirty-one kilometers per second, having accumulated a mass one and a half times that of the largest known asteroid, Ceres.

All those minds tearing each other apart, so close to the end and yet far enough away for madness to corrode all sense of civility, humanity. All the eyes staring up at the sky wondering who could save them. The rich ones, trapped in greed and selfishness in their bunkers. The powerful ones, boring into Gaskill's psyche with their weak, helpless hope.

<This doesn't feel right,> Cyral said.

<Why?> Gaskill asked from aboard his spacecraft 50,000 miles away. Cyral did not reply. Several seconds passed. <It may very well be one of the most righteous acts ever committed.>

More silence.

<What does it really feel like?> Gaskill asked.

<Everywhere,> Cyral said. <I feel like I'm everywhere.>

<Can you feel him?>

<No.>

Disappointed, Gaskill turned his attention to the moon, just outside the window to his right.

"Sean?"

"I've arrived sir," Sean replied from the moon's far side. "I've accessed the station on the northern rim of the Efe-2 caldera. Awaiting orders."

## "T-MINUS 12 HOURS THREE MINUTES AND FORTY-FIVE SECONDS UNTIL IMPACT."

Gaskill stared up at the moon. He wondered what the glowing volcanic Mare looked like on the other side. Had any of it cooled? What had become of the Ojun?

Just beyond the glowing cratered orb, Hermod's sparkling doom dazzled the black blanket of space. He was coming for them.

<Have you found him?> Gaskill asked.

<No,> Cyral replied.

Gaskill took a deep breath.

<How wide is the gap?>

<Fifteen hours,> Ade replied.

<Find him!>

*"T-Minus ten . . . nine . . . eight . . . seven . . . six . . . five . . . four . . . three . . . two . . . one."*

www.ingramcontent.com/pod-product-compliance
Lightning Source LLC
Chambersburg PA
CBHW031944260626
47157CB00017B/2300
*9798986611914*